Praise for

Sacrifice of the Lambs

by Joe Shumock

In Shumock's thriller, a former CIA operative investigates a series of strange deaths that may be linked to a secretive medical facility in Prague . . . "Thrives on suspense, with a capable protagonist who's more spy than detective."
—*Kirkus Reviews*

Where science and truth—stronger than fiction—potentially collide. Well researched, timely and tightly knit.
~Ruth Mills, M.D.

Shumock weaves the plot with insight and skill. The story captivates the reader from the first paragraph and makes you wonder if mankind faces this scenario in the future... or is it with us now?
~Linda Charest, Reader

Twists and turns – kept you wanting to see where it was going all the way to the end.
~Sharon Lapierre, Reader

Enjoyed this fast-paced thriller. A great read!!!
~Benjamin S. Citrin, M.D., F.A.C.C., F.A.C.P.

This fourth novel in Joe Shumock's *Letter Series* is the best yet. A superb storyteller, Shumock reaches down into the bottomless pit of what could be and exposes a secret reality to give the reader a glimpse into a scary future.
~Don Charest, Retired Securities Broker

Intriguing, thought provoking, and emotional in a setting of love and sadness. This writer, with anticipation and fear, keeps the reader on the edge of their seat.
~Dianne French, Alpha Omega Editing

A thriller unlike any other. A different kind of nail biter.
~Ray Lapierre, Lt. Col. (Ret) U.S. Air Force

A mastry of details with a historical backdrop of a Central European country and its people, complete with every twist and turn imaginable, intertwining medicine and romance... Joe Shumock's best.
~Pamela Struhbar, Teacher

SACRIFICE OF THE LAMBS

* * *

Fourth in the Letter Series

Joe Shumock

Silver Sage Media

Developmental Editing, Copyediting, Writer's Coaching:
Wayne South Smith, www.waynesouthsmith.com

Proofreading:
Dianne French, www.alphaomegaediting.com

Cover Design, Author Photo:
Barry A. Hodgin

Library of Congress Control Number: 2017914316

ISBN: 1976344344
ISBN 13: 9781976344343
CreateSpace Independent Publishing Platform
North Charleston, South Carolina

Silver Sage Media

To Norville

Norville H. Couey (1940–2016)

A friend for more years than
either of us wanted to count.
As children, we wanted to fly.
As a man, Norville did.
I am fortunate to have had such a
friend—such a brother—for all those years.

And, as always,
for Kathy

1

June 2015
Prague, Czech Republic

* * *

THE EXECUTION WAS SCHEDULED FOR 5:00 p.m. She glanced at the clock—3:03. Less than two hours…

The frosted window in the small room where they kept her did not allow her to see out. The young woman could tell it was cloudy, though, and earlier she had heard rain pattering against the glass. Several hours ago, a nurse had suggested she ask for something to calm her. Without a sedative, she expected she'd be climbing the walls by now.

There were people walking in the corridor. Her guardians were on their way to get her. One of the individuals coming for her was wearing shoes with leather heels. The distinctive clicks on the tile floor were easy to distinguish. The other three were less obvious, but she could tell there were four of them.

Looking down one last time at the prayer book she'd been reading, the young woman closed her eyes for a moment and then silently worded "Amen" with only her lips moving.

She leaned forward, preparing to stand.

Recent thoughts that had haunted her came creeping back, and she dropped back down onto the edge of the bed.

I've only begun to live, and…now I am going to die.

A sob…

Twenty-six years is not enough.

Without consciously intending to, she thought of friends recently lost—two—both were young men, strong and full of life. They were gone now as she would be soon.

It's as if there is a curse on those around me, she pondered, *and now it's reached out to claim my life too.*

She thought of her mother, wondering if any word about her situation had reached Elita. There were mixed emotions. Marta was not sure if she would want her mother to know what was happening. With sad eyes closed and a tear running down each cheek, she slowly shook her head.

Sleep had been scarce the last several nights. Over the last twenty-four hours, it hadn't come at all. She wondered if everyone felt this way when they were about to die.

I hope not.

She heard a key, and then the door opened. Though she didn't look up, the young woman could feel her keepers watching her from the corridor.

Finally, she stood, placing the prayer book beside a Bible on the cluttered shelf above the bed. Before turning toward the door, the woman crossed herself as she had been taught as a child.

Funny how old habits linger, even at the oddest moments.

The little priest who had been visiting her regularly led the group standing at the door. She only recognized one of the others. His name was Dr. Seifert, but according to the priest, he was generally referred to as the Warden. Though seldom seen, it was common knowledge that he was the unofficial administrator of this foul place.

The young woman glanced down. The Warden was wearing the leather shoes she had heard. She wasn't surprised. On two occasions, he had spent time with her in the days she had resided here. She recalled the clicking sounds in the corridor each time he came.

The priest acted as the group's spokesman. His words were Czech, the West Slavic language spoken in the Czech Republic and by most Czechs worldwide.

"Are you prepared to go, Marta?"

"Is there a choice?"

Marta's question went unanswered except for a slight embarrassed smile on the little man's face. His eyes averted, incapable of matching her stare.

Marta couldn't help feeling sorry for him. Father Anděl was elderly and appeared sad and out of place for this despicable chore.

The other two individuals were women, and judging by their pale green scrub uniforms, they were nurses. One of them had a stethoscope across her shoulders.

The women stepped inside the room and turned Marta away from the door. They helped her out of her clothing and into a hospital gown. Modesty was not a consideration.

Finished with the clothing change, each of the nurses took one of Marta's arms. Their grip, while firm, was surprisingly gentle though each stood close to a head taller than Marta's 5'4". Stepping back, Father Anděl and the Warden stood aside as the women walked Marta out and helped her onto a gurney. With a sheet covering her and belts fastened across her body and legs, one of the women pushed from the rear as the other guided the gurney along the corridor. The men fell in behind Marta and the nurses.

As the strange little group moved along, the priest opened a book and started to read religious words in a language Marta did not understand. She also did not believe the words were particularly relevant considering what was about to happen to her.

Their journey was short. The destination was a large antiseptically clean room. On one wall, there were two large viewing windows outfitted with drawn blinds. The room had a glass double door in a far wall and a table resembling those normally found in emergency rooms and surgical suites.

Marta had reached her final destination.

There were large overhead lights and trays with shiny instruments. Several white-coated technicians attended a number of humming machines located along a wall close to the table. The overall scene reminded Marta of some tragic theater production about to be played out on a stage with limited cast and almost no audience at all.

Unfortunately, Marta had the leading role. She was totally aware of the part she would play in this dark drama. Though her mind cried out to run—to escape and disappear—the young woman remained outwardly calm, knowing there could be no bolting from the calamity that was about to claim her.

This should not be the way life ends.

That thought had occurred to Marta many times over the last several days. Since the pronouncement was read, Marta had asserted a number of times that she was blameless and should not be here.

Nor was anyone else at fault, she reminded herself, *unless those who had contributed to her genotype—to her very existence—could be blamed.*

The women at her sides guided Marta off the gurney. Strong hands joined them and moved the young woman onto the operating table, helping her to stretch out on the cool surface. Bright lights made it difficult to see. There was a hum of activity all around, but for the moment it didn't appear to directly involve her.

A heated blanket was handed to one of the nurses, and then spread over Marta's body. It felt wonderful. She hadn't realized how chilled she'd become.

Activity was increasing. Lights were pulled closer to her body and trays rolled near the table. A different nurse moved to her side and swabbed her left arm with alcohol. No words were spoken, nor did the nurse's eyes connect with Marta's.

As she watched, an IV catheter was inserted into her arm. A fluid of some sort dripped into the device. Not feeling any particular effect, Marta suspected it was only a saline solution to keep the line open for what would come next.

Marta had come to the health clinic three weeks earlier for a job interview. A contact from the office of a respected labor recruiter had gotten the process started.

The woman who called said a health clinic's data department was searching for a new manager, and Marta's name was high on a list of prospects being sent to the hospital. Though she was one of several computer and internet specialists in her present company,

Marta's reputation as a software developer was known to many commercial organizations throughout Prague.

The recruiter hinted the starting salary as a manager would be significantly more than Marta was presently earning. When a 40 percent increase was mentioned, she agreed to an interview the following morning.

Marta had built her reputation in several ways, beginning with intensive study when she was at university. Always at the top of her classes, Marta had used her knowledge, combining it with hard work in the last four-plus years, to reach the advantageous situation she now enjoyed.

Dressed that morning in an attractive dark business suit with skirt and a cream-colored blouse, she added tall heels and checked herself in a mirror. Her make-up and hair were flawless. Then choosing carefully, a thin bracelet with a conservative necklace and matching earrings completed the outfit. Perfect. She certainly thought she looked the part of a manager.

Marta was an appealing young woman, and she knew it. Dark hair and striking blue eyes turned heads everywhere she went. Marta suspected her curvaceous body had something to do with that too.

Arriving early, she introduced herself and handed the secretary a business card. "I have an appointment with Dr. Hana Jirsa."

"Yes, I have you on her schedule," the secretary said. "I will let her know you are here." She picked up the phone.

Only moments later, Dr. Jirsa came and led Marta back to her office.

Marta was asked to fill out a short questionnaire, and then they moved into the interview.

Most of Dr. Jirsa's questions were routine, but a few caught Marta by surprise. She had never been asked where she grew up. When Marta said she lived in Dejvice, the doctor appeared pleased.

"Isn't that in Prague 6?"

"Yes, it is."

"And you lived with your mother?"

"Yes."

"You do not have other relatives in Prague?"

"No," Marta told her, "but I do not live with my mother now. I have my own flat."

"No roommate?"

"No."

Marta wondered, *Why does she need to know all that?*

They talked about the duties of the job for a few minutes. Marta quickly knew she could handle the position. The doctor agreed and said Marta was the most qualified applicant they had interviewed, and she could have the position if she wanted it.

Marta didn't have to think it over. The money had swayed her.

Finally, Dr. Jirsa asked if she'd had a tetanus shot recently.

"No, I have never had one," Marta said, a bit surprised at the question.

"We require a drug test and tetanus shot for all our employees," the doctor told her. "Is that a problem?"

"No, not at all."

Marta was happy to have the additional money and expected she would enjoy working with the hospital. The drug test and shot were small prices to pay for the new position.

Dr. Jirsa told her the drug test would come later, and a nurse would come and inoculate her with the tetanus vaccine while they talked.

Then she asked. "Are you expected back at work today?"

Marta said she was not, she had taken a day of leave so there would be no rush with the interview. This seemed to please Dr. Jirsa.

There were other questions about her family that surprised Marta too. She answered them truthfully but didn't elaborate. Marta didn't mention her father had died in an accident at work when she was very young. Her mother had told her. Marta didn't remember him, and they never talked about his death.

Since she and her mother had plenty of funds and a nice house, she had always assumed the money had come as a result of her father's accident. Marta had never asked for details.

The two of them had been happy, and her mother seemed to have plenty of money for whatever they needed or wanted. Their house was grand, and there was always a new automobile parked in the garage. They had often gone on lavish vacations, sometimes to beaches, other times to the mountains.

Funds for university were not a problem either. Her mother had insisted Marta pick one of the better schools in Central Europe. Elita hadn't wanted Marta to be far from home.

As the doctor and Marta talked, a nurse arrived and gave her a shot.

Within minutes, Marta began to feel sleepy. Dr. Jirsa noticed and stopped asking questions. She watched, making small talk for several minutes before moving around the desk and pulling a chair close by. Then she took Marta's hand.

The last thing Marta remembered that day was the doctor checking her pulse. Concerned, she tried to stand and leave the office but couldn't get to her feet. Nothing worked the way it should; she had lost all coordination. All Marta wanted to do was sleep.

Later, when she awoke, Marta was in a hospital room. There was a nurse watching over her who appeared nice but had to raise her soft voice for Marta to understand her. She assured Marta everything was all right. In a daze, she wondered if the nurse was being truthful.

Sleeping most of the time, Marta was seldom fully aware of her surroundings or circumstances.

Early one morning a doctor she didn't recognize came to the room. A different nurse was with him. Marta was fully conscious now and could talk without difficulty.

The man identified himself as Dr. Laska and asked several questions about her condition.

"Do you know where you are?" He watched her eyes as Marta shook her head.

The nurse's name was Ivana. She continuously checked vital signs as Marta and the doctor talked.

"Do you know why you are here?" A different question.

"No."

Marta had no idea why she had been so out of her head either. She had come to the hospital for an interview, but she doubted the validity of that now. The doctor didn't help.

He did say some of his colleagues would be joining them to discuss her future. She couldn't imagine what was coming.

A few minutes into the conversation, they were joined by Dr. Seifert, a psychiatrist. She recognized him—the Warden.

Later, as she tried to keep up, Dr. Laska basically told Marta her life was over. There was much Marta did not understand. Uninformed as she was, it was difficult asking relevant questions. She had thought she would understand her situation when the doctors left, but she didn't.

When the meeting was over, she curled up on the bed and cried.

Marta looked around the operating room, wondering about the specifics of what was about to happen. No one else had called it an execution, but for her, it was.

Though in her mind she knew she had done nothing wrong, that had not been a factor in bringing her to this moment. Now, unless some unexpected intervening act came about, she was destined to face an unknown darkness before evening fell.

Wanting to scream, a deep breath was her only outward expression of the distress she felt. Marta remembered the rain earlier on her window. Now darkness was closing in on her very existence.

The glass door between the rooms opened and three doctors entered—a woman and two men. The female was Dr. Jirsa who had interviewed Marta.

The nurse, Ivana, turned to meet them.

Gathering in a tight circle and glancing toward Marta occasionally, they were obviously discussing her situation and what was about to transpire. Dr. Jirsa was doing most of the talking; the others nodded, offering a word or two occasionally but mostly listening. Finally, they appeared to be in agreement, and the doctors returned to the other room.

The nurse came over to talk. She leaned against the table and took Marta's hand.

"It's time to start," Ivana said.

Marta nodded.

"We are going to strap you down," the nurse told her in an explanatory way. "Patients are sometimes inclined to get a little crazy."

Marta nodded again, a sob escaping her throat as a lone tear ran slowly down one cheek.

The nurse motioned to the two women who had escorted Marta here on the gurney. They moved to her sides and secured her arms and body with belts. Finished, they each patted her arm and then left the room.

Marta expected observers to gather outside the viewing windows. At a point the blinds would be opened. Her surgical procedure would certainly be fascinating to watch.

Ivana returned to Marta's side, this time carrying a hypodermic syringe.

"How much time do I have left?" *Anything to delay the inevitable.*

The nurse glanced at the clock, then said hesitantly, "You have another hour." Ivana pursed her lips, her forehead already drawn, giving her a sorrowful expression.

Marta could see the point of the needle as it entered the intravenous line. The nurse drew her eyes away with words.

"This will help you relax, and you'll feel sleepy."

"Right," Marta whispered. Tears edged to the corner of each eye. She couldn't help herself. "What time is it now?"

The nurse smiled. "Try not to think about it."

Marta turned her head as another sob escaped. "I wish I had never been born." Then Marta realized her tension was easing off. Ivana was watching her.

"Do you have children?" Marta asked.

The question appeared to catch the nurse by surprise. She hesitated but then answered. "I have a daughter. She's…your age."

Marta could see tears in Ivana's eyes.

The nurse gazed at her for several seconds. Marta wondered if she was thinking, *What if this was my daughter?*

Dr. Jirsa and one of the male doctors entered from the other room. The second male doctor followed moments later.

Ivana looked up, her eyes still misty.

"How are we doing?" Dr. Jirsa asked.

"We're fine," Ivana told her while glancing back at Marta.

Pointedly, and peering at the doctor, Marta asked, "How would you be doing if you were in my place?"

Though not expecting an answer, she got one.

Placing a hand on Marta's arm, and almost in a whisper, Dr. Jirsa said, "This is one of the most difficult things I will do in this life." Then she touched Marta's cheek adding, "Three times and it gets more difficult with each one."

Marta wondered what the doctor meant. *Three times?*

Then Dr. Jirsa left the room. One doctor followed her out. He had not spoken a word.

Marta watched the door close and then reflected on Jirsa's words again. *Three times...*

Her eyelids had started to feel heavy. An effort to keep them open was very difficult. Marta knew when she drifted into sleep, it would be for eternity.

"What time...is it?"

Glancing up at the clock, Ivana murmured, "Fifteen more minutes."

Marta's eyes slowly closed. This time she didn't have the strength to open them again. There was only a long sigh.

Ivana's sad expression was the last thing Marta saw.

The drug perfected specifically for this purpose was administered to the subject after she lost consciousness. EEG readings indicated a rapid lessoning of brain activity. All eyes were on the indicators telling their story as a green-line indicator edged its way across the equipment.

Taking up stations on either side of the table, the doctors had returned and waited as one watched the information narrow and become a straight line. All brain activity had ceased, and the heart was no longer beating.

A brief moment passed before that doctor gave the go-ahead. "We can begin."

When the blinds opened, more than a dozen observers were at the viewing windows. Other than the two nurses who had escorted Marta there, none of the onlookers knew anything about the patient on the table or the circumstances placing her there. A special screen hid Marta's face. The spectators believed they were there to observe a complicated surgery.

Three doctors stood at the table where the female patient lay waiting. Several other medical staff and technicians were busy monitoring equipment and carrying out various other duties.

Prepared for surgery, the patient's abdominal and chest areas were bared and ready. Betadine was evident from above the sternum to a point near the covered groin region.

Ready at last, a scalpel was slapped into the female doctor's outstretched hand. Without comment, she touched it to skin and guided it down the middle of the patient's body, leaving a thin red line in its wake.

2

Fall 1982
Cambridge, England

* * *

THERE WERE NINE OF THEM when they met for the first time.

Within a short walking distance of the University of Cambridge and its many schools was a favorite pub of several individuals involved with an about-to-be-formed exclusive fraternity. The pub had not been picked for its close proximity to the University or for the quality of the ale. Not surprising, the newly affiliated individuals had decided to meet there because of the pub's thought-provoking reputation regarding the discovery of DNA.

Opened originally as the Eagle and Child in the year 1667, the location was now one of the larger pubs on Bene't Street in the center of Cambridge, England. The name had later been shortened to The Eagle, and a plaque near the door rightly proclaimed it to be the location where Francis Crick interrupted lunchtime on February 28th, 1953, to announce he and James Watson had "discovered the secret of life." The announcement had come directly after they had claimed the scientific world's attention with their proposal for the structure of DNA.

For this '80s group of young students—three men and six women—discussion often centered on each of them doing something extraordinary with their lives.

These were not typical students. They had a number of exceptional traits in common. Superior intellect was one of these. Though it was never a topic of conversation, intelligence quotients within the group were all north of 160 utilizing The Wechsler Adult Intelligence Scale. By comparison, Einstein's IQ, though never tested, was estimated by scientists to be between 160 and 180.

Social status was another characteristic the young people shared. Each one was from a family of extraordinarily great wealth, though they were from several different countries and backgrounds. Each member of the group, with one exception, was an only child. That deviance was a young woman whose older brother had perished in a racing accident. In each circumstance, there were no siblings to share the riches.

At around twenty-one years of age, depending on their country of origin, each had received very substantial funds that were theirs to control and use in any manner they desired. The wealth came with social responsibilities and teachings that were not to be ignored. These individuals, not unlike other young adults across the globe, had visions of changing their world.

In the last weeks of their undergraduate studies, the group gathered to finalize a life's direction and consider a name for their organization. Though already established independently, it was acknowledged that graduate studies for the separate individuals appeared to meld into the overall life's objective the group was approving.

Most pursued single majors as undergraduates, but a trio were completing work in two fields before specializing as they began their advanced studies. Undergraduate course work among the group included the dual fields of genetic and bio-chemical engineering, political science and psychology, and computer science and software development. Single fields of study included architecture, international law, business, biotechnology, evolutionary anthropology, and the last, a young woman in pre-med pursuing a medical degree specializing in surgery and seeking a fellowship in organ transplantation.

After careful thought and with only a couple of chores remaining on their agenda, members of the new and purposefully secret organization chose simply to call their funding entity the Eagle Trust. This decision was based solely on the name of their meeting location.

The health and research facility they envisioned would have a Czech name since they had chosen Prague for its location. The unconventional hospital would be called *Výzkumné Centrum a Cambridge Zdraví,* or in English, the Cambridge Health and Research Center. It would become known worldwide simply as the Cambridge Center.

A Chairperson was selected, and the collective agreed the sole purpose of this person's life would be to run the everyday activities of their organization. A meeting would be scheduled annually where activities of the past year, as well as plans and expectations for the future, would be discussed.

The basic purpose of the Eagle Trust was ultra secret and to be fully known to only the nine original members. Bylaws stated if a member left the Eagle Trust for any reason other than death, the organization was to be abandoned and final funds disbursed to no more than two charitable organizations. These were to be named in the Eagle Trust's charter. Informal discussions among members emphasized the delicate nature of their goals, and how all necessary measures should be exercised to keep those objectives secret.

With all necessary rules for guidance and procedures in place, including the Eagle Trust's public purpose and expectations, it was time for funding. Banking and investment accounts were opened in Swiss international financial institutions. Major financial transactions would require signatures of the Chairperson and two other members.

Debate over the amount of initial funding took several hours spread among three separate meetings. Connected to those were secondary agreements for continuing monetary requirements. Additional investments were expected due to future construction, expanding facilities, and staff requirements.

There were also considerable discussions regarding placement of leftover funds if the Eagle Trust was dissolved. It was decided and unanimously approved that all assets would be sold and the funds disbursed equally to Doctors Without Borders and UNICEF.

Then, as agreed, each member of the Eagle Trust found a way to anonymously transfer multiple millions of US dollars into the newly opened Swiss financial accounts. Formed and funded, the Chairperson established temporary administrative offices in Cambridge, England, and with their member architect, began to draw plans for the Trust's new hospital. It was also agreed the facilities would be designed and constructed in a way that would represent old Europe as well as the new—the future. Their member architect was quite at ease with this unusual assignment.

Also by group decision, the Chairperson for the Eagle Trust would be a woman, Zuzana Balca. Five or six years older than other members of the newly formed organization because of a late start at university, Zuzana was pleased to accept the position. Considering it a challenge, she was happy to dedicate her life to the Trust's success.

Madam Balca was Czech in all ways, having been born in Prague of Romanian parents in the early 1950s. Her young father and mother had foreseen the coming German takeover of Romania. Gathering and secretly transferring their extensive wealth, the parents had gone to Prague for a holiday in 1935 and never returned to Romania.

Once established in the Czechoslovakian capital, Zuzana Balca's father carefully used his wealth to enter European financial markets. Again, the father saw bad times coming and moved his wife and their wealth to Switzerland in time to avoid the Germans again in 1938. After the Battle of Prague in 1945, Zuzana's father had made a return trip to assess the post-World War II city as a suitable location to raise a family and manage their significant financial holdings. Satisfied with what he found, they returned in 1946 and renovated the house they had fled before the war.

Then, in 1953 Zuzana Balca was born.

Zuzana was a strong individual virtually from the time she exited her mother's womb and experienced a significant slap on her rear end. She remembered being told as a child of age six that the doctor who delivered her said he had never heard a newborn scream so loudly. The doctor also said she had quieted only when placed at her mother's breast—only when she had what she wanted.

She remembered the need for being in charge developing early and in a robust manner. Zuzana also remembered her early ability to plan and utilize others in whatever scheme she was directing at a given moment. She quickly learned that education, effort, planning, and the ability to involve others and their talents almost always assured success.

The newly named Madam Chairwoman brought at least one other character trait of importance to her new position. That attribute was tenacity. Members of the Eagle Trust believed they could not have made a better choice.

Prague was the only home the Chairwoman had ever known and, though under communist control at the time the Eagle Trust was formed, the area was expected to prosper in the coming years with the lessening influence of eastern powers.

Projections by the members of the Eagle Trust became reality as the country peacefully split on January 1, 1993, becoming two nations: the Czech Republic on the west with Prague as its capital and Slovakia bordering on the east and slightly south.

The new nation and its capital would see the Eagle Trust as a shining example of new money and business savvy at work in the newly formed country. The Trust's Prague facility quickly thrived as a medical hospital and research center and was often mentioned with favor in financial publications and political speeches both locally and abroad.

Though the Eagle Trust had already become an operating reality in the mid '80s, its members, while pursuing their studies, continued to meet at The Eagle Pub. Many decisions, both major and minor, were made over a pint of ale along with the food standard, Fish and Chips.

An early tragedy struck the group shortly after they approved and funded the Eagle Trust. One of the young men, totally captivated by his studies of Evolutionary Anthropology, was killed while on holiday near the end of his time at university. Exercising his two avocational loves in life, hiking and mountaineering, a fall high along the trek up Mount Everest proved to be his undoing. Several pints were lifted in his memory.

In the ensuing years, the remaining eight members of the Eagle Trust completed their advanced studies at the University of Cambridge and then moved on to fulfill their individual destinies.

Some time later, on September 27, 1985, a second member was lost in the crash of a commercial jet about to land at Las Vegas' McCarran International Airport in the US. The young woman had finished her studies in Biotechnology at Cambridge and had moved on to a prestigious position in her chosen field.

The accident happened while she was on a much-anticipated vacation, a gift to herself upon completing her studies. She was visiting a favorite aunt, and while the two women were having coffee at the relative's kitchen bar, an Air Caribbean DC-9 jet was clipped by a smaller aircraft and crashed into the aunt's neighborhood, striking her home. Both women perished.

Now there were seven.

3

FALL 1985
PRAGUE, CZECH REPUBLIC

* * *

A SPECIAL MEETING WAS CALLED by Chairwoman Balca after the tragic loss of the second individual in their group.

The seven remaining members all made their way to Prague. A social get-together was scheduled on the first night around drinks and dinner at the Chairwoman's residence. Since winter and the holidays were approaching, mulled wine was served.

After much debate and several drinks, a conclusion was reached that the Eagle Trust should continue though its membership had been reduced by two. Their goals were no less valid now than they had been originally. The only change was in the number of members available for funding research and the medical facility. That, they decided, could be overcome with the specialized hospital now being a growing income source. Significant funds were also being realized from the development and licensing of various medicines to include drugs for use in organ transplant surgeries.

Patients at the ultra-upscale medical facility were increasing rapidly, leaving research as the area needing funding. There was no income from the work being accomplished within the core study. None was expected as that had never been a goal.

Yet outside of that secret focal experimentation, other research had rapidly begun to produce income for the Cambridge Center and Eagle Trust. Scientists employed by the Trust were gaining reputations that allowed the hospital to charge significant fees for lectures by these individuals. Requests for presentations were coming from groups and institutions worldwide.

According to accounting reports and projections, hospital income was expected to surpass its costs by mid-year 1987. Excess funds would reduce amounts required from Trust members. With the reduction in the number of contributors, an audible sigh filled the room as this information was reported.

"Where do we stand on the basic research?" a female member asked. Glancing at a report, the same woman added, "The expenditures for specialized equipment and staff have been horrendous. And that does not consider new construction for the research wing."

"I'm told we are extremely close," the Chairwoman answered. "We are being very careful concerning knowledge and details being shared and keeping departments isolated from one another."

"Are we talking about months or years?" a male asked in an upbeat voice.

The Chairwoman responded. "I am being told it will be at least a year, but I think a better estimate is six months."

After some hesitation, a statement was made on the subject seldom talked about by members of the Eagle Trust and certainly not at research conferences.

"To date, we have not burdened ourselves with concerns others have in our main research area."

Glancing at each of them, it was obvious from nods and spoken words that everyone understood her meaning.

"It was never our intent for newfound knowledge in this area to be available outside our group until we have reached our own goals."

The small gathering still agreed.

"Therefore, we have not considered religious or moral views in reaching our conclusions concerning the final use of our research."

More nods.

"Unless someone here disagrees as of this moment"—all eyes were on the speaker—"we will continue and hopefully have tangible results in a shorter time than we could have imagined."

A short pause, then, "Anything else?"

There was nothing.

Questions at dinner turned to the facility and staff with a push toward a tour for the gathered members.

The next day was agreeable with a cool morning and the temperature expected to peak around 45 degrees in the afternoon. Starting out early, eight o'clock in the morning, the Chairwoman drove to the hotel Residence Malostranská, parked near the entrance, and entered. The other members were waiting, congregated in a corner of the lobby drinking coffee or *horká čokoláda*—hot chocolate—as they speculated on their tour of the medical and research facility.

All eyes turned as Madam Balca walked into the room. As the other members gathered around the Chairwoman, asking questions and giving compliments, she greeted each of them. It was evident she was in charge of this meeting.

The architect member, though quiet and a bit shy, was drawn into the conversation by their leader. Madam Balca, her hand on the woman's shoulder, told the group they were in for a treat.

"You will be as proud of her as I am," she said. "Our hospital will soon be recognized around the world for its beauty as well as for the work we do there."

Most interest was, of course, directed to the research wing and the secret experimentation and, hopefully, to the final testing in progress there. Last night the Chairwoman had given them all reason to hope for short-term results.

One of the men asked if a hike to the medical center was even a possibility.

The Chairwoman smiled saying "Oh, you could reach our facility that way, but it would take much longer and be much cooler than you wish."

Everyone chuckled, even the individual asking the question.

Outside, the seven members crowded into the Chairwoman's Jaguar. Someone commented this was much like meetings at The Eagle Pub in their university days. Many times, they'd had to squeeze the nine of them into a six-person booth.

After Madam Balca took the driver's seat, there were only four places left. Jokes were passed as the six passengers jockeyed for the available seats. Two of the women ended up in the laps of the two men. Laughs, elbows, and long legs were all taken in stride. No one appeared miffed at the final arrangement.

There was even some chatter relating to impromptu parties at The Eagle Pub when they were in school at Cambridge. These usually came after exams and often lasted well into the night.

One of women observed that she had never sat on any man's lap back in those days. With significant laughter, one of the men observed perhaps she should have.

Madam Balca eased the car onto the street. Going away from the major flow of traffic and toward the western part of the city, they reached their destination thirty minutes later.

Operation of the medical center and creation of the research facility had begun in 1983 as soon as funding was established and available. Temporary space had been leased and outfitted in Prague with the idea that income should be generated as early as practical. The suggestion of the final facility being a very upscale construction on land purchased in a wealthy part of the city was immediately agreed upon and adopted as a standard. From day one, nothing was spared in terms of cost or requirements on the research phase or the other facilities.

Every item involved was state-of-the-art from the beginning. The most difficult undertaking had been the separation of departments and assignments to keep the final goals of the core research a secret. In some situations, staff was led to believe work being accomplished in the labs was on contract from other research facilities outside the country.

Having been kept away during construction and outfitting, the facility and grounds were an unknown to everyone except the Chairwoman and the architect member. The others had only seen plans.

Oohs and ahs were already sounding inside the automobile as they drew near. Passengers were pointing and touching the shoulders of everyone near them in the excitement of seeing the structures for the first time, even from a distance.

Moving slowly once they left the street, all eyes gazed at the gorgeous grounds and the main buildings. Two glass and chrome structures—wings—one longer than the other and three stories tall, stood attached to a central building that appeared very old, perhaps dating back several hundred years. The overall form of the three buildings suggested an exaggerated and inverted V shape. Other structures were visible behind the main buildings.

Grounds near the curving drive were planted and groomed to perfection. Though spring was months away, a few hardy blooms could still be seen given the temperate weather Prague had enjoyed prior to this current cool spell. Lawns filled the open spaces along with trees, mostly Cherry and Japanese Magnolias. Some were large and appeared quite old.

There were minimal parking spaces with reserved signage for guests near the entrance. The drive then curved to a ramp suggesting underground parking accommodations for management, employees, and others. The members were told there was also a large two-story above ground parking lot hidden by cedar trees along the right edge of the property.

The Chairwoman pulled into one of the visitor spaces, and everyone hurriedly unfolded themselves from the Jaguar and headed for the entrance. Inside, the main buildings were outfitted to agree with their exterior. The two modern wings displayed a similar style inside, with modern furniture, art, accessories, and window coverings.

The middle building was entirely different. Furnished with heavier pieces in the public areas, there were large dark and rough tables, with accompanying heavy benches instead of chairs. Bearskins covered stone-cobbled floors, and medieval swords, shields, and helmets decorated the walls and were scattered otherwise about the ground floor. Lighting, including chandeliers, flickered like candles although the power source was electric. Windows were decorated with stained and leaded glass depicting battle scenes from the Middle Ages.

The Chairwoman informed the group that upper floors in the building were made up entirely of offices, conference rooms, a small auditorium, and other administrative space for the Eagle Trust and its operations. There was even a suite of offices outfitted for the use of members of the Trust should they be on the premises. Finished with the details, she led the way to an elevator.

On leaving the public area, similarly heavy and dark wooden furniture also filled the offices and conference rooms of the two floors above, but furnishings there were very distinct from both the medieval pieces in the building's public area and the modern designs in the other two buildings.

Obviously proud of the signature facility, both its member architect and the Chairwoman explained there were already discussions of possible awards for both the structures and the interior designs.

Inside the privacy of the administrative offices, the Chairwoman gathered her group and reminded them of the Eagle Trust's goals.

"Even as we pursue our core research," she told the six other members, "we must not lose sight of the fact we also set out to do extraordinary good with our talents and our wealth."

A wave of agreement made its way through the small gathering.

The Chairwoman continued. "We are in the process of setting up two free clinics for the underprivileged here in the city. Young doctors will learn and gain experience as they care for those who seek our help." The clinics, Madam Chairwoman told them, would be a focal point that could be used to divert unwanted attention from certain areas of their research wing here at the Cambridge Center. She gave basic details and then proceeded with the tour.

The Chairwoman allowed the architect to explain many of the innovations incorporated into the Cambridge Center facilities. It seemed, though, the best ideas had come from the Chairwoman herself, at least in her own mind.

"It took me months to find this particular building with grounds large enough to accomodate our planned facility," she told them during one of her interruptions. Continuing, she took credit for having the old and the new represented in the structure of their hospital and research facility. The architect member stood quietly aside and listened along with the others. Several members glanced her way, some with knowing looks in their eyes.

Each of the others took time to congratulate the architect on the beauty and on her dedication to having their facilities exemplify both the history and the future of Prague and Central Europe. Standing idly in the background, the architect member's input was absent from most of the conversation as Balca agreed with, but also received, the accolades.

In the medical wing, up-to-date equipment was on hand for all needs and for the comfort of patients.

"After all," the members were told, "we want this to be the most sought-after facility in all of Europe and perhaps even the world. We want there to be a waiting list for treatment here."

Everyone agreed with her assessment.

The research wing of the building continued to hold the close attention of everyone in the group. It, too, had the latest equipment, and the best educated and trained staff available for its goals in experimentation, testing, and analysis. More than one of the members had thought of the prestige involved in having a plaque at The Eagle Pub beside the one commemorating Francis Crick's and James Watson's work regarding DNA. That specific discussion brought on a short flurry of handshakes, backslapping, and hopeful dialogue. Perhaps their plaque would come sooner rather than later.

Later that afternoon, the members returned to their individual countries and homes. The medical and research center teams settled into their respective routines and continued their endeavors, each aspiring to achieve the group's goals of making the world a more reasonable place to live, if even in their own interesting roundabout way.

4

SATURDAY, SEPTEMBER 19, 2015
COKER CREEK, TENNESSEE, USA

* * *

WHEN RAGE DOYLE HAD REASON to leave the seclusion of his log cabin, he normally stopped in Coker Creek to check his post office box. Relatively few items of importance found their way to him in this small, East Tennessee mountain community. Ads, coupons, and not much else made it to the box.

Not many individuals even knew he lived in Coker Creek.

Running low on coffee, which constituted a minor emergency in his world, Rage made a list that morning and drove down off the mountain for a few supplies he could purchase locally. On the way back to his cabin, the quick stop at the post office was more of a habit than a necessity to the former CIA Special Agent.

The mail clerk noticed Rage Doyle's vehicle pull up in front of the building. Doyle climbed out and said something to the three men standing on the porch. They laughed, waved, and watched him walk toward the door.

As Coker Creek's postmistress, she had been aware of Rage—Mr. Doyle—since he bought a secluded cabin and moved into the area more than two years ago. Guessing his age at the time to be sixty or so, she had been surprised to find out he was closer to seventy. An overheard conversation with another customer had confirmed the number.

She kept her eye on Rage as he entered and turned toward his mailbox. Tall at over six feet, he wore a thin mustache, a short beard, and a significant head of silver hair. At least the hair she could see was silver and full beneath the hat he always seemed to wear.

One time in jest, she had asked if he wore his fedora to bed. With a slight grin, he had glanced her way and said, "I don't remember. You'll have to come over one night, and we'll check." That was the closest he'd ever come to being personal.

He was trim and appeared to be quite muscular for someone his age. Several customers had mentioned seeing Rage walking and running on the mountain near his cabin, generally in the early morning.

As usual, today he was wearing his fedora and sunglasses. Missing was the long black leather coat he often wore.

A little too warm today, she guessed.

She had come to like Rage and thought he was handsome and interesting. A peculiar trait she had noticed was he reacted to his surroundings in an intriguing manner. Having watched, she decided he was always aware of everything happening around him. She had also decided it was not a conscious act.

Doyle's eyes were interesting too. She had seen him a couple of times without the sunglasses. His eyes were blue—sky blue on a clear day—and penetrating. And he had a small, half-moon scar just above the outer edge of his left eyebrow. She had fantasized a number of times about how it got there.

The thing about him that bothered her a little was no one seemed to know anything about his past. Despite the mystery around him, she would probably go out with Rage if he asked. It didn't bother her that she was twenty-five years younger.

But he hadn't asked…

"Who do you know in the Czech Republic?"

Rage looked surprised or confused, causing her to continue.

"You have an envelope postmarked from Prague in your box."

She was on a roll now.

"I was gonna call if you hadn't come in today. I thought it might be important."

Rage didn't comment.

None of the local residents knew his background. To them he was just one more retiree who wanted to live part-time in a log cabin in the mountains. He didn't bother the locals, and they didn't ask much about what he did before he became their neighbor.

Glancing through the material that had accumulated, Rage sorted out two pieces of regular mail. One was an addendum to his automobile insurance policy; the other was the now noteworthy envelope from the Czech Republic. It appeared to be a letter.

He checked one side then flipped it over. No visible indication of the sender. A cursory examination of the outside showed no signs of anything out of the ordinary. No suggestion of tampering or traces of powder.

Tucking the envelope into his jacket pocket, Rage said goodbye and headed for his vehicle.

She sighed and turned toward the small stack of mail that needed sorting.

While driving the mile back to his cabin, curiosity got the better of Rage.

Slipping the envelope from his pocket, he held it to the light but saw nothing strange about the outline inside, probably only a letter. Still, who could have sent it? And how did they come up with his location here in the mountains? He had other forwarding addresses, but the one here at Coker Creek was known to only a select few. Those he had chosen carefully and could count on the fingers of one hand.

The only person in the Czech Republic—and especially in Prague—who came to mind was a friend from long ago, Kateřina Bambenek. He didn't know if that Lambs still her name. They had only communicated a few times after he left Prague in the late 1960s.

At the time, she was a young woman of great beauty and even greater understanding. A torrid, though short, love affair with a young Kateřina had taught Rage a great deal about being in love and being new in the ranks of the CIA at same time. The most important lesson he had learned was the two very different undertakings couldn't be managed simultaneously.

They had tried. Both had wanted their time together to be special. Both had also known he would only be in Prague for a few weeks. Two months had stretched into three, but even that was not enough. They had fallen in love.

Rage and Kateřina had known from the moment they met their feelings for each other would not be just an affair. Neither had been in love before, and they would not be satisfied with something that would make them ashamed.

Each had wanted more, but like the young of all generations, they had thought their feelings could be placed on hold… at least for a while. But aroused passions can't be placed on the shelf for a later time, and therein one of life's contradictions was learned.

Back at the cabin with the car put away in his basement garage, Rage checked the downstairs windows and door for signs of someone entering. A string, a hair, or a small sliver of wood here and there were undisturbed.

He had considered living in Coker Creek under a false name but had discarded the idea. Having left the CIA years ago, he had decided to live the future as normally as possible. In part, that meant using his own name and being watchful.

Rage went upstairs and checked security signs. Satisfied no one had been there and he was alone, Rage went to the living room and tossed a couple of logs in the fireplace. Smoldering embers had a roaring blaze going in a matter of minutes, warming the small cabin, and giving off pleasant crackling sounds and a familiar smoky aroma.

With the fire going, Rage made coffee and with a cup in hand, walked to the French doors looking out on the mountains to the east. An early fall was evident with leaves changing colors. Most days were sunny, but this particular morning had been damp and cool. Rage had wished a couple of times that he had worn his leather coat.

As the fire grew warm, Rage walked over and sat on the rock hearth, his back to the blazing logs, and pulled the envelope out of his pocket. His small Swiss Army knife served as an opener, and the few sheets of a hand-written letter were soon in his grasp.

It began, *"Dear Raegene,"*

With those words, he knew immediately it was from Kateřina. Glancing out at the distant mountains, Rage fondly remembered she had always called him by his given name. Through the years, only one other person had ever normally called him by that name. That individual had died in his arms many years ago.

Glancing to the letter's ending, he stared at her signature. How long had it been? Forty-five, maybe forty-six years?

Rage remembered the morning he left her. He had made a promise, and she had believed him. Rage had said he would be back in six months, eight at the most. It had been over forty years now, and he'd never returned to Prague—not even to visit.

He thought of the few short months they had been together. How many times had they strolled across Charles Bridge in early evening searching for an out-of-the-way pub or café for a quiet dinner? As if only yesterday, he could still hear the sounds of the Vltava River as they stopped and watched the waters flow past. The couple often waved to partiers on the tour boats navigating the river. They had been there many times, talking, planning, dreaming, promising… He had made many special promises to her, only to have broken them all, one by one.

Forcing himself, Rage turned his attention from the memories and back to the pages he held in his hand.

Dear Raegene,

What a surprise this letter must be. If I had a koruna for each time I have thought of you in the years since we parted, I would now be wealthy beyond compare. I do wonder if you remember our short holiday in the country when we were very young. I have thought of those days often. You will never know…

But I am not writing this letter to discuss old times or promises—yours or mine. Instead, I contact you to ask an act of great kindness, one possibly involving danger. I should tell you, I ask this not for myself but for a dear friend who cannot request help because she no longer walks among the living. Her remains were interred a few weeks ago at the Vinohrady Cemetery here in the city.

This is the request, Raegene. I want you to come to Prague.

I must have help to solve a mystery and find those who killed my friend's daughter. My friend was Elita Melcer. Her daughter's name was Marta. As I wrote above, this letter is for Elita, so you should feel no special obligation because it is I who makes the request.

Marta was twenty-six when she was killed. She was anticipating the fall season and walking among the flowers on a thousand trails here in the city. That was her personality.

Then, I believe, this young woman's life was cut short for benefit and possibly profit of others. There is much more I will tell you if you join me here in Prague.

During the past weeks, I have questioned, searching for someone—anyone—who I might call upon for help. Raegene, yours is the name that came up, time after time. I need the wisdom I remember in the young man I knew for a moment in time those many years ago. If you could come here, even for a short period, I would believe there is hope.

My greatest concern is there are others like Marta who have died or are in danger—possibly even my own daughter, Ana.

I detest myself for begging, yet without saying more, this truly is a matter of life and death. Hopefully not for me but certainly for others. Perhaps you remember this about me, I am not one who exaggerates.

Appropriate information for reaching me is on another sheet.

And least I forget, you must wonder how I found you …

I too, have friends in strategic places. Favors were called, and you were located there in your mountains. I can only imagine your log cabin home hidden in a forest.

He stopped reading, staring out the window again for a moment.

How could she know someone who could find me here in Coker Creek? Someone at the Prague Embassy? Someone else? But who?

Perhaps he'd find out. He didn't like this location to be known.

Raegene, if this journey is possible, please let me know at your earliest convenience. Also, please send a letter rather than using the phone or the internet. I fear I am being watched, and certain communications could be dangerous for both of us.

If you cannot come, I will understand. Time must have dulled your memories of me. I would understand that too.

But I remember you... I will forever!

Sincerely,

Kateřina

Finished, he dropped the pages on the rug at his feet and then reached back down for the one that held her address and other personal information.

The street didn't sound familiar; that wasn't surprising. It had been so long ago, and she had shared a small apartment with another young woman when he knew her.

Suddenly, he felt a thin bead of perspiration on his forehead. The fire behind him was getting a little too warm to sit so close. Rage eased himself down onto the rug, gaining a little distance and then leaned back against the hearth.

Thinking about the letter, he quickly knew he would go. There was nothing pending to keep him from helping. He would pack and then call for reservations.

Picking up the letter and envelope again, Rage glanced at the postmark. Kateřina had mailed the letter seven days earlier. He glanced at his watch—11:10 a.m. Not even noon yet. If he remembered correctly, Prague was six hours ahead of Eastern Standard Time. That would make it just after 5:00 p.m. there. He wondered what she was doing, what the evening held in store.

When he was stationed in Prague those many years ago, when he and Kateřina were young lovers, they might have been sitting at some sidewalk café sharing a light dinner at this time of the evening. She would have a glass of wine at hand, and he would have been enjoying his black coffee à la Prague.

Drawing his mind back to the present, Rage thought of what would be required for a quick run to the capital of the Czech Republic. The less he had to carry, the better. Besides his MacBook Pro in its own bag, he needed his passport, a few changes of clothing and shoes, some extra underwear and socks, plus his toiletries in one decent sized carry-on to get him on his way. Experience had taught Rage to be prepared to rush out the door if necessary when he called for reservations. Often, a flight could be arranged instantly.

In fifteen minutes with his carry-on packed, Rage went back to the loft and entered the closet there. Moving four different boards in separate walls and in a complicated sequence, he was then able to remove a sizable section of the ceiling's slanted northern panel.

Secured on the back of the section, a small arsenal of weapons was available to him. Rage picked a Walther PPK 380 pistol and racked the slide a couple of times, assuring himself the weapon was unloaded and in perfect working order. It had been routinely cleaned and oiled just days earlier.

Rage then selected two empty magazines, several rounds of hollow-point ammo, and two lock boxes. He carried the items to his nearby desk. Returning to the closet, he carefully closed the opening in the slanted ceiling, returning the panel and locking boards to their original positions.

Back at his desk, Rage secured the pistol, magazines, and ammo into the lock boxes normally required by the CIA. He took those downstairs, slipping them underneath his clothing and shoes in the carry-on luggage and zipped the bag.

A dark thought crossed his mind: *Hope I don't need the PPK on this trip.*

He was packed except for his computer. Now what?

Thinking it through, Rage realized the nearly five-thousand-mile trip to the Czech Republic would take at least ten hours, maybe fifteen or more with layovers and aircraft changes. He would try to sleep on the flight across the Atlantic, and hopefully he would be refreshed and ready to hit the ground running when he reached Prague.

That was the hope and plan. In reality, Rage knew it almost never worked out that way.

Heading up to the loft again with his computer, Rage's thoughts were already on the calls he needed to make in order to set up the trip. Sometimes Rage wished he could just dial up a travel agent and let them do the legwork.

Unfortunately, his days with the CIA had taught him differently. Never let outsiders have your information and plans when it isn't necessary. Good idea then, good idea now.

Scheduling a flight to Prague from Knoxville, Tennessee, on the weekend was not easy. The best he could do was settle for one that would leave late Sunday afternoon and arrive in the Czech capital early Monday evening, local time.

It took over an hour to set it up. Finished, he checked his notes. If he could be at McGee Tyson Airport by 5:40 on Sunday afternoon, he would be on his way. Routing had been complicated. Rage had an itinerary that included Knoxville, Atlanta, JFK in New York, Dresden, Germany, and finally, Prague.

He had tried, but this was the best he could do on short notice. That would put him into Prague's Václav Havel Airport at around seven o'clock Monday night. If everything went as planned.

Rage didn't want to deal with his car. He had no idea when he would be returning, and Kateřina had mentioned danger. There wasn't a guarantee one *would* return from a trip like this. He had also learned that at the CIA.

Picking up his phone, Rage called his local friend who ran a gun store.

"Don, I need a favor."

"Name it," the man from lower Alabama told him.

Rage had a minor ownership in Don's weapons operation.

"I need to get to McGhee Tyson late tomorrow afternoon and don't want to leave my car there. Can you help me?"

"Drive over to our house. Linda and I will take you to the airport. We'll keep the car at our place and pick you up when you get back."

Don and his problem solving…

"You sure?"

"Yeah, I'm sure. Anything else? I'm busy."

Don was also direct and to the point when he needed to be.

"I'll be there around three."

"Okay."

5

MONDAY, SEPTEMBER 21, 2015
PRAGUE, CZECH REPUBLIC

* * *

A COLD RAIN WAS FALLING on Monday evening when Rage's flight touched down in Prague. The temperature was 36, about ten degrees lower than normal.

The attendant who made the announcement spoke first in Czech, then English, then two or three other languages. The former CIA agent understood most of the original announcement and then filled in the gaps when it was given in English. The gist of the information was that Prague was experiencing a cold early fall.

Glancing out a window, Rage was pleased he had worn his fedora and leather coat. *If the nasty weather continues,* he thought, *I'll need to pick up rainwear of some sort. Surely this drizzle will clear soon, and the temp will rise a little.*

Rage was among the first passengers off the aircraft and headed directly for customs. Passport in hand and bags ready to open, he approached the lone officer at the desk.

"Anything to declare?"

Rage showed him the pistol and accompanying paperwork.

"Anything else?"

When Rage shook his head, the officer waved him through.

So far, so good.

When he reached the taxi stand, three other travelers converged on Rage wanting to ride the same car into the city.

"But, I'm not going to a hotel," he tried to explain to them. It did no good.

His would-be fellow passengers gathered their English phrases to tell Rage he could drop them off at their hotels, and then the driver could take Rage to his own destination.

The driver wanted to do it that way too.

Without significant argument, Rage settled back and let the woman and two men get the show on the road. Kateřina wasn't expecting him, so he had no set time to arrive at her place. Since she hadn't wanted a phone call or email, there had been no way to alert Kateřina. His arrival was going to be as much a surprise to her as the letter had been to him.

The light rain continued, requiring the taxi driver to keep his wipers on. The deep grating sound each time the windshield was cleared was loud and difficult to endure, causing Rage to imagine fingernails on a chalkboard.

As the taxi moved along in the slow traffic, a sudden thought crossed Rage's mind. *I wonder if she has a husband or significant other?* It hadn't occurred to him, and it hadn't been mentioned in the letter.

Oh well, too late to be concerned now.

When Rage gave the street address, the driver whistled. Two of his fellow passengers glanced his way. They obviously recognized the area.

"Nice houses," the driver said in a broken English accent. He then rubbed a thumb and two fingers together, indicating money.

"Brevnov suburb," he declared, "in Prague 6 region." Then, bobbing his head up and down, he added, "Strolling easy to Charles Bridge. You will see."

Forty-five minutes later, the other riders were dropped off at their hotels. After a short ride into the rolling hills, the operator slowed and began checking for the number Rage had given him. The destination was several houses further along the street.

When the driver pulled to the curb, Rage sat for a few moments taking in his surroundings. A gorgeous pastel green manor house, significant in size, stood at the end of a meandering sidewalk that was bordered by handsome, though narrow, flower beds. Several mature trees were also a part of the landscape. Light from the street and gas lamps near the door illuminated the front of the house.

The residence was set back further than most of the others. Curving across in front of the dwelling, the circular cobblestone driveway continued around toward the back of the property.

The house itself was larger than those on either side. Rage briefly wondered if the structure could be a small apartment building or inn, then decided against it.

"You friends living here?" Broken English again.

Rage nodded.

"Very much money."

The driver's first comment had been a question; the second, an opinion.

"Someone from another lifetime," he said to himself more than to the driver.

Rage thought the fare was too high. The driver made assurances it was not as they settled up, and then he hurriedly closed the vehicle's door and drove away. Rage was pretty sure he had been taken.

Picking up his computer and the travel case, Rage started along the sidewalk toward the grand house. About halfway there, he heard a vehicle turn into the driveway and watched it slow as its headlights caught him walking toward the residence. The automobile stopped, as did he. Both Rage and whoever was inside the car watched each other for several seconds.

Inching forward finally, the dark Porsche 911 pulled near the steps and cut the engine. The driver's door opened, and a figure stepped out. Positioned between Rage and his destination, the individual stood as still as a statue. Only a few meters and the vehicle separated them.

Unsure if it was a man or a woman, Rage waited. At last, the vehicle's door closed. Three words were spoken softly with a voice Rage recognized after all the years between then and now.

"Raegene Dorryen Doyle…"

They stood still for several seconds more, staring at each other through the semi-darkness. Then Kateřina rushed toward him, arms opened wide. Locked in an embrace that had been nearly half a century in coming, no words needed to be spoken.

When they finally leaned back to look into each other's eyes, there were tears on Kateřina's cheeks. Rage's eyes sparkled too, perhaps with more emotion than just the excitement of the moment.

"Hello, Sweetheart," he said.

He remembered the favorite name he had called her all those years ago, and so did she.

She smiled. "Let's go inside and close the doors to the world."

He backtracked the few steps to the bags he had dropped. Kateřina followed, a step behind. She reached out for his computer. Then she turned to lead the way.

He couldn't pull his eyes away from this woman. She was as beautiful as when he had left her all those years ago. But now, a more apt description might be alluring. Mysteriously attractive.

There was…just…

She sensed something in his demeanor and turned.

"There will be time to talk," she simply said. "Let us get you inside first. You must be very tired from your trip."

"We can talk after I've rested. I just wanted to find you." He glanced at her as they started up the steps. "There wasn't time to let you know I was coming, and your letter sounded urgent. I'll get a hotel nearby,"

"I will not hear of a hotel." Her statement left little room for argument. "You will stay here with me. We have much to discuss."

He stared into her eyes. That gorgeous green color hadn't dimmed the least bit. He could see it even in the half-light of street lamps.

As they neared the entrance, security lights, triggered by their movement, brightened the entire front of her residence. Those eyes, the ones he had remembered so well, sparkled.

"I have to tell you about my friend and her daughter," she said.

"Yes."

She stopped, one foot on the porch. "There is something new you must also know." She hesitated, then obviously made some sort of decision. "But that will wait. At least until you are inside and settled."

Rage nodded.

"I didn't dare hope you would come," she told him.

A slight smile was his only response.

Kateřina smiled too, and then led her long-ago lover inside.

The interior of the dwelling was extraordinary. Marble floors, live plants and trees, a chandelier extending downward out of the ceiling of a third floor. And then there was the circular stairway, beautiful wooden hand rails, and a woven carpet runner beginning at the marble floor where they were standing.

Rage thought his entire cabin would probably fit in the entry of Kateřina's home.

He told her and was treated to the laugh he remembered from their days and nights together so long ago. *Funny how special memories streak across the years,* he thought, *and seem so fresh and new.*

Soft classical music wafted from further inside the house. A waltz was playing. Rage thought he recognized the Minuet Waltz by Chopin. He was proud of himself.

Commenting, Rage saw her expression brighten. "I keep music on most of the time," she said.

Kateřina had changed her shoes when they came inside and offered him the same. Rage picked a pair that looked like sandals. The box for shoes was near the front door. She called it a *botník.*

As Rage looked the house over, Kateřina said, "There is a story here."

I can certainly believe that.

The woman he had loved so long ago simply allowed Rage to follow her deeper into the opulence in which she lived. They walked without talking until reaching a large sitting area at the rear of the dwelling. Beyond, a sweeping multilevel terrace was lit past windows extending twenty feet upward at the rear of the conversation room.

A drink was offered, then refused, and coffee was agreed upon. The kitchen was only a few steps away, and Rage watched as she prepared a pot and poured them each a cup. Small talk filled the moments of waiting. With coffee in hand, Kateřina took a position at one end of a colossal settee and motioned for Rage to sit opposite her on a matching piece.

"Tell me about yourself," she said with a smile. "Preferably details that will not require you to kill me afterwards."

She sipped at the coffee and then set her cup on a side table.

"Without details," he said, "I'm afraid my life story is short and a bit uninteresting."

Rage couldn't take his eyes off her. She was watching him too.

He sampled the strong brew once and then again before also setting his cup aside. It was certainly different, bitter and strong, reminding Rage of New Orleans chicory coffee without the boiling milk.

"I worked with the Central Intelligence Agency for twenty-seven years," he told her finally. "Since then, I've been doing private assignments for almost twenty years."

Then he became silent.

Turning her head to the side, she questioned, "That is all there is of the life story of Raegene Dorryen Doyle?" Chuckling, Kateřina added, "Surely, you can do better!"

"Not without blood stains," he said with a wink and a grin. They both laughed.

Here in this house, sitting across from Kateřina, Rage was surprised at his thoughts and observations. So much of the beautiful young woman he had known all those years ago was still apparent in the mature lady across from him. Little things she did like the turning of her head to make a point in conversation and the ready laughter that seemed always an instant away.

Other things, too, like the seriousness in her face when time and subject called for it. And she still tossed her hair with a finger the way she had when she was so much younger.

Her pale and perfect skin, the flawlessly sculptured nose, and Kateřina's long neck were all still the same. Looking closely, Rage could detect tiny laugh lines, but the virtually invisible marks only give her face more character.

Even her figure seemed the same. She couldn't weigh five pounds more than when they had danced, almost as one, on the few occasions they'd had to do foolish and carefree things.

One evening she tried to teach me the tango. That hadn't gone very well.

"…there been many other women in your life since we parted?"

Rage realized she was asking a question. He had missed part of it.

"What? I'm sorry," he said, "I was thinking of another time. What did you say?"

Even in the muted light, he could see color come to her cheeks.

Quickly seeking to put her at ease, he said, "Don't concern yourself. I was only thinking of amusing memories."

Kateřina smiled, and her expression relaxed. The room seemed to get a little brighter.

"I was asking if there have been many other women in your life since we parted." She clarified the earlier question, and then seemed to get to the real point. "Did you marry somewhere along the way?"

"No… Did you?"

A slight shaking of her head. "No," she told him softly.

He noticed her squeezing her eyes closed for a moment as if there had been a pain. Then she looked at Rage again and smiled.

She held his gaze for an inordinate time and then told him, "I think I have always been waiting for you…but you never came."

It sounded so final.

After she'd said it, her mood brightened, a slight smile curving her lips upward.

"But you did come this time, didn't you?" The smile became even more scintillating.

After a moment's hesitation, she added, "The one and only time I've asked."

Another penetrating glance and then she walked across the room and adjusted the volume on the soft music.

"Tell me about your daughter."

Rage had noticed photographs of a young woman on a table in the entryway.

A momentary silence followed as Kateřina adjusted herself on the settee. Her shoes were kicked off and those long legs curled underneath her. She reached for the coffee and took a sip. Ready at last, her eyes looked past him, and she began to talk.

"Ana was a test-tube baby," she said, "and there was a..." her forehead wrinkled, "what is English for the woman who carries the baby?" She looked to Rage for an answer.

"Surrogate?"

"Yes, there was a surrogate mother involved."

Not quite knowing what he expected, Rage was pretty sure this wasn't it. He already had questions for her but kept his lips tight, letting Kateřina tell her own story.

"According to the information I was given," she now appeared in a rush, "a very wealthy couple wanted a child but could not have one of their own."

He was confused, but he waited for her to continue.

Nervous now, even agitated, her feet were back on the floor, Kateřina had her elbows resting on her knees. Looking into Rage's eyes, she appeared to be searching for the right words.

He waited.

"An agreement was reached with a surrogate mother, and everything proceeded without problems with an egg being fertilized and implanted." Kateřina stopped and reached for the coffee again.

"Did the surrogate mother know the couple?" He just *had* to get involved.

"I was coming to that," she told him. "They didn't want to know her. They said it would be better for the substitute mother."

Still not knowing where Kateřina's story was going, Rage reached for his own coffee. It was cold. He expected hers was too. Motioning for her to continue, he took their cups and headed for refills. She followed Rage to the kitchen.

"The pregnancy was uneventful and had reached eight months when the tragedy occurred."

He turned toward her, his eyebrows lifted. "A tragedy?"

"An aircraft cra…crash." Kateřina had trouble getting the words out, but she continued. "Everyone on board, the two passengers and the pilot, were killed."

"The baby's parents?" Rage asked.

"Yes."

Coffee in hand, they left the kitchen. Back on the settees, they faced each other again.

"What was your connection to this situation?"

Her words were slow in coming. "I gave life…to the baby."

He strained to hear Kateřina's next whispered words.

"She is my daughter." Kateřina held Rage's eyes for a moment. "She is Ana."

Time had slipped away; it was nearing midnight when Kateřina revealed she had been Ana's surrogate mother. It had come as a total surprise to Rage. There was so much more he wanted to ask, but he could read the exhaustion on Kateřina's face. She had rubbed at her temples several times.

At this point, moving and thinking on adrenalin alone, he was pleased when she suggested they call it a night. Though Rage had asked again about a nearby hotel, Kateřina wouldn't agree to it.

"There are six bedrooms in this house," she said. "I will put you at the end of the hall on the second floor."

The two of them retrieved his bags, and she walked Rage toward the room she'd suggested.

"My bedroom is here on the ground floor, on the wing past the kitchen and sitting area. It will be quiet upstairs," she assured him, obviously meaning he could sleep as late as he wanted.

She led Rage to the entry way and then started upstairs to his bedroom, but he stopped at the decorative table where the several photos of the young woman he'd noticed earlier were displayed.

"Is this Ana, your daughter?" Rage asked, picking up one of the framed pictures to look closely.

The young woman appeared to be in her early to mid-twenties.

"She's beautiful," he said, gazing at Kateřina.

"Yes," she said. "And Ana is lovely on the inside too."

The daughter was blonde. There were four portraits and a couple of other photos, one with a younger Ana holding a trophy. Another was a portrait of mother and daughter together—two beautiful women.

"She appears tall in the photos," he said.

"In your way of measuring, Ana is five feet and ten inches," she said. "That is tall, yes?"

"Yes," he laughed. "That is tall."

Kateřina took the picture, looked at it for a moment and then placed it back on the table.

"She is my treasure." Kateřina glanced at him. "I cannot lose her."

What an intriguing comment.

She turned to the stairs as he looked at her.

They continued up to his bedroom; Kateřina made sure he had everything he needed.

At last, before retiring for the night, they returned to the kitchen, and Kateřina prepared night-time tea.

"It helps me sleep and also eases the headaches I sometimes have in the morning," casually mentioning the problem had begun recently.

"Have you seen a doctor?"

"No. I am sure it's nothing."

He noticed a slight grimace as she turned back to the tea.

"There was something new you were going to tell me," he said. "Something you mentioned as we were coming inside earlier."

"Yes." She looked at him. "Ana is ill. She is in the hospital at her work location. It happened after I mailed the letter."

"Tell me about it."

The tea had steeped, and she handed him a cup, taking one for herself.

After a sip, she glanced at Rage over the edge of her cup. "Not now. I will give you the details in the morning when we are rested." Nodding at his tea, she said, "This will relax you after the long trip and our extended evening of conversation."

Like the coffee earlier, the hot tea was not anything he remembered having before. She didn't give it a name, only telling him it would definitely help him sleep.

There was a hint of orange and spices, and Rage even asked for a second cup. Kateřina seemed to enjoy watching him down the spiced drink.

Yawning several times before he left the kitchen, Rage told the lovely lady good night, kissed her on the cheek, and held her close for a moment. Then he went back upstairs to his new temporary quarters.

Usually one for long showers, he cut this one short and in record time, crawled into the big bed. He stretched out, and then a thought struck him.

I didn't do my exercises.

Rage had skipped his short routine.

I never do that but I'm not getting up for them now.

He didn't remember being this tired since he'd left the CIA. The flight, the hours they'd spent catching up, and now jet lag?

As he often did, Rage would plan tomorrow's itinerary when he awoke. Sleep came quickly. Though he was not prone to dreams, they interrupted Rage's rest during night and seemed very real.

6

TUESDAY, SEPTEMBER 22, 2015

* * *

HOURS LATER RAGE AWAKENED. IT WAS 7:00 a.m. He was still tired and also a little groggy. He wondered if it was jet lag or the tea Kateřina had brewed. Whatever, he hoped it would wear off soon.

He decided spending a few minutes in the shower couldn't hurt. Rage turned the water as hot as he could stand it. Easing under the spray, he leaned forward against the wall, head down with almost scalding hot water streaming over his body.

His thoughts turned to the day ahead and to Kateřina and the things she had told him. They had concluded the conversation after Kateřina said her daughter had been admitted to a hospital.

Now with a new day, more details about the overall situation needed to be forthcoming. For instance, what had happened after the deaths of the biological parents? How had Kateřina supported herself and a daughter? Oh, and the brief mention of a story regarding the house.

As Rage dried off and left the shower, a vague impression drifted across his consciousness. In his dream—or was it a memory?—it seemed he recalled his bedroom door opening during the night. A shadowy figure crept silently to his bedside. Once there, the covers had been lifted and a soft slim body nestled into the curve of his own. His arm was lifted and placed gently across the form beside him. Then, once again—in his dreams?—he had succumbed to the sleep his body and mind demanded.

Shaking his head, Rage walked to a window and stood looking outside for a moment at the gray morning. His mind twisted and turned, attempting to separate dreams from reality. Could she have come to him, sharing the bed and the warmth of his body? If only for a short time?

As Rage turned back to the bathroom, something tugged at his mind. Nothing visual, just…the certain awareness of a woman's presence…*Kateřina?*

Could she have been here during the night? Or, after all, this is her house. Why wouldn't there be touches of her in all the rooms.

Rage questioned his own thoughts, but…

Kateřina was in the kitchen. The aroma of coffee met him halfway down the stairs. It was certainly welcome. She was pouring a cup as he walked into the room. Motioning Rage to the counter, she passed the steaming brew across to him.

"Black and in your hand. Am I correct?" Kateřina laughed, remembering. "And all those years ago."

Rage chuckled too, lifting the cup in a salute.

"Any special requests for breakfast?"

"I'd be fine with something easy on the stomach. Toast or a pastry perhaps."

"Drink your coffee while I put something together."

Minutes later, they were enjoying dark bread toast with a variety of jellies. Small talk dominated the meal with none of the seriousness that had held them past midnight. Rage knew they would get back there soon enough.

"Why don't we go for a walk and continue our talk from last night?" she asked, clearing their dishes and topping off their cups.

She was talking fast and her hands were in constant motion. He could tell she was concerned. Who wouldn't be with a daughter in the hospital?

Indicating she needed to prepare for their outing, Kateřina started toward her bedroom. As she reached the doorway, Rage stopped her. "I had a strange dream during the night."

"Oh?" She turned and leaned against the frame.

"I dreamed you came into my bedroom and lay beside me for a while."

Kateřina stared at him for a moment before replying. Then, "Dreams are almost real sometimes, aren't they?"

With those few curious words spoken, she turned and walked on.

When it was time for them to leave, the weather was better. The sun was out, and only a few clouds were scattered about a bright sky. It was warmer too, but still not a time to be out without a coat and scarf. Kateřina found a muffler for him, and they strolled out to the street and away from her house.

"Let's walk toward Charles Bridge," she suggested. "It is only three kilometers away. Do you remember the bridge?"

Rage said he did as they headed eastward toward the Prague landmark and the Vltava River.

Since Ana was to be their main topic of conversation, Kateřina started with the airplane crash.

"Representatives of the parent's trust came to me immediately because the baby's birth was so near, only a month away." She walked slowly, her eyes cast downward. Speech was unhurried and deliberate, unlike earlier in the morning.

Wondering if she had ever told anyone the full story, Rage asked.

"No." She shook her head.

"Because they were still young, the parents had not yet planned for their own deaths, but they had made provisions for their new child's life."

Kateřina glanced over, a solemn expression on her face. The drawn look around her eyes suggested it was difficult telling this to him.

"I was informed the couple had no heirs, and their wealth was to be dedicated to various charities and to the child's health and well-being."

She stopped, standing for several moments as though in deep thought.

"I was surprised," she commented without looking at him as they continued walking. "Everything seemed to have been considered. The child, Ana, would be educated at Cambridge in England, and there would be funds for living. Everything had been considered except a family for Ana."

"Obviously, that's where you became important...for the second time," Rage said it aloud, speaking slowly as he thought the situation through.

"Yes," she said as they continued along the street. "The couple's representatives asked if I would consider adopting Ana." She glanced at him. "I told them I had little income even if the child's care was funded."

Looking briefly at Rage, she shared another bit of news. "The representatives assured me I would have ample funds at my disposal. A house and other necessities would also be provided."

She glanced over. "You have seen the house..."

Indeed, he had.

Then she added, "And a new automobile has been delivered each year since I agreed to the arrangement."

Rage had a question. "Has anything changed through the years?"

"Nothing," she said. "In fact, the latest automobile, the Porsche you saw last night, arrived only last week."

"What about the agreement? Is it written, and do you have a copy?"

"Oh, yes. I insisted on a written contract." Kateřina chuckled again, her head moving side to side. "It sounded too good. In the beginning, I had trouble believing it."

"What are the basics?" Rage was having trouble believing it, too.

She spelled it out in a sentence. "It provides the house, a car, pays all operating expenses, and allocates 200,000 euros each year for spending money and another 50,000 euros for travel."

Rage made a rough calculation. The figure came to about $270,000 spending money in US currency and close to $70,000 for travel. *Pretty decent money in anyone's estimation.*

Kateřina continued. "The Eagle Trust paid all expenses for Ana at the best private schools. Then everything, including her living expenses, was paid when she went to The Old Schools at Cambridge."

Gesturing with open arms, she said, "I could not have asked for more. There is even a substantial retirement fund in my own name. The Eagle Trust has no control over my funds."

Rage, as usual, was thinking ahead. "So you were provided for in case something happened to Ana?"

She cut him off. "Yes, and the same for Ana if anything happened to me."

"Some deal," he said.

"Yes," Kateřina agreed. "A very nice—how do you say it?—a nice deal?"

Talking as they strolled the streets, Kateřina and Rage walked all the way to the Vltava River near the western end of Charles Bridge. Both were ready for a break. She suggested they sit for a while at Café Márnice. When they were seated, the historic landmark bridge rose above them, casting its shadow across the outdoor tables.

Each ordered water and a loupák; Kateřina promised him it was just a sweet roll. Waiting, they settled back to talk more about Kateřina's daughter.

"When Ana completed her university studies, the Eagle Trust even found her a job," Kateřina told him. "One of the Trust's investments was an upscale clinical research hospital on the outskirts of Prague. Ana signed on to work as a research chemist."

Beaming, Kateřina added, "She loves her work."

"What does she do?"

"Ana experiments in the development phase of new drugs for use with organ transplant patients."

"How long has she been working at the hospital?"

"Three years plus three months."

Their refreshments arrived, and the conversation turned to Charles Bridge and Prague. Kateřina was obviously well versed on her city.

"The area around Prague has been occupied continuously back to approximately BC 5000," Kateřina explained.

"By whom?"

"Various Germanic and Celtic tribes," she told him. "Isn't that amazing?"

Wow! Hard to comprehend, Rage thought.

"Prague Castle," she had pointed it out to him earlier, "was founded in the year AD 870. The offices used by the President of the Czech Republic are still located there."

Rage had vaguely remembered the castle from the time he had spent here years ago. Having her tell him about it had more meaning now.

Kateřina was proud of her city too. He enjoyed hearing her talk about it.

"What about Charles Bridge?" Rage asked, "How old is it?"

Kateřina immediately warmed to the subject. "There were a number of crossings here before Charles Bridge."

Their waiter stopped by at that moment. He asked Kateřina if they needed anything and then left a ticket. Gathering up dishes and glasses, he overloaded himself. A cup rolled from the stack, bounced off the edge of the table and headed to sure destruction on the cobblestone at Rage's feet. A quick flip with the toe of his shoe bounced the cup just high enough for Rage to reach out and catch it in midair.

A few nearby customers heard the noise and watched the show. Several clapped as Rage deftly set the cup on the table as though his quick action was a common occurrence. He touched the edge of his fedora in salute to his admirers.

Kateřina patted his back and smiled before continuing.

"Judita's Bridge was the latest and best known of the earlier ones," she said. "It was only the second stone bridge in Central Europe. Its construction dated back to 1172. Unfortunately, it washed away during floods in 1342."

She looked at him. "I'm boring you."

"No," he assured her. "I'm interested. There was never enough time to learn about Prague when I was here with the CIA. I was always too busy with work…and with you." He winked.

Remembering, they both smiled.

"I will tell you more about Charles Bridge later."

Nearly noon now, Kateřina paid for the treats, and they began strolling along the old streets, walking back toward her house.

"When did you find out Ana was sick?" he asked. "I think you told me earlier."

"Only a few days ago—after I mailed the letter to your cabin in the mountains," she reminded him.

She leaned close and took his arm.

"Ana was perfectly healthy one day," she said, "then very ill with a life-threatening virus the next. She had been in London for a speech but was recalled for a project she was working on. After her return to Prague, there was an accident. Ana became ill. The doctors at the research center are concerned the virus is contagious. They are taking precautions."

She wiped at a tear.

"Ana has been living with me at the house, and we enjoy a good life." She glanced up toward Prague Castle in the distance. Standing proud there on the hillside, the old structures made for quite a view.

"How is she doing, or have you been able to talk to her doctors?"

Based on the answers to his questions, Rage would begin to narrow the situation.

Kateřina released his arm and stopped in her tracks, an angry expression causing her forehead to wrinkle. "I have not seen Ana since she left for work that last morning."

"Not at all?" Perhaps he had misunderstood.

"No!" She was shaking her head rapidly. "I have had no contact for a week except a brief phone conversation with her."

"She phoned you? Tell me about the call."

"Yes, she phoned me," Kateřina said. "There isn't much. She told me not to worry and Dr. Laska would keep me informed. It was a short conversation. Ana seemed rushed, and I believe something is wrong."

"Why do you think that?"

"It was something Ana told me at the end of our quick conversation," Kateřina said.

"What did she say?"

"She said 'I love you.'"

That one caught Rage off guard. "Why would those words cause you to believe something is wrong?" He watched Kateřina closely.

She hesitated and then said, "Ana and I believe those words are special."

Rage nodded, waiting.

"We only speak them when we are together, never on the phone or otherwise."

Rage slowed, turning toward her.

Kateřina slowed too, before asking, "Now do you understand why those words make me believe something is not right at the Cambridge Center?"

He glanced over, nodding. "I do. Did anyone explain the circumstances?"

"No. It became strange immediately." Kateřina looked up at him. "I wanted to see Ana and phoned Dr. Laska. I explained I did not have to be in the room with her. When I told him I did not mind if I saw her through a window, he still said no." Her eyes were misting. "He told me it was not possible because of the location and the room had no windows."

Her eyes held an imploring look as she glanced his way. "Help me, Raegene. Although I was told to come there this evening, I believe they are stealing my daughter away from me. I've called each day but always get the same answer: 'they are watching my daughter closely.'"

Back at her home, Kateřina asked Rage if he would ride with her to take flowers for her friend, Elita Melcer, and her daughter, Marta.

"This is the friend I wrote about," she told him. "I go to the cemetery each week on this day,"

"How did the mother die?"

"She took an overdose of sleeping pills a few days after she lost Marta. Until then, she had been trying desperately to find out what had happened to her daughter."

Looking at Rage, Kateřina motioned toward the settees.

"Elita was very close to her daughter, as I am to Ana," she said as they sat down. "She immediately went into a depression after Marta's death. I tried to see her, but she would not come to her door or take phone calls."

She looked at Rage. "I tried many times."

"Who found her?"

"The woman who cleaned her house."

Wanting to know more about the situation, he agreed to accompany her to the cemetery.

Kateřina had a standing order for flowers. After making a pickup, they drove to Vinohrady Cemetery, then walked some distance to a small plot with twin graves. The mother and daughter had been cremated, and their urns buried next to each other.

Many of the adjoining spaces were large and had elegant markers with designs and lettering detailing the persons entombed there. But not Kateřina's friends.

On the small headstone, there was only a plaque with Elita and Marta's names with their birth and death dates. A hook provided an area for flowers. Kateřina placed a single red rose and some greenery for each. Then she took a few moments, rearranging and making the blossoms appear even more beautiful, if only in her own eyes.

Rage spoke only once. "Always a single rose for each?"

"Yes," Kateřina said. "To me, there is something special about a single stem."

Interesting.

Finished, she turned and smiled at him. "Let's walk a bit."

He let Kateřina lead the way, wanting her to relax and express her thoughts. Rage needed more information to be able to help. Nothing was said for several minutes as they walked among the thousands of graves.

The grounds of the cemetery spread out before them, tombstones everywhere. His eyes were drawn to the years etched under the names. There were new graves and new dates interspersed among others that were very old. In some areas, graves were close, almost touching. Not surprised, he remembered Kateřina had told him the cemetery dated back to 1885.

Along the narrow roads and pathways, there were old trees providing shade with iron benches for the weary. Rage guessed they were placed there for the weary of body *and* of spirit.

Kateřina led the way toward a vacant one, beckoning Rage to follow. Near them, an elderly woman held the arm of an even older man, guiding him to sit and rest. They could hear the muffled conversation of the couple though Rage could only understand a word here and there.

Kateřina turned to him and said, "The man is her father. They brought flowers to his wife's grave."

The two of them sat quietly, unintentionally listening to the couple's conversation.

"He doesn't think he will have the strength to come again. He told his daughter he had said goodbye to his wife today." She paused and then glanced at Rage. "He hopes he will see her again in Paradise."

He let the sadness of the moment fade and then said to her, "Tell me more about you and Ana."

"Where would you have me start?"

"Let's try going all the way back to the beginning," he said. "How were you living before you were asked to be a surrogate mother?"

Glancing at the couple again, Kateřina took a moment to gather her thoughts. "It was several years after you left Prague. I worked at the General Hospital here in the city. I was also studying." Smiling, she added, "I wanted to become a nurse."

"How were you approached?"

"I do not understand...approach?"

"Why you?" He hesitated and then started again. "What made them ask you to be a surrogate mother?"

"I do not know why they picked me," Kateřina told him. Her eyes were squinted; a questioning expression was on her face. "Is it important?"

"Right now I don't know what is important," he told her honestly.

She settled back on the bench, fingers nervously moving about in her lap.

Trying again, he asked who had first talked with her about the idea.

"Dr. Sokol, one of the doctors at the General Hospital, called me to his office late one afternoon." Smiling, Kateřina glanced at her fidgeting fingers, then back at him. "I thought I was—how do you say it?—I thought I had done something wrong and was in trouble."

Rage smiled, allowing her to continue.

"The doctor assured me there was no problem, and then he told me about the couple and how they wanted a child but could not have one."

She gathered her thoughts again.

"It sounded so easy," she said. "And it *was* simple."

Kateřina stood, motioning Rage to follow. Together, they started along the path toward her vehicle.

"Dr. Sokol said I would be able to continue my studies, and I could keep my job at the hospital. The couple would even pay for time I might lose from work because of the pregnancy." She glanced at Rage, obviously seeking understanding.

He smiled and nodded.

"They would also pay me for doing this thing."

Given all the other money floating around, Rage figured they had offered her plenty.

"It was all so wonderful…"

Rage finished the thought for her. "Until the parents were killed?"

Kateřina glanced over and nodded. "Yes, until then."

They took a few steps without speaking.

Then Rage asked, "What happened next? Try to be specific."

Rage watched her face for clues. He often learned as much by observing as by listening.

"Actually, the pregnancy was easy."

She smiled again, this time without looking his way. He guessed Kateřina was remembering the good times, savoring special moments of pleasure and happiness.

"I was not ill with the morning sickness I had heard about." This time she glanced his way. "I did get a craving for gelato, but it lasted for only two or three weeks."

Rage recognized the name, an Italian dessert much like ice cream.

Interjecting himself into her thoughts, Rage inquired, "Nothing strange happened during the time you were carrying the couple's baby?"

She looked over, then back to the pathway, obviously considering his question.

"There was one thing. I did not consider it strange at the time, only precautionary—for the safety of the baby."

"What was this strange thing?"

"I was given a thorough physical exam every week."

"For the entire pregnancy?"

"Yes, each week!"

"That is unusual." Rage said it almost to himself.

Kateřina heard him and commented. "I wondered about the exams. At first I thought something was wrong. After several weeks, though, I decided the regular exams were just something the couple wanted. Dr. Sokol assured me there was no problem, so I did not worry anymore."

Perhaps she should have, Rage thought.

Earlier in the day at the Cambridge Center, there was a knock on an office door, and a well-dressed man entered. The language spoken between the two individuals was Czech.

Getting right to the point, the man said, "The subject that concerned us has happened."

The woman leaned forward, watching him, waiting. Elbows were propped on the arms of her large leather chair, her fingers forming a steeple beneath her chin. She was not overly concerned. Dealing with problems was her responsibility, and she was good at her job.

She stood and walked to the window. Almost as tall as her visitor, she looked to be in her late forties at most, not above sixty as she was. The woman was dressed befitting her position and the status it carried. Makeup and hair were all perfect, as was the blazer, blouse, and skirt she wore.

"Tell me what you have," she said motioning toward a side chair.

"Last night, key words triggered our listening devices. An extended exchange was then recorded."

The chief of security for the health center paused to give her a moment, but she signaled for him to go on, asking, "Where was this?"

A bit concerned, she returned to her desk.

"Kateřina Bambenek's home," he answered as she sat down. "The man is a stranger, but the Bambenek woman seems to have spent time with him in the past, perhaps even being a former lover. We do not know the individual, and his name was not spoken during their recorded conversation on the hidden house microphones. We did not get as much information as we would have liked. There was music playing in the room."

He leaned forward. "We will get a photograph and run it through an ID process."

Then he told her, "His accent makes me think he is an American and probably from the south in that country. I have heard the dialect before."

"An American…"

"Yes. Does it make you remember something?"

"Maybe…perhaps details in Bambenek's history," she said.

The woman was trying to recall details in the vetting material she had read on Kateřina Bambenek. She vaguely remembered something about a short affair years earlier with an American. The details escaped her. The vetting had been long ago, more than twenty-five years.

"What words triggered your recording? Is there a transcript I can read?"

The man handed her several pages. Taking them, she flipped through, studying a sentence here or there of broken conversations and random words. Finished, she turned away from the man and was quiet for a time. Finally, she swiveled back and tossed the transcript onto the desk. She sat forward in her chair directing attention to the man.

"This is rubbish. It's useless," the Chairwoman complained, gesturing toward the transcript. "Get a photo and identify the Bambenek woman's friend." Her voice had taken an authoritarian tone. "In the meantime, watch them. Record all conversations until we know where this is going."

She turned her chair slightly and stared out at the tree-covered landscape extending beyond the windows. Without looking back, she asked, "Do we also have equipment that allows recording of conversations when they are out of the house?"

"No, but I can have something by the end of the day."

She had picked the transcript up again and was scanning it using her finger as a pointer.

"Get whatever equipment you need," she told him without looking up. "I want them covered day and night, everywhere they go, together or separately."

"How often do you want to be informed?" the man asked.

"Every day," she said glancing up and thinking for a moment, "at one o'clock in the afternoon. If I am not here, call my cellphone."

He nodded. "Yes, Madam Chairwoman."

"Thank you, Karel. I will be expecting results soon."

Karel Vlasta closed his briefcase and left the office. Madam Chairwoman's eyes followed her chief of security until he was gone.

As the door closed behind him, the woman reached for the special gray landline on her desk. Leaving the receiver on its saddle, she activated the speaker, pushed one of several buttons on the front panel, and waited for the call to be completed.

These were calls she would rather not have to make. But they had agreed—any possible complication to their research project required Madam Chairwoman to notify each of the members of the Eagle Trust.

Since Number 4 was the most recent beneficiary of their research, Madam Chairwoman decided to reach out to her first. The woman's surgery had been performed only three months earlier. This would also be an opportunity to get an update on her condition.

As the call went through, Madam Chairwoman spoke her thoughts aloud. She smiled, thinking the longtime habit went all the way back to her time at Cambridge.

"Kateřina Bambenek's guest is probably only a friend visiting Prague," she said hopefully, murmuring the words softly. "It is of concern, given that her daughter is being prepared at the present." Madam Chairwoman shook her head, thinking of the complications Bambenek's visitor could potentially bring with him.

After three rings, there was a click, and a female voice answered. "¡Hola!"

"¡Hola, mi amigo. Esta es tu presidenta."

They each shifted to English after an initial Spanish greeting.

"Is there a problem?" the friend inquired. "This phone seldom rings."

"No problems although we are watching the next expected donor's mother."

"For what reason?"

"She has a visitor," the Chairwoman said. "The two of them have had discussions. Those conversations warranted our monitoring the situation. As agreed, I thought our members should know."

"Yes."

The Chairwoman assured her friend the situation was being watched and would be handled as necessary. Then she changed the topic. "How is your surgery? Are you convalescing satisfactorily?"

The woman had undergone an emergency heart transplant due to an attack of Viral-Myocarditis. She would almost certainly have died if a new heart had not been so readily available and with the surgery performed at the Trust's hospital in Prague.

The friend's voice changed noticeably as she answered the Chairwoman's question. It took on a lilt. A touch of happiness was apparent.

"My doctors tell me they could not be more pleased," she said. "All medications are at a minimum, and my vital signs are exactly as they should be, given the circumstances. I am exercising, and I feel wonderful, better even perhaps than before my illness."

The Chairwoman spoke up, "Our investments have been expensive, but they are now paying great dividends." She chuckled before continuing. "I sometimes forget what a great benefit it has been to have these supplies available when they are needed."

"I sometimes forgot too, before I needed mine," the woman said. "Now I only wish there could have been some other method of delivery." Her voice went quickly from words of happiness to laments for decisions the group had made and begun funding more than thirty years ago.

In an effort to redirect the thinking, the Chairwoman said, "Remember, your present ability to aid so many others in your country is due to our earlier foresight and planning. Even then we recognized the future potential of our investments. Now that we are using the assets, we must not lose sight of our original objective."

The Chairwoman could only hope she had been successful in restoring her friend's manner of viewing their original innovative ventures.

After concluding her conversation, Madam Chairwoman used two of the remaining buttons on her phone to directly contact the members who could not be reached locally. Those individuals were informed of their fellow member's condition, both physical and emotional, and the potential complications therein. Then they were informed regarding Kateřina Bambenek's visitor and the questions relating to his purpose for being in the Czech Republic. The Chairwoman assured each of those called that all necessary measures would be taken should problems arise.

With the calls successful, the Chairwoman had Ema, her secretary, alert a young woman on her staff she was needed in Madam Balca's office at once.

Pavia Balek was a trusted member of the Chairwoman's staff, more so than many others. She thought of her decision to bring the young woman into the organization early in her career. Madam Chairwoman had found her to be intelligent and extremely security conscious in addition to being trustworthy. Pavia was also a person with no other potential allegiances within the Cambridge Center.

Arrangements were in process for a small dinner party entertaining important members of Prague's government. Considering the evening to be very important, the Chairwoman felt at ease leaving Pavia to handle the details. They discussed the guest list, the menu, and the seating. Pavia brought her boss up-to-date and received approval.

With planning completed, the Chairwoman asked about Pavia's adoptive mother, whom she knew.

"Mother is very well," the young woman said. "In fact, she is leaving soon on a trip to Zurich with several friends from her church."

"Oh? That is wonderful."

As the young woman set about gathering paperwork and returning it to her briefcase, the Chairwoman watched, feeling her special connection to Pavia. The two of them had formed an unusual attachment in the time Pavia had been a member of her staff. The young woman, her right-hand assistant, had become someone Balca could depend on without question.

When he left the Chairwoman's office, Karel Vlasta visited the executive floor's coffee pot. Smiling as he stirred in a package of creamer, Karel surmised he would make several trips to various coffee pots before he left for the evening. He expected it would be that kind of day. Cup in hand, he headed to his office.

At his desk, Karel brought his computer online. A notebook of codes was opened and brought near the keyboard.

A cleverly hidden and innocuous appearing file on Karel's computer was opened. That allowed him to utilize additional codes. Working from the two sources, both individually and in tandem with fingers fairly flying about the keyboard, he opened several files. These contained very confidential information hidden behind varying levels of security deep in the organization's computer system.

Several days earlier, under the guise of checking security on the Chairwoman's personal station, Karel transferred an exact copy of her files to an external hard drive. In his office, the data was downloaded to Karel's personal laptop. It had been interesting to leisurely go through the private documents of someone as important as Chairwoman Zuzana Balca.

At a point, he was prepared to call it quits thinking everything worth a search had been examined. Then he discovered something of potential interest. A couple of common files seemed out of place. These particular files were quite large in size. The more he teased the depths of the information, the more it appeared to be at odds with other material. Only someone with his knowledge might have stumbled on the particulars appearing at the end of his search.

When Karel discovered the files and determined what they were, he could hardly believe his good fortune. At the same time, though, Karel immediately visualized the advantages to an outsider like himself being privy to this information. It was not unlike hitting a massive jackpot at one of Europe's grand casinos.

One of the Chairwoman's files contained a list of names of a very special group of individuals. One in particular, caught his attention. With Karel's intelligence and awareness of detail, he immediately realized how he could play this knowledge to greatly benefit himself and his plan.

It had taken three days to devise ways to cover the fact he could access and search for updates to this important data on the Chairwoman's computer. Prior to Karel's discovery, she was the only person who had the means of entry. Now there was another.

Leaning back in his chair, Karel thought of a particularly dark period earlier in his life. Considering his present situation, the security chief now realized the time spent incarcerated in a French prison several years earlier had not been wasted.

His cellmate, a Frenchman who called himself Henri Chevalier, had previously held a high position in finance at the International Third World Lending Bank's headquarters in Washington, DC. Chevalier's duties included the disbursement of funds to third world countries scattered across the globe. Henri had, over a period of years, devised ways and means to siphon off a few dollars here and there to accounts he controlled. To be accurate, the amount Henri accumulated was several hundred million dollars.

In telling the story to Karel, Henri appeared to think it entertaining, even a little comical in spots. His scheme had worked flawlessly. Henri had been pleased to give details.

The downfall, if it could be called that, had come when his superior, a member of the Bank's Board of Directors, had a chance encounter with him on a holiday weekend away from Henri's home in Virginia.

On a Saturday evening, the two of them met quite by accident on the sidewalk outside one of the most exclusive hotels in the capital. The Director, dressed in his tuxedo, was headed into the hotel for a meeting and ceremony. Henri, there for dinner at his favorite restaurant with a young woman on his arm, was exiting Henri's new Rolls Royce Phantom.

Henri and his boss locked eyes for a moment. Then the Director eyed Henri's vehicle. It didn't take the knowledge of a luxury car salesman for him to know he was staring at a half-million-dollar automobile. The Director also knew Henri earned approximately $100,000 a year. As Henri put it, the photograph was out of focus.

On Monday morning, the FBI came and took Henri from his office. Then someone went to Virginia and put special locks on the doors of his eight-million-dollar home. It was all gone: the house, the five-acre estate, the furniture, the Rolls Royce… and the girlfriend.

The photo was really out of focus now.

The best Henri could say of the situation was when the dust settled, he had been sent to France to serve a significant prison sentence in his home country. Until Karel Vlasta arrived, Henri had been the sole occupant of the cell they now shared. The Frenchman appeared quite happy to have gained a roommate who was both intelligent and interested in Henri's experiences and fascinating knowledge.

The men spent their first couple of days getting acquainted. Their life stories seemed to come easy. That was Karel's good luck.

Additionally, and unknown to most who knew him, Henri Chevalier was also a computer hacker extraordinaire.

Once he was firmly ensconced at La Santé Prison in Paris, Henri had been able to talk himself into a job in the library where the computers were located that could be used by low-risk inmates. Certain websites and other internet destinations and addresses were blocked, but that was not a deterrent for Henri. With his know-how, he could easily access any site and then erase evidence he had been there.

With the friendship of the two men firmly established, Henri procured a library job for Karel. Any free time for the two men was spent in the computer room. With encouragement from Karel, his friend taught him all about the interesting possibilities of what one could do with a computer and the right knowledge.

Henri had the right knowledge. After a few months, Karel did too.

Kateřina and Rage had reached the parking lot and her automobile. He held the door for her and then went around and climbed into the passenger seat.

"May I treat you to an early dinner at a favorite restaurant of mine?" she asked.

"Of course."

"I will take you for a ride first," she told him. Her eyes crinkled and the corners of her mouth curled upward into a happy expression. "I know a hill with a magnificent view of Prague and the castle. You must not leave the city this time without seeing it."

Kateřina looked over, her stare holding his. Then she reached out, long slender fingers touching his cheek and tugging him gently to her. When they were close, it seemed she was staring into his soul with those startling green eyes. Then she kissed him…with feeling.

For the brief moment, the time they'd been apart was wiped away.

He cupped her face gently in both his hands and kissed her back. *Yes,* he thought, *we're very young again!*

They parted, promises left unspoken, their eyes last to break. Then each of them breathed a deep sigh.

She started the engine and glanced at him one more time. Rage winked.

Memories were certainly in his thoughts. Then the years passed away, and in his mind, they were discovering each other all over again. Rage wondered if she was remembering too.

7

THE PRIOR THURSDAY, SEPTEMBER 17, 2015

* * *

KATEŘINA'S DAUGHTER HAD LEFT FOR London on a sunny Thursday morning, excited about the career-advancing opportunity ahead for her. Later that day, Ana presented a paper to fellow colleagues at an international symposium on the cutting-edge studies she was involved in at the Center's research labs. The presentation was a success with a number of individuals congratulating her, asking questions on several of the ideas she'd presented, requesting interviews for their publications, and offering her the opportunity to write for their academic journals.

Ana had signed up to attend several other presentations the following two days. She had also told her mother she would be visiting friends at the University of Cambridge before returning to Prague.

However, at noon the day after her speech, Ana was handed an urgent message. The note said her mother was critically ill—a stroke—and had been admitted to the Cambridge Center hospital where Ana worked. Ana needed to come home as soon as possible.

Fortunately, one of the Center's executives was returning to Prague late that afternoon on the company's Gulfstream G280 jet aircraft. The note said Ana was scheduled to be aboard the flight. The timing was helpful, cutting several hours of waiting from her journey.

The executive and Ana were the only passengers on the flight. They introduced themselves. He said his name was Vladan Kocian. She had heard of him; he was the Cambridge Center's Organ Transplant Coordinator. They began talking as the aircraft taxied out for the flight from London's Heathrow Airport to Prague.

As the jet waited in line for takeoff clearance, the executive questioned Ana. "Why are you having to rush home?"

She could tell Mr. Kocian suspected something was wrong. His eyebrows were bunched and his forehead wrinkled in concern. Ana glanced out the window before giving him the reason.

"My mother had a stroke," she told him when she looked back. "The message said it was serious." Ana knew her eyes were red and probably swollen too. She had cried several times since receiving the news.

"I am sorry," Kocian told her and then said his father had suffered a stroke just before he died. Seeing her expression darken, the executive hastily reassured Ana, saying his father had been 92 years old.

She breathed a little easier. *Mother is only 64.*

After a while, the executive excused himself and took a seat near the back of the cabin. Noticing he was on his cellphone, Ana closed her eyes and tried not to think of all the bad things she had heard about strokes. It didn't work. She was worried to the point of being physically ill.

Breaking Ana from her thoughts some time later, Kocian explained he had arranged transportation for her. There would be a limo waiting to drive her to the Cambridge Center. She thanked him, but he brushed it off and went back to his seat.

The two-hour flight seemed much longer. The sun was low on the horizon when Ana heard the chirp of tires making contact with the tarmac in Prague.

Grabbing her bags, Ana waved goodbye to Mr. Kocian and hurried through the terminal, stopping only long enough to answer a couple of questions at customs. Finished, she walked out into the coolness of early evening.

Waiting outside was her ride to the hospital. The chauffeur dropped her luggage in the trunk and held the rear door open. With Ana settled, he climbed behind the wheel. She was close now.

Exhausted and deep in thought, it was several minutes later when Ana realized they were nearing the hospital. The driver turned into the quiet, high-end area of business buildings not far from Kateřina's home and only blocks from the Cambridge Center.

Sitting forward for a better view, Ana glanced at the large complex as the driver turned into the winding driveway. Relaxing a little, Ana expected to be with her mother soon. Hoping for the best, thoughts turned to Kateřina's situation as Ana wondered what the possibilities might be. Everything she knew about strokes was bad.

Driving past the large main structure, the driver pulled under the cover at the entrance to the second building where Ana had never had reason to visit. Two individuals dressed in starched white coats appeared from the doorway as the limo came to a stop.

The vehicle's rear door opened.

"Ms. Bambenek?" the woman inquired as she peered inside.

Ana nodded. She didn't recognize either of them. "How is my mother?"

"Would you come with us, please?"

The limo driver had already retrieved her bags and handed them to Ana.

Giving herself over to the hospital personnel, Ana expected to be with Kateřina soon. This was unfamiliar territory for Ana. She routinely spent her working hours in the research wing of the main building.

The man, a doctor she guessed, led the way with the woman following Ana. The interior of the building was unusually quiet. Strangely, there were no medical types rushing about as she would have expected. No doctors or nurses, not even nurse's stations. And no patients, no one at all. Strange…

The trio stopped at a door near the end of a long hallway. Opening the room and stepping aside, the doctor allowed Ana and the nurse to enter.

It was a large hospital room but contained much more than a regular patient bed and accompanying medical equipment. Beyond the expected items, there was a crisply-made, three-quarter bed and beyond, a small round conference table with seating for four. Additionally, there were two comfortable leather chairs and a well-stocked bookshelf.

Obviously, she would be able to remain with her mother if that was necessary. Ana turned back to the two individuals.

"Where is my mother? Is she out for tests?" Ana glanced back and forth between them. Their hesitation gave her an uneasy feeling. "When will she be back? This is her room, isn't it?"

Something's wrong!

"Has...my mother...?"

"Calm down, Ms. Bambenek." The doctor said, closing the door. "Your mother is fine. This will come as a surprise, but there was never anything wrong with Kateřina Bambenek. No stroke, nothing."

"I don't understa—"

"It was you, Ana, that we needed here."

"Me? I..."

His words had caused Ana to feel very unsteady. She eased down onto the edge of the hospital bed.

"I know you find this difficult to comprehend."

He talked slowly, and his expression was serious. The woman, her arms folded across her chest, sat down and said nothing.

"I was selected to give you this extraordinary information."

"Huh?" She couldn't imagine...

"Ana, your entire life has been in preparation for the next several days."

Ana didn't know whether to cry, scream, or laugh. Thoughts ran rampant through her mind—good ones and bad. She didn't know which to follow.

The doctor and nurse were calm throughout her moments of distress and near panic.

What? Ana thought, her eyes drawn and facial muscles tensed. She knew there was a completely confused expression on her face. *What is he saying? What does he mean?*

When she had passed the agitated stage, the doctor stood and walked toward the door. The nurse remained seated.

He finally introduced himself as Dr. Laska as he prepared to leave the room, adding, "You will be monitored by cameras throughout the night."

"But, wait— "

"We will talk in the morning," the doctor said as he started to close the door. "There will be answers for all your questions."

Food came, and the attendant asked Ana if there was anything special she wanted.

Yes, I want explanations.

She shook her head. At the moment, thinking was somewhere between difficult and impossible.

She wasn't hungry, but Ana used the time to check the food. She needed to be busy. The meal consisted of a fried egg and cheese sandwich, a few vegetables in a cup, and fruit punch. Ana tried a bite of the sandwich before laying it aside. She tried the vegetables too. Then she finished off the drink. She hadn't realized how thirsty she was.

Without asking permission, the nurse began examining the things Ana had brought with her. Ana snatched her handbag away and held it to her chest. Then she moved in front of her luggage. The defiant stare she directed at the nurse left no doubt she would fight to keep anyone from going through her belongings.

The nurse sat down on the edge of the bed and motioned toward one of the chairs. "Please," she said to Ana.

Angry and showing it in her expression, Ana hesitated and then dropped down on the seat, the handbag still clutched in her arms.

I cannot stop them, she thought. Ana felt hot tears on her cheeks. *The nurse will only call for help and go through my things anyway.*

Ana was tired, sleepy, angry and frustrated, but she realized she and the nurse were at a standoff Ana couldn't hope to win.

"I can call security. They will restrain you while I make my search. The final result will be the same, but you could be injured, and you will certainly be insulted." The nurse watched as Ana thought about it. She added, "I only want to make sure you have nothing with which you could harm yourself."

She watched Ana for another moment and then said, "Let's do this and get it finished."

Ana considered the nurse's argument and shrugged. "Okay, do what you must," Ana said, handing the purse over, defeated for the moment.

The nurse took it, but before she opened the bag, she told Ana her name. "I am Nurse Tamara."

Seeing someone going through her luggage was demeaning. Tamara started with the handbag and immediately set aside Ana's iPhone.

"Can't I keep that? I want to let my mother know I'm back in Prague."

"I am sorry," Tamara told her, shaking her head. "No communications for now."

She appeared to be leaving some hope for later, but Ana doubted it.

Tamara went through the bags carefully. The phone and a nail file were the only items she kept.

Finished, she remained with Ana for a while but only answered questions about the room. Tamara indicated everything else would become clear the next day.

Ana climbed up on the hospital bed and wrapped a blanket around her legs. She had become chilled. There was nothing to say to the nurse. Ana reasoned Tamara had orders not to discuss anything about the hospital, the night's activities, or what would happen tomorrow. That didn't leave much for conversation.

After a while and obviously satisfied Ana was going to be okay, Tamara told her good night and left. There was the sound of a key in the door.

When she was alone, Ana examined everything in the room. Two doors turned out to be the bathroom and a linen closet. She tried the door to the hallway, but as expected, it was locked. When Ana tapped on the frosted glass of the one small window, it felt like a sheet of steel. The glass must have been a half-inch thick.

As tired as she was, Ana barely slept that night after being told her entire life had been in preparation for the next several days. What could those words mean? It couldn't be good, or they wouldn't be holding her in a locked room. Dr. Laska said she would have all the answers tomorrow. Ana cursed under her breath, angry again because she realized she didn't even know the questions.

Finally, tired to the bone, Ana slumped down on the bed and dropped into a series of restless naps. She found herself peeking at the wall clock often.

Awakening once again at 4:30 a.m., she forced herself up and went into the bathroom. Planning to only wash her face, Ana glanced at the shower and changed her mind. With clean under-garments in one of her bags, she decided to take a quick shower. Hopefully, that would make her more alert for whatever might be coming later in the morning.

Ana had no idea what to expect. Those daunting words Dr. Laska had said to her kept coming back to prey on Ana's mind.

Breakfast, consisting of toast, marmalade, and coffee, arrived at 6:30 a.m. A slot opened at viewing level on the door. An eye appeared and Ana was told to step back into the room. Obeying more out of interest than hunger, she sat on the edge of the bed and waited.

Tamara entered and set a tray down. Looking at Ana, she said, "I have to take your vital signs."

Producing a digital thermometer, a blood-pressure devise, and a stethoscope from a small medical bag, she approached the bed. Ana had already made up her mind to cooperate, at least for now. It was her plan to take whatever was happening one episode at a time.

As Tamara put the blood pressure cuff around her arm, Ana asked, "Can you tell me any details? Anything at all would help." She looked into the woman's eyes but got nothing in return. Checking the numbers as Tamara wrote them down, she saw 139/92 for blood pressure. Ana knew that was above normal.

Finally, the nurse told her, "There will be others in to talk to you after eight o'clock." Tamara packed her bag and left Ana alone with her cold breakfast.

Even the coffee was barely warm. A couple of bites of the toast and a swallow of coffee was all she could manage.

A knock at the door later in the morning brought Ana to her feet. This time it was Dr. Laska. He was accompanied by two other individuals—a man and a woman—and Nurse Tamara.

The nurse had a telephone in her hand and set it on the conference table.

"Hello, I hope you are rested," Dr. Laska said as he led the others into the room. "We met last night."

Ana nodded. *How could I forget?*

He introduced the others. "Ana, this is Dr. Seifert." He pointed to the man. "Dr. Seifert is a psychiatrist and is here to help you understand what will be happening in the coming days."

The man nodded. "I am Dr. Bruno Seifert. I will be in charge of your gift and parting."

What? What does he mean gift and parting?

Before she could ask for an explanation, Dr. Laska introduced the woman.

"This is Dr. Hana Jirsa. She will be in charge of your surgery."

"Surgery?" Caught by surprise, the word flew from Ana's lips.

She couldn't believe her own ears. *He said this woman will be conducting my surgery. What surgery? There is nothing wrong with me.*

Dr. Laska pointed to the small conference table. "Please, let's all sit down and get into the details."

The three doctors moved to the table. Dazed, Ana reluctantly joined them, leaving Tamara to perch on the side of the hospital bed.

Seated, Dr. Laska led off. Leaning forward, his hands cupped in front of him, the doctor said, "Ana, what I have to tell you will be difficult to grasp in one session."

Sitting directly across the table from Dr. Laska, she was watching him with an occasional glance at the others. Ana clasped her hands together to keep them still. She was uncomfortable under the doctor's focused stare, and she couldn't imagine what he would be telling her.

"Ana," he asked, "are you familiar with the subject of human cloning?"

Again, Ana wasn't sure she understood him. *First had come "gift and parting." Now "human cloning…"*

Dr. Jirsa reintroduced herself.

"As you were told, I will handle your surgery."

Ana found her voice this time. "But why am I having surgery? I am not ill. There is nothing wrong with me."

Both of the medical doctors now turned to the psychiatrist.

Dr. Seifert was a little man with a dark, neatly trimmed beard and about a dozen hairs on his head. The fact that there were few lines in his face and no grey in his beard caused Ana to think he was the youngest of the three and probably hadn't been out of university too many years. Ana suspected she was wrong.

"Miss Bambenek, these next few weeks will be difficult for you. I am here to help."

"Then open that door," she pointed, "and let me go home." Ana glared at the doctors individually.

Each of them met her angry glance, but no one commented.

Her head hurt, and Ana felt nauseous. She knew she was intelligent, but at the moment, she did not understand anything at all. It was too much.

The psychiatrist spoke again. "Dr. Laska asked if you are familiar with human cloning. Are you?"

It was taking longer each time for Ana's mind to catch up with their questions.

"No…well…yes," she said. "At university, I was exposed to the theoretical idea, but I have not studied the subject in depth. I think it deals with making a copy of a person."

"Though that is a simple definition, it is exactly correct," Dr. Seifert said. "It is only short on details." The psychiatrist gazed at Ana for several seconds, fingers pinching his lower lip inward. He appeared unsure of how to go forward.

Glancing at the other doctors, he said, "I believe the direct approach is most appropriate."

They each nodded, Dr. Jirsa a little more hesitantly.

Dr. Seifert turned back to Ana and said without hesitation, "Miss Bambenek, *you* are a human clone."

She looked at the others and then whispered, "What?" It was a rhetorical question. She understood the words he had uttered but had no idea of the concept as it affected her.

The psychiatrist continued. "Back in the early 1980s, a group of young people met and made some far-reaching decisions. It would be appropriate for you to understand these were individuals of great wealth."

Ana could only nod.

"Their riches allowed them the possibility of doing great good with their lives or perhaps, great evil." He caught Ana's eyes and held them. "This, of course, depends on one's point of view."

"I still do not—"

He held up a hand.

She dropped her head and stretched her hands out, palms up.

"These young adults were finishing their educations and preparing to return to their homes in various countries around the world. They were community oriented and eager to start their public lives and service."

Dr. Seifert stopped for a moment as if to give Ana a chance to comment.

She raised her head. "I still do not understand how all of this concerns me."

"You will," he assured her, "and soon."

Nodding again, Ana kept her eyes on the psychiatrist.

"Only illness or injury could stop these young adults, and though all of them were in excellent health, there was no way of knowing the future. Outside of traditional medicine, there was only one other way to try and insure their health."

Clarity was coming to her.

"These extraordinarily intelligent young adults could visualize the possible need for organ transplants under specific circumstances. The most advantageous and sure way to have replacement parts with the least chance of rejection was to produce them from an individual's own body."

Leaning her chair back slightly, Ana looked at the three doctors and stated the obvious, "I am someone's donor? Someone's spare parts?" Then, almost to herself, "A lamb to be slaughtered…"

Each of the doctors agreed: "Yes," from the psychiatrist; a nod from Dr. Laska; and a very slight nod and a welling of tears in the eyes of Dr. Jirsa.

"When?"

The psychiatrist again. "Soon, very soon. Three weeks at the most."

"What if I don't agree," Ana asked. "What if I pack my things and leave?" It was more of a question than a threat.

"Do you love your mother?" Dr. Jirsa leaned forward. "Your mother and you live well, do you not?"

Ana nodded slowly.

"You would like those circumstances to continue for your mother, wouldn't you?"

Ana looked the doctor in the eyes and waited.

"Do you know where your mother's money comes from?"

After a moment's hesitation, Ana told him, "My father was killed. I have always assumed there were funds involved at his death."

Dr. Jirsa paid little attention before continuing.

"The money comes from an organization called the Eagle Trust. Everything material the Trust provides to your mother will be taken tomorrow if you refuse. The house, the automobile, the funds, everything will be gone."

She watched Ana for a moment before continuing.

"As for your situation, you will be released with cause from your job, your bank account will suddenly go dry, and your investments will be worthless. Also, new career opportunities will not come."

Dr. Jirsa hesitated and then said, "You and your mother will be destitute, and there will be nothing you can do about it. The Eagle Trust has a very long reach…and many friends. The hospital and the Trust are big. You, as an individual, are not. No one of importance, including the authorities, will listen to you. At best, they will think what you have to say is preposterous."

The doctor hesitated, then added, "What I have told you will become true. You would not want that situation for your mother… or yourself. I promise."

She believed the stern expression on his face. Ana took a deep breath. "Do I have time to consider what you have told me.

"No!" The doctors said in unison.

Then Dr. Laska added, clarifying, "You will not be able to leave the hospital without the dire consequences I have described to you."

Looking down, Ana thought about her mother. She couldn't imagine how Kateřina could go forward with no income or place to live.

Dr. Laska surprised her again.

"Would you like to let your mother know you are back in Prague and here at the hospital?"

"Of course."

He told Ana what she could and could not say as Tamara plugged the phone into the wall outlet and prepared it for the call. The speakerphone had been activated so everyone could hear their conversation. At Dr. Laska's instruction, Tamara was prepared to cut the call short if the doctor signaled.

Her nerves already on edge, and with four pairs of eyes watching, Ana said hello to her mother and told her she was back from London and at the Cambridge Center.

"Are you well?" her mother asked. "There is a tremor in your voice."

The psychiatrist leaned forward, waiting for Ana's answer. Though visably nervous, her hands shaking and her voice little more than a whisper. Ana looked at him directly as she spoke with Kateřina.

"One of my projects here developed problems and demanded my personal attention. I had to leave the conference early," she told her mother

"So, you will be returning home tonight?" Kateřina asked.

"Unfortunately, not," Ana told her mother. "There was a minor accident, and I must remain under observation for the next twenty-four hours to make sure there are no complications." Then she added, "I will continue my duties while I am under observation."

"Will I hear from you?"

Her eyes finally left the psychiatrist as Ana brought the short conversation to a close.

"Dr. Laska will keep you informed," Ana said, and then added, "I love you," before telling her mother she needed to return to work and would see her soon.

She hung up wondering if she would ever see or speak to her mother again.

8

Tuesday, September 22, 2015

* * *

Driving across Palackeho Bridge in the late afternoon sun, they could see Prague Castle in the distance.

"Before I take you to dinner, I am going to drive us south for an even better view."

Fifteen minutes later, Kateřina rounded a curve on a small hill and pulled to the side of the road. Cutting the engine, she climbed out, motioning for Rage to follow. A short path led them through some bushes and trees to a point with a spectacular view. There was a bench with a couple just rising to leave. Kateřina spoke to them and then sat down. Rage joined her.

A vast expanse of the city lay before them with Prague Castle as its crown. Neither of them spoke, choosing instead to savor the moment.

Soon, she reached over and took his hand. "We never came here," Kateřina said, a nostalgic tone to her voice.

"Prague was a big place to see in only two or three months."

"Yes," she agreed, "it was."

Late afternoon was approaching; a chill was in the air.

They lingered a few minutes watching as Prague turned on its lights, one twinkle at a time. Dramatic and dazzling were words that came to Rage's mind. The view was not something that could be described. It had to be experienced.

Gentle pressure on his fingers reminded Rage of the beautiful woman at his side.

"Are you prepared to eat?" Kateřina whispered.

He nodded, a slight squeeze to her hand emphasizing his answer.

Driving north through the city, she traversed narrow cobblestone streets past buildings belonging to another era. Kateřina pointed out the American Embassy, an attractive three story building of light two-toned stucco and lots of windows. The one entrance to the compound accommodated vehicles as well as pedestrians. Strangely, there were no guards visible. The only signs of nationality were the flag and the Great Seal of the United States of America above the entrance. Rage vaguely recalled the building from his short stint in Prague all those years ago.

A few minutes later, they were at the restaurant, *Terasa U Zlaté Studně*. She translated the name for Rage: Terrace at the Golden Well.

"What's the Golden Well?" he asked.

Kateřina's eyes crinkled, and she laughed out, barely controlled, before touching his arm with her hand. The laughter continued for several seconds more before she could answer.

He hadn't intended the question to be funny.

"Other than a name, I have not an idea what it means," she said in her somewhat broken English and then laughed some more.

When she calmed, Kateřina told him, "I knew immediately you would ask me that question, and I was already certain I had no answer. To me, it was a comedy to think of the conversation in advance, and then have it proceed exactly as I had thought."

Rage chuckled with her this time.

"I should have called for a reservation," she told him as they entered the building and approached the elevator. "I hope they can seat us."

Kateřina was obviously well known at the very impressive establishment. Rage noted the restaurant encompassed the top two floors of the Hotel Golden Well. The top floor, known as The Terrace, was open to another stunning panoramic view of Prague.

The Maître d' greeted Kateřina using only her given name. She was assured the entire staff at the restaurant was happy to see her as always, reservation or not.

Asking to be seated at a quiet table on the rooftop terrace, Kateřina and Rage were guided to a reasonably secluded spot near the edge of the open dining floor. The scene across Prague's nearby tiled roofs and flowing down to the Vltava River was beautiful. A view in a different direction, also spectacular, displayed several of Prague's Vltava River bridges and down to the Old City.

Their drink order was taken: a Vodka Gimlet for Kateřina and a dark Czech hot tea for Rage. Waiting for the refreshments, they enjoyed the postcard panorama from their table.

"I am always in awe of the beauty," she said, "especially when I see this." She spread her arms to take in the scene before them.

"I understand," Rage told her. "This is certainly special."

Their drinks came, and the conversation returned to Kateřina's surrogacy.

"The baby, Ana, was due in a month when you were called in," Rage said clarifying his thoughts.

"Yes." Kateřina took a sip of the Gimlet. "There would be no one to take the baby."

Looking at Rage, her voice was low. He leaned in to hear.

"I understood the doctor's words," Kateřina said, "but not what he was meaning. How could there not be someone to take the baby I had carried?"

Their waiter returned to take the food order.

"We need to eat and return to my house." She reminded Rage she would be visiting Ana at the hospital this evening.

Kateřina suggested the Royal Steak from Argentinean Angus Beef for Rage and ordered Wild Scottish Salmon for herself. Then the waiter, speaking Czech, told them all the wonderful additions that would be served with their entrées. Kateřina translated.

When they were alone again, she assured Rage he would be happy and then said, "Now...where was I?"

"There was no one to take Ana..."

"Oh, yes," she said. Doing the motion to toss the hair back, Kateřina glanced at him, her forehead creased in the seriousness of the moment. "That was the time Dr. Sokol mentioned the couple's financial arrangements. An appointment had been set for me to meet with a representative of their Trust that afternoon."

Rage took a small notebook from his pocket and jotted down a few lines.

Sitting silently, she took a couple of sips from her drink before continuing. Even after all the years, it was obviously difficult for Kateřina to talk about the situation.

"I did not want to go to the meeting alone and asked Dr. Sokol to accompany me. I remember him saying he had intended to suggest that."

She sat still for a few moments and then reached over to touch his hand. Those astonishing green eyes begged for understanding. Down through the years and the many times he had thought of her, it had often been her eyes he remembered. There had been times when they haunted Rage.

"The Trust's representative was kind, but he only gave the smallest details. There had been a crash, and the parents were dead." She brushed at her hair again.

"Did he give a date or a location?" Rage asked.

"It was in the south of France on February 27, 1990," she said immediately. "I remember because it was exactly 25 days before Ana was born."

Rage nodded and made more notes.

Their food arrived and Kateřina asked if she could finish giving him the details when they were back at her home.

He had one question, "Are you telling me everything, every detail you can remember?"

She assured him she was and then said, "but I can tell you the remaining basics in only a couple of sentences."

Surprised, he beckoned her to continue.

"The representative assured me if I agreed to become the baby's mother, neither of us would need to be concerned about money for the rest of our lives." She hesitated for a moment and then said, "If I refused, I was told the baby I carried would be turned over to an agency for strangers to adopt."

Rage jotted even more in the notebook.

Kateřina gazed out at the city for a moment, then simply stated, "It was not something I could let happen."

Kateřina pointed Rage to the settees when they returned to the house. The music played softly in the background. Rage asked if he could turn it up a little as she detoured into the kitchen to get them a refreshment. Dark was settling in outside.

Rage hadn't realized how tired he was until he tossed his house shoes aside and sprawled across the settee's cushions. Twisting and turning, he stretched his back and limbs.

Ah, that feels good...

He glanced at Kateřina as she moved about in the kitchen preparing tea for them. She also appeared tired as she faced him from across the counter. He tried to imagine how she must feel with all that was on her mind and a daughter in the hospital under suspicious circumstances. Emotionally *and* physically, she had to be near the end of her resources. Yet there she was—doing something for someone else. She glanced at Rage and smiled as she steeped the tea.

Is she ready for the questions that need answering? Several had been taking shape in his thoughts. Slipping Kateřina's letter from his pocket, Rage scanned the handwritten pages one more time, then laid them aside.

The letter only stated a friend's daughter had been killed. Kateřina hadn't said how it happened. Perhaps she would give him the details now before her run to the hospital.

There were several unknowns bouncing around in the picture. How and where Marta died would be logical starting points. Certainly, there were factors involved that Kateřina had yet to mention. And if the daughter had been murdered as Kateřina believed, the question then became why? What could have been the motive?

He glanced at the counter and caught Kateřina staring at him.

"What?" he asked.

"Nothing," she told him. "I was just looking at you and thinking of our yesterdays."

She moved toward the settees, a tray in hand.

Setting their refreshments on the coffee table, Kateřina poured him a cup of tea. Passing it over, she then poured one for herself and settled back. Kicking off her shoes, Kateřina pulled her feet up beneath her.

"You must have questions," she said anticipating the conversation.

Rage couldn't help but chuckle. "You've been reading my mail."

"Oh, no." She sat up quickly, an expression of complete surprise and embarrassment captured her face. Her eyes grew wide, and her neck blushed a significant pink. "I would never read your mail."

Her tea was back on the side table.

He laughed as he shook his head and tried to explain. "No, you misunderstood. It's an expression we use back home. It means you're thinking the same as I."

Kateřina didn't appear convinced.

"Honest," he said staring into her eyes and nodding.

"All right..." She gave in, appearing to relax a little, but she wasn't totally persuaded.

He could almost read *her* mind.

"We have only a little time to discuss your questions before I leave for the hospital," she said jumping ahead while glancing at her watch. "My phone is off, and I also turned off the lights in the front of the house. I must change and have only a few minutes now. We can talk more when I return."

Rage leaned forward and came right to the point.

"In the letter," he pointed toward the sheets of paper, "you said Elita's daughter had been killed. You didn't say how or where."

She nodded while remaining silent.

"What brought you to the conclusion she was murdered?"

She took a sip of her tea. "Because..." she set her cup on the side table, "...because Marta was not the first of her circle of acquaintances to die or be lost under unusual circumstances."

Rage could feel the surprise that must have shown on his face. "In fact, Marta was the third."

Leaning forward, Rage nodded and indicated Kateřina should continue.

"The first to die was a young man of only twenty-two years. Marta knew him though they were not close. He was sent to Finland to work on an assignment for his and Marta's employer. His mother was told there had been an automobile accident involving speed," Kateřina said. "The young man died immediately."

Remaining silent, Rage allowed her to continue. Appearing reasonably at ease, Kateřina glanced at him occasionally, finally able to tell her story to someone who cared and might be able to help.

"The next was another male," she said, "a coworker of Ana's. It was reported he died of a brain aneurism while on a skiing vacation in Switzerland." Kateřina reached for her tea again. "He had gone there on a trip paid for by the hospital. I was told the outing was a reward for his efforts on one of their projects."

Wondering if he'd missed something, Rage held up a hand.

"Young people die all the time," he said. "They take chances. I don't see anything unusual about the three of them knowing each other or even working for the same organization."

"I am not finished," Kateřina told him. "There are two unusual circumstances involved with each of the young people and their deaths that connect them." She rose from the settee and walked to the large back windows overlooking the terrace. Standing there, her back to Rage and silhouetted by the bright lights outside, Kateřina raised her voice enough for him to hear.

"I suspect you will be as surprised as I was when this information came to me," Kateřina said. "The first could be just an unlikely coincidence. I am aware the second young man and Marta's body were both cremated." She took a few steps across the floor and then said, "No permission was asked or given for the cremations."

She glanced at Rage.

"A new friend, Adina Dobias, recently told me this was true for the other individual also—the one who died in Finland. His mother did not know about the cremation until she received his ashes."

Kateřina turned toward Rage then.

"The women were not given reasons for any of the three cremations." She held his gaze for a few moments and then turned back to the windows. Looking out across the terrace, Kateřina asked a question she didn't expect to be answered. "Why…why would they do that?"

Then she changed subjects.

"I learned the last coincidence quite by accident."

Finding it difficult to hear, Rage joined Kateřina at the windows. *Too many important similarities,* he thought.

"What brought the other young people to your attention?" he asked.

"I go to a large church," she said. "It provides aid of many sorts. There is a group for those who have suffered a death in the family. I am a member to support friends who have had recent losses. Adina, my new friend, and the mother of Ana's deceased male co-worker, is also a member."

Rage kept his eyes on her face but remained silent.

"Adina has mentioned something in confidence that was a surprise."

Rage started to ask a question, but she held up a hand.

"Let me finish," Kateřina said. "There was one other circumstance with the other woman that was like ours."

Rage couldn't imagine. "What?"

"She had also been a surrogate mother to her son," Kateřina said. "That makes four of us."

That information surprised Rage, too.

"Do you know the other woman?" he asked. "Have you talked to her?"

Kateřina shook her head. "She is also dead. It happened a few months after her son was killed." She walked back to the settee before continuing.

Dropping down, Kateřina curled her legs beneath her, and then she explained. "The woman was overwhelmed by the loss of her son. Obviously, she loved him and was very proud. She had been divorced many years and was the boy's only parent."

Not fast enough for Rage, he hurried her—a furrowed brow and a rolling gesture with his arm.

"Do you know the circumstances?"

At this point the answer didn't surprise him.

"She took her own life. The despondent mother hung herself."

His expression must have made Rage's thoughts obvious because Kateřina hurried to drop the last bombshell before he could stop her.

"Not only was that woman and my friend both surrogate mothers like me," she said, "they were each asked to adopt the child when something purportedly happened to the intended parents."

She held his eyes for a moment and then said, "They both fought hard to get more details about their children's death."

"Fought? With who?"

"The Cambridge Center, of course." She said the words as though the answer should have been evident.

Interesting…

With some hesitation, Rage asked, "When were the arrangements made for those adoptions?"

"Late in the pregnancy—as mine was."

Evening had turned to night.

Rage and Kateřina's talk had hit on several subjects that were of interest to him. Though he had tried to organize his thoughts as they talked, it had been difficult.

During the conversation with Kateřina, she spoke freely about her new friend Adina, and they had discussed the two other women. Like Adina, the women had each lost their children under unusual and similar conditions. Too many important factors involving Adina and the other women were not just similar, they were the same.

It was as if a sinister script had been followed.

Several details matched exactly. Adina and each of the other women were surrogate mothers. The three young adults—their children—either knew or were aware of each other. They were all connected through the health center or as friends. And their cremations had all taken place without permission.

Kateřina's daughter was friends with the three deceased individuals. Now Ana is in isolation at the health center. She could be next.

And as Ana's surrogate mother, Kateřina seemed to be making the first steps to join this questionable group.

Was it all a happenstance? Rage doubted it.

Through experience he had learned true coincidences are few and far between. He didn't think Kateřina's similar circumstances with these special women was an exception. There was something more ominous to it.

As she glanced toward her bedroom, Rage had one more question.

"Have you and Adina discussed the similarities in your circumstances?"

"No," Kateřina said, shaking her head. "Adina has not asked, and I did not tell her anything about my Ana." As an afterthought, she added, "Mostly I listened."

"Good," he said. Then he changed the subject. "Has anyone from the Eagle Trust been in touch with you since Ana's been ill?"

"Yes," she said, her eyes wide in surprise at his question. "Once."

"And…?" Rage was growing edgy.

"It was simple. They only wanted to know if I needed anything." She glanced at Rage, clearly wanting him to understand. Her head was tipped to one side, and she massaged her temples.

He hated to admit it, even to himself, but there wasn't much he understood about this entire situation.

She looked at her watch. "I have to go, and I'm afraid a headache is coming on. I can feel it." Excusing herself, Kateřina said she needed to dress for her trip to the hospital.

Rage was worried, but with all she had going on, her headaches could easily be stress.

Welcoming the time to organize his thoughts, Rage remained on the settee. Waiting and thinking, he glanced out the large windows occasionally.

Something was bothering him, a feeling he couldn't shake. He glanced out into the darkness several times. Rage had a sense he was being watched but doubted that was likely. Yet, on the side of care and without being obvious, he went to the windows and studied the yard, the trees and all he could see beyond. The property was like a forest behind her house.

Rage remembered having these sensations when he was with the CIA. Back then, they generally indicated trouble of some sort. Tonight, he tried to attribute it to the fact he wasn't coming up with solutions for Kateřina.

That only worked for a few minutes. The feeling came creeping back. He decided when Kateřina left for the hospital, he would take a walk. Perhaps he was suffering from stress himself.

Yeah, a little walk couldn't hurt.

Mentally trying to find contradictions in his thinking, Rage left the settee and paced back and forth in front of the large windows.

Grasping for a connection to the overall situation, he kept coming back to the Eagle Trust and its handling of Kateřina's finances. Rage wondered if there was a similar funding situation involving Adina.

But how can I find out without arousing suspicion?

Rage expected he would figure it out eventually. He usually did, but time was a factor here. After all, Kateřina's daughter is in the Trust's health center.

Kateřina returned from her bedroom wearing a fresh outfit and makeup. She appeared revitalized as she stopped in the kitchen. Rage heard activity for a short time before she returned to the settee with a small tray.

"I made more tea for you," she announced.

"Thanks." He came over and sat down.

Rage reached for the tea she offered, took a sip and set it on the side table. It was cherry this time. Very good.

"I will be back as soon as I am satisfied Ana is in good hands."

"Are you sure you don't want me to go with you?" he asked.

"Perhaps another time."

"All right."

Rage stood up and gave her a gentle hug.

"Thank you for asking." She smiled. "It is good you are with me."

With a kiss on his cheek, Kateřina turned and hurried out to her vehicle.

The security chief and his assistant were in their van this first evening since he told Madam Chairwoman of Kateřina Bambenek's visitor. They parked in a seldom used alley back of Bambenek's home where trees and bushes hid them from both the house and street. By the time they acquired and set up the electronics and photography equipment, it was eight-thirty in the evening.

The Bambenek woman had gone out before Karel and Alexandr had the equipment ready to record, but the assistant had also been busy with their cameras. He had photographs of the visitor from several angles.

Rage watched as the lights of the Porsche disappeared down the street. He checked his watch, waiting for another full minute to pass. Satisfied now she was well on her way, Rage hurried upstairs and unpacked his pistol. Loading it, he slipped the weapon inside his belt and slipped into a coat. Prepared for unanticipated circumstances, Rage turned off some of the interior lights and then slipped out the front door into darkness.

Leisurely in his manner, he strolled out along the sidewalk to the street. Anyone noticing him would think he was out for an evening walk. There were others out too, ambling along, couples and a few singles. Many spoke to him in their native Czech language. Rage returned their greetings, nodding to the men and tipping his fedora to the women.

As he walked, a thought edged its way into his consciousness. Two of the three surrogate mothers had been so depressed they had committed suicide.

What are the percentages of that happening?

Remaining on the sidewalk and strolling the equivalent of several US city blocks, Rage worked his way around to the wooded area behind Kateřina's house. There wasn't much to see—mostly the same trees and woods he had noticed from the house. He had about decided there was nothing unusual there when he happened upon a virtually unused vehicle path among the undergrowth.

Looking carefully and utilizing scattered illumination from the random streetlights, Rage could see an automobile had used the trail recently. He could tell by the direction weeds and sticks were broken that a vehicle had driven into the area but had not yet come out. At least it hadn't come out at this same location.

Rage walked several yards away from the path and then carefully entered the wooded area. He picked his way through in the general direction of Kateřina's back lawn. Several meters in, he spied a work van parked among the trees. Its interior was dark except for subdued light from what Rage expected were computer screens and other electronic instruments.

Watching, he detected two men in the van. There was also what appeared to be a large set of binoculars on a stand near a side window. Recognizing the instrument as night-vision goggles, Rage could also see a dish pointed through a small break in the trees toward Kateřina's house and its large rear-facing windows. The dish appeared to be a couple of feet in diameter—a listening device.

Kateřina's and his conversations were almost certainly being recorded. *But by who and why?*

Not expecting Kateřina back from the hospital for an hour or so, Rage settled down to watch the van and its occupants. Careful not to leave signs of being there, he remained hidden for thirty minutes.

The men in the van appeared to be tweaking their equipment. Their voices were low and could be heard only as murmurs outside the van. They were obviously expecting the occupants of the house to return to the surveillance area sometime during the evening.

Rage smiled. They'd be disappointed. There would be no more useful information available through the big windows.

Satisfied, Rage carefully eased back out to the street and walked casually to Kateřina's house. Inside, he put his weapon and ammo away and then went downstairs to make a pot of coffee.

Finished, he carried a small tray with the coffee over to the settees and settled in.

Kateřina's music was playing softly. Too softly, Rage decided. He went over and increased the volume. Now he had nothing to do but wait for Kateřina to return from the hospital.

Sitting there at last, his face turned away from the windows, Rage thought of his recent discovery. He smiled, hoping they could see him and wonder what *he* was thinking.

It was quite cool inside the hospital. As Kateřina walked through the entrance doors, she pulled her jacket closer to her neck. She went directly to the information desk and stopped behind another visitor.

When it was her turn, Kateřina asked for her daughter's room number. She had called the hospital earlier and expected to go directly to Ana.

The clerk checked her information and then looked up at Kateřina saying, "She is in quarantine."

She had been shaken by Ana's call a few days earlier, but Kateřina could never have envisioned this. It came as a complete surprise.

"Quarantined… She is quarantined?" Kateřina managed to get it out. The frown on her face expressed her frustration. She wasn't even sure she had heard correctly. "I do not understand."

"The person you ask for is in quarantine. What do you not understand?" There was a sarcastic tone to the clerk's voice.

"I was told my daughter was being watched carefully, but I would be able to see her this evening. Nothing has been mentioned of quarantine."

"When were you told that?"

"I spoke to someone connected with a Dr. Laska yesterday. This morning I phoned and was given the same report."

"Here it is." The woman turned the screen displaying Ana's information so Kateřina could see it.

"*V karanténě.*" The words "In quarantine"—and a room number—were beside Ana's name. They had not given a room number when she called.

Thinking fast, Kateřina thanked the woman and backed away.

There was an upholstered bench across the lobby. Kateřina walked over and sat down.

I have to settle myself. Being upset will not benefit my effort. She glanced back at the desk. *I must talk with someone in authority and ask questions.*

Kateřina returned to the clerk.

"Who may I speak to about my daughter?" she asked politely. "Is there someone in charge?"

The clerk thought for a moment and then said, "I will make a call for you."

Though she turned aside, Kateřina could hear parts of the conversation.

"The mother is here and insists…"

There was a pause as the woman listened. Then, "Yes, I will tell her."

As the phone dropped onto its cradle, the woman looked up. "There will be no one here who can help until morning. You are welcome to come back then. Around nine, I am told."

"Thank you," Kateřina said.

No way. I am going to find Ana tonight.

Kateřina started to walk away and then asked where the *toaleta* was located.

The woman pointed back past the elevator.

Kateřina glanced at the room numbers as soon as she was out of sight.

Good! According to the information she'd seen at the counter, Ana was somewhere nearby.

Kateřina had only walked a few meters when she was met by a broad-shouldered man in a suit and tie. He blocked her way and did not appear friendly.

"May I help you?"

"I am looking for the restroom," Kateřina said. "I must have missed it."

The man pointed back along the corridor.

Kateřina glanced in the direction he indicated, then nodded and started walking.

"Do not come back this way," he snapped after her. "The area is restricted."

Kateřina nodded again.

In the restroom, she activated the water and rinsed her damp hands. *They don't normally perspire this way.*

Thinking of her encounter, she hoped the man wouldn't be in the corridor when she left. He wasn't, but she had only taken a few steps in the direction of Ana's room when he reappeared.

"You were told not to come into the restricted area," the man said harshly.

Before Kateřina could speak, he reached out and gripped her arm. Younger and stronger, he forced her toward the lobby and then the building's entrance.

"If you return, it will not be good."

She believed him.

Outside, he released her with a push, saying, "Do not return."

Kateřina had no reason to think he was not serious. She was quite sure there would be a bruise on her arm but didn't give him the satisfaction of seeing her rub it. Standing for a few moments, she realized further efforts to reach Ana would be futile tonight.

And who knows what else could happen?

She glanced back toward the entrance.

The security man was watching her from inside.

Kateřina resigned herself to not finding her daughter tonight and turned toward her car and home.

And Rage.

Rain began falling as she drove out of the parking area. It increased along with the darkening of her mood. By the time Kateřina reached home, the car's wipers were on high, and tears were cascading down her cheeks.

How dare they keep me from my daughter!

Waiting on the settee, the lights low and the music playing, Rage immediately sensed something was wrong and then he saw her smeared mascara. Instantly on his feet, he took Kateřina in his arms and held her tight. She was shaking.

Guiding her over to the settees, Rage eased Kateřina down and tucked a blanket around her shoulders.

"I'll get something to warm you," he said.

When they were settled and she'd had a few sips of the brandy he'd poured, Rage handed her a note. Kateřina read it—"Don't say anything."—then focused on his eyes, a questioning expression on her face.

He gestured, palm down.

"If you feel up to it," he said, "let's go for a walk in the rain."

"Yes, let's do that." Her eyes were questioning.

She threw the blanket off and headed for the shoes she had left in the botník near the front door. She slipped into her jacket, and they each grabbed an umbrella and walked out to the street.

Glancing up and down as they strolled along the sidewalk, Rage would not have been surprised to see they were being followed. No one was visible; he knew where to look. He would continue watching until they were back in the house.

After a few steps, Rage explained everything about the new situation he had discovered. He told her about the men in the woods and that they could see the rear of her house.

She listened, her eyes drawn and a shocked expression on her face.

Warning her, Rage said, "Don't say anything in the kitchen or conversation room you wouldn't want others to know." Giving her the basics regarding the van and people behind her house, he told her they should keep the music on anytime they were in those rooms.

She nodded and wiped at her eyes with a tissue.

"Now tell me about Ana," he said.

Kateřina glanced at him. "It was terrible."

"The situation or Ana's condition?"

"The situation," Kateřina said. "I did not see Ana, so I do not know about her condition."

Finally, Kateřina told him she had been thrown out of the health center. She had to give him details on that one before he was convinced.

She was walking very slowly by the time she finished the story and appeared more relaxed and calm after her ordeal. She'd told him everything there was to know.

Rage glanced at her, considering it safe now to turn the conversation to Kateřina's friend and her son.

"Does Adina appear okay financially?" he asked. "I can't imagine a situation as good as yours."

"I have never visited her home," Kateřina said, "but she drives a very nice automobile. As for funds, I do not think I could ask her." She hesitated. "That would be too private."

"You do want to find out about Ana's situation, don't you?"

"Yes."

"Then you will have to help me."

Kateřina's head dipped as her eyes narrowed in a skeptical expression. "What would you have me do?"

"For a beginning," Rage told her, "we need to know Adina's circumstances."

Kateřina was moving her head from side to side, and her eyes were squinted. "No" was written on her face.

"Hear me out," he said.

"I will listen."

"Find a reason to spend some time with Adina," Rage suggested. "You could have her join you for dinner. You drive. You can see where and how she lives without asking."

A slight nod—Kateřina could see a way to gain information without asking private questions.

"During the evening, direct the conversation to your children."

Agreeing, Kateřina pointed out Adina had talked about her son when they met before. "She is proud of his achievements."

"Encourage her," Rage suggested. "You may be surprised at what she'll tell you."

They walked and talked for an hour before Kateřina told him she was exhausted. They were back near the house, and the rain had turned to a mist.

"We should get some rest," she said. "You must also be tired."

"I may want to send some emails and try to reach a couple of other people by phone. I'll need to get on your internet."

Inside and without a word, she gave him a slip of paper with her Wi-Fi password, and Rage went upstairs.

He decided he only wanted to call the US Embassy tonight, though he doubted anyone useful would be available before morning.

Karel glanced at his assistant monitoring the cameras and sensitive listening gear. Everything in the van had been trained on the rear of the woman's house since the set up. As head of security, he was less than satisfied.

Bambenek's visitor had disappeared for a while and then strolled back into the large conversation room. He seemed at ease as he waited for the woman, even looking through a couple of magazines.

The woman was upset when she returned, and there had obviously been a discussion. Unfortunately, most of it had taken place out of their range in other parts of the house.

The two security men remained in place, their new listening equipment trained on the large windows. All was not lost, though. The evening's exercise had been an opportunity to test the long-range listening paraphernalia while getting some of the couple's conversations on the hidden microphones in the kitchen and living room areas. Sometimes it worked, sometimes it didn't. Much depended on where the subjects were positioned and how loud they were. The music seemed to play most of the time now and was also a distraction.

Vlasta was used to favorable outcomes in his endeavors for the Chairwoman, but new achievements always thrilled him. Being able to watch as well as listen was a step forward.

After an hour with no detectable conversation, the security chief left Alexandr to monitor the situation. Vlasta returned to his office at the medical facility to analyze the photographs for his report to Chairwoman Balca.

Back in his bedroom, a call to the US Embassy confirmed Rage's expectation. He stepped into the bathroom, turned on a faucet, and took care to speak in a low tone, glancing occasionally toward the tree line at the rear of property. Asking for the head of security, he was told the individual would be unavailable until the next day. Rage said he would call again.

He had one more thing he wanted to do. After checking the date he had written in his notebook, Rage googled for aircraft accidents in the south of France on February 27, 1990. He found nothing. Further searching indicated there had been no crash anywhere near the location within several months before or after that date. Rage turned from his computer and looked out the window.

After a shower and with only a towel around his waist, he dropped to the floor and did fifty-count sets of push-ups and sit-ups. Rage seldom skipped the short ritual. Last night had been the rare exception. Finished, he slipped into his pajama bottoms and climbed into bed.

The book he had tossed in his bag was resting on Rage's chest only moments after he opened it. His thoughts had crowded out the reading and quickly returned to the evening's conversation.

He wondered why Kateřina and her friend had been asked to be surrogates. Taking the fact and adding wealthy infertile couples to the mix sounded like something from a novel. Unfortunately, Kateřina's and her friend's situations were not stories of fiction.

Yawning a short time later, Rage admitted to himself there was nothing more he could accomplish tonight. The book was moved to the night table as he switched off the light.

Sleep overtook him quickly; it always did. Then in three or four hours, he would awake and begin planning the next day. It had been that way for as long as he could remember.

He was just settling into the deep sleep when a soft squeaking sound came from the hallway door. Something stirred there bringing Rage awake instantly.

Without moving, he was immediately at full alert. Already lying on his side and facing in that direction, Rage saw a figure step into the room. Then he heard the sound again as the door closed.

As his eyes grew accustomed to the dark, Rage could see Kateřina standing near the door. In a long flowing robe, she was perfectly still, her back to the wall. She was staring at him, her hands behind her. In the soft light Rage could see the expression on her face and the contours of her body. She appeared relaxed and at peace standing there.

He could feel her watching him, probably assuming he had not awakened. Rage remained still. If Kateřina came to him, he would want the decision to be hers.

Though it seemed longer, a few seconds passed without either of them moving. Then Kateřina reached out and quietly opened the door again. Taking a step toward it, she paused, then looked back.

In a flash of memory Rage recalled the hesitation they had both experienced late on their first night together all those years ago. She was barely twenty, and he was only a few years older.

Kateřina had taken him from the Ambassador's party with a solitary soft command. "Come," she'd said, and then with a curling motion from her finger, she'd urged him to follow her.

Later, after walking and talking for hours, they had taken a room in a tiny hotel on a hill above Charles Bridge. Obviously having awakened the little man who ran the establishment, he was nonetheless cordial as he assigned a room with a view of the city. The bridge and the Vltava River were only a short distance below their window.

Memories…

Rage had opened the room's solitary window, and they had disrobed with only the light from the streets outside filtering through thin ornate curtains.

Kateřina had slipped out of her last intimate articles of clothing with her back to him. When she turned, Rage could hardly breathe. He would have sworn his heart stopped beating for a while. Kateřina was incredibly beautiful.

She stood watching him watch her for several seconds before she walked slowly into his open arms. Then, in their youth, they made love for hours before falling asleep. There in the tangled sheets, they had held each other tight, their legs intertwined beneath the covers.

I remember every moment of that night.

There had never been another like it for him.

A few seconds passed before Kateřina moved again. All hesitation gone, she tossed her hair back and silently stepped back into the bedroom, closing the door behind her.

As she approached, Rage lifted the covers allowing her to slide in beside him. A smile was on her face. Then a brief twist and turn ridded her of the sheer robe leaving only a short silk gown covering her still stunning figure.

The warmth of her body flowed over him like a blush he'd experienced at twelve when an older girl of his dreams had unexpectedly kissed him on the lips. Rage lifted himself onto an elbow and watched as she wiggled closer still.

She turned and kissed him gently. A tiny smile prefaced her words.

"I did not want to be alone tonight."

She hadn't wanted to be alone all those years ago either.

Kateřina turned toward him again. This time her face was buried against his chest, arms clutching him to her, and a leg thrown carelessly across his body.

"Hold me," she said.

They lay entwined for a while and then Kateřina turned and snuggled her back to him.

"Make me feel that I will never be alone again."

Holding her close, his arm across her with fingers gently resting on her breasts, sleep claimed them both.

9

WEDNESDAY, SEPTEMBER 23, 2015

* * *

RAGE AWOKE IN EARLY MORNING darkness and sensed Kateřina was no longer sleeping either. She turned, kissed him gently, and they talked softly about their lives and what might have been, Finally, the sun climbed above the horizon and brought the beginning of a new day. With her back to him again and his arms encircling her, they napped for a while longer.

She left Rage at last, telling him coffee and toast would be available on the terrace in thirty minutes. She also reminded him that a sweater or jacket would be a good idea.

His shave was quick. Dressed casually in gray slacks and an open shirt, he made his way downstairs and over to the terrace doors. She was waiting.

Scattered clouds of the new day were allowing the sun to play hide-and-seek with their little piece of the world. He let himself out and walked to the umbrella table where she had set out their breakfast.

Her first comment in the coolness was, "No sweater? I suggested..."

"Didn't bring one."

"Oh. Well, join me."

Stopping for a moment, he breathed in the fragrance of the damp foliage and stood astonished as he surveyed the numerous small trees scattered about the grounds. A smattering of Japanese Magnolias was interspersed among the others. Knowing dogwoods didn't grow here, Rage made a mental note to ask Kateřina about the winsome trees. He then turned to the table and breakfast.

There was jam—two kinds—and wild honey for the toast. The coffee was strong but not like yesterday. This was in tune with the type he enjoyed at his cabin in Tennessee, the kind he sipped as the sun climbed above the horizon on crisp mornings. Rage could almost hear the silence of the mountains broken only by bird sounds and red squirrels chattering in the trees.

Kateřina busied herself as he poured his coffee. She prepared toast and jam for each of them and then poured coffee for herself.

"What will you do today? Remember, I will be returning to the hospital this morning. Hopefully, I will see my Ana."

He knew she was not asking for a response, only for understanding. Also, they both knew the woods behind the house had ears. The question was whether the security van would be there during daylight hours.

She was unsure as she glanced at him. "I do not understand about the quarantine."

After saying he also hoped she could see Ana this time, Rage changed the subject. "I have a couple of calls to make," he told her, "and perhaps a visit with an old friend."

Kateřina nodded.

"Oh, I almost forgot," Rage added inquiringly. He pointed, "The small trees, what are those? They're extraordinary."

She smiled. "Those are cherry trees. Beautiful, aren't they? You should see when they are blooming in the spring."

They talked as each munched on the toast and sipped coffee. Mostly they were catching up on snippets of the years that had passed. After breakfast, they parted ways for the day.

Having shared his bed only a short few hours ago, Kateřina obviously hated to leave him now, but there were engagements she needed to keep after visiting Ana.

Kateřina admitted to herself she had spent much of the night thinking of her return to the hospital this morning. Her mind had been in turmoil since leaving the Cambridge Center last night. She was growing more concerned by the hour that something sinister was happening. Kateřina desperately wanted Ana back with her.

Early morning found Karel Vlasta putting the finishing touches on the upcoming day's report to the Chairwoman. The photos had been a disappointment. Bambenek's guest always seemed to be at an odd angle or facing away from their cameras. The couple's conversation in the house before the new equipment was in place had been useless. They had been sitting at the wrong end of the long settees and talking softly. The security chief shook his head hoping the new devices would be an improvement.

Karel had decided to partially disregard the Chairwoman's order to have Bambenek and her visitor followed. He only planned to involve himself and Alexandr in the operation. They would trade off and would follow the first one out each day. Arriving back at the house, the next one leaving would get an escort. This would keep the Chairwoman happy for a few days. Karel expected to be gone before Madam Balca realized he had his own plans and would be leaving for good.

Standing up and stretching, he considered his own alternatives. Glancing at his personal laptop, Karel marveled at the amount of damning information hidden there in password protected locations. The time was near for the security chief to make a move.

Karel's apparent devotion to the Chairwoman was evident to all of her staff and inner circle. Though his background and time spent in prison was common knowledge, it had not kept Karel from becoming a trusted employee of Madam Balca.

Several individuals were aware of his criminal record in France. The fact that the Chairwoman had overlooked those details and taken a chance when she recruited Karel spoke well for him. Up to the present there had been no reason for the Chairwoman or others to doubt her decision.

Now, and without anyone's suspicion, the situation was about to change. Karel had visited Switzerland on holiday four months earlier. While there, he had attended to some preliminary banking chores.

Utilizing false papers and an ability with disguises, Karel had set up several accounts with different international financial institutions. Security cameras, should they be examined later, would show two different men and one woman setting up his financial groundwork.

Within a matter of days, Karel expected to use those accounts.

Back in his room, Rage hoped he could find an expat friend he thought was living in Prague. He also needed to find a particular type of electronics store. There were some things he needed. An idea had come to him after he discovered the hidden van last night.

In the meantime, Rage unpacked the two lockboxes from his suitcase again. First he retrieved the pistol. After a quick inspection, he reloaded both magazines and palmed one into the weapon. He then pumped a cartridge into the chamber and replaced it.

A final check, safety on, and a nod. He slipped the pistol under his belt. His blazer covered it and made the weapon difficult to detect. The second magazine went into his coat pocket.

With the chore complete, Rage reached for his cellphone and walked into the bathroom, perching himself on the side of the tub. From there he began a search for his old friend.

"Who?"

Marty Cutler didn't recognize the caller's name.

"Doyle…Rage Doyle?" Cutler's memory shifted into gear.

Smiling, Rage remembered Marty's full name: Martin Mayhem Cutler. When they'd met back in the 1960s, Marty had explained the unusual middle name by saying his father had a quirky sense of humor. In Marty's case, the moniker had seemed quite appropriate. Violence and chaos seemed to follow him throughout his career at the CIA.

"Rage! You old son-of-a-gun." He was remembering now. "How are you? *Where* are you?"

"Actually, I'm in Prague hoping to help a friend."

Rage guessed it had been over twenty-five years since he'd spoken to Cutler. They had both been with the CIA, though in very different roles at the time. On the surface Marty had run a small tour business in Panama City, Panama. Rage was running the covert operation.

In reality, Cutler was a member of Rage's team. Marty had been acting as an informant to help bring down Manuel Noriega's drug empire and ultimately, the leadership of the Panamanian government.

It was the late 1980s, and Noriega was already close to losing control of his country. Still there were a number of CIA operatives and informants on the ground in the Central American country. All of this was happening before Noriega was arrested in early 1990.

Information had reached Rage that Cutler's cover had been compromised, and he had been designated for assassination. In fact, according to the source, a death squad had already been dispatched to Cutler's location.

With less than five minutes to spare, three operatives under The Author's personal command and plan entered Marty's business premises. They took cover, and with Cutler bravely sitting at his desk, The Author's men eliminated the members of the death squad when they entered the offices.

In those days, Raegene Dorryen Doyle had been informally known as The Author within CIA circles. The nickname had nothing to do with literary composition but was instead for his ability at planning and carrying out clandestine operations like the one involving Marty Cutler. Only a few insiders knew President Lyndon Johnson had been the first to pin the nickname on Rage.

"Prague? You're here in Prague?" Cutler was beside himself. "You son-of-a-gun!"

The former operative, though quite nervous before the raid, had been very grateful to The Author for saving him from a certain death at the hands of Noriega's men. Cutler had said at the time he owed one to Rage. "Anytime," he had emphasized. "Any place."

They both knew he meant it.

"I might need your help," Rage told Cutler. "I'm checking out a situation for a friend. It may not amount to anything, but one doesn't know until the facts are in."

"True," Cutler agreed and then asked, "Can you meet me for a drink? Maybe talk over old times?"

"Sure, I can do that. I'd like your thoughts on a couple of things anyway."

Since Cutler was familiar with Prague, Rage let him decide on the location.

"I'll pick you up at your hotel," Cutler suggested.

"That won't work. I'll need to meet you. Name a place."

"Have you visited Charles Bridge?" Cutler asked.

"Been near there," Rage said. "Had coffee and a roll in the area yesterday. A place called Café Márnice. Didn't go up on the bridge, though."

"Good enough," Cutler said. "Can you meet me there in an hour?"

"Sure."

"There's a little place nearby where I go for a glass of schnapps now and then. Too early for schnapps now. We can have coffee." Then he added, "This is more of a Czech neighborhood place. Not touristy. The kind of place we used to like, except you always drank water."

Rage heard him chuckle.

"You still on H2O?"

"Yep."

"See you in an hour."

Arriving at the information counter a couple of minutes before nine, she was third in line. While Kateřina waited, she gazed around the lobby. An older man and woman were tidying up the area. The man was pushing a heavy polishing machine back and forth across the floor. He appeared too old for the effort.

The woman was dusting and replacing magazines that had been tossed about. As Kateřina watched, the woman took a wide broom from against a wall and started to sweep.

There were several people sitting about the lobby. Kateřina thought it would probably be interesting to hear their individual stories. *Some would be happy,* she imagined, *some sad.* She was trying everything to keep her mind off Ana's situation.

Finally, it was her turn at the counter.

Kateřina asked for her daughter again. The clerk looked for Ana's name, read some information and then turned back to Kateřina.

"I am sorry," she said. "Ana Bambenek is in quarantine. Are you her mother?"

Kateřina nodded, tears already misting her eyes. *It is happening all over again.*

The clerk was saying something.

Wiping away tears, Kateřina calmed her emotions. "Please… what were you telling me?"

The woman began again.

"Dr. Laska asked to speak with you when you are here to see your daughter. I will call his secretary." She dialed a number.

Kateřina could only wait and wonder.

The attendant spoke a few words and then hung up the phone. Looking up she said, "The doctor is coming for you."

Returning to the bench she had used the night before, Kateřina didn't have long to wait. She watched a man in a white doctor's coat walk to the counter. A few words were spoken and the clerk pointed toward Kateřina. The doctor turned and strolled over.

"Ms. Bambenek? I am Dr. Laska, Ana's physician."

He shook her hand and then glanced around the lobby. It was becoming crowded and noisy.

"Perhaps my office would be better for speaking about your daughter." Gesturing, he said, "Come with me."

In his office, the doctor offered coffee and then sat down at his desk. He immediately began to explain about her daughter.

"Ana is very sick," he said. "As you have already learned, she is in quarantine. The measure is temporary. Once we are sure of Ana's illness, she will be transferred to intensive care or to a room."

Kateřina started to speak, but Dr. Laska interrupted.

"Let me finish," he suggested. "I'm sure I will answer most of your questions."

"Yes," she said, "Please continue."

He is very sure of himself when it is my daughter's life he is discussing.

Dr. Laska took a breath and then set about explaining.

"Ana became ill while working in our lab. She was being instructed on a new procedure for conducting certain tests. There was an accident potentially exposing Ana to a serious strain of SARS. If you are not familiar, that is Severe Acute Respiratory Syndrome. Unfortunately, the potential exposure was to the most extreme form of SARS."

The doctor leaned forward and appeared to give a possibility of hope.

"We expect Ana to be well in a few days when the tests and treatments are concluded, but as a precaution for herself and others, we set her up in temporary quarantine quarters in our facility. We are prepared to deal with her exposure here." He leaned back in his chair.

"The only complication comes from having no dedicated quarantine area, therefore we must use temporary quarters. Given that, we cannot have visitors as there are no interior windows, and we cannot allow you to enter the quarantine space."

A thousand thoughts were flooding Kateřina's mind. None of them were good. Mainly she didn't believe he was telling her the truth.

The doctor continued. "Hopefully, we will find Ana clear of all complications within a few days. We are expecting that. I am sure she will return to you in a couple of weeks at the most."

He paused for a brief moment, but it was enough for Kateřina to ask a question.

"I thought Ana was in London to present a research paper. Is that not true?"

"Yes," Dr. Laska said, "she was." He glanced at her, then away. Kateřina thought he seemed suddenly off his game, not as sure of himself as he had been moments before, but he continued.

"There was a sudden need for Ana's expertise back here in our labs."

Kateřina realized she must have looked surprised because the doctor hurried on to answer her unasked questions.

"An important project of Ana's reached a critical stage sooner than was expected, and she was needed for the next step."

Dr. Laska looked at Kateřina, held her eyes for a moment, then glanced away. He appeared to gather his thoughts before turning back and holding her attention this time.

"Ana accidentally exposed herself to a virus. She was working in the lab and had opened a vial of body fluids from a patient who had SARS. We are concerned your daughter may have touched the material and then herself, thereby contracting the virus. Unfortunately, to protect her and others, we had to put Ana in quarantine until we can see if she develops the virus."

Watching her now, Dr. Laska appeared to think that was all the explanation Kateřina required. "I am sure your daughter will be home soon and in your care."

He smiled but without holding eye contact. Kateřina didn't believe this new assurance was sincere either. After adding a few additional details, the doctor ushered her out of his office with a promise to keep her informed.

"But when can I see her?" Kateřina asked as they walked along the corridor.

"Soon," was his reply. "As quickly as she is cleared from quarantine."

Wondering why she hadn't been allowed to speak with Ana by phone again, Kateřina asked.

"We are too busy with the real needs of both patient and medical personel," Dr. Laska told her. "Anything your daughter touches or is near when she coughs or otherwise expels bodily fluids must then be sanitized. We try to keep that requirement at a minimum."

Kateřina realized she was leaving the hospital with more questions than answers. She could almost feel the print of his shoe on her rear end. She recognized when she'd been kicked out of someplace, and this qualified. Without thinking about it, Kateřina suddenly realized she was rubbing the arm where the security guard held her last night as he escorted her out of the building.

Driving home, she took her time. There was no particular hurry. Rage said he had things to do. She hoped his friend could help make sense of her situation. Ana's friends and acquaintances were dying and having accidents at an alarming rate. Now Ana was sick and being kept from her.

Waiting at a traffic light, she touched fingers to each temple in a feeble attempt to ward off the discomfort she felt coming her way. The headaches were becoming difficult to endure without going to her room and closing the draperies. Only darkness seemed to help.

She thought of Rage but did not think he was aware of her condition, except perhaps just this symptom. When she wrote the letter, Kateřina had chosen not tell him. Now she decided to talk with Rage only if he became aware of her condition on his own.

She was not sure when Rage would return from meeting his friend, but the time would be easy to fill. She had things to do too. A call to Adina was first on the list. She could not leave everything to Rage.

Parking near her front door, Kateřina let herself inside and headed for the kitchen and some hot tea. A nap could come later. The headache was back and had brought its friends this time.

No use putting it off, Kateřina thought. Fortified with a cup of fresh tea, she turned on the stereo's classical station. That done, she took her usual place on the settee and punched Adina's number into her phone. *I wish Rage could be here to give me assurance.*

Answering after several rings, Adina's voice was low; she sounded depressed. Kateřina thought of how Adina's son had died. News of his death had passed around to her when it happened. That had been a couple of years ago. Adina and Kateřina 's chance meeting at church had come later and was now progressing to a special friendship.

After asking how her friend was feeling, Kateřina shared, "I do not want to eat alone this evening. Would you do me the favor of joining me for dinner?"

Finding the experiences with their children to be so similar had initially surprised them both. Now Kateřina felt guilty for what she planned if her friend agreed to the outing.

"Well…" Adina was hesitant.

Kateřina remembered Rage's words. *"…You will have to help me."* She pressed her friend to join her. "Come on. We will have good food and a nice wine. It will be good for both of us."

"Yes," Adina said finally. "It does sound appealing, and I should get out of my house."

"Good! What time shall I come for you?"

"Do you know where I live?"

"No, but I have GPS in my automobile."

Adina gave her the address, and they agreed on a time. After exchanging a few pleasantries, they said goodbye.

Remaining on the settee and reaching for her tea, Kateřina drew her legs up and considered what she was about to do. *It's lying,* she thought, *but I must know if the doctor is doing a bad thing to my Ana.*

A friend of Kateřina's knew someone who worked in maintenance at the health center. The individual had said there were areas at the facility and even one entire building specifically off limits. No one could go to those locations unless they had special credentials. The man who talked to her friend had made it sound sinister, mentioning security patrols, cameras, and guards at the entrances. Kateřina could certainly attest to the part about certain areas being restricted. She rubbed the sore arm the security guard had gripped the night before.

Kateřina thought the restrictions seemed extreme.

On the other hand, Cambridge Health and Research Center had a reputation as *the* place for the wealthy along with celebrities, politicians, and others in high positions to come for serious surgery, including organ transplants. The female President of Chile had received a new heart just a couple of months earlier. News of the procedure had circulated.

In fact, the health center had been in the news just recently. Ana's situation had encouraged Kateřina to search out and read stories about the hospital. Cambridge Center's global standing in the health community was exemplary, garnering coverage on Reuters, the BBC, and all of the largest media organizations in Great Britain and America.

But there was a downside.

Rumors had also quietly made the rounds regarding the medical center getting many of its donated organs locally. Kateřina had not paid attention to those stories until Ana became ill. Once it happened, Adina had mentioned seeing some coverage on the internet and in the Prague newspaper. She told Kateřina about the articles.

There had also been other disturbing news in various publications about the worldwide black market trade in human body parts. Kateřina wondered if the Cambridge Center might be involved in some way.

If it were possible, would they take organs from Ana if she did not survive the SARS virus? Perhaps Dr. Laska and others would not give Ana the care she needed in order to steal her organs. And would Kateřina even know?

Her head dropped and tears flooded her eyes. If she lost Ana, life would not be worth living.

If the suspicious illnesses had only involved Ana, Kateřina might not have been dubious about what was happening. But it wasn't just her daughter. There was Marta Melcer and Adina's son, Kamil. And there was also the son of the woman Adina knew who had hung herself. Kateřina thought she remembered the young man's name was Ivan Relek. This made three.

Now there's Ana... and perhaps even others.

Like a dark mist, the dreaded idea hung over Kateřina as her head pounded.

I must know...

In an attempt to get it off her mind, Kateřina laid back and turned her thoughts to the individual who had come to help her, the mysterious lover she had not seen or spoken with in years.

Kateřina couldn't believe she had crept up the stairs last night to Raegene's bedroom and then to his side. But then, she also remembered it had been her, not Raegene, who had been the instigator of their short but torrid affair all those years ago.

Though she had been the younger of the two, it had been love at first sight for her. Literally, she had taken Raegene by the hand and made him the love of her life. Then all too soon he had been called away by the real love of *his* life, the CIA.

In time, she had learned it did no good to hate a shadow.

There had been other men Kateřina cared about during the ensuing years, but there had never been another Raegene. Though several tried, no one stood a chance of replacing him in her heart.

Her thoughts flew back through the years, and Kateřina remembered how they had made love in the tiny hotel all those years ago. *A thousand times I have relived those moments…*

In her memories, Kateřina returned to the night before last when he arrived at her home.

She had climbed out of her own bed and reached for her robe. Her desire to be with him made walking to the stairs easy, but the first step had been very difficult. Three separate times she tried before conquering it. Then, one stair at a time, she made her way to his door.

Then the door became a barrier. It was almost as if the handle was too hot to touch. She had reached out several times before finally entering his room. But even then, Kateřina had almost commanded herself back to her own bedroom downstairs.

And last night, I can't believe I closed the door behind me and stood there watching him sleep.

She wondered if he'd really been asleep or if Raegene had been watching her too.

Even then, I started to leave…the years and the doubts…as I opened the door to leave and then looked back, I suddenly knew this was where I belonged at the moment.

She smiled.

He had been watching me; I am sure he was.

Raegene had lifted the blankets for her when she came to him. All the hesitation was gone as she slipped underneath the covers to lie beside him.

It was me, Kateřina thought suddenly, almost surprised as she remembered. *I wanted more. I wanted Raegene to make love to me.*

Leaning back, Kateřina closed her eyes, almost in a dreamy state. Her thoughts continued to drift through the night, reliving the moments. It was as though her mind had photographed and recorded every special word, each touch, every emotion.

The years had seemed to fall away, and we were young again. But this time with a special appreciation of life's experiences.

A smile touched her lips as Kateřina recalled something Raegene said at one special moment in the near darkness. With her head resting on his shoulder, he had whispered, "I can truly say passion is not all lost on the young." They had both laughed out loud.

Moments later, they had turned to face each other, eager to hold the other close again. Time and space meant little as they lay there touching and emotionally exploring the new while vividly recalling the past. Their warm bodies brought their strength of feeling to a heightened fervor Kateřina doubted either had known before.

But they had not made love. Maturity held them back. Each had wanted to make love, but they had expected there would come a better time—when Ana was home and Kateřina was well.

They had embraced and held each other close, spending their time in each other's arms and playing the mind game of *What if?* Kateřina finally summed up their hours together with one perfect thought.

She whispered to him, "The passion of our youth, though wonderful, could not have been better than these sweet hours."

He smiled, understanding and knowing she was right.

Leaving him as the sun brightened, Kateřina attempted to push certain particular thoughts away but found them creeping back to disquiet her mind and memory. Could it be—was it within the bounds of reason she still loved him as she had when they were young? She understood it was different now, they had changed, but she wondered, *Do I care for him the way I did back then?*

Remembering the way he touched her and the soft words uttered in the stillness of night, dare she hope Raegene might feel the same?

Is it possible…?

Rage was a few minutes early and standing near the large tree at the gate entrance to Café Márnice. A very large man approached him shortly after he arrived.

Cutler was tall, probably 6'4" as Rage remembered, but he must have put on at least a hundred pounds since they said goodbye in Panama. A slap on the shoulder staggered Rage. Then Marty spoke.

"Except for the grey, you haven't changed much."

"You have," Rage countered as he glanced up at Cutler.

The big man laughed and patted his belly.

"It's Jolana's fault," he said, referring to his wife. "She's Czech, you know." He pointed to the sidewalk and led the way as he continued. "Gravies and sauces. They're gonna kill me. Her, too. She outweighs me by a good twenty pounds."

Bragging, Marty told Rage he still works out. "There's a gym near my house. I go there and beat up on a body bag a couple of times a week. I'm tougher than I look," he said.

The schnapps place was about half full with most of those present having an early lunch. There were salads, vegetables, and soup, some of it being served in bread bowls. Everything looked scrumptious and smelled even better. Rage remembered he had been venturesome with his eating when stationed here with the CIA.

Cutler ordered first. He asked for coffee and a spinach soup.

Rage chose Goulash in a bread bowl and a bottle of sparkling water.

"Are you in touch with any of our people?" Marty asked.

Rage shook his head. To go into detail would require saying more than he should. Rage made it a rule not to go there. Cutler understood and let the subject drop. Remembering Rage had said he was helping someone, Cutler asked if he could be of service.

"I know my way around the city and even have a couple of friends with the police," he said.

"Good," Rage responded. "Do you think your friends could get me a temporary permit for my pistol while I'm here?"

Rage opened his blazer, letting Cutler know he was carrying the weapon. Marty lifted the left side of his Hawaiian shirt a couple of inches; he was carrying too.

"Doesn't have to be temporary," Marty said. "Your profession will qualify you. There's a 30-day waiting period, but I know someone we can get to waive it." He was bragging a little.

Marty pulled out his cellphone and dialed. When he closed the phone, he told Rage to hurry with his soup. They had an appointment with Colonel Tibor Repa of the Prague police in thirty minutes.

At the station, the officer had some forms for Rage to sign, and those appeared to cover the weapon matter. There was also a form Rage should carry with him. Otherwise, he was to be a careful and obedient visitor to the Czech Republic.

Marty's friend asked about the weapon, giving Rage a chance to show him the Walther PPK he carried.

Looking at the pistol, the officer glanced up and said, "This is James Bond's weapon of choice." Impressed, the Colonel asked several questions about the weapon before the conversation lulled, and the participants went on their way.

As they left the police building, Rage asked about a specialized electronics store. Marty said he knew where one was located though he'd never been there. Rage was a bit skeptical when Marty drove directly to the location.

Inside, Rage browsed along several aisles before motioning for Marty to come and interpret for him. He picked a few items with Marty's help and took them to the checkout counter. Walking out, Rage carried two medium bags, and Marty had a third.

On the way to the car, Marty asked, "You starting a business?"

Rage smiled and shook his head. "Just a little extracurricular activity."

Marty glanced over but didn't ask any more questions.

Rage was starting to think Marty Cutler might be handy to have around for the next few days. Watching Cutler handle himself in casual situations, Rage decided his friend's size would not be a deterrent to having him as a traveling buddy. Another upside was Marty's bulk could definitely keep possible disagreements low-key from the start. Rage would need an interpreter too. Marty spoke the Czech language fluently and said he could handle a little French.

Back in his friend's vehicle, Rage asked if Marty was familiar with the Cambridge Health and Research Center. When Kateřina mentioned the hospital where Ana worked and was now quarantined, Rage assumed it was small and probably private. In his mind, he was doubtful there would be a reason for Marty to know about it.

"*Výzkumné Centrum a Cambridge Zdraví?* Oh yeah, the Cambridge Center," the big guy exclaimed. "I hope you don't need to go there for treatment. The place is for the wealthy, and I mean the very wealthy."

"How do you know about it?"

"A cousin of Jolana's is a nurse there," he said. "He was one of the first medical employees hired when the Cambridge Center opened back in the 1980s."

A male nurse and on the inside. Good to know.

"Want to see it? We could drive by."

"Sure. Let's go."

Getting on one of the main streets, Marty headed west out of the business district. They drove for several minutes before turning off and entering an exclusive area consisting of stylish buildings no more than four stories tall. Most were on large tracts of land and all were landscaped and well manicured.

Reminded of an upscale business district, Rage looked about as his friend drove them deeper into the area. Signs giving the names of occupants were small and uniform. Buildings appeared reasonably new, mostly constructed to suit the new era in Central Europe. Of the little he remembered of Prague from his short stay here in the 1960s, what he was seeing now spoke of new money and new ideas.

Everything about the neighborhood visually verified what Marty had suggested about the medical facility being for the rich. Most of the signs fronting places of business carried the Caduceus symbol of medicine.

Rounding a long curve lined with trees, flowering beds, and meandering driveways stood a group of buildings needing no signs of identification, but there was one. Not unlike other markers, this one gave only the name of the occupant— *Výzkumné Centrum a Cambridge Zdraví.*

"Cambridge Health and Research Center," Marty said under his breath. "Wow."

Though he had never seen the hospital, Marty said he had heard of it. Milan, the cousin, had mentioned it on occasion but had never gone into detail. He appeared totally surprised.

Marty braked, stopping dead near the curb. Glancing over, Rage realized his friend was as stunned as he.

"Man!" was all Marty said before dragging in another deep breath.

The entrance was at the crest of several sloping hills falling gently away from the street. The entire complex was visible from where the two men were sitting.

Rage, too, was mesmerized.

The front set of buildings, three stories tall and attached, drew Rage's eyes from the expanse of single-story structures that spread out behind and made up the major portion of the complex.

Glancing at each other momentarily, Rage and Marty quickly looked back at what they had discovered. This was a full-blown hospital and a big one. That would also account for the other medical businesses that seemed to be gathered in its shadow.

"Did you know it was this size?" Rage asked.

"Nope." Marty was shaking his head. "This is mind-boggling."

"Yeah."

"The center part of the main building looks old," Marty said, "like it was already here and the others were added."

Looks like something right out of the Middle Ages.

Stones and stucco covered the exterior of the structure. Large wooden beams obviously held it together and were the frames around windows and the entrance doors. The doors themselves must have been nine feet tall with the upper half consisting of leaded glass images depicting another era. Though they were too far away to appreciate detail, the building was unlike anything Rage had seen before. He guessed it was the administrative section of the complex.

They were still at the curb and staring at the hospital when a car slowly passed them and then stopped. The driver's door opened, and an individual walked back toward their vehicle. Lowering his window, Marty had a short conversation Rage didn't understand except for the last few words.

"*Děkuju,*" Marty said. "*To je nádhera.*"

Rage caught a "Thank you" and was pretty sure Marty had told the man the complex was beautiful.

Before leaving, the man leaned over and looked across at Rage. Walking to his car, he glanced back a couple of times.

"We need to move on," Marty said. "This guy is with security, and I told him we were just admiring the place."

"Good. Did he sound suspicious?"

"Didn't seem to be."

The security man pulled out from the curb. The two men left the hospital and drove deeper into the complex. Karel Vlasta eased his car down toward the health center and parked behind some shrubs. The strangers would be coming back; he knew that. All the streets in and around the Cambridge Center led to deadends. There was only one way in and out.

Ensconced at a good vantage point, Vlasta pulled a small set of binoculars from the glove box and climbed out of his vehicle. Resting one foot on the step of the car and the other on the ground, he leaned his elbows onto the vehicle's roof and waited. He could easily see the street, but it would be difficult for passersby to see him.

Though Karel didn't have a name yet, he was confident he recognized the passenger in the automobile. He was almost certain it was the American guest of Kateřina Bambenek.

Waiting for the men to reappear, Karel began to form a new idea.

As they pulled away, Rage noticed everything seemed to be under one continuous roof except the three-story set of main buildings and one other. This one appeared long and narrow and was set between the main building and the rest of the complex. At one end of this particular structure, almost hidden behind the main edifice, was an important feature Rage had not noticed before.

Remembering Kateřina's explanation of how Ana's young friend's remains had been returned, Rage stared at the far end of the narrow building. There, only partially visible from their position on the street, was a tall narrow chimney stretching skyward.

The hospital had what appeared to be a crematory.

Rage was familiar with crematoriums and wondered why the hospital would need one. He knew furnaces like this one could be used to incinerate medical waste, but this had the look of a full-blown crematorium—one designed to incinerate bodies.

In Prague 10, only a few kilometers away, Vinohrady Cemetery had Strašnice Crematorium—in area, one of Europe's largest. Kateřina had pointed it out when they brought the roses to the cemetery earlier.

So why would this hospital need its own crematorium?

As Rage and Marty drove past the health clinic on their way out of the complex, Rage spied the individual who had checked them out a few minutes earlier. He was behind some tall bushes, almost hidden, and watching them with binoculars. The security man obviously thought he couldn't be seen there. Rage was satisfied to let him think that.

Back on the main street, Rage glanced at Marty. "Tell me about Jolana's relative who works at the hospital."

"Yeah, a cousin."

"Do you know him?"

"Sure, I know Milan," Marty said. "He's always at family functions. He likes to eat." Marty glanced over at Rage. "Oh, yeah. He's as big as Jolana. The whole family tends to be large as I think about it." He looked at Rage and chuckled. "Even their spouses are big." Marty patted his belly and laughed.

"Does he talk about the health clinic?"

"Not much," Marty said while checking the traffic around them. "He's mentioned it on occasion. I've heard him say it's a good job, and like I told you earlier, he's been there since the place opened."

As they drove back to Charles Bridge to part, Rage was taking in the scenery as he questioned Marty.

"Does the clinic ever get mentioned in the news?"

Marty glanced over, his eyebrows lifted with a bit of surprise. "Funny you should mention that."

"Why?"

"Remember, I said you need to be rich to go there? Well, they treat celebrities and politicians too."

He glanced over to see if Rage was listening.

Marty continued. "The President of Chile had heart transplant surgery there recently—two, maybe three months ago. It was a big deal."

"Did it go well?" Rage asked.

"Super from what I heard." He glanced over at Rage again. "Did you know Chile's President is a woman? The Prague Post said she went to university in England with the woman who's in charge at the Cambridge Center."

Coincidence or otherwise? Rage wondered.

Marty added, "Milan likes beer if you want to talk to him. One problem, though."

"What's that?"

"He doesn't speak much English. You'll need an interpreter."

"Know one?"

"You buying the beer and schnapps?"

"I can make it happen."

"Then I know one!"

"Set it up."

After Kateřina left for dinner, Rage finished assembling the equipment he had purchased earlier at the electronics store. It was exhilarating to have a clandestime operation going, even a small one.

And this isn't a small operation for Ana and Kateřina. It could be life or death for them.

Reaching for the almost empty bag, Rage checked the small listening device detector he had purchased. Satisfied, he switched it on and started a hour-long search taking him through the many rooms of the house. One of the upstairs rooms was outfitted as an art studio. Kateřina appeared to have talents unknown to Rage.

The only place he found a problem was in the conversation room and kitchen. He found three hidden devices spaced about. Rage guessed they had been there for a long time. Glancing around, he decided the situation could be handled with the music, lowered voices and holding conversations in other rooms inside the house. The front porch with its large chairs would also work as an alternative.

Now Rage was prepared to get the main plan into operation.

The result of his earlier assembly efforts was a small package including a video camera, a small but powerful listening device, and a transmitter. All of these components were battery and solar powered.

At dusk, Rage was in the woods where he had gone the prior evening. As expected, the van had not arrived. The men would be concerned about someone seeing them if they arrived during daylight hours.

Rage worked quickly but with care. Small night-vision goggles purchased that day allowed him to work with an economy of effort and at a rapid pace. His tiny flashlight gave all the additional light he needed.

He had picked a location before leaving the woods last night. He installed the equipment and then quickly cut a branch to cover his efforts as he heard the van approaching. Rage hoped they would park close to the spot they had used last night. The location gave them a small but clear shot to Kateřina's back windows. It also allowed Rage to zero in on their position.

The tree Rage had picked was old and quite large. The low limb he used was at chest level and allowed him to install the equipment pointing head-on toward the van.

When the vehicle pulled in and stopped, Rage had just flipped the switches to activate operation and stepped back into the bushes. He heard the vehicle's door open quietly and then close. Then Rage sensed trouble; someone was walking toward him.

Without a sound, Rage moved behind the big tree and drew his weapon. The footsteps came closer. He waited, breathing quietly through his nose.

Then he heard a sound. Rage didn't recognize it for a moment—then he did. Someone was peeing against the tree three or four feet from where he was standing.

Rage smiled, relaxing a bit.

Could'a been worse.

Kateřina rang the bell. Moments later Adina opened the door, and the women hugged and voiced hellos. Though they had met under unusual circumstances concerning their children, the women were not yet close friends. This would be their first opportunity to spend quality time together. Kateřina was looking forward to getting some of Rage's questions answered and also some of her own.

Without appearing to, Kateřina scrutinized Adina's home and decor. The house appeared larger than Kateřina's from the street, and the classical decor was certainly as nice as her own. Adina's neighborhood was also in Prague 6 and not very far from Kateřina's. She had driven there in a matter of minutes. If the outing was pleasant, Kateřina guessed they might become good friends.

The tantalizing aroma of fresh coffee greeted Kateřina as her host led the way through the house to the kitchen.

"This will carry us over to dinner," Adina said as she handed Kateřina a small china cup and saucer and poured coffee for her. Sugar and cream were on a small tray.

There was a table and chairs nearby, but the women remained standing at the lovely white kitchen counter. They discussed living in Prague 6.

"It is convenient here," Adina observed. "Almost everything is at hand. I seldom drive more than a few kilometers."

"This is also true for me," Kateřina agreed. "Except I drive weekly to Vinohrady Cemetery to visit the graves of a friend and her daughter. They both died recently."

Her new friend glanced Kateřina's way.

"My son is at Vinohrady also, but I can barely make myself go there."

A bit surprised, Kateřina inquired why.

Adina looked at her but remained silent for a moment. Then glancing away, she said, "I don't believe the story the doctors told me of my son's death." She took a breath. "Someday I will know the truth, and then I will go there." A glance at Kateřina showed the sadness in Adina's eyes.

A breath caught in Kateřina's throat causing a distinct sound.

"What is it?" Adina asked.

"A cough…almost." In recent days Kateřina had started to develop a respiratory condition to go along with the headaches. She glanced away, also not wanting Adina to know how intriguing the comment had been regarding her son and the doctors.

"Please, let's sit," Adina said, motioning toward the nearby table. They each took a chair.

"Your taste is exceptional. You have a special talent for decorating." Kateřina was sincere. The house was beautiful.

Smiling, Adina said, "I had help in the beginning, and now you can see I spend much of my time and too many of the Trust's korunas enhancing this large dwelling. It is beautiful, but it is emotionally empty."

Skipping a breath, Kateřina was uncertain if she had heard Adina correctly. "You are funded by a trust?" Kateřina asked. "This is a good thing."

"Yes, the Eagle Trust has always been at my side. I could not have lived otherwise."

This was all she had to say about the Trust, but it was enough.

Adina glanced at Kateřina as if deciding whether to voice her next thought. Then she said, "I sometimes speak with my son as I walk about these rooms."

Almost as an afterthought she added, "Kamil loved it here."

When Kateřina didn't reply, the mother continued. "I understand how conversing with my dead son must appear to you, but it gives me solace."

Wanting to keep her on subject, Kateřina told a small lie, saying she often spoke to her daughter when Ana was away and working. She didn't tell Adina, but there were moments too, when she had been tempted to speak with Ana since she had been sick. But no, she had not spoken out to Ana in the empty house.

At least not yet.

"When the Cambridge Center's doctor called and said Kamil was dead, I was sure there had been some mistake." Adina's eyes were downcast, the tone of her voice searching for understanding. "He was young and healthy. How could Kamil be dead?" she asked. It was almost as if she wanted Kateřina to tell her.

With her eyes back on Kateřina now, she said, "I was sure he was talking about some other young man and they had used Kamil's name in error." Kateřina reached over and caressed Adina's hand as a tear slowly made its way down the disconsolate mother's cheek.

Dabbing at her eyes, Adina continued. "A priest, Father Anděl, and Dr. Laska became my contacts with the hospital as they brought my son's body home from Switzerland."

Kateřina took a sip of the coffee to hide her recognition of the doctor's name.

Adina said, "Swiss authorities had procedures, and there were forms to submit. Still there were surprises."

"What sort of surprises?" Kateřina asked.

"It took so long," Adina said, her eyes squinted in thought. "I did not receive my son's ashes until three weeks after his death. Thanks to their good heart, the clinic took care of the paperwork. They said there were many of the Swiss forms."

Each of the three mothers who had lost children had spent an excruciating period waiting for their loved one to be returned.

I do not know if I could survive such an ordeal.

Then Kateřina remembered though the circumstances were different, she had already suffered through several days of angst.

Ana has too.

Kateřina suggested they continue the conversation over dinner. She sensed Adina was tiring, and there were still many unanswered questions. She would pursue them after her new friend had a glass of wine.

Pavia Balek was aware of the special consideration she enjoyed from the Chairwoman. On several occasions, coworkers had mentioned the situation in joking, yet pointed ways. At times in conversation with her friends, she detected a touch of envy.

Pavia had not knowingly done anything that should account for the special treatment she enjoyed. Yet, she realized it was there, having become a reality within a year of the time she joined the staff. Whatever; it was nice to have the favor of the Chairwoman.

The eyes of her boss were not the only ones Pavia had garnered. Karel Vlasta had been playfully pursuing Pavia for the past couple of months. Though she had not been interested initially, just within the last week she had begun to see him from a different perspective.

Having broken a two-year relationship with a young man from University, Pavia was now feeling differently about Karel's attention. Being young and alone was not a situation she handled well.

Though he was a few years older, when Karel asked her to have dinner with him this evening, Pavia readily accepted. He had asked her to pick a restaurant. She named a small place, a pub she knew near her apartment. The eatery's specialty was a schnitzel, grilled and served with potatoes in a secret sauce. The dark bread they served was always soft and warm. Pavia liked it brought to the table fresh, a couple of slices at a time. A delicious, locally brewed ale was served throughout the meal.

Afterwards came fresh *sněhový pudink*—steamed meringue pudding—a special Czech dessert. As the American tourists so aptly put it, the pudding was "to die for."

He was waiting when Pavia edged her way through the pub's front door. A wave and then Karel was at her side.

He was interesting and had an unusual sense of humor. With a grin, Karel introduced himself. Acting as though they had never met each other, he even asked if she would like to join him for dinner. Pavia laughed at his teasing.

They chose a table near a back corner, and he held her chair. She could grow to enjoy his manners.

Liking Karel immediately, she was surprised at her own feelings. Pavia had thought about it on the way to meet him and had tentatively decided if there was chemistry, she would go out with him a few times and see where it might lead.

"Was this a good day?" he asked as he slipped into his chair.

Pavia told him about her activities in general terms. Even though Karel was head of security, she didn't talk about the work she did for the Chairwoman with anyone. Most of her duties were common knowledge, but still she didn't think it proper to discuss the details of her job.

Pavia thought about the arrangements she had made for the Chairwoman's special dinner. Only a few others even knew. She suspected Karel was aware of it because of his job. Still, Pavia did not mention the small gathering.

A young waitress appeared, and they ordered the schnitzel and pudding. The young woman was dressed in Germanic costume with a short, checkered dress and a white puffy blouse with a low neckline. She brought ale and bread to the table and then left them to their conversation.

Pavia noticed Karel deftly checking out the young woman's cleavage. She grinned as he looked back at her. Having been caught, a blush began at his neck and spread upward.

Men. She shook her head and chuckled.

His face grew a couple of shades darker.

Obviously hoping to move on, Karel asked Pavia about soccer. "Do you go to the games?"

"I have been to a few." She didn't tell him her recent boyfriend had bragged about going to the matches, yet he hardly knew anything about the game.

Karel obviously enjoyed the competition.

"I am a fan of the Slavia Prague Club," he told her. "They play their home games at Synot Tip Aréna out in Prague 11."

"I have been there," she told him.

She didn't tell him about the terrible argument she'd had with her boyfriend at the stadium recently. Pavia had told him she would have to work during the weekend and would not be able to stay over at his family's country estate near *Cesky Krumlov.* It was the last time she saw him. Too bad in some ways. The country in the south of the Czech Republic and his family's estate are beautiful.

Catching her attention, Karel said in passing, "I even know a couple of the players but only through friends."

Glancing his way, she smiled. He didn't make the games sound overly important in his life, just a pastime. She liked that.

"Is it exciting working so closely with the Chairwoman?" he asked. "I've noticed you travel often."

"Yes, I like doing things for her, and travel is always exciting."

"I find her very serious about business," he said. "No smiles and few pleasantries."

She was starting to feel uncomfortable. Anything she might say here would sound as if Pavia had negative feelings about her boss. She didn't want to go there.

"Tell me about your work," she prompted. "It must be exciting to be responsible for the security of an organization such as the Cambridge Center."

"Yes," he said, smiling. "It is."

Pavia thought he had a nice smile.

Then she surprised him with a pointed question. "How long were you imprisoned in France?"

He looked into her eyes but did not answer for several seconds. There was no hint of what he was thinking. Pavia started to fear she had crossed some line.

Finally, "Nearly four years." A serious look was on his face.

She remained silent, wondering if he would say more.

"Four years is a long time. I was lucky to have an interesting cellmate. We talked, and he told me about America. He had worked and lived there."

Pavia gave a little. "Of all the travels with my work, I have never been to America. Did your friend like it there?"

"Very much," Karel told her.

"Why was he in prison?"

Another hesitation and then, "He took something that did not belong to him."

"Oh." Pavia then asked a question for which she did not expect an answer. "Why were you there with your new friend?"

They both knew what she was asking. Still, his answer stunned her.

"I...killed a man."

Pavia felt her eyes widen and, in reflex, she drew a hand to her face, touching parted lips. Dropping the hand back to her lap, Pavia's impulse got the best of her again.

"What...happened?"

She probably shouldn't have asked the questions, but it was too late now.

"Do you really want to know?"

"I guess." She could feel him watching her.

"I had been hired to protect a young woman, the daughter of an important person in France. An individual got too close to my charge and then made a sudden move. I thought I saw a blade and reacted. The thing I saw was a card, but my bullet had been lethal. The authorities did not see it as an accident. They found me guilty of careless use of a weapon resulting in a death and sent me to prison."

When Pavia did not respond, he asked, "Do you wish to leave?"

She thought about it and shook her head. "I am sorry I asked you to tell me."

He started to speak, but Pavia reached out, touching his lips. "Let me finish."

Karel appeared to relax as she continued. "It was not my business, but I had assumed it was something uncomplicated. It was not simple, and it was not for me to ask or to know. Again, I apologize."

He made a gesture as though brushing away her words.

At that moment, their food arrived. They enjoyed their dinner as though her questions and his answers had not been a part of the evening. She told him about the secret sauce, and he complimented her on picking this pub. He said he liked it. Karel seemed to enjoy the conversation. For Pavia, the schnitzel was wonderful. And the pudding, well…

Karel asked if he could walk Pavia back to her apartment. She said yes. She even took his hand as they neared her door.

Surprising Pavia when they arrived, he said he would like to see her again and kissed her on the cheek. Then he was gone.

Watching him walk away, Pavia was disappointed. She had grown to like and respect Karel in just one evening.

Rage arrived to a silent house. Kateřina would be well into her outing with Adina by now. This was good; he would have time to eavesdrop on the goings-on in the hidden vehicle.

He had silently slipped out of the woods after the man relieved himself and returned to the van. Taking a moment, Rage had watched and realized there was only the single individual manning the equipment tonight.

Rage was disappointed. Two would have meant conversation. Now, unless someone else showed up, he would have to rely on overhearing one side of phone calls for any new information.

Back in his bedroom, Rage activated his own equipment. There was a brief hum and then he heard movement coming from the van. He heard a voice too. Rage could see enough to verify there was still only one occupant. The man was either talking to himself or was on the phone.

Though he only understood a word here and there, Rage checked his small receiver and the recorder. The equipment was picking up every sound, including each word the man uttered.

The tiny video camera and recorder were doing their jobs, too. As a bonus, Rage could even watch the action in the van in real-time on his computer screen.

He had decided not to involve Kateřina in the investigative process. She had enough on her mind. With Ana hospitalized and Kateřina having serious headaches, she had more than one person should have to handle.

Rage's thoughts turned to Marty Cutler.

He could be Rage's interpreter for the remainder of his stay. The big man would be working with him anyway. Rage was confident Marty would jump at the opportunity.

As The Author sat watching the computer screen and planning his operation, a phone rang in the van. The man inside keyed the device, answered and then listened. Glancing at his own equipment, Rage confirmed again that every word and sound was being recorded.

He wondered what the conversation was about. After listening for several seconds, the man in the van went into a lengthy explanation of some sort. Rage smiled, anticipating a valuable interpretation when Marty could listen to the recording.

Though it was just beginning, Ana knew she was in for another sleepless night.

This was the strangest and certainly the most hopeless situation she had ever encountered. She was a prisoner, but…she was not a prisoner. Ana shook her head.

Though Dr. Laska had assured her this was true, Ana could not imagine being allowed to leave under any circumstances. She knew too much. Someone might believe her.

But even if they were telling her the truth, how could she do that to the only meaningful person in her life?

Agitated, she stood up and began pacing in the confines of the room. Ana considered the available options.

Though the door to her room was locked, Dr. Laska had indicated she could still escape the situation with only a decision and a signature. Again—if they had been truthful—she and her mother would lose all the material things they had come to depend on and enjoy. But they would have each other. It was one alternative, and it was a good one, except…

The second was Ana could allow the doctors to have their way. It appeared she had been destined for this since conception. Even with the medical explanations, Ana had trouble getting her mind around the idea.

As she walked, Ana remembered something from her past.

On a cold winter night when she was nine, Kateřina has awakened her. Ana had been wet with perspiration and was freezing. Her mother had stayed with her through the remainder of the night, alternately holding her and then bathing her body with a warm damp cloth. Ana remembered seeing her mother's face each time she opened her eyes.

Could she take away everything material her mother owned in this world. Ana didn't think so.

Even if she did it, there was no real assurance she would be released. There was no guarantee she would be allowed to leave under any circumstances. No, Ana reasoned, there could be no walking away from this. It was—it must be—her destiny.

After the doctors left her late that morning, she spent most of the day alone. With one exception, Ana's only interruptions had been medical personnel. Blood was drawn on three separate occasions. Each time Ana asked why, and each time she was reluctantly told lab technicians were doing tests on some of her major organs.

Father Anděl, the diminutive little priest, had been her lone visitor. He had come to her room during the late afternoon after her earlier meeting with the doctors. Remembering what she had been told, Ana had not been nice to him.

Angry already, she had aggressively asked how a man who purported himself to be God's representative could be involved in something so offensive as stealing body parts from the living.

His answer surprised Ana.

"Sometimes sacrifices must be made for others who are most important."

Staring at him in disbelief, Ana could not imagine Father Anděl believed his own words. She certainly didn't. To sacrifice a living human being because someone had deemed another life to be more important was outside the bounds of Ana's imagination. She also believed it was outside of God's will.

"Get out!" she shouted.

The little man tried to speak, but Ana had passed the point of listening to him.

"I cannot believe you are a priest. You are the antithesis of a man of God."

She stared angrily at Father Anděl. Ana's face was drawn, her eyes so focused they were almost closed. Her lips were pressed and tight against her teeth.

She approached him. "You have no words I want to hear."

Ana shoved the priest toward the door and then slammed it as he left.

She walked back and sat in one of the chairs. It took several minutes for her heart rate to fall back to a normal level.

Mixed with the disbelief she was experiencing, Ana found herself wondering who would be claiming her organs—who was this special person who could bring about such disregard for another's life.

Thinking different thoughts, Ana also couldn't help but wonder if there was someone out there she resembled, or acted like, or *was* like? This probability was also past Ana's understanding.

Broken, yet strange as it seemed, Ana knew she could never crush her mother's life by attempting to refuse the doctors. She suddenly dissolved into tears, sobbing like a bullied child.

Ana let herself cry out the frustrations building since she arrived at this evil place. She had never been so discouraged.

Then amidst her disconsolation, there came a knock at the door. The sound was soft, almost as if the individual did not mean to interfere with the sadness coming from the room.

"Are you all right?" The voice was soft too, and feminine.

A sob caught in Ana's throat as she stared toward the door.

The individual in the hallway knocked again. A gentle tap and then, "I said, 'Are you all right?'" There seemed to be real concern in the question. Then there was silence.

Was this a trick by the doctors to see if I would try to slip out without telling them?

She decided to remain quiet and see if the individual would try again. If there came one more knock…

But there wasn't.

Ana strained to listen, hearing only silence. Whoever had been in the hallway was gone now.

Ana couldn't help wishing she had responded in some small way. If for no other reason, to have a friendly contact outside the door. The sobs, though softer now, found their way back to her throat.

Her opportunity had been slight, but now it was lost.

Kateřina drove herself and Adina to the *Restaurace Chapadlo*. Asking for a quiet location, the women were seated near the pub table section at the far edge of the dining floor.

Known for its great food and welcoming atmosphere, the restaurant was easy on the eye, too. Dark wood, both in the structure and the furniture, gave the large modern rooms a sense of warmth and simplicity. The wood was everywhere with touches of polished brass accenting its beauty.

Kateřina liked coming here; it was one of her favorite places in the entire city. Adina appeared to appreciate *Restaurace Chapadlo* too.

After acquiring wine, they each ordered the Roasted Chicken with fresh herbs and a side of mashed potatoes. The wine, *Andrea Formilli Fendi*, a superior Sauvignon Blanc from Italy, satisfied them both. It would be relaxing for the conversation Kateřina hoped would follow.

"How old was Kamil?" Kateřina asked when they were settled.

"Twenty-four, almost twenty-five." Tears instantly moistened the mother's eyes as she said, "His birthday was twelve days after his death."

"I'm sorry." Kateřina sensed there was nothing more to say on the subject.

They each tried a sip of the wine.

"How old is your daughter?"

"Twenty-six."

Another sip.

"May I tell you something?" Adina searched Kateřina's eyes as she spoke.

With a hand, Kateřina motioned her to continue.

"I believe my Kamil's death was suspicious, and I do not think he died in Switzerland as they told me."

"Oh?" Kateřina questioned, twisting her legs under the table so she could face Adina directly. With wine in hand and her gaze steady, she gave the boy's mother her full attention.

"I also question if Kamil died of a brain aneurism at all."

Setting her wine down before an almost certain dining catastrophe, Kateřina struggled. She wanted to ask the many questions flashing through her mind. Still, she remained quiet, allowing her new friend to go on with her story.

"It's all unreal," Adina said and then took a long breath. "Everything became so confused."

Why wouldn't you believe the doctors about what happened to Kamil? Kateřina wanted to ask, *as I have with Ana?* But she, too, realized she didn't really believe them.

Kateřina decided to take a chance and raise some questions.

"Where do your suspicions come from? And why do you think Kamil did not die in Switzerland?"

Glancing around as if she might be overheard, Adina softly disclosed, "I received an email from Kamil."

Kateřina nodded. *An email. Huh. No big news there.*

Then, leaning forward and staring into her eyes, the mother whispered, "According to the information I received from the Trust, Kamil died before his email was sent to me."

Leaning back in her chair, the information caused Kateřina to glance around for other listeners too. Hiding shock, she asked,

"Are you quite sure of the timing?" She leaned forward again. "Perhaps in grief, you may have reversed the two incidents."

"No." Adina had checked, saying the times were as she stated them.

"What did Kamil say in the message?"

"He was concerned about something involving the health center. He said he would be leaving Interlaken for Zurich within the hour and then on to Prague." As an afterthought, she added, "He had been skiing the Jungfrau in the Bernese Alps near Interlaken. When Kamil sent the message, he was already off the mountain."

Her mind in a spin, Kateřina could feel one of the headaches coming on. Forcing her conscious thought to the three suspicious deaths, she hoped the pain would go away quickly as it most often did. She wanted to ask questions and understand the answers. Feeling a bit uneasy, though, Kateřina couldn't help but be reminded the headaches were coming often now.

Ignoring the discomfort, she surmised if the sequence of events were as Adina had said, it meant Dr. Laska had lied about Kamil's death.

Why would he do that?

More wine was poured, and the conversation drifted to other topics surrounding the youth's death.

"Had Kamil shown any symptoms of health issues before he left on holiday?"

Adina shook her head.

"What about a problem after he left or during his travels?"

"None."

Adina's answers were becoming brief. She appeared tired now and reluctant to pursue the matter. Their children passed from the women's conversation. But the circumstances surrounding Kamil's death had not passed from Kateřina's thoughts. She wanted to tell Rage what she had learned.

After driving Adina home and promising to repeat the evening soon, Kateřina turned her car back toward her own house and Rage. She intuitively knew he would find meaning in the new information she had discovered.

The evening had gone even better than Karel had hoped. He knew Pavia would continue to see him, and he expected she would become conversational about the activities of their boss. Also, she would feel she owed him after the questions she had asked. He would make sure that worked to his advantage.

Walking to the nearest Metro stop, Karel began to organize his thoughts for involving the Bambenek woman's visitor in his plans. First he needed to know the individual's identity and be sure there were no complications. One name—first or last—and he could start gathering information.

Karel had a friend at the airport who worked with the computers there. Everything involving flights in and out of Prague, even passenger lists, ran through those computers. As luck would have it, the friend worked nights, preferring the additional income it paid and also the relative quiet routine accompaning the hours.

Metro 22 was pulling into the stop just as Karel crossed the street to the boarding dock. Jogging the last few steps, he swung aboard the tram and found a spot near the back of the car. Pulling his cellphone out, he called Alexandr in the security van. Karel asked if the woman had used any name for the man staying with her.

"Yes," he was told, but it was not clear. "Something like Raging or Rushing. I have listened to the recording at length, but each time it sounds like the woman is calling her visitor Raging or something close to that." He sounded sure. "I do not know if it is a first name or a last."

"Keep trying."

Consumed with thoughts of his own project, Karel had changed the surveillance plans and assigned a young woman to work with Alexandr. She was waiting when Kateřina Bambenek pulled out of her driveway that morning.

The individual was sure the Bambenek woman had not realized she was being followed. In the hospital's lobby, Bambenek was observed being directed down a corridor toward staff offices.

Approaching the counter, the woman knew how to get the information she wanted.

"My friend just came in, and I don't see her here in the lobby. Could she have gone to someone's office?"

The clerk was very helpful. "Yes. Dr. Laska came for her."

"I'll wait."

Karel's helper took a seat among several other people and flipped through a magazine. Gone for several minutes, the Bambenek woman was obviously upset when she passed through the lobby on her way out. Several people were leaving at the same time. Vlasta's young assistant was able to reach her vehicle and follow without being noticed.

Bambenek went directly back to her house. The shadowing vehicle parked down the street, and the woman watched for several hours before her target left again. This time she picked up another woman, an obvious friend, and they went out to eat. At the restaurant, the young woman remained in her vehicle except a quick run inside to a restroom. After dinner, the Bambenek woman drove the friend home and returned to her own house. The rest of the evening was quiet after the Porsche went into the garage.

Several photos had been taken on the assistant's iPhone camera during the day and later in the evening. Notes were made of all addresses and other information she thought might be useful to Karel. Each time she found herself waiting, the young woman would upload the camera content and her comments to Karel's computer. The only photos of consequence were probably those of the friend who accompanied Bambenek to dinner.

Karel was on the tram when she phoned to report. The late call from the young woman indicated there probably wasn't much to be gained by following the Bambenek woman. He told her he would handle future surveillance, and this was all right with the young woman as it had been a boring day. Karel knew he would probably do no more than feed the Chairwoman a little false information to keep her happy until his own plan came to fruition.

Looking up, he realized it was time for his transfer at the Malostranská Station. After changing lines, he rode for a while in deep thought. He knew all the loose ends would have to be accounted for, but if he did this right, Karel would soon have all the funds he needed for life.

Arriving near the clinic, he exited the Metro with several others and began the fifteen minute walk to his office and vehicle. When he entered the main building at the hospital, Karel went directly to his desk on the second floor. He was anxious to get a name for the mysterious man.

Though Karel was expecting to request a callback, his friend answered when he phoned the computer facility at the airport.

"Karel." The friend was excited at the call. They had been biker buddies and members of the Black Dogs motorcycle club a few years earlier. "I have not heard your voice in months. My wife asked about you just yesterday."

When he got an opening, Karel asked if his friend could phone him back using a cellphone. He did not want the possibility of having their conversation recorded.

When the return call came, Karel asked about the name his assistant had gotten from the recording. Could the friend help? Probably, Karel was told, but it would need to be in the wee hours of morning. The friend did not want the possibility of a supervisor asking why he was accessing those particular records. If he found anything, it would be on Karel's voice mail when he awakened. Vlasta thanked him and they disconnected.

Before leaving for the night, Karel did a quick inspection— his fourth of the day—to know if anyone had accessed the Chairwoman's special files since he last checked them. Nothing showed up.

Janalynn Dusa had received her nursing license only six months earlier. The job at the Cambridge Center was a dream and had come to her by way of a friend. The research wing at the health facility was adding a nurse to its Intensive Care Unit. Surgery in the research wing was confined almost entirely to organ transplant cases. The facilities were state of the art. It was a grand opportunity.

Dusa's friend and fellow nurse had said the Cambridge Center's patients came from all over the world. "Many are politicians," she was told, "including several heads of state."

Then the friend said, "The President of Chile received a heart transplant there only weeks ago." The nurse also bragged, "World known entertainers and business tycoons walk these halls on a daily basis."

As Dusa was applying for a spot on the nurse's roster, the news was conveyed a new patient had just arrived. The English singer and entertainer, Victoria Lancing, had checked in a day earlier and was being prepped for a liver transplant. An American comedian was there too, and on the list for a new heart.

Hired on the spot, pending a security check and drug test, Dusa was now in her second week. As nursing positions go, this one was special. On every shift in the intensive surgical care unit, three nurses were assigned to each patient.

Dusa was initially charged with watching for deviations in her patient's temperature, blood pressure, pulse, and respiratory rate. Those were her only duties, but they were extremely important since deteriorating vital signs often preceded cardiac arrest. Pain and distress would be watched by the entire team.

On this particular evening, proud of her new job and contemplating the 12-hour shift she had completed at 8:00 p.m., Dusa made a wrong turn as she headed for the parking area. As she realized her mistake and turned to go back, Dusa thought she heard sobs coming from a room along the corridor.

She paused in mid-stride. The door opposite her was without signage of any type. *Probably maintenance,* she thought. Attempting to twist the knob, she found the room locked.

Then Dusa heard sobs again, and they were coming from the unmarked room. This time she was sure. It sounded like a woman crying. Nervous, she glanced around her. She had been told certain sections of the building were restricted; she hoped this unit was not one of them.

Still she tapped softly on the door and asked, "Are you all right?" The question was just above a whisper as she glanced in both directions.

There was no answer, but the sobs quieted.

After several seconds, Dusa knocked again, and then, "I said, 'are you all right?'"

If silence was audible, the closed door and beyond would have screamed out to her. Dusa raised a hand to the back of her neck. Nervous, her fingers moved up and down, her body feeling the chill and emptiness of the hallway and the sadness of the sounds she had heard from the room.

She'd had this sensation before. Just two years earlier, a man had pointed a gun in her face at a bus stop and started to assault her. Thankfully, the bus had arrived and scared him away. The sensation she felt had never preceded anything good.

Finally, hearing nothing more, she took the first steps back toward the exit and her automobile. Glancing back as she turned a corner, Dusa vowed to knock on the door again the next night. Sobs like those she'd heard had to have meaning.

Kateřina closed her eyes for a moment as she waited for a traffic break on *Milady Horakove*. This headache was serious. Her vision blurred with the increasing pain in her head.

When the car behind her tooted its horn, Kateřina instinctively opened her eyes and punched the throttle.

Bad timing. The last car on the main street had not cleared the intersection. The ensuing crash seemed minor, but Kateřina dreaded looking at the damage. Seeing the other vehicle had only a scrape along the side, she hoped for the best on the Porsche.

She climbed out. The man in the car behind her, the horn blower, walked over and kneeled down to look.

"Not too bad," he said, touching the dent and scrapes with his fingers. "I am so sorry, but you appeared distracted and had missed two opportunities to merge into the traffic."

Excusing him with an arm gesture, Kateřina confessed, "I should have been alert and more careful."

She didn't mention her head was throbbing and she wasn't sure how long her eyes were closed. There had been no vehicles behind her when she'd reached the intersection, Kateřina remembered.

I could have been here for a couple of minutes. I'm not sure.

Now the pains were starting to worry her.

The police came and made a report. Finally, she was on her way home again. Having not been asked by the officer, Kateřina did not mention her headache being the real cause of the accident.

Rage had prepared a pot of coffee and was waiting for her. Music was playing in the background. Obviously anxious to know if she had new information from Adina, he walked over to help with her coat. That's when he saw the tears.

He held her at arm's length and asked, "Are you all right?"

Kateřina stared up into those welcoming blue eyes and sobbed, "Oh, Raegene. It has been a terrible evening."

His tenderness had been one of the most endearing traits Kateřina remembered of him. She had shed many tears when he left her all those years ago to embrace the CIA. Being quite young, she had not understood how he could love her, as he professed, yet leave her alone a world away with only vague and unfulfilled promises of returning.

Looking up into his eyes now, she acknowledged he had returned when she needed him…and reached out to him. Kateřina also realized there was so much in this mature man that she remembered of the young Raegene Dorryen Doyle. Burying her face in his shoulder, she couldn't quiet a sob, nor did she try.

"What is it?" With a finger, he tipped her chin up so he could see her face. "What happened, Sweetheart?" he asked in his soft, drawn out way of speaking. Kateřina loved the endearing term when he used it.

He gave her a moment, not pressing, rather allowing Kateřina to gather her thoughts and feelings.

She started off by telling him about the accident.

He was concerned, but she was obviously more upset than injured. Kateřina mentioned the headache, and Rage wondered again if she should be scheduling a visit with a doctor.

"It's nothing," she said. "But something is very wrong at the—"

Thinking of the van parked in the woods, Rage quickly cut her off, suggesting they sit in the chairs on her front porch. He reached for both their coats.

They walked back outside. When they were settled, he let her continue.

"I'm listening." That soft masculine voice again.

Light from the porch's gas lamps illuminated her face, allowing him to watch Kateřina's changing expressions as she described the evening.

The first thing she told Rage was about the Trust. Kateřina repeated part of her conversation with Adina. She told him about being afraid to ask more and then moved on to other subjects.

Drawing on the strength of his attention, Kateřina said, "Forty minutes after Adina was notified her son was dead, Kamil emailed her saying he was leaving Switzerland immediately on his way home."

Kateřina's statements about Adina's email and Dr. Laska's call to her were each disturbing. Obviously, both pieces of information couldn't be correct. Different time zones couldn't be the problem. Interlaken and Prague were in the same zone. Something was very wrong, and someone was not telling the truth.

Intuition had served Rage well throughout the years, and he felt whatever happened in Switzerland must have gone wrong for the Cambridge Center's staff. Dr. Laska was involved, too, because he had delivered the contradicting news to Adina.

Perhaps Adina's son had discovered something involving himself, something causing Kamil to leave Switzerland in a hurry. Rage suggested this to Kateřina.

He stared at her for a moment and then asked, "Do you think you got all the information Adina had?"

"Yes…I think so."

"Then it's something she doesn't know about."

Those big green eyes focused on Rage. "It must be."

With pursed lips, she glanced away then looked back. "There is something else," she said.

Rage watched her, waiting.

"Adina used the words 'the Trust' when speaking of decorating her house. She even called it the Eagle Trust."

He was immediately interested. At least he knew the Trust was involved in both of the women's lives. *How many others?*

"I was afraid to ask more questions."

She was tired. Rage could see it in her movement.

"Want a nightcap?" he asked. "We can start again in the morning."

"Yes, please." She kneaded her fingers at the back of her neck as they walked inside.

Looking up at Rage, Kateřina said, "I will return to my own bedroom for the night. I don't want to disturb you if I'm restless."

"Sure," Rage said. He was concerned. He had not seen her like this.

As an afterthought, she said, "I think I will skip the nightcap too." She stepped over and gave him a kiss on the cheek. "I'll get a shower and then go right to bed. I've had this aching pain for hours. Perhaps sleep will make it go away."

Rage watched as Kateřina headed for her bedroom. It was probably his imagination, but the lady seemed a little unsteady on her feet. He thought he saw a slight stumble.

Some rest probably is the answer.

As Rage climbed the stairs to his bedroom, Marty phoned. He had reached Jolana's cousin, and they could have an ale when Milan finished work the next day.

1 0

THURSDAY, SEPTEMBER 24, 2015

* * *

ANA HAD SLEPT LITTLE SINCE the mysterious encounter with the stranger outside her doorway. She knew it must already be past midnight. Soon she would face a new day of unknowns. The little time she had left was racing by.

Ideas and notions of all sorts were running rampant through her mind. Crazy thoughts. She wondered why someone would bother to knock on her door unless they had been called. The individual had likely heard her crying. That had to be it. Maybe the person *had* wanted to help.

There was the other possibility too. If she had been right and the doctors were testing her, then Ana had surely served their wishes for a compliant subject. But if the visitor was a stranger and was concerned, then she had missed an opportunity. But for what? There seemed no hope anything she might do or say at this point could make a difference in her situation.

Ana's world was in turmoil.

Her eyes straying back to the small table in the corner, Ana locked in on the notepad and pen left there earlier.

Hmm. *Žádné riziko, žádná odměna,* she reasoned. *No risk, no reward.*

She walked over and settled into the chair. Her legs crossed for comfort, an idea began to build. Still forming her thoughts, Ana picked up the pen and began writing.

The psychiatrist had said she might want to jot down her impressions. Dr. Seifert had even suggested writing about her feelings could calm her. Much relating to the sudden radical changes in her circumstances was beginning to make sense now.

The doctor had said she might deal with the coming events in terms of the good they would serve. "Think of it in terms of the research," the psychiatrist had said. Seifert even had the audacity to suggest she consider it a privilege to be instrumental in saving the life of some important figure. The priest had suggested it too.

Ana didn't think so.

What she did think was the psychiatrist should see a psychiatrist, and the priest should pray for forgiveness.

Ana glanced at the door for a moment, then back at the notepad. All at once writing down her thoughts seemed a good idea. If for no other reason, perhaps she could make some sense of them for herself.

Once pen met paper, Ana lost all interest in time. The importance of her own situation was forgotten too; all thoughts of signing their papers and leaving this place ceased to exist.

She had known almost from the beginning she would never do that to her mother. Conceivably, the knowledge had formulated in the early hours after she learned her fate. It must have been there all along, if only subconsciously.

Now suddenly, Ana only wanted to reassure her mother she could never be unhappy with her. Though Ana wouldn't go into detail, she wanted Kateřina to know going forward this way was her decision. Her mother could not have known in the early years what would come later in their lives. At this point, the decisions were Ana's alone.

Ana realized there was so much Kateřina would not have known. She would never knowingly allow her mother to suffer the anguish she had encountered within the confines of this room.

She wrote slowly but thoughtfully, seldom lifting pen from paper. When she rested, there were actually two letters.

Knowing there were security cameras, Ana had been careful to have anyone watching assume there was only one letter, but she continued writing straight through into another. She would separate them later. Besides the one to her mother, the other dealt mostly with the suggestions Dr. Seifert had made. Ana didn't expect this letter to be read by anyone other than the doctors and the psychiatrist. She did, though, want there to be some effort made for them to understand the horror of what they were doing. Ana wanted those in charge to view their deeds from a victim's eyes and point of view. Completed, she read the words over and was satisfied. Finally, Ana put the pages aside.

With both letters finalized, the young woman turned her eyes to the door again, almost willing there to be a soft knock like the night before. She wanted to hear the woman's voice again.

Sadly, only silence filled her room and the hallway beyond.

There was no assurance her mother would receive the letter written for her. Perhaps the medical group would also be left to read the thoughts Ana expressed to her mother in her very personal message. She questioned if they would recognize her teardrops on the pages. Doubtful. She also doubted if they were capable of recognizing the emotions and thoughts behind those tears.

The letter thanked Kateřina for all she had done for Ana. Without saying it directly, she referred to all those recitals her mother had attended when Ana was learning to play the violin... and with no talent.

Oh, how her mother must have suffered.

Ana smiled, remembering.

And later, the teen years and the shallow girl's emotions they brought with them.

There was so much more.

She wondered if the doctors would even care.

Deep in thought, Ana failed to hear a key in the door until the last moment before one of her nurses stepped into the room. Acting on instinct, she slipped the pages into a book she had been reading.

The nurse noticed and asked about the book. Ana assured her it was not a very good story. Nodding, the nurse appeared to lose interest and continued about her duties.

Soon, Ana was alone again. She would have to be more careful. Ana realized the staff probably had orders to report anything out of the ordinary.

A couple of last thoughts were added to both letters. When she finished, Ana tucked the pad inside the same book and placed it on the shelf.

A new day was evident through the thick, frosted glass window. Light was coming quickly, and when she held her hand near the glass, there was a slight hint of the sun's warmth.

There seemed to come a lessening of anxiety with the new day, too. In her situation, Ana realized it was a false assurance, but it was better than the night.

To recharge herself, Ana took a shower and donned fresh undergarments. Bathing always invigorated her. Now—here—it was the same.

Finished, she pretended to be reading when anyone came into her room. Ana didn't like having the staff know of the deep depression she was experiencing. She didn't want anyone feeling sorry for her. Ana had lived proud, and she wanted to finish that way.

Breakfast came soon. It consisted of dark bread with butter and jelly—not among her favorites. There was a slice of salami and one of ham. Coffee to drink and a dish of yogurt finished off her tray. She picked at the food.

After pushing the tray away, Ana, mindful of cameras, carefully hid the two pieces of writing in separate places. She pondered how to get the letters where they needed to go.

The one for the doctors could be left in the room. Someone would find it.

She so desperately wanted the other message to reach her mother. It would be Ana's last communication with the woman who had tended her as a child and hugged her as a university graduate. Wiping at sudden tears, Ana was defenseless against her despair.

Having been up with the writing for most of the night, she climbed into bed and hoped for a couple of undisturbed hours of sleep throughout the morning. She knew there would be needles and other interruptions as she tried to rest.

Ana was living and would be dying by someone else's schedule now.

Rage checked his recording equipment just before dawn. The van had remained quiet except for the one man's movements and a few phone calls. He would get Marty to listen and tell him if there was anything important in the calls.

The video camera had only picked up a small amount of activity. The man had spent most of his time moving about monitoring instruments inside the van. He had also made three trips outside to the old tree.

There had been no visitors to the van throughout the night.

After checking the equipment, Rage went downstairs early and made a pot of coffee. He had brought his notepad with him. Questions have a way of popping up unexpectedly. He added three while having coffee.

Music was playing. Rage was beginning to enjoy the classical mix drowning out their voices to the receivers in the walls.

A few minutes after nine, Kateřina had still not come out of her bedroom. Rage was concerned; he remembered the head pains she'd had before going to bed. Starting on his second pot of coffee, he could wait no longer.

Knocking softly, he leaned in to catch any sounds coming from her room. Hearing nothing but seeing her bed had been made, Rage assumed she would be out soon. He started back toward the kitchen and had only taken a few steps when Kateřina swung the bedroom door open. She was tying the sash on her robe.

"Good morning," she said. "I smelled the coffee." There was a pleasant lilt to her voice this morning.

He stopped, asking, "How's the headache?"

"Good…I think," she said. "It is still with me, but I believe it is much better."

"Then come have some coffee," Rage offered. "Maybe the cafine will help."

"Let me do some things first. I will be out shortly."

Rage started toward the kitchen for a second time as he heard the bathroom door close. Moments later, he heard a crash. Hurrying to her, he knocked at the bathroom door.

"Are you all right?"

There was hesitation and then sounds of movement before he heard her voice. "Yes, a slight accident. I dropped a bottle from my vanity." Her voice was low, strained. "I am fine," she said.

She didn't sound fine. He waited a few seconds before walking away.

This time he made it to the kitchen. Though worried, Rage was hungry; he hoped Kateřina was too. Maybe food would help her, at least a slice of toast. He reached for the bread hoping he could talk her into something more.

Kateřina ambled in after a few minutes and dropped into a chair at the small breakfast table. *A bit unsteady*, Rage thought.

"I usually have tea in the morning," she said, "but I think I will have some of your coffee today."

The toast was almost ready, but she declined. "I'm not hungry."

"You need to eat something," he told her. "How about a banana or an orange?"

"No," she said with enough emphasis Rage realized she wasn't going to change her mind.

He sat down at the table with her.

Now he was worried. Being around her for a few days, he knew she usually enjoyed eating at all meals. But this wasn't the time to push, he realized. She would eat when she was hungry enough—if the problem was just a headache.

Just then, Kateřina reached for her cup. As she started to lift, it slipped from her fingers spilling the contents. The cup scooted across the table, then dropped and shattered on the floor. The coffee followed like a flooded creek across the tabletop and then to the floor.

Rage grabbed a cloth from the counter and hurried back. He covered the liquid on the table first and began to wipe it up. Then he did the floor. A rinse, a final wipe down and the accident had been cleared except for the broken cup.

Kateřina had carefully, but silently, dropped to a knee and gathered the broken pieces into a small pile. Rage brought the waste container and got rid of them.

"I'll get you another cup," he said.

Rage heard a sob and saw her tears.

"It's just a cup," he said, moving over to kneel beside her. His arm encircled her shoulders and a hand touched hers.

"It is not the cup," Kateřina sobbed as she reclaimed her chair and looked at him. "I think I am sick," she said. "Very sick."

Moving back to his chair, he reached out for her hand. For several seconds, Rage could only look at her.

Then, "How do you know? Wh…what makes you say you're ill?"

Her voice was little more than a whisper. "I have been having the headaches for some weeks now. I have also been sick with my stomach. Sometimes it has been very uncomfortable."

"But—"

"And I *have* been to a doctor—a few days before you arrived," she disclosed. "He is doing tests."

"And…?"

There was hesitation. "The doctor cannot tell me an explanation until the tests are complete."

Pulling a tissue from her pocket, Kateřina dabbed at her eyes. "I am very afraid."

He scooted over and dropped to a knee again at her side. Rage gathered the one love of his life into his arms. He was afraid to speak least he lose control of his own emotions.

This can't be happening.

Yet it was. He saw it in her eyes.

"I have fallen several times," she revealed with a sob. Reaching out, Kateřina took his hand and dropped her head to his shoulder.

"I sometimes get…how do you say it? I get dizzy." She pulled back to look into his eyes. "That was the noise you heard earlier. The bottle fell as I struck it on my way to the floor. I had fallen again."

Making an effort to control his voice, Rage asked, "When do you see the doctor again?"

"They will phone me when the tests are complete," Kateřina told him. "Perhaps today or tomorrow." She sounded hopeful.

They moved to her settee; Rage joined her, sitting at her side. He wanted to watch her face and expressions. He brought her a fresh cup of coffee and set it on the side table.

"It could be so many things," Kateřina said. "At first, I thought blood pressure, but the physician almost immediately said this is not the cause."

"Why not?"

"After the first exam at the doctor's office, I was told it was more serious." She glanced out the rear windows and then back. "They obviously found another problem and did not want to alarm me until they know the cause."

Rage forced himself to remain quiet and listen.

"You are the first person I have told," she said.

Not having someone to talk with must have been difficult.

She spoke again. "It has been very lonely." She got up and walked to the windows. "First I worried about Ana's situation and her friends, and then the headaches began to come more often. Falling is only recent."

She glanced his way.

"I thought it could be stress too. The physician said he doubted if stress had anything to do with it."

"And you have not told anyone?"

"No, Raegene. You are the first."

Kateřina continued explaining as she returned to the settee. "I hope you do not mind if I tell it to you." Then she confessed, "There is no one else I would trust."

She looked into his eyes then and held them. "How do you tell a stranger… you fear for your life?"

"You can talk to me," he told her.

She dabbed at a tear and then finally smiled.

Rage's phone rang, startling them both.

Motioning him to take the call, Kateřina stood and walked toward her bedroom.

He watched as she moved from chair to table and to door frames, all the while holding on, obviously afraid of falling again. Rage watched, in his own mental turmoil, as she haltingly made her way out of the room.

He was listening on the phone as he watched her. Rage had been expecting Marty to touch base regarding their meeting later today with the cousin who works at the health center.

"Hey," the big man said when Rage answered. "Milan's getting off early. We can meet him around four o'clock. Does that work for you?"

"Sure," Rage said as he glanced toward Kateřina's bedroom. He'd rather not leave her but knew she would insist.

"Where do you want to meet?" Rage asked.

"Why don't you give me the address where you're staying; I'll pick you up."

Rage thought about it for only a moment. "All right."

He trusted Marty now. He gave him the information and some sketchy directions. Marty said he knew the area. They agreed on a time and hung up.

Rage walked out of the conversation room and listened from the hallway.

It was silent in Kateřina's bedroom, but the door was slightly ajar. Rage could see the bed. She was lying there. Doubting she would mind, he tapped lightly and then walked over and sat down beside her.

Resting an arm across her body, he waited for a reaction. Kateřina's eyes opened slowly, and she looked up at him. Then she smiled, only the second one of the morning.

"I'm worried about you," he told her. "Did you take something for the pain?"

"Yes. The doctor had said it might get worse, so he gave me some pills to use until we know more." Her eyes closed for a few seconds.

"I have to go out later," Rage told her.

"Take my vehicle," she said. "I have no plans."

"It's okay," he said while caressing her shoulder. "Someone is coming for me."

She nodded and closed her eyes. Then she opened them and said she would call the dealer and have them pick her car up for repairs.

"They will bring us a replacement," she said.

Why is she worrying about the car? Maybe it's the medicine?

Rage tucked the blanket close, then kissed her cheek. Her face was cool to his touch. He stood watching her for several seconds. She was very still, her breathing almost indiscernible.

He would try to make the meeting short and get back to her.

Marty wouldn't be arriving until early afternoon. He planned to give them plenty of time to listen to the recordings from the van and do some prep work. It was only a few minutes after eleven o'clock now.

Rage went to the kitchen and retrieved the writing pad and questions. He came back and settled in one of the chairs near her bed. He would keep an eye on her while he worked.

Using the minutes, Rage jotted down more questions and ideas. He also gave thought to the situation at the hospital. What might have led to Ana being quarantined and unavailable?

If Kateřina's suspicions were correct, someone at the Cambridge Center could be behind the deaths of other individuals—perhaps three more. In addition to Marta Melcer, there was Adina's son and perhaps the young man who was purported to have been killed in Finland. As Rage considered the situation, he realized there could be two other connected deaths Kateřina had mentioned—the surrogate mothers. Of the three who had lost their children, only Adina was still alive.

A thought occurred to Rage. Supposedly, two of the young people had died out of the country—in Finland and Switzerland— and one had died at the hospital. Just a hunch, what if all three had died at the Cambridge Center.

Remembering, he thought of the cremation chimney he had noticed there.

Suppose…just suppose…

Rage also wondered about the two mothers who had died tragically. Though reported to be suicides, suppose their deaths were a part of something more intricate, more sinister? Perhaps something would come up during his investigation of Kateřina's friend and her young daughter.

The notes Rage had written were all over the map, both literally and figuratively. One questioned if the three deceased young people had ties other than their loose connection at Cambridge Health and Research Center? Several other questions concerned the Eagle Trust: Where and when had it been established and for what purposes? Who are its members? And since the Trust financed both Kateřina and Adina, could there be others receiving funds from the same source? It could be investigated, but was there time?

Ana…

Leaning back, Rage wondered where he could get private information on the Eagle Trust.

I'll get on the internet tonight and see what I can turn up. But first, I'll reach out and see if I can connect with Idona47.

The *Idona47* connection was a holdover from his days at the CIA. The procedure involved contacting and presenting coded questions over the internet. It was an interesting activity.

Glancing at his watch, Rage realized he probably had time to begin the steps now. Correspondence with *Idona47* was always initially accomplished using gaming communication boards on the web.

After checking on Kateřina, Rage hurried upstairs to his computer. Within minutes he had left enough information on the internet for *Idona47* to know *Corda* would communicate at 10:20 p.m., Prague time. Based on standing rules, *Idona47* would look for *Corda* at a certain gaming board on level 51 at two hours and three minutes prior to the time stated in Rage's email—8:17 p.m., in this case.

Rage was *Corda*. He had no idea who *Idona47* was, only that he or she was a friend, and they had worked together over many years and projects. Rage knew there had probably been several *Idona47s* over the years, maybe even more than one at a time. A connection might initiate a case identification to be worked until closed by someone on the other end. Rage only knew how helpful having *Idona47* had been in the past.

Finished with the setup communications, Rage slipped down to Kateřina's bedroom and looked in on her. He found her breathing comfortably. Her eyes seemed still behind relaxed eyelids. All in all, she appeared to be resting without the pain she'd experienced earlier.

He left a note for her on the kitchen counter and folded his page of questions. Shoving it into his pocket, he was now ready for Marty. His watch showed 12:25 p.m.

Rage went outside to wait.

Surveillance covered virtually every meter of the surgical facility. Security, both inside and out, was almost as tight as in the research wing.

Cameras operated 24/7, but they were not monitored on a minute-by-minute basis. Certain alerts were set to become part of a computer-generated report updated each morning at 3:00 a.m.

An alert had triggered when Janalynn Dusa entered and then exited a restricted area at 8:22 the prior evening. Upon examination, other cameras indicated she had apparently entered the restricted zone in error. After all, she was new at the Cambridge Center.

One problem, though. Discovering her error and on returning to the main hallway, she had stopped, appearing to listen outside a doorway. Dusa had leaned close and said something but apparently received no answer. Hesitating, she then knocked and spoke again. Evidently not receiving an answer this time either, she turned and found her way to the exit. Hopefully, no harm done, but the security chief still had to report the occurrence to Madam Balca.

With the video downloaded to his laptop, Karel called Madam Balca's secretary and was immediately put through to the Chairwoman. Briefly explaining the breach of security, he was summoned to the Chairwoman's suite.

"Show me," she told Karel when they were seated. Nothing was said while the sequence was running. Finished viewing, the Chairwoman turned toward the window. After a couple of minutes, she turned the chair back to her desk and leaned on her elbows.

"Watch her," she said to Karel. "I do not want to make it an important incident at this time."

She hesitated once more and then became more specific.

"I don't want any action reflecting back on our operation here. Make sure the woman in the room only communicates with individuals on the access list."

Karel closed the laptop and nodded. "As you wish."

Back in his office, Karel made some notes on the computer report, giving details but leaving the Chairwoman's name out of the narrative, a matter discussed when he was hired. The Chairwoman should never be mentioned in security correspondence. According to orders, Karel always acted as the final authority concerning anything untoward happening at the hospital or on its grounds.

Finished with the report, there were orders to give.

Alexandr was at his desk across from a wall of security screens. The assistant listened closely as Karel said he wanted to be informed of any suspicious behavior on the part of Nurse Dusa—any hour, day or night.

"Understand?"

The assistant nodded.

Returning to his office, Karel slipped on his rubber boots and heavy coat. He readied himself for the daily tour of the grounds around the facility. As he left his office, the security chief decided to make a detour over to the next building and check on the door Dusa had discovered. It had probably been an accidental wrong turn as far as the nurse was concerned, but Karel couldn't take that chance. Keeping her under constant surveillance for the next several days should answer the question.

Reaching the unmarked room where the nurse had stopped the night before, Karel listened and then tried the door before he knocked. As he was about to leave, a soft voice from inside said, "Who is it?"

Thinking fast, Karel replied, "Maintenance. We thought the room was empty. We will clean later."

As he walked away, Karel wondered about the woman who had answered him. This was not a regular patient's quarters. He considered the situation as it possibly related to the information he had discovered on the Chairwoman's computer. Karel now knew the name of the woman in the locked room. Perhaps Ana Bambenek was to be the next donor in the unique group he had discovered several days ago in a file on the Chairwoman's hard drive.

As it had then, Karel's mind immediately went to ways he might use the information.

After his stroll around the grounds, he returned to his office. Sitting at the desk, Karel phoned his assistant

"Anything new on the nurse?"

"Nothing."

"I will come by for an update later."

"We will watch her closely."

Satisfied the situation was under control, he made a second call.

"Pavia Balek."

Karel smiled upon hearing the voice of the Chairwoman's assistant.

"It is Karel."

"I look forward to seeing you tonight and having dinner again." Her voice was low with a seductive tone.

"So am I. Are you sure you want to walk to the pub?"

"I'm sure."

"There may be rain," he warned her.

"I enjoy walking in the rain," she said. "I will bring an umbrella."

"All right. I will be there at eight." Karel wanted time to stop by the security van on his way to meet her.

With the evenings arrangements made, Karel strolled down to the security center. When he entered, Alexandr saw him and pointed to one of the video screens. It showed a broad view of the critical care unit.

"Our nurse is at the center of the screen," the assistant said.

Nodding, Karel watched the young woman as she approached a patient and proceeded to take a pulse reading. Obviously, she was on the job and where she was expected to be for now.

"What are her hours?" Karel asked.

"She finishes the shift at 8:00 p.m. They sometimes work extra hours if the unit is busy."

"I will be away for a few hours this evening," Karel said, "but I want to be kept informed."

He watched as Dusa moved about the ICU. Then he said, "If she strays as she is leaving tonight, have someone prepared to follow her, and call my cell immediately."

"Consider it done."

Marty was several minutes late. By the time he pulled into Kateřina's driveway, Rage had begun to pace along the porch. Feeling the redness in his face, Rage was not surprised when Marty climbed out and immediately began to explain.

"They were working on the street a couple of kilometers back," he said. "I got caught."

"It's all right," Rage told him in a tone indicating it was not all right.

"The cobblestones make repairs difficult." Marty still wanted to explain. "Each stone is separate. Makes work very labor intensive. I stood and watched them one time for about an hour. It's pretty fascinating."

Not to Rage. He was ready to drag his friend upstairs to listen to the voice recordings.

Finally prepared, Rage started the playback. Marty sat down and became serious, reaching for a pad and taking notes as he told Rage what was being said.

One of the calls was the security assistant's wife—they were going to Mama's on Saturday night. Another was a friend inviting the man to go to the club soccer game on Sunday.

A third call was what Rage had hoped for. The caller obviously asked about activity in Kateřina's house. The man in the van didn't use his caller's name in the beginning but later slipped and called him Karel a couple of times. Rage had the identity of the caller now. He was sure it was the chief of security at the Cambridge Center. Rage had been curious about the man asking questions on the street in front of the Cambridge Center and then hiding to watch them. Marty had called Milan after they left the area. He had given them the name of the security chief.

Marty's translation was only one side of the recorded conversation, but it was still interesting and informative. Karel Vlasta was obviously hoping to identify Rage and his reason for being at Kateřina Bambenek's house. So far, they didn't have an identity for Rage.

There had been a couple of follow up calls from the security chief. The equipment operator in the van told him Bambenek's visitor had been alone for most of the evening. The woman had gone out. That much had been picked up in the recorded conversation. Otherwise, the occupants had done most of their talking in other parts of the house.

When they finished the translation, Rage made a few notes before starting a thorough planning session for their meeting with Milan.

Later, Rage glanced at his watch and said they should go. "I'll meet you at the car," he said.

He couldn't leave without checking on Kateřina. She was still resting, apparently comfortable and without the pain she had been experiencing earlier. He tucked the covers around her. The note he had left on the kitchen counter earlier still covered the situation.

On their way to meet Milan, Marty started talking about cobblestone streets and sidewalks again.

"Will we be on time?" Rage was trying to change the subject.

"Sure. We're in good shape." Marty said. "It's not far."

Marty shared he thought the cousin was unhappy working at the health clinic. "It's changed dramatically over the years," he told Rage. "Milan says there are a lot of off-limits areas. Most of those have to do with research."

Rage relaxed and took in the sights as he listened to Marty. Many of Prague's buildings were centuries old. It was interesting to Rage that in Europe they commonly used structures built hundreds of years earlier. Interesting, too, was the fact most of the streets were narrow, giving thought to horses, wagons, and carriages from another time.

"What kind of research is done at the Cambridge Center?" Rage asked.

Glancing over, Marty said, "I've never asked Milan."

He pulled onto a side street and parked.

"Come on," he said to Rage as they climbed out and headed down the cobblestone sidewalk.

The stones are pretty, but kind of dirty too. Rage had not noticed before, but sand held the stones tight. *Not too level, either.* Glancing up and down the sidewalk, Rage saw few women in heels. *They could break an ankle walking here.*

The pub was down a narrow alleyway between two buildings. There was a traffic light, green and red, for patrons and others going to and from the pub. Walking space was too narrow for individuals to pass each other. Really large people would have trouble too. Rage glanced at Marty. They might need bandages for his elbows when they reached the pub.

When Rage came to the end of the narrow space, he saw several outside tables. The place was busy.

The Author recognized Milan before they reached him. Even sitting, he seemed as wide as he was tall. Short, he couldn't have been much over five feet when standing.

"Dobrý den, Milan," Marty called out.

There was more Czech speech, and then Milan reached out to shake hands.

"Dobrý den," Milan said. The handshake was firm.

"Hello," Rage returned.

"Tell him his city is beautiful," Rage said to Marty. "You can also tell him I was here for a few months in the 1960s."

Marty translated. Milan said something then, and the two of them laughed.

"He said he was a mere child when you were here."

Rage chuckled as he removed his shades and winked at Milan.

They ordered a beer for the nurse, and Marty had a glass of schnapps. Water for Rage.

After a few minutes of conversation, Rage suggested they talk about the Cambridge Center. Milan immediately glanced around the pub and then leaned forward and lowered his voice, saying something to Marty.

Finished, he watched as Marty translated in a lowered voice.

"He will try to help us, but he must be careful. He can't afford to lose his position."

When Marty finished, the short man gestured, arms out and palms up.

Marty added, "He doubts if he knows much that can help us."

"Ask if he knows anything about the research being done at the Cambridge Center?"

The nurse talked for a couple of minutes before finishing and taking a sip of his beer.

"He says he's heard the research people are perfecting a line of drugs for use with organ transplant patients. He says rejection is a problem, and they're trying to make the problem go away."

Rage nodded.

Marty finished the translation. "He also says they are doing something secret in one set of labs. Only the people who work there are privy to the research. The area is heavily guarded."

"Ask if he's worked in most areas of the hospital at one time or another."

Their heads together, Marty and Milan held a short conversation. When they finished, Milan took a sip of his beer while Marty translated.

"He had just gotten his license when the Cambridge Center opened. I think I had already told you Milan was one of the first employees. Another nurse, a friend, suggested they apply to the health clinic. Neither of them expected to get hired, so they were surprised. They both got a job."

Milan was nodding.

"In those early days they did whatever needed doing, everything from assisting in surgery to carrying out bedpans."

Rage interrupted, "Who were the early patients? Where did they come from?"

Marty turned to Milan again, asking questions and getting answers. At one point, Milan turned and spoke directly to Rage.

Marty gave Rage the English version. "The word around the clinic was most of the patients were from wealthy families in Europe. Then later, patients were showing up from all over the world." Marty glanced at Milan, took a sip of his schnapps and then turned back to Rage.

Milan's mug was already empty; he appeared ready for another. Marty was low on schnapps too. Rage took a swallow of his water and waved to their waitress, motioning for another round.

"Go on," he said to Marty.

"The clinic keeps suites at a small exclusive local hotel," Marty told him. "Often, one or more family members accompany patients. They stay at the hotel and the hospital furnishes transportation."

Rage jotted a couple of notes. He would have Marty go to the hotel and gather whatever info he could from the staff.

Milan seemed to have thought of something new. He jostled Marty's arm and said, "Victoria Lancing, *bavič z Anglie je tady. Ona stále transplantaci jater. Drby označuje, že je opilec*"

Marty turned to Rage again. "Victoria Lancing, the entertainer from England, is here now. She will be getting a liver transplant. Gossip says she's a heavy drinker. Milan says she smokes too."

"He seems well informed about what goes on at the clinic," Rage commented.

Marty told Milan and then listened.

"Jsem tlustá a zábavný. Všichni mluví ke mně. Někdy jsem klást otázky."

Marty grinned as he told Rage, "He says he's fat and funny. Everyone talks to him. Sometimes he asks questions."

"Ask him how they got a donor for Victoria Lancing."

Words were exchanged again as Milan opened his hands wide. Then Marty told Rage, "Sometimes he hears about things, sometimes not. He doesn't know about the entertainer, but he will ask."

Rage nodded as their drinks arrived.

When the waitress was gone, Rage pointed to Milan and said, "Ask about the donor for the Chilean President's new heart."

As Marty asked, Milan leaned back in his chair and seemed to withdraw. A smile left his face, and he slowly moved his head from side to side. When he spoke again, the words were slow, almost angry.

"Něco špatného se stalo."

Marty translated. "Something bad happened, and Milan thinks it has happened before."

Watching him, Marty and Rage sat waiting. Milan looked away for a few seconds before saying more.

"Jeden z našich nejlepších sester přestat, a mladý výzkumník prostě zmizel."

"One of our best nurses quit, and recently, a young female researcher disappeared."

"Ask him why the nurse quit."

The two men leaned in and talked for a short time. When they finished, Marty turned to Rage. "The gossip was the nurse didn't like the way surgery was handled on the President of Chile. She wouldn't get specific, but it had something to do with the organ donor."

"Is she available?"

Marty's translation, hands outstreached. "She left the country—disappeared."

"What about the researcher?"

More conversation in Czech, and then Marty said, "They were told she caught a virus of some sort and died."

"Did he hear her name?"

Marty turned and asked Milan.

Milan lowered his voice to a whisper. "Ana Bambenek."

Rage didn't need an interpreter.

As Marty drove them back to Kateřina's house late in the afternoon, Rage explained his plan for the local hotel where patient's families set up camp.

"Your time may be wasted, but see if anything interesting has been said around the hospital staff. We have to cover all the possibilities."

Marty was excited now that they had met with Milan. "What are we looking for?"

"I'm not sure. What I do know is three young people with connections to the Cambridge Center have died under unusual circumstances. You could certainly call their deaths suspicious."

Marty glanced over, his mouth agape.

Rage continued. "And the researcher Milan talked about?"

"Yeah?"

"Remember her name?"

"Ana…" He shook his head. "Ana… something."

"Her last name is Bambenek," Rage told him. "She's my friend's daughter, and she works at the Cambridge Center."

"You gotta be kidding."

"Nope." Rage looked at his former team member. "It could be a fluke, but as you may remember, I'm not a strong believer in coincidence."

His face drawn and grim, Marty took a quick look toward Rage, "I do remember that."

Back at Kateřina's, Rage climbed out of the vehicle and then leaned down to ask Marty one more question.

"Do you know someone who can do a little surveillance job for us?"

Marty thought for a moment. "Yeah, I know a guy."

Rage explained the details. The big man nodded and said he would take care of the situation within the hour.

Marty waved as he drove away.

Hands in his pockets, Rage stood in thought for a few moments as the car disappeared.

He smiled, remembering a time in Colombia when Marty took down three men at one time—two with knifes and the third with a pistol. By the time the brawl was over, the men were begging someone to get Marty off them. They were more than happy to be locked inside a barred police van where the big man couldn't get at them.

It's good to have someone with me who knows the ropes.

Rage found Kateřina on one of the settees, the music playing and a blanket wrapped around her. Her eyes followed him as he walked over and sat beside her.

"Better?" he asked in a soft manner.

"Yes, better." Kateřina kept her voice down too.

"Headache gone?"

"Not completely."

"Can I get you something? Coffee or tea?"

"You did not offer coffee, tea, or me," she said. "I might have taken the latter."

She's definitely better.

"Actually, I will take the offer of tea." Her pretty smile was back. Her green eyes seemed more alert too.

When he returned with a cup for each of them, Kateřina hoisted herself into a sitting position.

"Did you learn anything?" she asked.

The note he'd left her had said who he was meeting and why.

"A little," he said. "A nurse quit at the clinic recently. The rumor was she didn't like the way surgery was handled on the President of Chile."

"What did she not like?"

"I asked the question," Rage told her. "Milan didn't know, and it's a dead end. The nurse left Prague, and no one knows where she went."

She took a sip of the tea. "It is good. You are learning." She glanced at him over the lip of her cup and smacked her lips.

After another sip, Kateřina asked, "Did the nurse know about my daughter?"

"Yes, he did." He nodded and then glanced away.

Like mothers from the beginning of time, Kateřina sensed a problem.

"What did he tell you of Ana?" Her eyes were focused hard on his face.

Not quite knowing how much to say, Rage kept it brief but truthful.

"They were told she caught a virus and didn't survive. No one has seen her."

Kateřina's breathing became rough and unsteady, but it only lasted for a few seconds. There were tears, but she wiped them away with a sleeve.

"No one saw her? My Ana? Then she could still be alive."

"I got the impression Ana has not been seen since she disappeared," he told Kateřina, "but it means nothing. Remember… you have spoken with her doctor. He only said she was in quarantine."

Her expression seemed to brighten a little.

"Yes, he did say that." Kateřina smiled, hope in her voice and a sparkle returning to her eyes. "Then Ana is still alive unless I know otherwise."

Rage watched. *I hope you're right.*

They continued talking on the porch—some things about Ana and some about their life that might have been. Evening was settling in, the last rays of sunshine had dropped below the horizon, reflecting off the undersides of clouds above the rolling hills as street lamps were coming on too. It was beautiful.

Kateřina, at least for now, let herself believe Ana was still alive and being cared for at the Cambridge Center. That she was being held in quarantine had become a distraction her mother could live with in the short term.

Tiring, Kateřina nestled down in the pillows on the settee when they came inside. She covered herself with a blanket. The music, as usual now, was playing in the background.

Her eyes blinked slowly, and she appeared ready to sleep. Thinking she should be in her own bed, Rage kissed a cheek, lifted her up, and offered support.

On the way, he slipped his right arm under her left and took several slow steps to a waltz playing on the sound system. Recognizing this one, Kateřina asked him if he knew "The Blue Danube." She said it was one of her all-time favorites.

He hadn't known that.

Glancing down, Rage saw her eyes were closed as they made slow dreamy turns to the music. A slight smile curved the corners of her mouth upward. Though tired, she was obviously enjoying these brief moments in his arms.

The tune ended all too soon.

When she looked up, Rage smiled. "Would you like to try a tango?"

He reminded her of the time she had tried to teach the sexy Latin dance to him. They laughed about the result.

Rage walked her to the bedroom and tucked her underneath the blankets. He could tell by her breathing she was asleep before he left the room.

As he closed her door, Rage decided to take a walk. Though he could check on the van utilizing the recording equipment upstairs, he also needed some breathing and heart exercise. A stroll could satisfy both issues.

Outside, he hiked vigorously to the area where the surveillance van normally parked. Rage slowed his pace and glanced along the street. There was no one in sight on porches or otherwise. The cool temperatures probably…

He pulled his collar tight. Taking care then, Rage surveyed the area one more time and then stepped into the bushes. One moment he was on the sidewalk—then he was gone. Rage had done it countless times while on missions. He smiled, knowing he was still capable.

Satisfied no one had seen him, Rage crept to within twenty feet of the van. As he kneeled down behind some bushes, the side door on the vehicle slid open. The man who had been so close to Rage one other time glanced around and then walked to the big tree.

That time again.

Rage remained still and quiet.

Zipping up, the individual returned to the van.

At almost the same time, Rage heard a vehicle door close somewhere along the street not far away. Seconds later, he heard slight sounds of someone coming his way through the undergrowth. Rage drew his weapon as he spread himself under bushes on the damp forest floor. With his pistol ready, a finger on Rage's left hand pulled a bushy limb down to cover his face. Darkness completed his camouflage.

Close enough for him to see a rubber boot as the individual passed, Rage waited a moment and then raised his head to see the man tap on the van door and then climb in.

He was only in dim light for a moment, but it was enough. The man who had stopped to question them in front of the Cambridge Center was now in the security van. Karel Vlasta, the same person they had heard on the recordings

One other piece of the puzzle.

Rage had been away from the house for over an hour, but he had kept an eye on the time. He would need to hurry. It was now a little before eight o'clock.

The communication with *Idona47* would come at 8:17 p.m. if Rage's message had reached its destination. If not, it would automatically reset forward by twenty-one hours and sixteen minutes. The new arrangements, if they became necessary, were coded into the earlier message.

He could hear conversation in the van. The two men's voices would cover his exit. Rage climbed to his feet and eased out to the street. Walking fast and even jogging a couple of times, he arrived back at Kateřina's with minutes to spare.

Kateřina seemed to be resting easy, leaving him to hurry upstairs. Rage wiped beads of sweat off his forehead as he sat down at the desk.

He did a quick check. The computer was up and running at the appointed time. A new time arrangement was unnecessary.

As he watched, an innocuous advertising email landed on Rage's screen at the set time. Connection made, he had his message from *Idona47* decoded in just a couple of minutes. The communication he sent back took a bit longer.

Now Rage wanted to have a good grasp of who and what the Eagle Trust was.

It won't be easy. He coded questions for the information he needed. Rage asked for details normally requiring days to pin down. He was pushing *Idona47* to have the information within hours.

It was easier to communicate now. Once an initial message was passed from each of them, a different set of rules governed the sending and receiving of new information. Given very specific coding, there was no waiting time involved on future communications.

He struck the button to send. Even with the misdirection embedded, the message would be at its destination almost instantly.

Rage could almost hear swearing on the other end of their communication. It was probably heating up *Idona47's* laptop too.

Regardless, he knew the Eagle Trust would get a thorough examination over the next few hours. He would probably know more about Kateřina's daughter when this was over as well.

As always, Rage committed the details to memory when he finished. To the obvious chagrin of his superiors, this had been his method since the early years at the CIA.

A little after 10:00 p.m., Rage signed off and closed his computer. Unless he received a message resetting the time, much of the information would be available in a few hours.

Rage quietly went downstairs and checked on Kateřina. She was still resting. He smiled thinking she could use the down time.

Back in his bedroom, he shook his arms out to the sides, relaxing and stretching them. Rage still had to do his daily exercises. Dropping to the floor, he began the crunches.

"One, two, three…"

Though she was on time, Karel was waiting again when Pavia walked down the steps and entered the pub.

"Hello."

He stood, kissed her on the cheek and then pulled out her chair.

She smiled. "Hello to you."

Lights were low. Other couples were scattered about the dining room, heads lowered, involved in quiet conversation.

Karel ordered drinks and asked about her day.

"It was good. I am doing marketing research for Madam Chairwoman." Then, chuckling as she thought about it, Pavia said, "Madam Balca is always in a hurry."

"What kind of marketing?" he inquired.

Pavia didn't think it would be out of order if she told him.

"The Chairwoman wants to do a special mailing campaign to some of the wealthy individuals and couples here in Central Europe. She expects the effort could produce a new source of patient income for the Cambridge Center."

"Are you finding possibilities?"

"Yes, many."

"Do you like your boss?"

Strange questions again, Pavia thought, remembering their prior meeting.

"Yes, of course. She is very good to me."

"Does she do more for you than others who work with you?"

Another interesting inquiry. She answered him anyway after giving the question some thought.

"Yes." Pavia nodded her head. "She does more for me."

Still considering Karel's question, she said, "But I think it is because I work so closely with her. We see each other almost every day." She hesitated for a moment and then said, "…and I work very hard for her."

"Yes…that is probably the reason."

I bet there is more he wants to say.

Instead, he changed the subject. "Shall we order?"

They both asked for the Sausage Plate with sauerkraut and potatoes, including fresh drinks, and then they talked.

"Is she good to work for?"

"For me, yes." Then she added, "For some of the others, not so good."

These drinks are strong, she thought.

"I work very hard to please her." With a hand dipping side to side, she said, "Some of the others, not so hard."

He asked other questions, making conversation, and then their dinner came.

Karel talked about travel, inquiring about places Pavia had visited. She named several—Paris, Amsterdam, London, Munich—and as they enjoyed their food, she described the historic island of Lindau in Bavaria.

Thinking of the few days she had spent there, in her mind's eye Pavia could still visualize Lake Constance surrounding the island. The clear lake and luscious green hillsides were fresh and beautiful in her mind. She did her best to describe the panorama of the snow-covered Alps stretching out behind the unique harbor entrance with its white lighthouse and Bavarian lion. For her, it was so distinctive Pavia was near a loss for words describing the location.

Karel asked questions and appeared interested in the things she was telling him. He was fun and entertaining and seemed to enjoy flirting with her. She was beginning to like him very much.

Pavia listened as Karel talked about places he had visited too. He had even been to South America.

Too soon, it was time to go.

The day was busy for Nurse Dusa. She alternated between three patients throughout her shift. One man was almost lost when his new kidneys threatened to shut down.

Dusa had watched in admiration as one of the younger doctors stepped in, giving orders while talking to the patient, assuring him everything would be all right.

"Stay with me," the doctor had said several times.

It was like that all day, one crisis after another. As such, there had been no opportunity for contact with the individual she had encountered the previous evening.

The incident was on her mind all through her shift. She was nervous and a bit afraid, but Dusa knew she could not avoid a situation where she thought someone was in peril.

Throughout the hectic shift, she thought of the sadness emanating from inside the mysterious locked room. Dusa was determined to go that way again tonight. She would find a way to let the person inside know someone was concerned.

Just before it was time for the shift to end, there was another emergency. The patient was snatched from death by the same young doctor who had impressed Dusa earlier in the day. Everyone breathed a sigh of relief when the danger was over.When she was finally able to leave, it was almost 10:00 p.m. She signed out and headed to her vehicle.

Walking as though she knew the way, Dusa intentionally made the same wrong turn and headed for the mysterious room. A few meters before reaching the door, she started to change hands with her large purse. She had made sure it was open and things would spill.

A slight stumble and the hoax was on. The dropped bag and its contents went everywhere but mostly toward the locked door. Lip gloss, her keys, a mirror, billfold, even some loose change skipped across the polished floor.

On her knees, Dusa muttered under her breath and tossed the billfold into her bag, pretending exasperation as she gathered her belongings. Dusa managed to knock on the door as she scooted along the floor.

Now the nurse held her face close to the surface as if looking for anything that might have gone under the door. She had already glanced down the corridor.

Listening for a moment, she then whispered, "Are you there? Are you okay?"

Unhurried, she continued picking up change and other items. All the while she hoped for a response, but none came.

Deciding the individual had been moved, Dusa picked up her lip gloss and started to stand. A movement under the door caught her attention. The edge of some folded sheets of paper appeared.

A halting voice softly commanded, "Get this to my mother."

Without a moment's hesitation, Dusa put the pages into the purse as though they had spilled out along with her other belongings. She would check them later when it was safe.

One last time she asked, "Are you okay?"

"No."

The hesitant one-word reply sent tingling along Dusa's neck and down the spine as the encounter had the night before.

She waited, seconds ticking off, but there was no other response.

After taking a few steps in the direction she had been going before dropping her handbag, Dusa stopped. She glanced around as though confused. Then, a finger to her lips, she shook her head, pointed a finger back and then went in the direction she had initially come from. Though listening, she passed the locked room without a glance. Dusa continued out of the building to the employee's parking lot.

There were two or three other individuals headed for their vehicles. She felt safe now, but examining the pages for a contact could wait until she was away from the hospital.

Nearing her car, Dusa slipped a hand into her bag for keys. She heard footsteps and the tingling returned. Glancing back, she realized it was just another weary worker on the way home. The man she'd heard walked near her as he passed. Relieved, Dusa hardly took notice of him. She was too busy climbing into her vehicle and getting out of the parking lot. Dusa wanted the bad feelings behind her.

Traffic was light, and twenty minutes later she was approaching her neighborhood. Though they had been having their problems,

Dusa hoped her boyfriend was already home; she needed his arms around her. Dusa wanted to feel safe.

The evening was going according to plan. Karel had watched Pavia enjoy four drinks by the time they finished dinner. She didn't appear to notice he had not ordered for himself on the last two rounds

With her a little tipsy, she should be open to his questioning.

After paying the ticket, he took her arm as they left the pub and climbed the steps to the street above. On the sidewalk and with the alcohol taking hold, she clutched his arm and leaned close.

Asking about her boyfriend on the way to her apartment, the conversation drifted to the family estate in the south of the Czech Republic. She described it in detail as they walked.

"It is large and very beautiful," she told Karel, adding, "He taught me how to fire a gun. There was a shooting range at the estate."

She stumbled on the uneven cobblestone, tightening her grip on Karel's arm for support.

Pavia glanced his way. "They are wealthy. Too bad I was not able to keep him," she joked.

In a short time, I will be wealthier than you would believe, Karel thought.

As they neared her building, Pavia brought out a key. With a minimum amount of fumbling, she opened the door and stepped aside to let Karel in. He heard the door close and then she was back, clutching his arm even closer now.

"Would you like a drink?" Pavia asked as she released him, swaying as she headed into into the kitchen.

"Let me make the drinks," Karel suggested as he nudged her toward a barstool.

"Yes," she said, "I think it would be a good idea."

Karel mixed one for her and poured a cola over ice for himself. Finished, he set the drinks on the bar and joined her.

As he watched, Pavia downed a third of hers in one large swallow. She came up grinning.

He may have erred in giving her more to drink. She appeared already past the point of answering any pertinent questions about Madam Chairwoman.

Despite her condition, Karel gave it a try.

"Does the boss ever mention me?" he asked.

Rolling her head, Pavia seemed to think about it.

"Neeww," she giggled. She was holding her head at an angle and fluttering the lashes on her upturned eyes. She offered, "I will talk about you, if you wish."

She was well past intelligent conversation.

With her face turned toward him, Karel leaned forward and kissed her, softly at first, then with more fervor. Pavia responded immediately, her tongue demonstrating the passion she must be feeling.

He was obliging, pulling her closer and matching her kisses.

She slipped off her stool and moved between his knees. Her continued kisses were demanding as their bodies pressed together at all the right places.

After a few moments, Karel leaned her away from him. She watched him closely.

He stared into her eyes for several seconds and then did something Pavia didn't expect. Starting with the top button on her blouse, Karel slowly undressed her…with his eyes.

He could tell she was imagining the heat from his fingers. But he wasn't touching her—his hands were at her back, fingers holding her at a distance while his eyes stripped away her clothing—piece by piece—the blouse, the lacey camisole and then the thin bra she wore. Finally, she was as bare as she had ever been—in his eyes and in her imagination.

With her own eyes narrowed and focused, the look she gave him was nothing if not wicked.

Their eyes locked on each other then and held fast for several moments. Finally, Karel broke the stillness. Releasing her with one hand, he moved the back of his fingers to the neck of her blouse. Palm out and nails stroking, he raked them slowly downward across her breasts to the waist of her slacks.

Pavia drew in a deep, raspy breath as Karel felt a shiver pass through her body.

Her breasts virtually reached out to him as her long fingers cupped his neck and pulled his face to her chest. Her head thrown back, a soft moan escaped her slightly parted lips.

Her body begged to be touched—to be held and caressed.

Karel and Pavia were both where they wanted to be. Kisses grew more passionate by the moment. Pavia moaned again…softly, caught in the depths of her wanting. Karel pressed her close, feeling the heat as she leaned against his body, encircled in his arms.

Sharing her bed suddenly seemed overwhelming to both of them. Perhaps on another occasion she could be enticed to talk and tell secrets but not tonight.

Forgetting his questions, Karel eased them into the bedroom and down onto her bed. With his attention back where it belonged, Karel reached out to satisfy both their desires.

At that very ill-timed instant, he felt vibrations from the cellphone in his pocket.

In the heat of the moment, Karel had forgotten he'd left orders to call him if the nurse approached the special room again. Though he didn't want to, Karel turned onto his elbow to check the phone. As he feared, it was Alexandr.

The text was short and to the point. "Call me. NOW!!!

He quickly tucked his shirt and ran the fingers of both hands through his hair.

Pavia tried but didn't have much luck standing. She watched him start toward the front door with sad eyes imploring him not to go. Her arm reached out toward him as Karel closed the door.

Outside, Karel hurried back to his vehicle. In the first few steps, he pulled out his cell and called the security office.

Karel glanced at the phone. There had been three messages before this one.

He punched in the numbers. "It's me," Karel said.

"I have been trying to reach you," Alexandr told him. "She did it again. This time some papers were passed to her under the door. I have one of the contractors following her."

"Patch me to him and stay on the call."

The man following Dusa answered immediately. He was directly behind her vehicle.

"I need the papers from her purse. There may be several pages," Karel told him. "Handle it."

"No problem." The voice was calm and confident.

The connection with the contractor was broken then, leaving only Karel and Alexandr on the line.

Karel said he would be at the office shortly. He had reached his car and squealed the tires as he headed for the Cambridge Center.

Twenty minutes later, Karel approached Alexandr's desk. The assistant was focusing on the wall of video screens.

After checking in, Karel told him, "Let me know when you hear from our man."

Karel headed for his private office. After closing the door and dropping into his chair, Karel picked up the phone and punched in a different number. The call was answered on the third ring.

"Hello." A sleepy woman's voice.

"We have a problem."

"Oh?"

"The nurse stopped by the secured room again. The patient passed some papers to her under the door," Karel said. "I have someone following the nurse."

"Keep me in the loop."

"A suggestion," Karel said. "Move the patient to a different location immediately."

"Of course. I will. Inform me when anything changes."

"Yes, I will." Then, "We may be up late tonight."

Without a response, Karel heard a click as Madam Chairwoman's phone disconnected.

She was second in line at the intersection. The first car pulled away allowing Dusa a clear view of the heavily traveled street. She wanted to make a left turn and waited for a break in the traffic. The papers in her handbag rested heavy on her mind, expecting there would be an address or phone number.

As Dusa sat watching the traffic and thinking of the sad sounding woman, she was struck from behind.

"Oh, no!" she said, realizing this was her second accident within a month.

The car that hit her already had its emergency flashers on, and someone was climbing out. In her mirror, she saw a man walking toward her car.

"Are you all right?" he asked as she lowered the window.

"Yes, I think so."

As Dusa started to look up, something slammed into the side of her face. Darkness surged over her.

Only minutes after the call to the Chairwoman, Karel's phone rang. It was Alexandr.

"We have the papers," he said.

"Good. And the nurse?"

"She was left on the street with her vehicle."

"Dead?" Karel asked.

"Doubtful. Probably just unconscious. I just spoke with our man. He took her bag and left her vehicle to look like a robbery. The papers were in the handbag."

"Good. Call him back and have him clean out the bag and discard it."

They hung up, and Karel called the Chairwoman, bringing her up to date.

"Good." A long sigh indicated her relief.

"How do you want me to handle the nurse?" Karel asked. "Shall we dispose of her?"

He had explained the orders he had given regarding the scene.

"No, you made the right call," Madam Chairwoman replied. "I think we must let her continue as normal. I will have her supervisor reprimand and put her on notice for being in a restricted area on two occasions. Otherwise, we will watch her."

"What about the papers?"

"I am on the way to my office. I will call when I arrive," she said. "You will bring them to me."

A few minutes later Alexandr brought an envelope and dropped it on Karel's desk. It was open.

"Do you think he read this?" Karel expected he already knew the answer.

Alexandr nodded. "Of course. The pages were in an envelope. It was open when it came to me."

Almost as if he was talking to himself, Karel said, "I wonder if the nurse read them too?"

Alexandr obviously heard him.

"I doubt it," he said. "Our man said he watched for lights in her vehicle. She hadn't stopped until the intersection where he took the bag."

Karel was relieved. He hadn't wanted to deal with the nurse. It would have been difficult to explain.

Holding up the pages, Karel asked if their man was still in Alexandr's office.

"No. He said he was going home."

"Good." Karel was looking at the pages.

"I need to get back to my desk," Alexandr said and headed toward the door.

Karel knew the man who had followed Dusa. He had worked as a contractor several times when Karel did not want a connection to the hospital.

A few clicks on his computer gave Karel an address. He jotted it on a small stick-it note.

Karel spread the recovered sheets across the desk and studied them. The note was a plea for understanding. It was obvious Ana Bambenek had been distraught when she wrote the thoughts to her mother. He copied the young woman's letter and placed the original pages in an envelope.

When she arrived, the Chairwoman summoned Karel to her office. As he entered, the Chairwoman was saying goodbye to someone on her cell. He handed her the envelope without commenting.

Madam Balca fished the pages out and began to read. Finished, she looked up and asked if he had read the letter.

"Yes," Karel told her. She ran through it again and then asked how many others had access.

"Two. My assistant and the man who followed the nurse."

"Do you trust them?"

"My assistant? Completely. We have a close working relationship." Then Karel said, "I do not trust the other man."

She glanced at the letter a third time, studying it even closer.

Looking up finally, Madam Chairwoman told Karel she would decide what to do with the pages and he should deal with the individual who retrieved the letter.

Karel understood he was dismissed.

When the door closed, the Chairwoman immediately reached for the letter and unfolded it again, studying the words even closer this time. Her first thought was Ana Bambenek had nice handwriting. It closely resembled her own.

An idea quickly formed. Could she rewrite the letter giving the mother reason to think her daughter had met someone undesirable and run away? That would leave the Cambridge Center with a clean slate.

But, Madam Chairwoman remembered there are several others who knew about the upcoming surgery. Victoria Lancing was being prepared, too.

She shook her head. *Too dangerous to make changes now.*

Madam Chairwoman picked up the pages and read Ana Bambenek's letter again.

To Katerina, My Dear Mother,
I am sorry you are involved with me in
this difficult situation and decision.
Many things are happening I do not understand. There
is so much of my beginnings I am only now learning. Also,

there must be many details about my birth you did not know. Otherwise, you would have objected years ago.

At a time in every life, once circumstances have reached a crucial point, there can be no going back. Unfortunately, we have reached that stage. I cannot go back, and you <u>must</u> not. It could serve no worthwhile purpose for either of us.

Though you may never understand, please trust me. I am taking the right course for myself and for you, and you must let this be the last words between us.

I know you love me and would do anything for me. No one could ever have a more wonderful parent. In all ways, you have been both mother and father to me when I had no other. I am eternally grateful for that. Thank you for my life.

In closing, only you will understand why I must say these words:

I love you.

Ana

When she finished, the Chairwoman dropped the short letter onto the desk. She turned back to the windows; two new thoughts rushed into her reasoning.

Why would I change it? The daughter said caring words for both of them. She also told her mother to leave the situation alone.

And in the young woman's closing, what meaning was there that only Kateřina Bambenek could understand?

Madam Balca couldn't imagine.

The Chairwoman only considered the two notions for a few moments. She could find nothing more that gave her concern, and these were not enough to stop her. The young woman had said everything beneficial.

Send the letter out and let the situation go, the Chairwoman thought. *Watch her mother, though. And…watch the American stranger.*

Stopping back by security headquarters, Karel spoke briefly with Alexandr and then said he was going home to get some rest.

In the parking lot, Karel started his vehicle and then pulled out the slip of paper with the contractor's address. Reaching over, he programed the GPS. A few moments later, he had directions.

When Karel reached the entrance to the building, he used a gloved finger to ring the buzzer to the man's apartment.

A sleepy voice inquired, "Who's there?"

"Karel Vlasta. I have another assignment for you. May I come up?"

"Sure," the voice answered. "I was asleep, but come on."

There was a buzz. The door clicked and unlocked.

Karel glanced around. It was an older building. He doubted if there were security cameras outside or in the small lobby.

Shoving his way through the door, Karel took the elevator and was soon at the apartment's front door.

The man was waiting and stepped aside. He motioned toward a sofa and asked if Karel would like something to drink. The man suggested coffee or tea. He said he also had vodka.

Karel walked toward the sofa. When he turned, he was holding a pistol with a silencer attached. Confused, the contractor stepped back. "What are you doing? Why the weapon?"

Karel motioned toward the bedroom. "Are the nurse's purse and other belongings in there?"

The man nodded. "The things I kept are there."

Though it was cool in the apartment, Karel could see a touch of sweat on the contractor's upper lip and forehead. His hands were shaking, and his voice trembled slightly as he started to explain. "I only kept her billfold and credit cards and the money," he said. "I was told to get rid of her handbag. I tossed it into a dumpster several kilometers from the nurse's car and my apartment."

"Were you wearing gloves?"

"Na…No," he said as he swept a hand across his forehead to get rid of the sweat. "I did not think…"

"Show me her things." Karel gestured toward the bedroom with his weapon. "Where is your pistol?"

"On th…the shelf in the closet," he stammered.

Karel could see the nurse's belongings on a table in the corner. While keeping an eye on the man, Karel opened the closet and stuck the man's weapon inside his belt.

Turning, Karel asked, "Did you read the note?"

"No…" Karel saw the man's expression take on a resolute look. "No, I didn't read it. But what if I did? What would it matter now?" His words were challenging.

Karel listened, but the man was right. He didn't believe him and couldn't take a chance.

Then the individual softened. "You're going to kill me anyway, aren't you?"

Without saying another word, Karel shot the man once in the chest and another time in the head as he crumpled to the floor.

Karel walked to the table and pocketed the nurse's things. Then he methodically took the room apart searching for valuables. He slipped several of the contractor's personal items into his pockets.

Standing at the front door, he looked back at the room. It looked like a robbery had taken place except for one thing. Karel exited the apartment and locked up using a key he had found on the eating table. Then he turned and leaned against the cheap door, breaking it open with his shoulder as any competent burglar might do. Very little sound accompanied the act. He tossed the key back onto the table and left.

Leaving by the building's stairway, Karel hurried to his vehicle. In addition to the pistol, his pocket bulged with the man's money, billfold, a watch, and two rings. Investigating police would easily draw the conclusion the victim had been killed during a robbery.

Karel removed the gloves. A bead of perspiration had now formed on his own brow. He wiped it off with a finger and pointed the automobile toward his apartment.

11

Friday, September 25, 2015

* * *

THEY MOVED ANA DURING THE night. Security had arrived unannounced and walked her to the new room. She suspected the security camera had caught her slipping the letter under the door. Ana knew in her heart the only chance of reaching out to Kateřina had been the brief message.

Ana hated the letter to her mother was so short. There was so much more she would have said if there had been time. It was a blessing the individual in the hallway had come to her aid. Ana could only hope the letter would reach Kateřina.

If her mother believed she was still alive, Kateřina would use any means available to locate her. Ana knew that. She had used the letter to take away her mother's hope and with luck, any danger to her. Ana had no doubt Kateřina would be in jeopardy if she came searching.

She couldn't help it; Ana's mind kept bouncing from thought to thought.

Having been told she was a human clone, Ana knew enough to surmise an unknown biological parent was out there somewhere. How did that fit into the situation? She and her mother were only two pieces of the puzzle.

Who is the other person? she wondered, knowing the question would probably not be answered in the time she had left.

"Three weeks," the psychiatrist had said. *Three weeks at most.*

A week and two days had already passed.

There was so much she had planned for. Ana had been studying or working her entire life. If she had been fortunate enough to live to 70 or 75, this would have been only a small part of a normal life span.

Thinking of the places she had planned to visit brought a thin mist of tears to her eyes. Ana was interested in history and had dreamed of strolling the streets of Rome, Athens, and even London with its 2,000 years of importance in the history of the British Isles. She had wanted to go to Jerusalem, too…and America.

There were so many places and so many things.

Now it was all gone.

Her thoughts were interrupted by a knock at the door. Then Ana heard a key rattle. The nurse entered, and they went through their usual routine.

"We have you scheduled for x-rays early tomorrow."

There had been tests and a few x-rays at intervals every day and night since she'd returned from London. Ana thought of the story she had been given to get her back to Prague: her mother had suffered a stroke. Then the trip back and the limo waiting to bring her here to the hospital—Ana had fallen for it all.

In the less busy times, Ana had been offered books to read and a Bible to study. Nothing held her attention like the knowledge of what was to come. After the first four or five days, Ana had found some comfort in reading scriptures she'd remembered from childhood.

Though she knew reading the bible could not redirect her fate, Ana thumbed through it anyway. She looked for familiar words and then read them fast. Doing that crowded out other dark thoughts.

In another part of the hospital, Victoria Lancing awaited surgery too. She stood clutching a walker in the doorway of her room. This was unusual. Her illness and lack of energy was keeping her bedridden most of the time. Other than the nurses and doctors who attended her, she was seldom seen. There were family and friends at the hotel, but they were only allowed to visit occasionally. Even then, anyone coming to see her was required to wear a medical mask.

Turning back to her bed, Victoria moved slow, the walker keeping her upright, her feet dragging across the tile floor. Apparently without energy, her body slumped, and an extended belly made her appear pregnant.

Nurses were in and out of the room every few minutes. Victoria had been asked to not leave her bed without a nurse at her side, but she didn't listen. The walker allowed her a small amount of freedon to relieve her nervous state.

She was scratching at her hands and fingers continuously; they had become red and irritated. On this particular morning, she had been nauseous since she awoke, but her heaving had been wasted since there was nothing left for her to expel.

The entertainer was registered with the health clinic as Elizabeth Ackerley from Southampton, England. It was a useless attempted deception since Victoria's presence had become a known fact within hours of her arrival. Many on the clinic's staff were fans of her acting and angelic singing voice.

Glancing toward the door, Victoria realized she would give anything for a shot of scotch right now.

Years earlier, a need for drinking had come with her fame. Over time Victoria had slowly slipped into the bottle, preferring Dewar's Highlander Honey, a blended scotch. She had been introduced to drinking after her first successful music album. Over the years, the whiskey had become a trusted friend of sorts.

Initially, she would only have a drink to celebrate something wonderful and new in her life. As time passed, Victoria came to enjoy the feel of sipping one or two shots over ice before she turned in for the evening. After this came a need for more. Finally, over a twenty-year span and the success coming with those years, the signs of liver damage became too prominent to be ignored.

The goals of the Eagle Trust had been lost in Victoria's case. Research at Cambridge Health and Research Center was directed toward ultimately proving to the world human clones could allow brilliant individuals to live almost indefinitely. Little was gained from using the young clones to prop up self-destructive participants, even gifted ones like Victoria.

Remembering, she thought of the career she had expected in psychology when she was studying at Cambridge. She was going to save the world from itself. Glancing out the window, Victoria recalled the talent show that had changed her life. If she had only known…

There had been interventions for Victoria by her family and by the other members of the Trust. Several times she had committed herself to abstaining from alcohol. Victoria had tried, but the whisky had always proved stronger.

Now she had another problem. Victoria had finally accepted the fact for her to survive, her clone would have to die. This reality disturbed her more profoundly as the surgery drew closer.

A short time after returning to her bed, Victoria's transplant specialist came to discuss her upcoming surgery. With initial greetings out of the way, the two old friends and fellow members of the Eagle Trust got down to business.

"Must we do it this way?" Victoria asked.

"Only if you wish to continue living," Dr. Jirsa told her.

"How is my donor doing?" Victoria asked. "Have you visited her?"

"I do not think we should go there," Hana said. "The fewer details we know of these young people, the easier it will be to go forward psychologically when this is over."

Victoria stared at Hana for several seconds before replying.

"Can you really not think of those people, Hana? Have you never considered your own clone?" Victoria kept her eyes firmly on her friend.

"We are killing, no, murdering them to save ourselves. Do we have the moral right to do that?"

Hana broke the stare before answering.

"I think of mine occasionally," she finally said, "and I also think of the good I am doing and will continue to do. If I develop a condition or have an accident, my clone represents a hope for me to continue my profession and be able to help others."

"But a young person dies each time one of us needs something they have," Victoria declared. "I have given much thought to this since I have been in Prague and in this room."

Dr. Jirsa remained silent, listening.

Victoria looked at the surgeon, took a deep breath and seemed to tug at her own courage.

"Your situation is very different from mine." Her words were well thought out. "You save lives with what you do. Your work is important for people. I...only entertain them." She hesitated. "I give them enjoyment, but if they do not come to my concert or my play, it will not change their future. What you do..." She spread her hands in front of her in a gesture "...what you do allows your patients a future." Victoria looked at her friend for several seconds.

The doctor remained silent.

"I do not know if I can go forward with this surgery," Victoria finally said. "I am not sure I can allow this person to be sacrificed to save me."

When she left Victoria Lancing's room, Dr. Jirsa went directly to the psychiatrist's office. It was important she speak with Dr. Seifert now.

"Is he in?"

Five minutes, the secretary signaled with a hand raised and fingers spread.

Dr. Jirsa nodded and grabbed a magazine.

She didn't like the situation that appeared to be developing with Victoria Lancing. The donor was already at the stage where she knew her fate, and other facts made going back impossible. If Victoria refused the liver transplant, her donor's organs would have to go to others on waiting lists.

What a waste if it happens, Dr. Jirsa thought. *Victoria is such a talent, and we will lose her without this procedure. She is almost too ill for surgery now.*

The doctor slowly shook her head.

Minutes later, the psychiatrist walked his patient to the outer door and turned, motioning Dr. Jirsa into his office.

"Now, what is so urgent?" He pointed to a chair.

She explained the circumstances and her concerns involving Victoria. Finished, she waited for his comments. Though Dr. Seifert was not an original member of the Trust, he had been one of the first outsiders hired, becoming an important member of the Cambridge Center's staff.

He knew everything there was to know about their research and about the human cloning experiments. His contract with the Eagle Trust and the Cambridge Center swore him to secrecy though this had never been an issue for Dr. Seifert. He recognized the opportunity here to be on the leading edge of the medical phenomenon they were dealing with in the research labs at the Cambridge Center.

He had written several papers and was considered a world-renowned expert on cloning in general and on the theoretical subject of human cloning. He was also considered an expert practitioner of psychiatry.

"I have been expecting this," he said. "It was only a matter of time before one of you hesitated to use your clone. I expected the morality of what you originally did and what you are doing now would overwhelm one of you."

He stood and paced back and forth behind his desk.

"Ms. Lancing is the ideal individual with circumstances to make this decision likely."

He stopped, waiting, she thought, for some reaction from her. She nodded and motioned for him to continue.

"Psychologically, she is emotionally weak," he stated. "The drinking only adds to her medical and mental problems. With time on her hands, despondency causes Ms. Lancing to be mentally sensitive to the perceived problems of others—in this case, her clone and donor."

His arguments made sense. Dr. Jirsa was considering what her next step should be when he spoke again.

"Where do you stand as far as preliminary testing is concerned?" The psychiatrist scratched thoughtfully at his beard.

"We need another week."

"I do not think you have a week with this one." Then he stared at her and stated, "We must deal with Ms. Lancing's surgery as soon as possible. Do not waste an hour."

She knew he was right. This had been her own argument to herself after she left Victoria.

Finally, jabbing a finger toward her, he emphasized, "Meanwhile, she must not be allowed time for thought."

Dr. Jirsa returned to her office and sat at her desk. She immediately reached for Ana Bambenek's chart and leaned back thoughtfully studying the details.

The remaining tests could be completed in a matter of hours. Several of the lesser ones could be skipped entirely. Results could be rushed too. So in only a short time, a day or two at most, they could perform Victoria's transplant surgery.

Now, Dr. Jirsa thought, *how can we keep Victoria occupied during the interim period?*

There was a way. It wouldn't help or hurt Victoria, but it would keep her out of trouble. The doctor picked up the telephone and told a nurse what she wanted.

"I will be there in a few minutes to sign an authorization."

The injections Dr. Jirsa ordered would keep the patient in a sleepy state. When she was not resting, Victoria would be too groggy for remorse.

The shots had already been prepared when the doctor authorized them minutes later.

Victoria Lancing was crying when she was approached by the head nurse. Victoria's regular attendant had accompanied Ivana and stood watching. After vital signs were taken, Victoria was told the doctor had ordered sacred medication to help her overcome the nausea and the tenderness in the right side of her stomach area. Victoria thanked her and obviously looked forward to the relief.

Ivana left almost immediately, leaving the regular nurse to keep watch on the situation. Victoria was in a deep and steady sleep within minutes. Ivana was informed and reported the results to Dr. Jirsa. Hanging up the phone, the nurse thought she could hear relief in the doctor's voice.

At midmorning, Tamara came to Ana's room again. The vital sign routine had become normal for both of them.

Ana had gone for x-rays earlier and was back for breakfast. Though she was not hungry, Ana ate the toast, one small sweet roll and some cheese.

The nurse stayed, talking small talk and keeping her company. Finally, Tamara said she must go.

Looking back as she reached the door, Tamara said, "I was told to inform you your surgery has been moved up. Only a short time now."

She glanced at the floor.

"I am sorry," she said simply, and then she closed the door.

As Ana heard the lock engage, she equated it to drawing the curtain on her future. This play, this drama she was in, was about to come to a close.

Ana walked over, picked up the Bible, and dropped into a chair. She sat there, the book on her lap. Then she began doing something, a ritual of sorts. Ana mentally began saying goodbye to everyone she knew.

All those individuals—friends and others—could not hear her and had no way of knowing what Ana was experiencing. But she knew. Ana felt better for saying her goodbyes.

It took time. Even after she initially finished, others came to mind. She realized, right up until the end, new names would probably drift from her memory.

Ana hoped so.

Finished—at least for the moment—she opened the Bible. Ana wasn't looking for a particular verse or story, but as she scanned the page, her attention jumped to the shortest verse in the Bible. Ana became teary when she read it.

John 11:35. "Jesus wept."

Milan had been curious since Marty brought the American to see him. Obviously, they thought something bad was going on at the hospital. Judging from their questions, it was probably something illegal.

Interesting, because Milan thought this too. He had to remain careful, though, and in the background. He couldn't afford to lose his job.

Milan had worked in the transplant ICU for the last several years. With his studies, he had advanced in his present position and situation but had also avoided going into any sort of management. Milan just wanted to do his job and help patients. He wasn't interested in telling others what to do.

Yet, taking a chance, he had departed from his regular routine, doing something he normally avoided. He didn't usually get into the business of others.

The situation had started innocently enough. Someone was sick and one of the newer nurses had been called in on her day off. She had shown up sporting a very bruised face and a black left eye. She had tried to hide the injuries with makeup, but the bruising was too pronounced.

"Wow," he'd jokingly said when he saw Nurse Dusa's injuries. "Have you been in a fight?"

Dusa immediately swung her focus toward him, color left her face, and her eyes grew wide in surprise…or fear. Quickly gathering herself, she replied, "No…no, I…was mugged last night near my apartment."

He could tell by her changing expressions and tone of voice something was wrong. Perhaps it was more than a mugging, maybe a boyfriend problem. Whatever it was, Milan doubted if she was telling him the truth.

He let it go until break time, and then he stepped out on his own.

The transplant ICU was empty. The last patient, a kidney replacement, had been released from the ICU two days earlier. The staff was cleaning and resupplying, a forever job.

"Let's get a cup of coffee," he suggested to Dusa. Critical care employees had a small lounge and coffee bar off the ICU. Other than the coffee lounge, they were not allowed to leave the area during their shift if there were patients.

Milan and Dusa were the only ones willing to chance having the strong coffee this late in the morning. It was several hours old. The joke was it could be lethal after ten o'clock.

They had the break room to themselves.

Mindful of security, Milan pointed to a table out of camera range. He opened a cabinet and pulled out cups. Dusa poured the coffee. Lots of sugar and creamer might overcome the brew's age.

"What really happened to you?" he asked in a voice indicating he didn't believe the earlier story.

"I told you," she said. "I was mugged."

He looked at her, then he shook his head ever so slightly.

Dusa held his eye for a moment, then glanced away. When she looked back, there were tears on her face.

"I tried to deliver a letter, and I was mugged." A moments hesitation, then, "Something is happening here," she said softly. "Something very bad."

"Like what?"

"I do not know. I tried to help someone. I was asked to deliver a letter." She hesitated. "…I think I have become involved in this bad thing."

Milan waited for a moment, then asked, "Would you feel comfortable telling me about it?" He touched her hand reassuringly.

Milan couldn't believe he was having this conversation. He would not be here if Marty and the American had not come to him with their questions.

Dusa took a napkin and dabbed at her eyes. She glanced back, her forehead wrinkled and a look of uncertainty on her face.

Then she sat up straight in her chair, took a deep breath and said, "I have to tell someone. If anything happened to me, no one would ever know what I did or what happened."

For a moment Milan thought she had committed some terrible act.

She told Milan in the short time she had been working here she had heard things. "Others talking in the break room and in the restrooms," she explained. Clarifying, she added, "Not to me but just talking to others."

"What are you hearing?" Milan did not expect there would be much of consequence. The young woman had only been working at the Cambridge Center for a short time.

"I have heard tidbits of gossip about three individuals, two young men and a woman. These things all happened before I came to work at the Cambridge Center."

Milan's interest began to increase.

"It is strange." She glanced at him. "A young woman was admitted a few weeks ago. She was given lots of tests, something almost daily, and then she suddenly disappeared. One day she was in her room; the next day it was empty."

"What else?" Milan asked.

"It is all so confusing," she said, "but it might have been because there was so much excitement at the time. The President of Chile was having surgery when the young woman left the hospital."

"What about the two young men?"

"I only heard it happened," Dusa said, adding, "The circumstances were similar to those of the young woman."

"Who told you?"

"A nurse who is no longer with the hospital. I met her at a party before I came to work here. She was moving to the United States."

Milan immediately thought of the story he had heard. He wondered if it was the same nurse who left after the Chilean President's surgery.

"What about the letter you tried to deliver? Tell me about it."

Dusa began with her unintended wrong turn in the hallway the first night. Then she told him the rest of the story, watching his reactions.

"I would have missed her if I had not accidentally gone into the restricted area." Dusa described the crying and the lack of response on the first night. Then the nurse told him all that happened up to the moment she was assaulted a few hours earlier.

"The woman in the room wanted me to take the papers to her mother. I never saw the mother's name or address," she said. "I was going to look at it when I arrived at my apartment. I did not make it to my apartment."

Dusa touched her bruised face.

"When I woke up, I was still in my car, but everything was gone." Dusa held out her hands. "My purse, all my things…and the letter."

Almost pleading for understanding, she added, "I did not know what else to do, so I drove home and then came to work today."

She glanced at Milan. "There is one other thing."

He remained silent.

Dusa focused on his eyes, holding his attention, and said, "I have wondered if the individual in the locked room might be the researcher who disappeared?"

Now Milan wondered, too, given the gossip he had already heard.

Dusa felt relieved after having told her story to someone who listened and appeared to care.

"On the way home, I decided to tell my boyfriend I was mugged when I parked the car. I couldn't tell him the truth." Dusa glanced at Milan. "He would only scream at me for opening the car's window to a stranger."

Now she was angry at the boyfriend.

"'Not even for an accident,' he would shout. He always thinks he knows best. 'Never do that.' He always repeats himself too." Dusa's eyes begged understanding. "I just couldn't tell him."

Milan touched her outstretched hands again. He did understand but resisted an urge to tell Nurse Dusa to run, not walk, away from this boyfriend. The guy sounded like disaster waiting to happen.

Instead, Milan asked, "Do you want to do anything? Tell anyone else?"

Eyes down, she thought about it for a few moments and then shook her head without looking up.

"I doubt if anyone would believe me." She glanced at Milan and then lowered her eyes again. "Everyone probably thinks my boyfriend hit me."

She glanced at Milan again. "Isn't life strange? Even with his temper, he has never hit me, not even once." With a slight grin she said, "He just yells."

This is an opportunity. Milan wondered if he should make a phone call.

Instead, he told Dusa, "I know some people who will listen, and I think they can help."

She gazed at him, studying the look he was giving her.

"Let me think about it," she said. Dusa stood up and started back toward the ICU. After taking a few steps, she slowed, turned, and asked, "Do you trust these people?"

"Yes."

"Do you think they can do something about what is happening here?"

"Yes."

She seemed to relax.

"Then tell them."

Kateřina slept longer than usual. It was midmorning before she put in an appearance.

Rage was on his second pot of coffee. He had looked in on her twice. She seemed to be resting peacefully, so he hadn't disturbed her.

Around nine, he had given up and made himself breakfast of toast and jelly. As he reached for the last bite, she said hello.

"Morning, sleepyhead," he said, kidding her.

"What is this sleepyhead?" she asked sincerely.

"You don't know."

"I do not," she said.

He explained, and they enjoyed a chuckle. She agreed the term had been appropriate over the last few mornings.

Rage poured coffee for Kateřina before clearig his dishes. Then, with a knowing wink, he suggested they move to the front porch to finish off the prior night's conversation. Though the music was playing, he glanced at the locations where he had detected the listening devices. Sometimes it was easier to find a different place for conversation.

The sun had warmed a rather cool early morning. Sitting outside was a nice change, too.

Seated and sipping their coffee, she glanced over and began the exchange. "Perhaps I am only being a mother hoping my beliefs will become real. I continue to have this thought in my head that Ana is in the hospital and wishing she could come home to me."

Rage didn't disagree. After all, they *had* been getting mixed signals.

"I understand your feeling. Milan told us he heard Ana had died of a virus. Yet the doctor tells you she is in quarantine at the hospital and will be home soon." Rage glanced at Kateřina. "I do think you're right. I believe Ana is alive and is being held at the Cambridge Center." He glanced away. "We need to find her."

Kateřina smiled hopefully, wiping away tears.

Asking questions, Rage led her down every path he could and finally decided he had everything she knew. They had gone over the deaths of Marta, Kamil, and Ivan Relek, all of whom were loosely connected to the Cambridge Center. The circumstances of their deaths and the manner of how the bodies had been returned were of special interest.

Before either of them had realized, it was time for lunch. Though Kateřina said she wasn't hungry, they agreed she should eat something.

Combining talents, they prepared a meal. Kateřina directed the production from a barstool while Rage handled the actual preparation. Sandwiches and salads were easily within his range of expertise. Wanting Kateřina up and active for a few hours, Rage thought having her direct him in the kitchen was a good diversion.

To keep her involved, he asked questions about her life in Prague after he left, even when he knew the answers.

When their food was ready, he asked, "Would you like to eat on the terrace?"

Her smile was his answer. Then a finger came up to flip her hair back.

He gathered everything on a tray and followed her outside. When they were settled at the table, Rage took a bite from his sandwich and then asked, "Have you heard from your doctor?"

She picked up a carrot stick and nibbled at it before answering.

Without looking at him, she shook her head and said, "No, and it makes me afraid. I think perhaps no news is bad news in this case."

Kateřina glanced at Rage and then out at the trees. "This is an American expression, is it not?"

"I think the actual phrase is 'no news is good news.'"

By the time they finished eating and brought their dishes in, Kateřina was yawning again. Rage had decided she was struggling with a lack of strength and with depression. He offered to help her to the bedroom, but she wanted to try it on her own.

"I will call if I need you," she said.

She must have made it; he didn't hear from her.

Early that afternoon, Rage cracked her door before he headed upstairs. She appeared to be sleeping soundly. He smiled, happy she seemed better than the night before, even with the mixed signals about Ana.

When Rage sat down at the laptop, it was not yet time for the email from *Idona47*. Waiting, he pulled up last night's recordings of conversations in the van and phoned Marty.

His friend listened, translating the assistant's four phone calls, two outgoing and two he had received. One of the outgoing was to his wife again, the other to his office asking about an ongoing project. One of the incoming was the update he had called about earlier. The other had been Karel Vlasta letting Alexandr know he was on his way to the van.

Rage thought about almost getting stepped on last night when Vlasta arrived. The security chief had also made a call after he arrived on the scene.

The remainder of the night's recordings mostly covered Vlasta's conversation with someone at the airport. Marty said the security chief apparently had a contact who worked with the main data system, which included passenger lists. Vlasta was trying to identify Rage and the reason he was with Kateřina. The only thing they had so far was a mispronunciation sounding like "Raging," which the assistant had come up with using the long-range sound recording system in the van.

Finished with the translations, Rage said goodbye to Marty and sat back to digest the information.

Soon it was time for the internet meeting with *Idona47*. Rage had his computer up and ready for the communication he expected. Only moments after he opened his email, a message landed.

After passing the information through three decoding programs, he glanced at what he had. Rage turned his screen and leaned forward, his face only inches from the monitor. His attention focused on the information *Idona47* had been able to acquire.

The Eagle Trust was the first item on the list.

The Trust was formed in Cambridge, England, in 1983. There were nine unnamed original members, and the purpose of the organization, loosely put, was to do good throughout the world and specifically to do extraordinary things with the lives of the Trust's original members.

A narcissistic approach to life, Rage thought.

After those bits of information, *Idona47* shared almost every other detail about the Eagle Trust was secret. *Idona47* had been unable to locate a list of the nine original members. Research was mentioned but not in detail. There was still not enough information in the message to draw conclusions.

Prague was the city named as headquarters for the Trust, but the establishment of *Výzkumné Centrum a Cambridge Zdraví*—Cambridge Health and Research Center—was not disclosed in the original agreement.

Perhaps it was not in their plans at the time. Or it was, and the members didn't want its goals known, Rage thought. *I'll have to consider it both ways.*

He glanced out the window before returning to the task at hand.

Why wouldn't everything about the Trust be in the founding document?

Suddenly Rage rose up so fast and with such force, his chair flipped on its side and skidded across the floor. He moved to the window and looked out, thinking...

An idea had occurred to him that was almost too stunning to consider. It was an extraordinary possibility, completely out of the realm of ordinary thinking, and Rage wasn't sure where it had come from.

But what if... just what if...?

A few minutes at the window and then Rage turned, picked up his chair, and was back at the computer's keyboard and *Idona47's* email.

He carefully went through the message again. Rage paused, considering what he knew and what he didn't. He needed the names of those who started the Eagle Trust and what the hidden goals were for those individuals.

He wondered, *the Chairwoman, the person in charge here in Prague, could she have been one of the unnamed original nine?* It was easy to surmise this idea. And Milan had said she was in charge when he came to work there. So she had probably run Cambridge Health and Research Center since its beginning.

What else had she been running?

Milan had told Rage and Marty another interesting piece of information. There had been an article in Prague's newspapers at the time the President of Chile received her heart transplant. It stated the Chilean President had been a friend of the Chairwoman when they were at the University of Cambridge.

This could also indicate the two were members of the Eagle Trust. One might speculate the other seven members had passed through Cambridge also.

Since Rage knew the Chairwoman's name, Zuzana Balca, and could get the Chilean Presidents name, two of the original members of the Eagle Trust might just have dropped into Rage's lap.

Hmm…

Much to think about—a lot of questions.

Rage started a list he would email to *Idona47* later.

1) Get the name of the Chilean President.
2) Using this name and Zuzana Balca, delve into the two women's circles of friends in the two or three years before and after 1983. Search specifically for a group of nine who were close friends and perhaps even appeared to be making plans of some sort.
3) How was the Eagle Trust funded?
4)

He left number four open for the moment.

Rage started his email to *Idona47* and added to it, coding as he went. He was nearing the end of the material when he heard an unusual sound coming from downstairs.

He charged out of his chair and rushed to Kateřina's bedroom. Taking the stairs two and three at a time, he tripped and almost fell near the bottom.

The sound he had heard grew in intensity as he neared the ground floor. It was coming from the bedroom.

Kateřina was on the bed, but she was tangled in the sheets and didn't recognize him. In fact, she appeared frightened when he bent over her.

"Who are you?" she asked. "Where is Raegene?" Kateřina flailed both fists at him, trying to fight Rage off. Her eyes were wide and uncomprehending.

She had a great deal of strength for someone so ill, but he was able to corral her arms after a few moments. Speaking softly, he said soothing words, calling her name several times and telling her he was there to help.

Rage eased himself down to lie beside her. Finally, she calmed and seemed to understand. She was perspiring, and her skin was hot to the touch.

Several times she rubbed at her temples as though trying to rid herself of the pain. Rage wondered if he should try to reach the doctor who was treating her.

He talked to her, touching her arms and caressing her neck and shoulders. Over the next thirty minutes, consciousness and recognition seemed to come and go. She would appear to be sleeping one minute and awake the next. One moment she would know him and then she would be afraid of him.

Rage was afraid for her.

At last Kateřina seemed to overcome the stupor that had held her. Rage wondered if she might have overdosed on some medication or if the condition had been brought on by an illness. Neither possibility was inspiring.

Finally, she looked over at him and smiled. It was like she had returned from some far-off place. She was pale and exhausted. Kateřina was back though, and she recognized him.

"Would you do something for me?" she asked softly.

"Of course."

"Will you help me shower?" Her voice was unsteady. "I do not think I can do it without help."

He slid off the bed and reached back for her. Her eyes on his, Kateřina held up her arms like a child.

Rage slipped between them and lifted. She held onto his neck as he brought her upright. Once she was in a standing position, he moved her to his side and walked her into the bathroom.

The situation became complicated once they were there.

Rage had realized he would need to get in the shower with her, but both of them were still fully clothed. He decided to go first and then help Kateřina into the shower and out of her clothing there.

First, he eased her down on the side of the garden tub.

"Can you hang on for a moment?"

With a hand on each side balancing her, Kateřina nodded an okay and sat very still, obviously afraid of falling.

Rage was out of his shirt quickly. Then he kicked off his shoes and unbuckled his belt. Everything he'd been wearing was soon on the counter.

Glancing her way, he noticed she was watching him, but with a flirtatious expression accented by slanted eyes and with her head tilted that special way.

"What…?"

"Nothing…" A grin curled the corners of her mouth. She finished the thought. "I realized I've never watched you get undressed."

He grinned, his eyes dancing. "Well, you've gone to a lot of trouble to make it happen this time."

"Yes I have, haven't I?" Her grin was gone. "I'm sorry I'm no longer the girl you knew in the little hotel so many years ago." After hesitating for a moment, she added, "We have both missed something very special."

Rage stood still. "Yes, we have." Sadness was evident in his voice,

He got towels in place and opened the glass door before giving Kateřina an arm for support. He walked her into the large tiled shower. There was a bench long enough to lie on and shelves with everything one could need for bathing.

As he attempted to avert his eyes, she dropped down on the bench and began to undress. With his help, she was quickly out of her clothes and handed everything to Rage.

"If you are going to help me, we must get used to this."

He nodded, turning, and at a definite loss for words.

He helped her reach for the faucets and hold on to lift herself. Rage heard the water start as he carried Kateřina's things to the counter. He felt awkward. She had recently shared his bed, but they were not totally undressed there.

Turning, Rage had his first clear look at the beautiful woman he had left behind so many years ago. Just for a moment he questioned the wisdom of his decision. Both their lives would have been infinitely different if he had made her his first love.

She was turned away, a washcloth in her hand, preparing to step under the spray. She was still a beautiful woman.

Without speaking, he approached and encircled her with his arms. Hands cupping her breasts, she molded her body against him, feeling his desire and moaning softly as her own longing flooded her emotions.

Then she stumbled.

Rage held her tight as she regained her balance.

"Maybe you're rushing things a bit?" he said. "Perhaps I should stay close and hold on to you."

She turned toward him, unclad and unashamed. Her hands were on her hips as his were protectively poised to catch her if needed.

"Are you attempting to place yourself in a gratuitous situation, Mr. Doyle?"

Not completely sure of the answer himself, Rage could only smile.

"Well," he said after a moment, "that wasn't the idea at the time, but it does have its merits, don't you think?"

"You are still quick with your mind and your words," she told him and then added, "Not an unappreciated trait to this observer."

She stepped into his arms, each of their bodies longing with desire. The embrace they shared was one for all the years they'd been apart. Ending it with long sighs and remorse in their eyes, a soft kiss seemed proper even in their current state of undress.

"I love you," she told him.

"I love you too."

They both were smiling as she turned to continue soaping herself.

"Hang around to scrub my back?" she asked over her shoulder.

"Yep! I can do that."

They finished Kateřina's bath without further drama. Rage soaped her back when asked and held an arm when it appeared she needed the support.

When they were ready to begin the drying, Rage had expected he would steady her, and she would handle the actual deed.

It didn't happen that way. Wiping with the big soft towel turned into a group effort and was not without its rewards for both of them.

"Here," she said, passing him the towel at one point. Rage began, his eyes drawn to her shapely body. When he glanced at her face, she broke into a cute but sly little grin.

"Caught you," was all she said.

They finished drying Kateřina, and he helped her into a gown. Rage dried and slipped into the clothes he had been wearing when this all began.

The shower seemed to help gain back some of Kateřina's strength. She walked with a somewhat jaunty gait that had not been there thirty minutes earlier. In fact, it hadn't been there since the head pains struck.

Though she apparently felt better, Kateřina decided she would try to sleep for a while. Rage agreed the rest would be good for her and tucked her into bed with a parting kiss.

Scanning the internet after lunch, Karel Vlasta discovered his plan to make the contractor's death appear to be a robbery had worked better than he expected. The police were trying to tie the crime to another recent burglary and murder in the same area of the city. Newspapers and TV were keeping close tabs on the story since the current version involved two killings.

At 1:00 p.m., Karel was sitting across the desk from Madam Chairwoman for their daily meeting.

"Nurse Dusa has been a model employee since the incident," Karel told the Chairwoman. "Her face is badly bruised. Makeup doesn't come close to covering it. She is telling others she was mugged in her neighborhood."

The Chairwoman listened but had not commented, so Karel continued.

"I have put more guards to watch the restricted areas and the patient in her new location. The room where you had her moved is easier to watch. We also have a camera targeted on the corridor."

Karel had surmised Ana Bambenek to be the donor for the next transplant. The secrecy surrounding the young woman made it a logical explanation.

"What have you found out about Kateřina Bambenek's visitor?" the Chairwoman asked.

"My contact at the airport is having difficulty giving me an identity, even with the pictures and a partial name," Karel told her. "This makes me think he is someone important and perhaps involved in some secret division of the US government."

This surprised the Chairwoman. Her expression changed, her forehead creasing, and the corners of her lips turning down.

"Why would someone from their government be involving themselves with our hospital?"

Karel gestured with open palms.

"Perhaps he is just a friend of Kateřina Bambenek. It could be simple."

On Karel's suggestion, they decided to give the van surveillance another night and then temporarily halt it. Karel was concerned the van had been discovered. Music played constantly now in the backward facing rooms, and their subjects had recently taken their conversations to other parts of the house. The fact the Bambenek woman was ill could account for part of it, but who could tell?

The security chief had discontinued the effort to follow the Bambenek woman and her visitor after only a couple of days. He told the Chairwoman it would be too easy for Karel's people to be noticed. He said he did not want to alert the American visitor.

What he wanted was to have the individual available for his own planning.

The best Karel could tell the Chairwoman was he would report any information as soon as he received it.

"Get me an identity," she told him. "We have to know who we are dealing with."

Karel certainly got Madam Chairman's message. He would be expected to have information in time for their next meeting.

Long night, tonight, he thought.

There had been another evening with Pavia Balek in his plans. Given the manner in which the last one ended, Karel had been looking forward to a night of wine and desire with the Chairwoman's interesting assistant. Now there would only be a phone call of apology and regrets.

Back in his office, Karel called his friend from the airport. Not wanting to wait until evening, Karel phoned the man's apartment. The data manager was in a hurry, but a contact seemed to be on his list of priorities.

"I would have phoned you later this afternoon," he said. "I have news."

Karel was elated momentarily. Perhaps he would not have to make the call to Pavia after all.

Continuing, the man said, "I have his name. It is Raegene D. Doyle, but there is a problem."

Karel listened, his happiness quickly fading.

The man continued. "I was curious and tried to identify him using the name. There was not much info available." Karel's friend had been with the Prague police for several years before going to work at the airport.

"What did you find?"

"He is a trouble shooter of some sort." Karel could hear papers rustling. "There is no list of clients or anything of the sort. It usually means names are too important to be disclosed."

Hmm. We get a lead, but we then come to a deadend.

"Give me the name again. I will do some tracking of my own."

"Raegene D. Doyle," the friend said, spelling his name. "The D is for Dorryen. He has done work for the US Government, including the CIA. The lack of information could mean he is very important...or very dangerous."

Karel was left with an uneasy feeling.

"One last thing," the friend said. "He has a postal address in the mountains of eastern Tennessee in the southern United States. The address could indicate he is retired. Another alternative is he goes there to disappear from time to time. There may be friends in the mountains to protect him."

"Is this all you have?"

After a moment, the friend added, "Yes, but be very careful if you have to deal with him."

Karel turned off his phone and walked around to the leather sofa opposite his desk. With some thinking and planning to do, he lay down facing the window and closed his eyes.

So, who is this man we are dealing with, and does he pose a threat?

Karel realized he did not know the answer to either question nor did he have the time to find out. He quickly decided his own plan needed to move forward right away.

Karel thought of the Chairwoman. He was not prepared to tell her about the stranger yet. She might send him chasing details when he needed to have his own plans working.

"I will see her later this afternoon," he said aloud.

Karel locked his door. Tonight would be an ideal time to set his plan in motion. Henri could get things started while Karel was having dinner with Pavia. He looked forward to continuing where they had left off.

Moving back to his desk, Karel quickly executed the steps on his computer to take over and work from the powerful laptop at his apartment. He was pleased he'd had the foresight to set that up after his trip to Switzerland. Only minutes later everything was prepared for the operation and a coded note had been sent to an unusual location in Paris.

Surely Henri Chevalier would be checking his computer in the coming hours. If their plans went as expected, Karel could flee Prague and would never need to work again. For Henri's part, he would have the funds to buy his freedom. Perhaps they would even reunite for a drink at some point in the future.

Finished, he put in a call to Pavia.

She answered, apparently pleased to hear from him. She also seemed ready for another round which might end more favorably than the last.

Yes, she can meet me at 7:45.

Quietly closing the door, he turned toward the stairs and the unfinished email to *Idona47*.

When Rage opened his laptop, there was a short regular email waiting. Rage didn't recognize the name but immediately knew the sender.

"Are you okay? You ceased communicating in mid-sentence and sent your message as though something unexpected had happened. Inform us if there is a problem."

Us? Who would be us? Hmm…

This was the entire email. Rage would have bet the message could not be traced by the best hackers available.

To have communicated openly, *Idona47* was obviously concerned.

Rage coded and sent a short, reassuring message and then turned back to his thoughts and the list.

With the file open, Rage added question number 4 to the list: fields of study.

He anticipated a number 5 and wrote it down too: present occupations of known members.

Finished, Rage leaned back and wondered what he had missed. Experience had taught him there was always something more. Not knowing what it could be at the moment, he completed coding, closed the email and sent it on its way.

Then he called Marty.

"I spent almost four hours out at the *little* hotel," the big man said excitedly. "It's not small, and boy, is it luxurious. Great location, too. It's within walking distance of Prague Castle."

"Wh…?" Rage tried to ask a question, but Marty was on a roll.

"Remember, Milan told us Victoria Lancing is at the Cambridge Center for surgery. Well, guess what? Several people are there from Great Britain, an entourage of sorts. Her agent and her hairdresser and several family members, sort of hangers-on, I'm told. The hospital won't let them stay with Ms. Lancing at the Cambridge Center, so they're sort of taking a vacation. The hospital's driver said he's taken them all over Prague. The place they are staying is the Grand Luxury Palace Hotel. That's what it's called. They're taking up a couple of suites, and this place is pricey, but it's worth it. The hotel is beautiful. I got a guy to show me one of the smaller suites."

Rage caught Marty taking a breath and asked, "Were you able to speak with any of Lancing's relatives?"

"Of course, my friend. Do you think you're dealing with an amateur here?"

"I keep forgetting," Rage said with a sarcastic tone. It didn't seem to faze the big guy.

"There was a group of Lancing's people in the lobby having drinks. I walked in on happy hour, and then I slipped into my British accent, got a scotch on the rocks, and asked some questions."

The big man had a way with accents, but Rage wanted to slap him on the back to hurry the rest of the story. His friend didn't work this way. Rage heard him take a deep breath.

"Lancing's transplant must be coming up soon," Marty told him. "A couple of days, someone said. Maybe less. One woman seemed to know they already have a donor and most of her tests are complete. This woman was bragging it will be young organs Victoria Lancing is receiving."

Rage caught the reference to the donor being a female. He slipped in a question. "Did anyone mention seeing the donor or hearing a name?"

"Nah. I asked several different people about it. None of the Brits appear to know anything specific about the donor. She appears to be anonymous. They only know she's there and available."

Then Marty's tone changed.

"There is one interesting thing."

"What is it?" Rage asked.

"Victoria Lancing's almost gone."

"Gone?"

"Yeah, as in dead." Marty paused. "She's in bad shape—a drinker, a real lush. If she doesn't get this transplant soon, the consensus is she's a goner."

For some strange reason Ana Bambenek came to Rage's mind. *A strange time*, he thought, *for a thought concerning Kateřina's daughter.* But Rage had learned through experience to respect unusual and suspicious feelings. He only hoped his premonition was not a forebearer of bad news about Ana.

Thinking ahead, Rage told his friend, "I have another job for you,"

Marty was ready. He always enjoyed the chase.

"What is it?"

"See if you can catch up with Milan again. I won't be with you this time. He might be a little more open if you are alone."

"It's possible," Marty agreed. "What do you want to know?"

"I want Milan to do some investigating. Have him attempt to find out if Ana Bambenek did catch a virus and die, or has she just disappeared?"

"What are you thinking?" Marty asked, his voice moving down an octave, suddenly sounding very serious.

"I'm not ready to say yet."

If I'm right, Milan and Marty may learn more than we want to know.

Finished with the message to *Idona47* and having talked with Marty, Rage went downstairs to check on Kateřina again. At first glance she seemed okay. Then she took a breath. It was rough, hard to get in and out. Her skin was warm—probably too warm. Rage touched her cheek causing Kateřina to open her eyes. He thought about the way she had felt earlier.

"It hurts," she said, looking up at him.

"What hurts?"

"My head. It is killing me."

"I think we should get you to a doctor."

"No," she said emphatically. "They called while you were upstairs."

Rage thought he had heard her phone ring.

"I have an appointment for my test results tomorrow. I will go then."

There was nothing to be gained by arguing.

"Okay, no doctor," he said. "How do we help you tonight?"

She told him where to find her capsules. Rage hurried off to get the medicine and some water. Glancing at the label, he recognized the common mid-level pain prescription. Rage had used it himself on a couple of occasions.

His cell chimed while he was drawing the water for Kateřina. It was Marty again.

Rage answered and said, "I'll call you back."

"Hurry."

She raised herself to an elbow and took the capsule.

"I think I will stay in bed and try to sleep," Kateřina said. She glanced up at him, a concerned expression on her face.

Turning onto her side, she sighed and settled herself into a comfortable position.

Watching her for a few moments, Rage decided she would be all right for a time. He made sure she was covered properly and then eased to the door. Glancing back, she had not moved, so he quietly left the room.

Rage dialed Marty as soon as he walked into the kitchen. With the phone on his shoulder he listened while making himself a cup of tea. "Go" was all he said.

Marty was excited because he had received a call from Milan. He had talked with another nurse in the ICU at the hospital. They had hardly said hello before, but today they had communicated privately. Milan told Marty it had been a very interesting conversation.

"The nurse may have found Kateřina's daughter."

The nurse's name was Janalynn Dusa. The revelation communicated to Milan was she had accidentally discovered a female locked away in an unmarked room on one of the restricted corridors.

"Did Milan get a name for the female?" Rage asked eagerly.

"It was the first thing I wanted to know," he said. "Sorry, no name.""

Rage uttered an expletive under his breath. Quite unusual for him.

Marty probably heard the comment but let it slide.

"Anything else?"

"Yeah," Marty told him, "a couple of things. Both of them could be pretty important."

"Tell me before I come over there and choke you," Rage threatened.

"The locked room is in the transplant surgery wing."

"What?" Rage exclaimed. "Say it again." He couldn't believe what he was hearing.

"Yeah," Marty confirmed, "the transplant wing."

There was silence for several seconds as Rage considered the possibilities.

"What's the other important thing?"

"This nurse found the woman one night but couldn't get a response other than hearing her crying."

"Go on."

"Nurse Dusa decided to try and make contact again the following night," Marty said. "The woman in the room was obviously prepared. She slipped a letter under the door. The nurse had dropped her handbag as cover for the contact. The woman in the room begged for whoever was there to get the letter to her mother. Afraid she would get caught, Dusa gathered her things, slipped the letter into her purse and scrambled out to her car."

"So she made it okay?" Rage asked.

"Well…not exactly."

"Tell me." Rage was resigned to a problem.

Marty gave him the details as Dusa had given them to Milan. The accident, the assault, then regaining consciousness to find she had been robbed.

"Dusa wasn't sure how long she was unconscious," Marty added.

"Let me guess," Rage said. "When she woke up, the letter was gone."

"You got it," Marty agreed. "End of story."

"I…don't think so." Rage countered.

It was late afternoon. Kateřina had been awake for close to an hour. Ana and questions about her situation were always on Kateřina's mind. This afternoon had been no exception.

Believing Rage had told her all he knew, she could only hope for the best with a mother's faith. Though there were reasons to think otherwise, Kateřina was desperately holding to the unfounded belief her daughter was still alive. The news Rage brought about the Cambridge Center nurse seemed dark. Still, with no hard evidence of Ana's death, there was hope.

After a while she raised herself to an elbow. There had been no movement or noise in the house for a while. Rage was either being very quiet, or he had gone out. She would look for him later when she tired of the bed.

A plan had taken shape as Kateřina rested. She had decided to return to the hospital and demand to see Ana. With dread, Kateřina visualized the first time she was there. She didn't like the feeling of being escorted out and warned not to return.

She would not accept it again.

That visit was three nights ago. Dr. Laska had basically told her the same thing a day later. Whatever might happen now, she was determined to return. She was also resolved not to leave the hospital without answers.

Kateřina's immediate concern was whether to ask Rage to join her. Based on the previous trip, she could easily end up being incarcerated. If Rage came along, they could end up in the same lodgings.

With her mind focused, Kateřina eased out of the bed and reached for her robe. She glanced at her watch—already mid-afternoon. She found Rage staring out at the terrace from one of the rear windows.

Hearing her, he turned. They looked into each other's eyes. Then without hesitation, she walked into his arms and let him hold her. It was the closest she had felt to being secure since this terrible state of affairs began.

Finally, she leaned back in his arms and looked into those blue eyes. "I need to do something," she told him, "but you do not have to be involved."

"What is it?"

"I must find out about my daughter."

"You're going to the Cambridge Center?"

She nodded.

"Did you think I would let you go alone?"

"I…hoped not," she said softly and then nestled her head back onto his chest.

It was good she had mailed the letter to the Tennessee mountains.

An hour later, they were walking into the hospital. Rage had driven, and Kateřina had rested her head against the back of the seat for most of the way. She had pointed, giving directions though he had been there before.

Along the way, Rage asked Kateřina about a shopping center. She said there was one on the main parkway near the hospital. She pointed it out. He parked and went inside one of the general merchandise stores. When he returned with a small bag, she was resting.

Easing into an empty parking spot at the hospital, he came around and held the door for her. Kateřina seemed okay after a couple of unsure steps. Holding her arm, Rage guided her to the information desk.

Rage noticed she made a special effort to pull herself erect as they approached the counter. Imagining the difficulty Kateřina must be experiencing, he watched as she spoke to the clerk.

"My daughter is here. Her name is Ana…Ana Bambenek."

Even her voice sounded tired.

The clerk hit a few key-strokes, paused, then struck some more. She glanced toward them. Then she punched at the computer even more as she spoke to Kateřina.

"Are you sure you have the correct hospital?" the clerk asked. "I do not show a patient by that name."

Kateřina spelled the last name. Still no result. She was already disturbed.

Rage stood slightly behind her.

"But I was here just recently. The person here at this desk showed me Ana's name and information." Kateřina didn't mention Ana was in quarantine at the time. She didn't say she had been thrown out of the hospital either.

Rage leaned over Kateřina's shoulder while the clerk continued searching on her computer. When Kateřina glanced up, he whispered, "What was the room number when you were here before?"

She understood and mouthed it to him.

Number 1037.

Rage nodded.

Without saying anything, Rage moved away and sat down on a bench.

Kateřina continued with the clerk, determined to locate Ana.

Appearing bored, Rage picked up a local newspaper and pretended to read it.

Several people were waiting with questions, and the clerk asked Kateřina to step aside.

Dispensing with the others in short order, the clerk turned her attention back to Kateřina and then made a phone call. Motioning toward a hallway, the clerk gave Kateřina a slip of paper and sent her on her way.

Several new people entered the lobby simultaneously, giving Rage a moment to make his own move. As Kateřina started down the corridor she had been directed to, she glanced over at the bench again. Rage was not there.

Unnoticed, he stood up and casually walked down one of the hall-ways. Rage avoided security cameras when he could or did things to make it difficult to get a good view of him otherwise. The fedora was always useful. Rage knew he couldn't let them catch him stroll-ing up and down the corridors.

He came to a room with one word on the door: *Dodávky.* He was pretty sure it was Czech for supplies. Rage turned the knob and slipped inside. He had been right.

Moving down the second aisle, he found what he needed and quickly slipped into a starched white coat. Then Rage folded his fedora and stuck it inside his belt, making him look heavy through his middle. Next he put on a pair of reading glasses he'd brought from Kateřina's house. His appearance had changed significantly, but he wasn't quite finished.

A moment more and he had pinned on a badge he'd purchased at the store. He had been lucky. The name tag was about the right size and color as those worn by doctors at the hospital. One final touch—a towel casually tossed over his shoulder to partially hide the tag.

Back outside the supply room, he walked purposefully toward the hallway leading to Room 1037. After a few steps, he slid the glasses down on his nose. Now he could see where he was going.

Glancing both ways, Rage picked up a patient folder he found on an unmanned counter. Now he looked like any other doctor at the hospital.

Passing two nurses on his way, Rage smiled. They nodded but kept their serious expressions.

Rage wasn't sure what to expect when he reached the room. Ana had probably been there when her mother was at the hospital three nights ago, but it wouldn't mean she was still in the same room tonight. This was assuming she was here at all.

No one else crossed his path along the way. He breathed a sigh of relief as he reached the room. Again, glancing both ways, he turned the knob and swung the door open.

That he was able to walk into the room surprised him. Rage had expected the door to be locked. Then he saw the reason.

There was nothing in the space—no equipment, no furniture, no supplies, not even towels in the bathroom.

And there was no Ana.

Kateřina walked along the hallway until she reached a secretary who appeared to be guarding the area past her along the corridor. The woman took Kateřina's slip of paper and then dialed a number.

"I will send her in," was all she said before hanging up.

Motioning then to Kateřina, "Down this way to Office E. The doctor is expecting you."

The door she had been sent to had a name and specialty inscribed on it—Dr. Bruno Seifert, Psychiatrist. Kateřina tapped on the door. A moment later the doctor opened it and waved her inside.

"Please sit," he said gruffly and indicated a side chair. Then he sat behind his desk. "How may I help you?"

"I am trying to locate my daughter," she said. "I have had only one short call from her since she went to London."

The doctor had a blank expression on his face.

"Ana works here in research," she added. "Ana Bambenek."

"Ah…" He leaned forward, a slight smile coming to his face. "Your daughter is Ana Bambenek?"

Like he does not know! she thought.

"Yes, she is here at the Cambridge Center. I came here three nights ago looking for her," Kateřina said. "Your security people threw me out of the hospital."

He moved closer to the desk. "Go on."

She described the earlier visit including being shown on the computer that Ana was in quarantine at the time.

The doctor listened, nodding and asking an occasional question.

"I even asked if I could see and talk with my daughter, possibly through a window at her location. I was told I could not. That's when I tried to find Ana on my own and was escorted from the hospital."

He chuckled and said, "I am not surprised security took things in hand. There are areas off-limits and restricted to all but certain hospital personnel. I am sure you understand." He smiled.

Kateřina nodded, not wanting to argue her case with the psychiatrist.

"Now," he said, "about your daughter, Ana…"

He stood up behind his desk. All hints of a smile were gone as he gazed down at Kateřina.

"Your daughter is very sick, Ms. Bambenek, and she is in quarantine as you were told. We are not sure what she has at this time. Until we are certain, we must protect Ana and all those who come in contact with her. This is the reason for the quarantine."

"May I see Ana or at least talk to her?" she asked.

Her question received the same answer Dr. Laska gave her Wednesday night.

Seifert returned to his chair and then effectively closed the meeting. "I will personally keep you informed."

Dr. Laska had said the same thing.

Then he dismissed her with a few last comments. "Tests will be finished in a few days. Then we will know more."

As Kateřina stood, she asked a question that had been bothering her.

"Why is my daughter not on the register at the desk as she was earlier?"

He looked surprised, hesitating for a moment before answering.

"I am sure it is because she is not in a regular hospital room and is restricted from having visitors. It would be confusing to the clerks."

With this explanation, he walked her to the door and closed it behind her.

Thrown out again, and I still have not found Ana.

Somewhere along the corridor, a thought came to Kateřina.

Dr. Seifert did not give me reason to believe I have lost Ana. Actually, he gave me hope she is still alive.

Her steps came a little easier.

The security officer did not recognize the doctor moving along the corridor toward him. He knew many of the physicians by sight, but not this one. The man had a patient folder under his arm and was walking close to the wall. A towel hanging across his shoulder partially hid his identity badge.

Only intending to ask questions, the officer reached out to stop the individual.

Suddenly, the man was behind him with the officer's right arm much higher up his back than he thought it would go without dislocating the shoulder. Then a thumb was on his neck.

This was the last thing he remembered.

He awoke inside a stall in the men's room. He was sitting on the toilet and leaning against the wall. There was a sore spot on his neck, and his pants were around his knees. And he had absolutely no idea how he had arrived here. The only explanation was the individual he approached had carried him there.

Startled and groggy, he listened for others. There were no sounds, threatening or otherwise.

He climbed to his feet and pulled up his pants. Then he walked out to the mirrors where he checked for injuries to his neck. There was nothing visible, just the tender spot and a red mark about the size of a man's thumb below his right ear. His right shoulder was sore too and felt strained. He had no idea how long he had been unconscious. According to his watch and blurred memory, it had been several minutes.

Outside in the hallway there was no one in sight. The security officer felt alone in more ways than one.

When Kateřina returned to the lobby, Rage was waiting, a magazine on his knees and wearing his fedora. He stood and took her arm as they walked to the exit.

"Did you tire of waiting?" she asked. "I was gone for several minutes."

"I managed to entertain myself," Rage said. "How did you make out? Did you learn anything about Ana?"

"Yes," she said as they returned to her vehicle. "Let me tell you about it over a glass of wine back at my home. I need to think as we drive. I am quite tired too."

Rage glanced at her when they were in the car. Kateřina's head was back and her eyes were closed.

A second look revealed more wrinkles around her eyes than he'd noticed before.

Though it made no real difference, Ana did not like the new room. It was smaller and darker. There were no windows here, not even a thick frosted one. At least there had been light from that one. There was also less furniture here. Only a hospital bed, medical equipment, and two chairs, unpadded and uncomfortable and a few books.

Ana was sitting in one and trying to get through one of the books. She wondered if she would finish it before time ran out. Glancing down, she noticed her hands were trembling.

Little changes in Ana's own behavior continuously caught her by surprise. Like the trembling of her fingers, new and un-expected tears had a way of sneaking onto Ana's cheeks. Feeling them now, she wiped her eyes with an already damp tissue.

She enjoyed reading books and had always had one of some type in progress throughout adulthood. Now it was a few pages at a time. She had only read three chapters of a 300-page novel. It was in her hand, but she had not read a word in several minutes.

She still had the Bible too. Ana read a few verses each day. Her thoughts running unchecked, she wondered if her mother had re-ceived the letter. Ana could only hope.

She was still remembering friends and others. Ana would pic-ture them in her mind and say a few words before telling each one an individual goodbye.

Each hour Ana thought of things she wished she'd said in the letter, important things. Important to her at least, and perhaps, to her mother.

Ana wondered if she'd said she loved Kateřina in the letter. Memory was slipping. Her mother certainly knew Ana loved her, but that was not the point. Ana worried she didn't write it; she wished she had.

She wiped at the tears again, realizing she needed a new container of tissues.

There came a knock at the door, and it opened. Ana glanced over expecting it to be the nurse.

Instead, Dr. Seifert sauntered in. She hadn't heard his leather shoes this time. The psychiatrist murmured hello, motioning Ana to remain seated as he took the other chair. He began to thumb through a folder he brought with him. Ana's name was on the tab.

"It is almost time," he said glancing up, unsympathetic in his tone.

He could have as easily been telling her to have a nice day.

"All your tests are finished, and we have most of the results." He was immediately back to the folder, flipping pages. Glancing up again, he asked, "Do you want anything special?"

"Do you mean like a special last meal?"

He looked up again, holding her stare this time. She looked right back. Ana did not intend to go down easy.

"When is the big day?" she asked.

"We do not have an exact time."

"Oh?"

"Two or three days, I expect. Perhaps less."

Her heart skipped a beat.

"Why so soon?" she asked. "I was told two or three weeks initially."

"The other patient is not doing well," he told her.

"I am so sorry. We certainly need to hurry," she said. Then she asked, "Is the other patient a woman?"

He looked at Ana, apparently deciding whether to tell her.

"Yes, a woman," he said after a few moments. "Why? Does it matter?"

Ana didn't answer him.

Ever the psychiatrist, she thought.

He moved on to another subject.

"Would you like to sleep more? I can give you something if it would help."

"No," Ana told him. "I want to be aware of everything. I want every moment of my life."

He wrote something in the file. Then he stood up and walked to the door. Opening it, he turned back and looked at her.

"I had a visitor a few minutes ago."

Ana got a strange feeling in her stomach. She was not sure she wanted to hear what the doctor was going to say.

"It was your mother."

Ana would have fallen if she hadn't been sitting.

"Would you have liked to see her?"

She absolutely despised him. And she had tried hard to remove the emotion from her heart. She had tried so very hard.

"Of course, I would have wanted to see my mother." Ana glared at him. "Why did you tell me this?"

"I am a doctor, a psychiatrist. I study people."

He watched Ana for a moment. Then with his chin lowered and eyes drawn, he gave Ana a sly smile. "I am studying you. You and your mother make an interesting case."

The door shook for a moment when he closed it.

What he had said shook Ana's mind. Her faith in anything medical was gone forever—if it mattered.

Even with Rage holding her arm, Kateřina almost fell as they were going up the steps to her porch.

She glanced at Rage and with a trembling voice said, "I am so clumsy these days."

Once they were inside, he asked, "Are you sure you want wine?"

"Yes," she insisted. "I want to relax, and I need to tell you about Ana."

Rage walked her to the settees and then went to the kitchen for her wine. On the way, he turned up the music. He carried a tray back and handed Kateřina her wine. He had water for himself

"Ana is there at the clinic," she told Rage when he was sitting beside her. "As they had told me earlier, the psychiatrist said she is in quarantine. I do not believe him, but I do think they are holding Ana. Though I don't believe everything, Dr. Seifert answered my questions and said he would personally keep me informed."

"This sounds good, but you did not believe him? Why would he say Ana is quarantined when she is not?" Rage asked.

"As the nurse told your friend, I believe something sinister is happening there. Something that cannot withstand scrutiny."

"Did he say why you are unable to see or talk to Ana?" *So many questions,* Rage thought.

Kateřina told Rage about her conversation with the psychiatrist, attempting to leave nothing out.

"But if he's sincere?"

Her head shaking slowly and thoughtfully, Kateřina added, "If Ana really has something contagious, then isolation would be a proper precaution until they know the cause."

Isolation would also be a useful alternative if the good doctors are doing something else, Rage thought. *Something vile and not admirable at all.*

Though early evening, Kateřina said she wanted to go to her bedroom.

"I have a headache coming, and my stomach is feeling sick."

For several days now he had watched the headaches and the nausea grow worse.

"I will be seeing the doctor early tomorrow," she reminded Rage as he walked her to the bedroom.

"Good."

"I did not want to worry you," she said, glancing his way. "I also did not call you here to be my keeper."

Rage must have looked sad because she took his hand, pulled him to her, and kissed his cheek.

Smiling, she said, "But since you are here, I think I will let you care for me. Just this one time."

She started to smile again, but a grimace took its place.

Rage embraced her, kissing her this time, and it wasn't on the cheek.

She took his hand as they walked to her bedroom.

Turning back the covers, he took her sweater and helped her into her gown. Then he tucked her in.

Kateřina reached for his hand one more time. A kiss on his outstretched fingers seemed to make her happy.

It was time for Karel to toss the dice. Hopefully, he would soon be doing it for real.

Karel loved the casinos of Europe, especially the Monte Carlo in Monaco. He once read the same architect designed both the Monte Carlo Casino and the Paris Opera House. The classical style beauty of the buildings was virtually beyond compare. They each reminded him of historical European castles except the two structures were more beautiful than most of the castles.

Thinking of previous excursions, Karel loved arriving at the Monte Carlo after darkness had set in. The well-lit casino reminded him of a mammoth carved golden nugget on a pedestal overlooking the Mediterranean Sea.

What Karel loved most of all was the way he felt when he was there. The staff went out of their way to lend an air of importance to all their guests. They never failed to achieve their goal with Karel.

This was the sensation he was looking for now. He was betting everything on this one action. Whether he won or lost was in some aspect less important than the excitement of taking the risk.

Karel had spent the afternoon hours with his office door locked after his meeting with the Chairwoman. It had not gone well. Perhaps the one they would be having now would be better.

He called and asked if he could come see her. Chairwoman Balca grudgingly told Karel she could only give him a few minutes as she had plans for the evening.

She motioned him to a chair when he arrived.

"What do you have? Is this something involving Kateřina Bambenek's American visitor?"

She would not be easily pleased, but Karel thought he could do it this time.

"I have his name," Karel said. "Raegene Dorryen Doyle."

"What?"

He said the name again and watched her eyes light up. Then he spelled Doyle's name as she penciled it on a notepad.

She was obviously surprised. "Wonderful. Tell me about this man."

"He has worked for the US Government at some time in the past," Karel said. "Probably with the Central Intelligence Agency."

She lost her smile. "What else?"

"My contact thinks the little information available could mean he is or could be dangerous."

She appeared concerned now. "Dangerous in what way?"

"Physically, almost certainly," Karel said, "Otherwise, in any number of ways. He may have been one of the CIA's field agents."

She had her elbows on the desk now, leaning toward Karel.

"As an agent, he is probably experienced and trained in investigative techniques."

"Find out more. We cannot let him interfere with the operations here at the Cambridge Center. Our research must not be interrupted." She leaned back. "It cannot happen."

Returning to his office, Karel locked the door again and returned to his own work. Various financial accounts were coded and instructions were forwarded. Then the accounts were set to receive and transfer the funds Karel expected. The final destinations were scattered across Europe at various financial institutions in several different cities.

On his way out for the evening, Karel stopped by to have a word with his assistant.

"Is Nurse Dusa still behaving herself?"

Alexandr looked up and nodded.

Then Karel asked if there was anything new on the identity of Kateřina Bambenek's friend. He wanted to see if Alexandr had turned up anything new. The security chief was holding information close on the American. At this point, only Karel and the Chairwoman knew his identity. The assistant had not yet been made privy to the visitor's name.

Alexandr told him some of the same information Karel already had, nothing new.

The American was a dark mystery—almost. Karel smiled. He expected the American would be arrested in the confusion surrounding his own disappearance. That's if Karel didn't have to kill him in advance. Raegene Doyle might even be charged with Karel's death if he could arrange the proper circumstances.

Pleased with the way details were working out, Karel left to shower and dress for dinner with Pavia. He had high hopes for the evening.

One question Karel wanted to ask Pavia was if her boss had mentioned the Bambenek woman's friend. It could be useful to know if the Chairwoman was involved in her own search for the blackmailer.

He did feel a little sorry for Pavia. Karel enjoyed her company, and he would probably miss her, at least for a while, but he couldn't take her with him. He couldn't take anyone. No one, especially Pavia, could know when or where he was going, and Karel wasn't coming back.

When Rage had Kateřina tucked in and comfortable, he phoned Marty.

"Are you available this evening?" The Author had always been inclined to cut to the chase.

"Sure," Marty told him with a tone of excitement in his voice. "I'll have Jolana record our TV shows. We've probably seen them anyway."

Rage explained what he needed. Marty said he would handle it.

At 7:45 that evening, a large well-dressed man entered the lobby at the Cambridge Center's hospital. Waiting in line at the information desk, the individual struck up a conversation with a much younger woman in front of him. As they talked, and without appearing to, the man checked out the entire lobby and the hallways leading off it for as far as he could see. For future reference, he now knew where security cameras and guards were located.

The line stalled and after several minutes, the big man said he had enjoyed the conversation and told the young woman goodbye. He moved off to stand near the elevators. From there he had a view of corridors in all directions.

The hospital was busy with visitors coming and going. Also, it was time for a personnel shift change. Nurses, aides, a few doctors and numerous other hospital employees were coming to work or going home.

The man moved about the corridors with relative ease knowing some areas were restricted. Those were the locations he wanted to explore. He wanted to know where he could go with ease and where he might be challenged.

Obviously, the evening shift change was an ideal time to make this review. The man had reached almost every area he wanted to visit and had only been challenged twice. Even those were soft encounters where security personnel respectfully pointed out he was in a restricted area. In each case, he was directed to the public hallways.

Fifteen minutes of this was all he needed to make a map and do a report. With his assignment complete, the big man strolled to the front entrance and out to his vehicle.

Rage would find his report interesting.

They had both anticipated the evening together. Karel had different reasons than Pavia, but he didn't let it show. She appeared delighted to see him. He expected them both to be happy later.

Complimenting Pavia on her outfit, he kissed her cheek and hugged her close when they met. She returned the hug and slipped an arm around his waist as they were directed to a table.

A waiter came and took drink orders. Pavia asked for a glass of wine and Karel followed suit. Soon, their entrées arrived. They each savored the perfectly prepared fare.

Engaging in small talk, the evening seemed to slip away. Karel was able to casually ask if the Chairwoman had mentioned a man named Raegene Doyle. She appeared a little surprised by the question but thought about it and said no.

It didn't seem to bother her that he had inquired. Karel told Pavia he wondered if the man had made contact with the Chairwoman. Though Pavia had seemed a little surprised, she didn't appear to be suspicious.

Time seemed to slip away in everyday conversation about the hospital, and their everyday lives and experiences. A couple of hours passed, and then it was time to go.

When they reached the cobblestone sidewalk, she took his hand in a natural way that made it seem they had known each other for a long time. Within a few steps she had snuggled close to his side. Pavia had obviously enjoyed the wine and drinks she'd had during the evening.

Wondering if heavy drinking was something she did often, Karel looked down at the attractive woman beside him and slipped an arm around her waist.

Glancing up, she moaned softly, wanting more than they were allowed along the street.

After a few steps, she asked, "Are you going to get a phone call and rush away tonight?" Her words were a bit slurred.

"Not tonight."

"You are sure?"

"Yes, I left orders. I told them 'only if it is an emergency.'"

"How will they know it's an emergency?" she asked.

He grinned at her and winked. "I told my assistant any crisis requiring a call tonight should also involve a dead body."

She stopped and turned, staring at him.

"You didn't really say it, did you?"

Karel laughed at her seriousness. Her open-mouthed expression was priceless.

"No, but I did say I would kill one of them if it was not an emergency."

They both laughed this time.

Inside Pavia's apartment door, she stepped into his arms. She was very compliant. Their passionate kissing soon included touching. Then their clothes were coming off.

This time Pavia started the unbuttoning, but she didn't do it with her eyes.

First his coat was tossed on a chair. She tugged the shirt out of his trousers and then it came off too, one button at a time until she could open it.

With his chest bare, she stared into Karel's eyes, his neck captured with one hand. Her other arm and hand reached to the top of his chest, pointing fingernail extended and touching, dragging slowly like a knife…downward…*way down…*

By now, breathing was difficult…for both of them.

Anticipation is a mighty beast.

Pavia had dreamed of it that way. A predator hunting, then hiding and reappearing. Never quite out of mind, never really within reach. Waiting, and then capturing and consuming.

Now the beast was upon her. And she didn't want him to go away.

Karel had thought of her often since the first night when they'd met for dinner. She had a way about her. Now they had been together for an entire evening. They had spent time getting to know each other. They'd felt the lust, then the satisfaction of having each other's body.

Karel lay awake long after peaceful sleep came to the young woman beside him. His future twisted and turned in his mind.

Being with her without interruption was outstanding. Maybe he could take her with him after all. But no, this was not a decision to make. He would find another Pavia out there somewhere.

Everything was in place for the life he planned. Pavia might have a place in his future but not in the way she might hope. Her connection to the Chairwoman could not be overlooked or replaced. He would use it if necessary. He could leave the Chairwoman wondering what could come next.

The next few days would be crucial. He needed a particular set of conditions to give him a true hope of success. Those details could be coming together soon, possibly within hours.

Taking a deep, confident breath, Karel knew he was prepared.

Dusa had arrived with the other employees for the evening shift.

The bruises from her recent encounter were still evident, even under makeup. She wondered again if the thief had been after her money or the message she had planned to deliver. Deep inside she continued to think it was the letter.

She had been careful in case this was true. Had the offender caught sight of her in the restricted area and seen her slipping the papers from under the door? She had not given much thought to security cameras and restricted areas until she was mugged.

Now she noticed everything. Like tonight…

As she came in for her shift, there was a man she had not seen before in one of the restricted hallways. Dusa knew she would have noticed him because he was very large, and she thought he looked out of place.

Though the individual was careful, he was doing something that caught her attention. He had taken a small notepad from his pocket and made an entry on it. Then he turned and started back the way he had come. Even with the shift change traffic, Dusa had noticed and considered it strange for him to be there.

She would not report what she had seen; this was security's business. Though she had not talked to Milan since their conversation in the coffee room, Dusa considered mentioning the chance encounter to him.

She would be paying more attention in the future.

As an afterthought, Dusa wondered if anyone was watching her.

His cellphone rang a couple of minutes before 9:00 that evening just after Rage had checked on Kateřina and found her sleeping soundly.

He took the call as he walked into the sitting area at the back of the house. Music, almost constant now, played in the background.

Rage dropped onto one of the long settees and answered the phone.

"I have a nice map and some other good information for you," Marty announced.

"I need to see it."

"Same place where I dropped you off before?"

"Yeah."

"Twenty minutes?"

"See you then."

He closed off Kateřina's bedroom, hoping she would sleep through the short meeting.

Minutes later the doorbell rang. Marty was standing there looking nice in a suit and tie.

"Oh...I'm sorry. I was expecting my friend Marty Cutler." Rage stuck out a hand to shake. "May I help you in some way?"

"Funny," Marty said with a touch of sarcasm. "A fellow tries to help, and this is what he gets in return. My best suit too." He touched the lapel.

"Kidding. You do look very businesslike."

Rage led him into the house and asked if he'd like coffee.

"I would rather have schnapps," Marty said. "My second choice would be the coffee."

Rage opened Kateřina's cabinet and found a bottle of Marty's favorite liquor.

Holding it up for inspection, he asked, "This okay?"

"Pour..." Marty told him.

With drink in hand, Marty followed Rage into the dining room.

Marty asked for a sheet of paper and drew a map as he remembered the building and hallways of the hospital. His small notebook helped. He added security cameras and was quite detailed. Rage remembered that of him when they worked together.

"You can move into the corridors safely at about ten minutes before eight," he told Rage. "The new staff will be rushing in, and the employees getting off will be leaving. Visitors will be all over. It'll be crowded."

Rage was studying Marty's map.

Pointing, the big man showed him the places where he thought they might be holding Ana. The locations would probably be the same whether she was actually sick, in quarantine, or for other reasons.

"I want to get involved," Marty said. "It's been too long since I've had any action."

"What do you suggest?"

Marty had obviously considered the situation and had a plan. Rage thought it would work. One in, one out, and ways to make it happen. Not particularly difficult or dangerous, but they would still need to be on their toes.

"When?" Marty inquired.

"Tomorrow night," Rage answered. "It's a Saturday night. There should be more visitors than usual, and that will be to our advantage. If Ana is still there and okay, we need to get her out."

"Right."

"So," Rage said finally, "we go in a few minutes before eight while the shifts are changing."

Marty nodded.

"The more traffic," Rage said, "the better."

The big man agreed saying, "So The Author likes my plan?"

Rage smiled. Marty was so excited he virtually had sparks flashing off him.

Rage would give the plan more thought overnight, but unless he found a problem, it was a go.

Watching Marty's taillights disappear, The Author decided to take a walk. Careful entry into the trees and bushes behind Kateřina's house disclosed an empty spot where the van had been parked last night. This came as a relief to Rage after the several nights of the security van watching them.

How long would it last…?

1 2

SATURDAY, SEPTEMBER 26, 2015

$* \quad * \quad *$

THEY WERE UP AND DRESSED early. Rage could tell Kateřina was anxious. Her speech was rapid, and she had checked herself in several mirrors.

The appointment was set for 10:00 a.m. The oncologist wanted to discuss the tests.

Kateřina had asked Rage to go with her.

They were having tea and toast when the doorbell chimed above the classical concerto playing on the sound system. Rage glanced at his watch, 8:25 a.m. They were already running close on time.

"Are you expecting someone?"

Obviously surprised, Kateřina shook her head.

"I'll see," he said and headed for the door.

A UPS driver was standing on the porch holding an envelope.

As Rage closed the door, he glanced at the letter-sized package. It was addressed to Kateřina. He carried it into the kitchen and handed it to her.

"It does not say who sent it," she said.

"Open the envelope."

She did and pulled out three small sheets of note paper.

Kateřina flipped through them. Rage could see her face turn pale and her body slump.

She glanced up at him. "It is from Ana," she said. Her voice was calm, perhaps resigned.

Without saying a word, she slid off the bar stool and walked to a chair near the windows. There, Kateřina sat down and read the pages. Finished, she dropped them into her lap and turned to look out the windows.

Rage watched her from his stool. He could almost see her growing older before his eyes. Something had hit her hard.

He waited as long as his nerves would allow. Walking over to her, he picked up the message. It was written in Czech—not unexpected. He would have to let her tell him about it. He turned to the settees and sat down.

Neither of them spoke as time ticked away. He glanced at his watch, nearly half past nine.

"We should go," he told her softly. "You're due at the doctor's office soon."

The drive was silent. When they arrived, she touched his arm before opening the door. "When we return home, I will read Ana's letter to you."

As they walked into the medical building, she touched his hand and gazed up, focusing on his face. "I want to deal with the doctor before I consider Ana's words."

Rage nodded.

She checked herself in, and they were escorted directly to the oncologist's office instead of a treatment room. Kateřina obviously didn't see this as a good sign. She avoided his eyes. Rage was quiet, waiting.

They had just seated themselves when the doctor arrived.

"Dobrý den, Kateřina." He spoke in Czech and without a smile or any other form of assurance or encouragement. Then he introduced himself to Rage in broken English.

Turning back to Kateřina, he leaned forward a little and then began what Rage expected was an explanation of her problem. Early in the conversation Rage heard words he expected were probably medical terms - *Multiformní glioblastom.*

Kateřina seemed stunned for a moment and then turned to Rage, taking his hand.

"The doctor says I have Glioblastoma Multiforme." She explained with tears in her eyes. "It is cancer of the brain."

Then she turned back to the doctor.

His explanation went on for several minutes. Then the oncologist paused and glanced at Rage.

Kateřina turned in her chair and told him, "I have a bad cancer."

Each statement seemed to have a question mark behind the words. It was as if she couldn't believe what the doctor was telling her.

Rage lowered his eyes, then took both her hands. "I'm sorry."

"In English it is called Glioblastoma Multiforme, "she said again. "It is a tumor on the brain." Kateřina glanced at the doctor and then back at Rage. "Pressure is causing the pains in my head and also the other problems. I will let him finish explaining, and then I will tell you when we leave."

"Yes," Rage said. "Let him finish."

Kateřina turned back and gestured for the doctor to continue. She spoke several times, obviously asking questions. Occasionally, she wiped tears from her eyes.

Rage guessed they were nearing the end when the doctor glanced at him, made several other comments, and then leaned back in his chair. Kateřina spoke, obviously asking another question, and the doctor answered her.

Finished, she and the doctor stood up, and he shook hands with her. The oncologist then shook hands with Rage as Kateřina moved toward the door. Rage offered his arm, and they walked solemnly to the car.

She climbed in and leaned back onto the headrest. He heard a sob. Rage reached over and pulled her to him. For several minutes Kateřina cried softly there in his arms.

After a while, she dried her eyes and said, "Take us home, please."

The drive back to Prague 6 was quiet. It had rained earlier and started to sprinkle again as they came out of the doctor's office. The light drizzle continued most of the way to her house.

Kateřina didn't say a half dozen words, nor did she shed more tears. She sat still and looked out the window, deep in thought.

As Rage turned onto her street. He heard her breathe a long sigh. Now they were close to home and whatever peace she would have considering the diagnosis.

With the rainfall growing heavier, he pulled into the garage. Rage opened her door and helped Kateřina inside.

Dropping her handbag on the kitchen counter, she walked over to the pair of chairs near the settees. Rage eased her down and sat beside her. He offered a pillow to rest her head on.

"Tea?" he asked. "Or something to eat?"

Eyes closed, she shook her head.

"You eat something," Kateřina urged him. "You must be hungry."

He shook his head. "Do you want to talk now?"

She remained still for several seconds.

Perhaps she didn't hear me, Rage thought. He glanced her way.

She looked at him then, saying, "Yes, I think I am ready."

Rage steadied himself.

Kateřina pulled herself erect and turned toward the one person she could tell her innermost thoughts.

"As I said in the doctor's office, I have cancer. I told you what it is called."

Rage listened.

"The headaches are a symptom of the disease," she said. "There are others, too, such as the times I have stumbled and fallen. And dropping things also and when I have had trouble writing." There was a frightened look in her eyes.

Rage remembered she had mentioned having problems holding her pen. With Kateřina spelling the words, he had written a couple of notes for her.

She stood up and walked to the windows, remaining there for only a couple of minutes. Then she returned to the chair.

"I will probably forget things," she told him, "and I may become angry for no reason." She glanced at him, a sad expression on her face. "Please know it is not me. It is the disease." Then she stared down at her nervous fingers.

Kateřina continued. "The cancer is the reason I have been sick and losing my stomach. I have not told you, but I have been forgetting things often."

He didn't mention he had noticed her forgetfulness. There had been a couple of times when she failed to make tea right after she said she wanted some. The anger she had mentioned had come on several occasions when it was unexplainable.

Now he understood.

She stood up again and walked to the kitchen counter. Once there, Kateřina looked about as if searching for something. After a time, she shook her head and walked back to sit beside Rage. She took his hand in hers.

Glancing over she said, "It just happened. I forgot what I wanted."

Kateřina smiled then. "I hope I will remember later, and then I will get whatever it was."

"I sometimes forget, too," Rage told her. "A part of this is the years for me." He was trying to pump her self-esteem up a notch or two.

Rage waited and listened.

"There is much more, but I am tired now. I also want to read Ana's words to you. Do you wish to ask any questions about the cancer?"

"Can the doctor help? There must be some treatment."

"Perhaps," she said. "The oncologist and his associates are meeting this afternoon to discuss those possibilities. They want to see me again tomorrow to tell me what I must do."

She looked away.

"If I have no treatment, my life could last only a few months. Perhaps less," she added.

She caressed Rage's hand while looking into his eyes.

They sat there, not moving for several minutes. He remained quiet, letting her emotions settle.

After a while, she looked up, holding his attention for what seemed a very long time. Kateřina loved him with her eyes in a way only he could understand.

Finally, she said, "I wish I had written to you many years ago. I do not want to give you up now that you are with me."

She smiled at him again, this time with tears in her eyes. "I can only wish."

Kateřina was ready to talk about her daughter.

"May I read Ana's letter to you?" she asked. "There is much about it I do not understand."

He nodded. Rage moved to the settee and streached his legs.

Rage knew Kateřina had been thinking about the letter even as she was contemplating her own dire future.

She walked to the counter where she had left the pages.

Back beside him on the settee, Kateřina read Ana's letter aloud.

Crying by the time she finished, Kateřina looked at Rage and asked, "What does she mean? I do not understand most of it."

He asked her to translate the entire letter again, and she did, slower this time.

She searched his face as though the answers might be there.

Breaking it down in pieces, Kateřina asked, "In what difficult situation and decision am I involved?"

It was the next paragraph that had caught Rage's attention. Something about Ana "only now learning about her beginnings" and then about "details of Ana's birth Kateřina must not have known."

He asked her to read the paragraph again. Rage didn't tell her, but he thought he was starting to understand. Ana's words and thoughts fit with his own theories of what was happening in the shadows at the Cambridge Center. There was a reason certain areas at the hospital had such tight security. If his theory was right and she had known, he expected Kateřina would never have agreed to participate as a surrogate mother. Also, if he was right, Rage knew the doctors at the Cambridge Center would never have told her the truth.

Ana obviously thought this too. Now it was too late to change the past. "Ana couldn't," she had written in the letter, "and Kateřina *must* not try."

Why? he wondered. *Did Ana foresee danger for her mother?*

Rage asked to hear the rest of the letter again.

Kateřina read it, sobbing now and then as she did so.

When she finished, Rage stood and walked to the windows by himself. He looked out, thinking…

Hearing the pages shuffle again, he glanced back.

"She said she loved me at the end. Did you notice?"

He nodded.

Rage realized Ana knew the end was already in sight when she wrote the letter. They would never again have the chance to say those words while looking in one another's eyes. Ana obviously wanted to say "I love you" to her mother one more time.

Ana apparently had the power and ability to make some sort of decision, and she was making it for herself *and* for her mother. According to the last paragraph, Ana knew and understood Kateřina had been her only true parent.

Poor girl…poor mother…

He turned back to Kateřina again. She stood, and they walked into each other's arms.

Karel had used the morning to refine his plan. The last stop had been to check with his assistant. Karel watched the wall of security monitors for a while. Almost nothing at the Cambridge Center was out of sight for more than a few minutes.

Before he made his daily report to the Chairwoman, Karel went back to his office. There were a few more things to do.

The email Karel sent took a circuitous route to the library at La Santé Prison. Henri Chevalier had been alerted to expect this particular message. Upon receipt, Henri would take the next step in their plan. Ultimately, Karel's boss would receive a very special message. If all went well, the Chairwoman would then make Karel a very rich man. Even after sharing with Henri, Karel would walk away with a veritable fortune.

In the confusion, Kateřina Bambenek's American friend would be blamed for the blackmail being paid for the Eagle Trust's information. Karel had Rage Doyle set up as the fall guy for the perfect ploy. He chuckled as he leaned back in his chair, imagining the ways this would play out.

Karel had also asked Henri earlier to see if he could find anything on Raegene Doyle. Henri had found several small pieces of the information that had not turned up earlier.

The Chairwoman would be pleased to get anything, Karel thought.

The midmorning call caught Milan by surprise. Things had been busy. Scuttlebutt said a transplant surgery was upcoming. They were making preparations.

Milan had just stepped out of the ICU for a cup of coffee when he received the call. He glanced around to make sure he was alone and then moved away from the solitary security camera in the break room.

He let Marty do the talking.

"We need your help. My friend wants you to do some investigative work."

There were several seconds of silence.

"What is needed?"

"Watch and listen, maybe ask a few questions."

Milan went quiet again.

Marty broke the silence this time. "Have you heard anything new about the young researcher who caught a virus and died?"

Milan's attention level jumped several notches.

The first thing coming to mind was his recent conversation with Nurse Dusa. Milan had already told Marty about the note Dusa tried to deliver and her assault.

"Can you move around the hospital and listen?" Marty asked.

Milan made a quick decision. He could walk some of the hallways this afternoon and see if anything caught his attention. He had access to most of the corridors in the hospital, including restricted areas.

"I will call later," he told Marty. "Perhaps I will find something."

"Is it possible for you to phone me later this afternoon?" Marty asked.

Milan thought about it. He could walk out to his vehicle for the call. "Is five-thirty this afternoon all right?"

"I'll be waiting."

"It will not be long." Dr. Seifert had stated when he left Ana's room.

There was nothing for her to do now but think. This was not what Ana wanted. Remembering Marta Melcer, she imagined the two of them walking in the parks of Prague. As friends, they had been there often. Remembering those times was so much better now than the dread she was being forced to endure.

Knowing she could walk out at any time only made being here more difficult. Imagining she could leave but knowing she never would was maddening.

She thought of her mother. Ana wondered how much Kateřina knew of her past. She also wondered how her mother had been selected, and if there were choices involved. Surely Kateřina must not have known the mysterious perils and possible dangers facing each of them.

Ana considered the thought. There had never been any indication her mother knew.

There was a tap at her door, the sound of a key, and then it opened slowly.

The little gray haired priest peeked in, only his face and the hand holding the door were visible.

"Hello, Ana."

She had thought about his last visit. Why bother to get acquainted when she would only be here for a few days. Father Anděl had said he would answer questions for her and hear Ana's prayers.

She had not been very nice to him. "I have no questions," she had said bluntly, "and there will be no prayers for you to hear." He had suffered her anger and then left, saying he would be back.

And here he is, she thought.

"Father Anděl." She chose not to smile. "I thought I had seen the last of you."

"No, my dear," he said, "I am like a good dream, returning when you least expect me." He smiled at her then. His teeth had been yellowed by the cigarettes she could smell on his much-worn clothing.

"I have been told your time is near," he said. "Are there still no prayers?"

"None," she told him. "I am ready for this to be over. I will give what is destined for me, and then I want to be gone."

"And that is all?"

"Yes."

The sadness in the tired priest's eyes made him look very old.

Ana suspected Father Anděl knew much more about this place than he would ever say.

The Chairwoman was waiting when he arrived. Karel had phoned to let her know he had more information on Kateřina Bambenek's visitor.

"Again, his full name is Raegene Dorryen Doyle," Karel told her. "He is better known as Rage Doyle."

"What is his job?" she asked anxiously.

"Doyle is an intelligence consultant. I believe he is retired. He appears to travel and visit friends most of the time."

"Why is he here with Kateřina Bambenek?" She asked. "Is she a friend?"

"It seems they were lovers many years ago when he was in Prague for a short time. He may only be here this time to visit, but my opinion is he came here to help his friend in some way."

"Why does she need help?" the Chairwoman asked. "Is this because of her daughter?"

The Chairwoman had mentally stumbled. Karel was not privileged through regular sources to the information regarding Ana Bambenek and others like her.

Karel acted as if he was uninformed about Bambenek's daughter. He had dealt with the daughter's letter as if she was just another patient under quarantine. Karel also knew all about Victoria Lancing and the President of Chile. And he knew about the two young men and the young woman who had died earlier. Karel knew about them all.

He had other things to tell the Chairwoman. "I think the woman's concern is more than her daughter having a virus," Karel told her. "I think Kateřina Bambenek is ill herself. In fact, I believe she has cancer."

The Chairwoman sat up straight, her eyebrows lifted, an expression of surprise on her face. "Why do you think this?"

"Something was mentioned on one of our recordings. On a hunch, I had my assistant follow them this morning. They visited an oncologist's office."

"Did the American go with her?"

"Yes. This is why I believe he may be here because she is ill."

"Put the security van back in place," she told him. "Perhaps they have grown comfortable enough to say something we should know."

"I will have someone there tonight," Karel lied. Having given the possibility prior thought, he had no intention of doing that. Trying to oversee the surveillance and furthering his own agenda would be too distracting to handle either adequately. "I have been concerned and have not had our van there during daylight hours. It would be too easy for someone to spot us and call the police."

"Yes, I know," she said. "We must not have the authorities involved."

Early in the afternoon, Milan took a walk. This was not uncommon. He often strolled around the hospital's campus, but this afternoon there were rain showers and a strong wind. It was natural then for Milan to do his walking indoors.

Perhaps he would chance upon something he'd not noticed before. Over the years with his walks and natural curiosity, he had become familiar with and knew workers in most areas in the medical facility.

Milan had watched the Cambridge Center grow from six buildings, including the main structure, into the complex it was today. Though the entire facility was connected by enclosed walkway shelters, he had lost count of the individual structures making up the hospital. Twenty or twenty-five would not surprise him.

But it is different now. Something bad is happening.

Milan had given the present situation a lot of thought. Whatever sinister thing was happening now may have been going on since the beginning of the Cambridge Center. Close security on the research center had been there all along, but it had increased significantly a few years ago. Milan knew something had changed requiring the increased security, but he had no idea what it was.

He rubbed a hand across his forehead. Milan glanced at his watch and realized he had been walking for over an hour, going places he'd not been in years. Some were locations he had never visited.

In the research center, signs were ominous.

Entrance Forbidden
Must Have Proper Authorization

What could they be doing in there?

Even in the organ transplant ICU, security had been tightened at about the same time. The subject had never been discussed at his level. Milan had just noticed the changes.

A few minutes later, he had completed a circuit of the entire hospital, every hallway and corridor, and had wound his way back to his own general area.

As he strolled along a corridor in the transplant wing, a door opened ahead of him. One of the nurses came out balancing a small tray with a vial and hypodermic needle on it. She also carried a stethoscope and a portable BP monitor.

Glancing past her into the room, Milan saw a young woman sitting upright at the head of her bed. She had her long legs pulled up and arms clasped around her knees. In the moments he had to notice her, it appeared her eyes were downcast, and her blonde hair looked unkempt. The patient glanced toward him.

Then the door swung closed and the nurse looked at Milan, obviously surprised he was there.

"New patient?" he asked in passing.

The nurse's eyes darted to his face. "Yes."

Milan waited, but she didn't offer more. Without being obvious, he noted this was Room 1011 and walked on.

Behind him, Milan heard the nurse lock the door. *This was unusual.*

There was significant activity in the nearby halls, various medical types passing as they went about their duties. Milan had worked there for years and could tell preparations were underway for transplant surgery, probably in a day or two judging by the activity. Action in the area became intense as surgery drew close. There was not yet the air of tension accompanying the short hours before and after the actual surgery.

The rumors were right again.

The only transplant patient waiting was the entertainer from the UK. Milan had seen her a couple of days ago during his walk. She had not looked well at the time.

Walking on, nothing else caught his attention. He returned to the ICU and completed supplying the shelves and baskets he had been working on earlier.

Before heading out to the parking lot for his phone call to Marty, Milan checked the desk. There was no notice of an incoming patient or of an upcoming surgery. He was surprised at the contradiction to the hustle and bustle he was seeing.

Soon it was nearing 5:30 p.m. He headed toward the parking lot. Milan had information to pass on that Marty and his friend would find interesting.

With the phone call occupying his mind, Milan turned a corner and ran directly into a well-dressed woman. He almost knocked her off her feet. As he caught an arm to keep her from falling, Milan recognized Chairwoman Balca. He had not spoken with her in more than a year.

"Milan…" She recognized him too.

He knew his face must be very red.

"It is you, Milan." Gathering herself after the near fall, she was pleasant but did not smile.

The Chairwoman had been young when he came to work at the hospital.

In those days, she and I talked a lot.

He smiled. The two of them had mopped floors together. In those days, everyone did whatever needed doing…even the Chairwoman.

"How is Lidmila?"

She even remembered his wife's name.

They chatted for a short time. He hurried the small talk, wanting to get to the parking lot and his call to Marty.

The Chairwoman excused herself soon—a meeting to attend, she said.

As Milan walked to his car, the dark thoughts following him before were at it again. His mind went back to the young blonde woman he'd seen a short time ago. It was unusual for there to be a locked room near the ICU. Remembering the occurrence, the woman had appeared depressed in the moments he had to see her.

There really is something wrong in this place. Something very bad!

Thinking about his many years here, Milan thought his bad feelings went all the way back to the time the Cambridge Center's architect had been found dead near the furnace doors inside the crematorium. She had committed suicide. No one had ever said why.

He shuddered even remembering it.

I should probably tell Marty about the architect.

Milan couldn't shake the sinister feeling following him now. It was coming much too often.

Marty was antsy. Something was wrong. It was 5:44 p.m., and there was still no call from Milan.

When his cellphone rang, Marty punched the talk button hard. "Hello…hello."

"Dobrý den. I have information for you."

"Where have you been?" Marty was past being concerned.

"I ran into the Chairwoman," Milan said.

"So?" Marty countered.

"No, you are not understanding," Milan said. "I almost knocked her down."

He explained, and they both had a laugh.

Then Milan talked about his afternoon journey.

"I walked the inside of the entire hospital complex today. I was prepared to give up when I stumbled across something you need to know."

Milan told Marty everything he had seen in the room.

"Oh, one other detail," Milan added in an excited voice. "The woman is in Room 1011."

Milan then talked about the ICU preparing for a transplant surgery though their records did not indicate having one scheduled. "This is not the way it is normally done," Milan told him. "Something strange is about to happen."

"Milan, you told me the young woman was blonde and she was sitting on the bed looking depressed. Now," Marty told him slowly, "I want you to close your eyes and tell me every single detail you can remember about the patient again."

Marty gave Milan a moment and then finished off his requirement. "I want you to remember how tall she appeared to be, what color her eyes are. I even want to know if she had lines in her face. I want every little detail about the woman in Room 1011."

For several seconds, there was no sound on Milan's end of the call. Then he gave Marty everything he had asked for.

Marty issued some instructions. "Watch the transplant area closely. If there is any indication a procedure is at hand, get in touch with me."

Milan expressed his concerns about the hospital again and said, "If I can help you and your friend, you have but to call."

Finished, he surprised Marty, telling him about the architect's suicide.

Marty listened but made no comment other than to say thanks.

After his meeting with the Chairwoman, Karel returned to his office. Circumstances were in place for him to prepare Doyle's computer. Karel was aware this particular notebook was not an average laptop. He used one like it.

Expecting this day would come, Karel had given Henri the task of obtaining the American's IP address for his laptop computer. It had taken some time, but Karel's old friend had sent the information along to him in a coded email message.

With the material Henri provided, Karel began by connecting to the internet. Doyle's equipment had a number of manufacturer-installed features making the chore he planned difficult, but Karel moved along at a steady pace. He'd had a great teacher in Henri Chevalier, and Karel had been a gifted student.

His first forty minutes were spent working his way into Doyle's computer and making sure he was not using it at the present time. He also needed to be sure the American had not set any traps or alerts to keep anyone from attempting what Karel was about to do.

In reality, it was easier than Karel expected.

Obviously Bambenek's visitor is not an expert on computers.

Karel cruised quickly through the list of items he wanted to accomplish on Doyle's computer. It was so simple he smiled most of the time. With his chores completed, Karel carefully worked his way out of the computer. Just in case Doyle was better than Karel thought, he took great pains to make sure there were no telltale signs left behind.

Finished, Karel stood up and paced to the window and back a few times. All the while his mind was reeling with questions regarding anything he could have missed. Nothing jumped to his attention.

Marty called the moment he broke the connection with Milan. Rage was waiting, and Marty shared Milan's updates before they went over their plans for the evening. Ideally, the two men planned to locate and remove Kateřina's daughter from the Cambridge Center's transplant wing. Milan's information would help immensely, especially the room number. Rage couldn't wait to reach Ana's location.

Marty asked, "We're gonna get some action, right?"

Never one for excessive words, Rage countered, "Probably."

Kateřina had been at the forefront of his attention at the same time he was planning to rescue her daughter. She'd been sick since they had returned from the oncologist's office. A debilitating stomach problem was coming on as the evening drew near.

Growing worse by the hour, Rage recognized he couldn't leave Kateřina alone while he and Marty went to the Cambridge Center. Someone would have to be with her. Rage could only come up with one name.

Kateřina knew he was planning to go out, and he had told her where he was going. They had not specifically discussed what he would be doing.

"You need someone with you," he told her. "You should call Adina."

She looked at him for a moment before pulling herself upright and reaching for her phone. Holding it close, Kateřina punched in the number.

The stomach problem must be bad, Rage thought as he watched her. She had stayed close to her bathroom most of the afternoon. He had heard her trying to vomit several times.

She reached her new friend, and Rage attempted to listen as they spoke

"Adina?" Then she slipped into Czech. The conversation between the two women was short, but he heard his name mentioned a couple of times.

"Adina will come this evening," she told him. "Will six o'clock be early enough?"

When he nodded, Kateřina added, "She will stay until you return."

When Adina pulled out of her driveway she noticed a white Volvo with a damaged left front fender parked down the street. Giving it no particular thought, she had her mind on the evening with Kateřina. Traffic was light and Adina was making good time until she came upon an accident. With nothing to do but wait, she happened to glance in her mirror. Four vehicles back was a white Volvo.

Almost immediately, she dismissed thoughts it might be the same one she had noticed in her neighborhood. Traffic began moving slowly and she was on her way again. As Adina reached Kateřina's street and made a turn, she noticed headlights behind her in the quiet community. Something made her glance back. The headlights she'd seen appeared to be the Volvo again. And there was a damaged fender.

A chill ran down her spine. *Could someone be following me? Why would they?*

As Adina pulled into Kateřina's driveway, the car giving her concern swung into a driveway down the street and its lights went dark. She breathed a sigh of relief, and the incident slipped from her mind.

The Volvo set there for several minutes. Adina had closed Kateřina's front door when the car backed out and repositioned several hundred meters further along the street with hedges hiding it there.

Adina arrived on time and was sitting near Kateřina's bed when Rage left them. Kateřina smiled after him and waved a subdued goodbye as he went outside to wait.

Before Marty's latest conversation with Milan, Rage had told him to ask for a couple of patient's names. With those, the two intruders could sound legitimate when they approached the information desk. True to form, The Author was already out ahead of the mission.

Marty picked him up in a rented car at 7:00 p.m. At Rage's suggestion, Marty had used an assumed name so the vehicle could be abandoned if necessary.

As Rage climbed in, he glanced into the back floorboard. There were two bags of flowers and also two small radios on the seat.

"Got everything?" he asked.

"Everything but the kitchen sink," Marty quipped, adding, "Jolana wouldn't let me bring the sink."

Rage glanced over and grinned. Same old Marty Mayhem Cutler.

"Did you prep the tape?"

"I did."

They were carrying tape for use if they found Ana and needed binding to keep her quiet.

They discussed a set of signals for radio communications and went over their plan one last time as Marty drove toward the hospital.

Rage stopped Marty and climbed out before they reached the driveway to the employee's parking lot. The maneuver was close to the entrance yet reasonably inconspicuous.

The Author slipped one of the radios into his pocket, reached for a bag of flowers and headed for the lobby. Rage's Walther PPK pistol was in his belt.

The mission was on.

Walking casually, Rage went directly to the counter to ask for his patient's name.

Timing was right—visitors were lined up and numerous others were standing about the lobby in conversation. There were even some medical types entering and leaving by the front entrance. Rage waited his turn and watched the action in the lobby. The night shift change was in full progress. He glanced at his watch—7:45 p.m, just right for the 8:00 rush.

Timing was important, and the two former operatives had agreed on a specified duration for their mission to find Ana. Rage clicked his radio once as he left the information counter. The signal began their prearranged operation time—twenty-five minutes and counting.

Marty had suggested a route out of the transplant building if they found Ana. He had marked it on the map. Their parked vehicle would only be a few meters from this particular exit.

Rage hoped the patient's name Milan picked for him would be near the corridor housing Room 1011. Unfortunately, it was in another corridor. Marty hadn't thought to specify the locations. This wasn't the first time The Author had to improvise at the last minute on a mission.

Checking the signage, Rage moved purposefully toward the corridor he needed. His confident walk and the flowers he carried made it appear he would be visiting a patient.

As he entered the correct corridor, two tall nurses with a patient on a gurney came toward Rage. They were followed by a third nurse walking behind but apparently with them.

The nurse held up a hand stopping Rage.

"*Zde nejsou povoleny.*"

He had no idea what she said and had to do some quick thinking. Rage knew he wasn't allowed here and expected the nurse did too.

"Do you speak English?" he asked.

She spoke with a heavy accent. "A lit'tal."

"Ah…"

Remembering Kateřina's conversation with the Center's psychiatrist, he told the nurse, "I am meeting Dr. Seifert here."

She gave him a disapproving look but nodded slightly and hurried on to catch up with the gurney. As Rage turned the corner, he glanced back. She was watching him. He waved and tipped his fedora.

Raising her chin, she said something and then turned away and continued along the corridor. He could almost hear the *harrumph*.

Rage checked the room numbers and breathed another sigh of relief. He was in the right corridor now and wouldn't have to go back where the nurse might see him. Room 1011 was coming up on his left. Without seeming to, Rage checked both directions in the hallway. He was alone—at least for the moment.

A hand in his coat pocket brought forth a very small lock-pick set. Turning the knob, Rage found the door locked as he expected. He was not surprised and immediately went to work. Using the flowers as a shield in case someone came by, he had the lock picked mere seconds later.

The door opened, and Rage stepped inside and put his tools away. Glancing around, it was evident he was alone unless there was someone in the bathroom. The blanket and sheets on the bed were rumpled. Disappointed, Rage listened and then visually checked the bathroom.

His thoughts were racing. *Where's the young blonde woman Milan had seen earlier?*

At a loss for a moment, Rage then remembered the gurney and the nurses he had passed. He was almost certain the patient on the stretcher was a woman. She'd had some sort of covering on her head. Rage had no idea if she was blonde.

Ana? Perhaps…but where were they taking her?

Running a hand under the bed sheets, Rage felt his heart speed up a beat. It was still warm beneath the covers. Someone had been lying there recently.

He glanced around. There were some books on a small table against the wall. A chair was pulled out. A writing pad and pen was also on the table.

Stepping over, Rage picked up the pad and held it to the light. There were indentations on the top page indicating something had been written on the one before it.

He lightly moved the pen back and forth across the marks. Rage recognized the closing from Ana's letter. Kateřina's daughter had been in this room.

Carefully tearing the page off, Rage slipped it into his pocket. Later, if he needed, he could compare it to the last page of the letter.

He quickly scanned the room. Nothing else caught his attention.

Rage checked his watch. There was still nineteen minutes available—not much time to find one thin young blonde woman somewhere in this very large hospital.

What are my options?

Unfortunately, gurneys didn't leave tracks on tile floors.

There had to be a way to trace three nurses, a gurney, and a patient. Where could they have been taking Ana? Could she be going for a test, or…?

Rage felt himself shudder a bit when he thought of the alternative.

He needed Marty with him to translate the language. Reaching into his pocket, Rage came up with the radio, clicked it three times and headed toward the lobby.

Marty was waiting, his face scrunched up—no smile—and looking worried.

"What is it?" he asked. "Are we in trouble?"

"Not yet." They walked across the crowded lobby avoiding security cameras. Standing side by side and looking in different directions, Rage told Marty what he had found as other visitors shielded them from security.

"I located the room. It was empty. We need to find the patient and hope it's Ana Bambenek."

"Yeah," Marty agreed, "and we better do it fast. I can't believe guards haven't been all over us."

"It's the shift change," Rage commented.

"Yeah," Marty said. "but we need to be out of here in the next few minutes."

"Any ideas on finding where they took Ana?" Rage asked. "I've about exhausted mine."

"Show me the last place you saw the gurney?" Marty said. "And walk a few steps behind me. Maybe the guards won't think we're together. I speak the language. I can occupy anyone we run into. You can point me in the right direction until we're in new territory."

Rage headed them back toward Room 1011 with Marty up ahead and watching. When they reached the right corridor, Marty glanced back. Rage nodded to the location where he'd last seen the gurney. Rage was about ten feet behind Marty as they headed into the unknown.

Sitting in one of the chairs, Ana had been reading the letter again before returning to her study of Bible verses. Somewhere along in her contemplations, Ana had settled on Psalms 23 as her favorite. Leaning her head back, a thought came. *It is certainly true I am in the valley of the shadow of death here. I can only hope God is watching over me.*

A knock interrupted her thoughts. When she heard the clicking of The Warden's leather-soled shoes, the second letter she'd written—the one to the doctors—was in her hand. Ana slipped it between the pages of the Bible, which she quickly placed on the table.

All five of them had come to Ana's room at the same time: Father Anděl, the two tall nurses handling the gurney, the head nurse, Ivana, and the psychiatrist. Ana already hated him for the smug way he obviously thought of her and others like her. She also despised him for the way he had spoken about Ana and her mother.

The two nurses helped Ana into a gown and settled her on the gurney. The head nurse gave Ana an injection, saying it would calm her nerves.

The others turned their attention away as Father Anděl said a short prayer for Ana. Then there was no reason for further delay.

The Warden announced, "It is time."

The little priest and Dr. Seifert left first. They had other places to go.

The nurses maneuvered a drowsy Ana out of the room and into the hallway.

Ivana was the last to leave. She noticed the Bible on the table with the folded paper sticking out. Curious, the nurse pulled the note out, opened it, and read the words.

Finished, she glanced toward the door. The nurses were starting to move the patient away from the room. Without a second glance, Ivana tore the message into small pieces as she caught up with the others. A few meters along the corridor, the head nurse tossed the waste in a trash container.

Ana, her thoughts quickly starting to cloud, had only a vague notion of moving along the corridor.

Time had become unimportant.

Everything was like a dream until loud voices drew her groggy attention. Then a jerking bump, and a vague sensation of falling.

The crowds of the earlier rush were starting to thin. The big Czech security officer wore a uniform and had a short well-groomed graying beard. He also had a loaded equipment belt which included a pistol. Standing near the intersection of four corridors, his eyes were scanning all directions.

The officer watched as Marty approached. A hand up, not allowing him too close, the man stood facing Marty and ordered him to halt. "Where are you going?" he said in Czech. "This area is off limits to visitors."

Marty was also a quick thinker. He motioned Rage to his side and spoke to the guard.

"This man has a relative here," he said in the Slavic language. "She was just brought to this area on a gurney. Dr. Seifert sent us here."

The guard looked Rage over carefully and asked, "Do you have authorization?"

Marty answered. He chuckled while motioning toward Rage. "Uninformed American. He does not speak the language. We are friends from the past. He asked me to come to the hospital and help him find his niece."

Marty glanced around and then engaged the guard again. "Has a gurney accompanied by three nurses passed during the last few minutes?"

The guard's eyes darted toward one of the corridors.

Marty noticed and sought to push the man's thinking.

"Dr. Seifert will be here soon. He will give authorization for us."

The guard's attention shifted back to the men in front of him.

Marty took full advantage of the situation. "Do you wish to answer to the doctor if the niece dies without speaking to her uncle?" He shuffled his feet and waited expectantly for the guard's decision.

After a short hesitation, the man pointed to the hallway where he had glanced earlier. "The gurney went to the transplant surgery suite—the third set of doors on the left."

Marty glanced at Rage and then back at the security officer.

"Then we are still in time. Are you sure that is where they went?"

"Of course," the guard said indignantly.

They walked a few meters before Marty turned and brought Rage up to date. The conclusion was they might already be too late. Pushing Rage ahead, the two former colleagues hurried after Ana Bambenek.

The double doors where the guard pointed opened into an equipment and surgical preparation room. A set of doors on the opposite wall were closing as Rage and Marty entered from the corridor. The nurse Rage had spoken with earlier was keeping the doors clear of the gurney.

When she saw him, the nurse's expression turned dark, her eyes slanting as her lips pulled tight.

Rage remembered her name tag read Ivana.

"Why you here?" she asked in her broken English. "Do you wish to make trouble?"

"No," Rage assured her. "This is my niece." He motioned toward the patient. "I wish to see her before the surgery."

"How do you know of medical procedures?"

He glanced around the room and through the doors leading into the next area.

"It is evident," Rage said. "I can see the surgical tables and set-up."

"You must leave now. You cannot stay here." She walked toward Rage making a pushing motion toward the corridor.

She was angry, yet unsure, and she also seemed a little scared. She had glanced at Marty several times. His size and his presence obviously concerned her. More than anything else though, she wanted them out of there.

She stepped forward and pushed Rage, saying something to him in Czech.

Marty translated. "She said they are preparing for a transplant procedure. She's concerned we may have already contaminated this space."

The nurse reached out for Marty's arm. Already standing in the second doorway, he stepped back and turned. Then he glanced at Rage…and winked.

Appearing to catch his foot, Marty—all six feet, four inches and three hundred pounds of him—fell backward toward the swinging door and the gurney. There was a loud tearing sound as the top hinge broke loose, bringing down the heavy door.

For a moment, Marty appeared to be regaining his footing—until he reached the gurney and its patient. Then it was all over.

The door fell, Marty went down, and the gurney tumbled over on its side. The noise was horrendous. Fortunately, the patient was saved by straps holding her fast to the gurney.

Ivana screamed words that sounded like a prayer. One look at her face caused Rage to doubt she was asking God for guidance. The woman appeared more inclined toward killing.

Marty was apologizing as he climbed to his feet. "*Promiň, promiň.*"

"*Zmizni!*" the head nurse screamed. She repeated it in English. "Get out!"

Marty was on his feet by now and headed toward the corridor door. The Author was right behind him.

Glancing back, Rage saw nurses lifting the patient and setting the gurney back onto its wheels. Obviously drugged, the young blonde woman appeared none the worse for the experience.

From the photos he saw of Kateřina's daughter, he knew they had finally found Ana.

There was no way to get her out of the building though. Too much going on and too many people were coming their way. Security would be there in seconds.

Marty looked back at Rage as they hurried away from the action. There was a grin on his face.

"I don't think the surgery will go off on schedule tonight, do you?"

"I doubt it," Rage agreed. "Now let's get out of here and try to stop it completely."

Others had come running when they heard shouting and the horrific sounds. Dr. Jirsa was furious. If possible though, Head Nurse Ivana appeared even angrier than the doctor.

"What a mess!" the doctor exclaimed as she surveyed the damage. "What happened?"

The head nurse explained, even using a couple of expletives in her dialogue. Nothing like this had ever happened on her watch.

"Who were those men?" the doctor wanted to know.

Again, Ivana explained as well as she could. The part about the uncle/niece relationship was patchy at best.

Frustrated, Dr. Jirsa started to walk away but then turned back.

Waving her arms about, encompassing both rooms and all of the equipment, Dr. Jirsa commanded, "Get this cleaned up and sterilized as quickly as possible." She then pointed at the door, adding, "Get this repaired too."

Then, stepping over the door, she stomped away from the debris and along the corridor.

Looking back, she said, "The surgery will have to be delayed but only until this is cleaned up." Glancing at the gurney, Dr. Jirsa said, "Take the patient to her room and make her comfortable." As an afterthought, she added, "And have a security guard stationed at the door."

The nurses who brought Ana to the transplant suite now returned her to Room 1011.

Ivana took only a few minutes to organize crews to handle the work. Some were sterilizing instruments and stainless steel pans and trays. Others were washing and wiping down anything possibly affected by the calamity.

Ivana looked around the room thinking, it could take three or four 12-hour shifts to be certain they had found, repaired, and sterilized everything.

Ivana said it out loud. "I only hope Dr. Jirsa will be understanding."

Foot traffic, most of it hurrying, was going in the direction of the disaster they had caused. Rage and Marty kept moving along the corridor, through the lobby and out to the parking lot.

As they reached their vehicle, Marty observed they had run a little over on their time limit for the mission. The Author glanced at the big man, a bit of a grin on his face.

"Will they make a police report?" Rage asked.

"If you're right about what they are doing here, I doubt it. They wouldn't want anyone asking questions, especially the authorities."

When they were away from the Cambridge Center, both Rage and Marty took deep breaths. Though they hadn't thought it would happen, each would not have been too surprised if the police had been called and they'd been arrested.

As they drove out of the complex, Marty said he had an idea. Rage motioned for him to continue.

"Would the young woman's mother file a complaint?"

Rage was immediately interested. "Tell me more."

"My police friend who helped us with your weapon…"

Rage gestured for him to keep talking.

"…he might be convinced to go talk with the doctors."

Quiet for a few seconds, Rage was thinking. "Probably couldn't get charges at this point."

"Maybe not," Marty said, "but we might get them to turn her loose. Or at least delay the situation."

"They could hurry whatever they were planning."

"So what? Do we just wait and hope things turn out okay?"

Rage became quiet again. He was thinking of Kateřina and how he had left her. Apparently, she would lose her daughter if they did nothing.

Rage was very afraid he was losing Kateřina.

What an upside-down world.

"We shouldn't wait too long," Marty said. "How about if I just touch base with Officer Repa? He's a Colonel. He could be very helpful.

"Do it," Rage told him.

As Marty drove him back to Kateřina's house, Rage told his old friend a little about what was happening there. Marty seemed genuinely surprised and concerned.

"Someone is staying with her?" he asked.

Rage told him about Adina and how she was with Kateřina until he returned. Rage also told Marty a little of how he and Kateřina had come to know each other all those years ago.

Rage told him honestly, "We were more than friends."

Marty appeared to understand without judgment. Rage thought again of how fortunate he had been to locate the big man.

Dropping Rage off, Marty left to contact his friend with the Prague police.

Adina met Rage at the front door. They walked to the bedroom as she told him Kateřina was getting worse. Adina was very concerned. A routine trip to the bathroom earlier had almost resulted in a serious fall. A stumble had thrown Kateřina off course and almost into the tub. Fortunately, she had been able to grab onto a safety bar and save herself from injury. Adina had been nearby and helped her back to the bed.

Rage listened, feeling he should have been with Kateřina. He couldn't help feeling guilty about not being there even though he had been trying to locate Ana.

Kateřina was pleased he was home, but Adina had recently given her medicine to sleep. As Kateřina dozed, Rage walked with Adina out to her vehicle. The friend asked questions indicating she was aware of Kateřina's condition. The women had talked while Rage had been on his mission. Kateřina had told her friend everything.

Adina said she would come anytime and stay as long as she was needed. From her car window, Adina told Rage not to hesitate to call.

As she was driving away, Rage noticed a light-colored vehicle pass along the street in the direction Adina had gone, but he didn't give it any particular thought.

Kateřina was snug in her bed when Rage came inside. Sitting beside her, he ran his fingers along her shoulder and neck. Her hair was spread across the pillow framing her pretty face. Those eyes followed his every move.

She was beautiful, but he could tell she was slipping beyond his reach.

"Did you find my Ana?" she asked, her voice hardly above a whisper.

Kateřina had known about the trip to the hospital. Now she needed answers.

"We found her," he said. "She is still at the hospital, but she is safe for the present."

Looking at him, she took Rage's hand, kissed it softly and then lowered it to her breast.

"Hmm…" With a smile, she looked into Rage's eyes as if searching for something hidden there.

He loved this woman but agonized with feelings he had come too late.

Continuing to watch him, Kateřina seemed to be memorizing every feature of his face. She drew his hand close to her cheek and closed her eyes again. Rage could feel each breath pass gently across his fingers.

"Do something for me," she said, her eyes still closed.

"Of course."

"Prepare for the night and then come and lie beside me."

Leaning down, he kissed her forehead.

"I'll be back soon."

Kateřina was sleeping when he returned. There were tears on her cheeks. She awoke when he wiped them away and eased into the bed beside her.

"I dreamed you did not come back."

He understood her meaning, having left her all those years before and never returning.

"I won't leave you again," he told her. "No promises to break this time. Just know I'll stay."

She turned on her side and nestled back into his arms. Closing his eyes, Rage knew he would be here for as long as she needed him.

When he looked again, Kateřina had turned her head and was watching him with one eye, a smile accentuating her momentary contentment.

She turned to him, and her fingers moved, gently inviting him to touch them. He took her hands, cuddling closer to touch and to be close to the only woman he had ever loved.

He knew it, and she knew it. This was all that mattered.

1 3

SUNDAY, SEPTEMBER 27, 2015

* * *

MORNING LIGHT WAS CREEPING INTO the room when Rage finally closed his eyes. He hoped to sleep for a few minutes before Kateřina awoke.

She had settled down an hour earlier, having slept fitfully for short periods throughout the night. Moving often, she managed to stay close to him. Even in her sleep, Kateřina had kept herself in his arms. She called his name often, even as she turned and twisted.

Rage hoped she wasn't hurting, that the unease might only be a result of the medicine. He was concerned it was not the cause, perhaps something darker.

He had googled Glioblastoma Multiforme. The information indicated a high and rapid mortality rate. Rage refused to imagine losing her.

Finally, in the early morning, sleep enveloped him like fog sometimes covers a valley at daybreak. Like the haze, his sleep didn't last long.

Rage had been awake for several minutes before he opened his eyes. Kateřina was awake too and had turned and moved a short distance away. She was watching him, the slightest of smiles on her face. Without moving, he smiled back.

"Miluju tě."

He recognized her words.

"I love you too," he said, and he meant it.

Rage realized he had loved her since those few weeks they had spent together so many years ago. What a strange relationship.

He helped her out of bed, and they prepared to see her doctor again, this time for possible treatments. Kateřina would learn if she had a future today. Neither of them were optimistic.

The Chairwoman unlocked her office door a few moments before seven in the morning. She came in early even when she was working on weekends. This had been her routine since the 1980s when the construction project for Cambridge Health and Research Center's main building was first completed and occupied.

Chairwoman Balca sat down at her desk and immediately brought her computer online. She had almost been late this morning. There were a few things in the Chairwoman's world even she could not control.

The café she often went to for breakfast was closed for renovations. They were unfamiliar with her at the eatery where she stopped this morning and had lost her order. The Chairwoman had finally walked out without even a cup of coffee. Now she was both hungry and stressed.

Normally scanning the news and weather, this morning she skipped most of the news and all the weather. Only one item caught her eye. Though it didn't affect the hospital at this moment, it might in the future. This made it worth reading.

The conflict involving the Soviets and their earlier, and not so subtle, move into Crimea and now the Ukraine was of close and more personal concern to Chairwoman Balca. There were those who wondered if Vladimir Putin might also have designs on other European countries, including the Czech Republic. The Chairwoman was among the concerned group.

After all, the Czech Republic and Ukrainian borders are only three hundred kilometers apart.

Thinking of the possibilities only stressed her.

She checked. There was nothing new on the overnight news.

Scanning her recent emails, one captured her attention immediately. The message was in Czech and the subject line read: The
Eagle Pub, Cambridge, England, Circa 1982 - The Eagle Trust.

The Chairwoman's heart seemed to twist in her chest as she
gazed intently over the words. A chill was suddenly upon her, encompassing her entire body. She wrapped her arms in front of her.

Then she leaned in and read the message:

*I know about your specialized research and the acts you have com-
mitted at various times over the years. I also know what you are
doing currently.*

*Take note. You will receive another message within twenty-four
hours involving a requirement for substantial funds with instructions for their delivery. You will be required to act quickly when the
message is delivered. I assure you everything required is within your
immediate capability.*

*Make no mistake. This is serious. Your future and the
Cambridge Center, as well as Eagle Trust and its members, depends
solely on your actions.*

*You must contact no one regarding this matter, absolutely not a
single individual except the Eagle Trust's members. I will know and
act immediately and accordingly.*

*In such case, I will simply disappear. The world will then
be informed of everything transpiring since the early 1980s at
Cambridge, England, and forward to the present in Prague. This
information drop will include particular individuals and families
in countries across the globe, as well as everything involving the
hospital, the transplant wing, the research center, the Eagle Trust,
and its surviving members—everything—all your secrets.*

I Trust I have made myself clear.

I am here to verify you comply with all instructions.

The Chairwoman glanced back at the way "Trust" had been used
in the next to last sentence. It was an obvious attempt to be sarcastic and to make a point at the same time.

The person certainly succeeded.

The Chairwoman glanced at her monitor and realized there was no address for the sender. Looking further she searched for other emails like this one. There were none.

She doubted if this one could be traced, but the sender, he or she, had made one mistake. The email sounded as if the individual had recently come to Prague.

I am here to verify…

The mystery man visiting with Kateřina Bambenek immediately came to mind.

What's his name? She pulled it out. *Raegene Doyle—Raegene D. Doyle.*

She turned away from the desk and her computer, thinking…

He fit the situation: new in Prague, little known about him, and difficult to identify. There is also the fact Kateřina Bambenek's daughter is being prepped for surgery at the time he shows up.

What does he know, and how did he get his information?

The message had also stated substantial funds would need to be transferred.

I wonder what the demand will be? Perhaps I should set up a conference call? she thought. *No, I will wait until there is more information. The sender mentioned a second email.*

She glanced around, suddenly concerned with the security in her suite.

The office could be wired.

She looked down at her phone.

Calls could be recorded. I will have to use my cellphone for communicating.

She picked up her cellphone and then walked to the private bathroom. On the way, another thought came to mind: The sender had said "…all your secrets." This, she assumed, included her own.

The Chairwoman could feel a sheen of perspiration on the back of her neck. She couldn't fathom that her own secret could be disclosed for all the world to know.

She had held it so close. The remaining members of the Eagle Trust knew and a few others. Madam Balca thought of the initial research and how the clones had been carefully watched through the years. Now it could all be for nothing. The Chairwoman shook her head in sadness.

She closed the door to the bathroom, turned on the water in the sink, and then called the security office.

"Is Karel Vlasta in today? This is Chairwoman Balca."

Karel answered a few seconds later.

"Come to my office," she demanded.

"Now?"

"Yes, now."

Colonel Repa had not been on duty when Marty called the night before. Repa didn't answer his cellphone either.

The Colonel returned Marty's call very early Sunday morning. He suggested Marty join him. They settled on Café Savoy in *Mala Strana*, Prague's Little Quarter.

Marty was there thirty minutes later. Colonel Repa was waiting, sipping a cup of coffee. They shook hands.

Marty asked, "Can we talk off the record for a few minutes?"

His friend gave Marty a questioning look before nodding.

"I think a young woman is being held against her will at the Cambridge Center."

The Police Colonel was obviously surprised and interested. His wide-eyed facial expression belied his calm demeanor.

"Cambridge Health and Research Center?"

Marty nodded.

"Why?"

"We are not exactly sure," Marty said. "She may be the donor in a transplant surgery."

This startled the policeman. "With permission given?"

"That's the question," Marty told him, "and we don't know the answer."

"Who is we?" Repa asked.

"Rage Doyle and me." Marty told him. "Doyle is the man you arranged a weapon permit for a few days ago."

"Yes, I remember him. Who is the individual you think is being held at the Cambridge Center?"

"The daughter of Doyle's friend, Kateřina Bambenek. The daughter's name is Ana."

Marty ventured to tell his friend about the previous night's action. Repa listened, shaking his head when Marty finished. Any opinions he may have had, Colonel Repa kept them private.

Marty suggested the fact the police were not called might be a sign of unlawful activities at the hospital. The Colonel appeared to give it some consideration.

They talked for a while, but the conclusion was there would need to be a complaint for the Colonel to contact the hospital. There was also some question about the complaint coming from the mother since the daughter was of age, in her mid-twenties, and capable of making her own decisions.

Marty did get his friend to say though he had doubts, he would approach hospital administration if the mother would give him a letter of complaint. Repa sounded doubtful of getting anywhere with the staff or the Chairwoman, even with a letter. Colonel Repa indicated there had been previous complaints filed against the hospital without results.

They parted with Marty saying he would get a letter to the Colonel during the day. Marty hoped he could. He knew Rage's friend was ill.

The big man called, but it went straight to voicemail. He left a message explaining what he wanted, and he needed it as soon as possible.

Smiling, Karel had expected the call earlier.

The Chairwoman will be on edge, near panic, but holding it inside. She is already violating the main command of the email—contact no one outside the members of the Eagle Trust.

Karel wanted to be ahead of Madam Balca.

She will want me to find details about the email.

He smiled as he closed and locked his office door.

Karel already knew the particulars, every one of them. One of the most interesting involved newspapers in particular selected cities around the world.

Now came the interesting part. Karel would carefully convince the Chairwoman to do what the second email would demand. He already had the process organized. Karel was set to give up the information and have it look as if Doyle was the blackmailer.

When he ran out of details, Karel would allow the Bambenek woman's friend to be exposed—and killed. By this time the blackmail money would already be making its way through Karel's financial accounts.

He smiled. Karel would do whatever was necessary to let Madam Chairwoman discover Raegene Doyle as the individual demanding the funds in exchange for her organization's future.

He would lead his boss directly to Kateřina Bambenek's friend—after the money had been transferred.

Then Karel would dispose of Doyle for her.

Looking as somber as he had the day before, Kateřina's oncologist led them to a small conference room. Though it was early on Sunday, two other doctors were waiting.

Introductions were made. The woman was a radiation oncologist, the man a neurosurgeon. Kateřina told Rage they would be discussing whatever treatment she might choose. Both of the new doctors spoke fluent English.

"Would you rather have this discussion in English?" her doctor asked Kateřina. He glanced at Rage.

"Yes," she told them. "Raegene has agreed to be my temporary caretaker."

Her oncologist leaned forward and said, "Your cancer is quite advanced. With aggressive treatment, you may have twelve months. Without, three months or less. Even with treatment, it could be only a few weeks."

Rage reached over and took her hand. She squeezed and glanced at him, tears in her eyes.

"I cannot tell you these will be good times," the oncologist said. "Radiation will be difficult, but it will extend your time."

"What about surgery?" Rage asked. "Or chemotherapy?"

The neurosurgeon shook his head immediately. "She is too far advanced," he said. "Ms. Bambenek was too far along for surgery to be beneficial when the cancer was discovered."

"Radiation and possibly chemo are the only reasonable treatments," the radiation oncologist said.

Kateřina asked several questions about the effects of the treatments and whether she should have one or both. The doctors gave details and suggested having her receive radiation.

They answered all her questions and a couple from Rage. Kateřina's choice apparently would be to take the radiation treatments and hope for the best or not to take them and accept the inevitable.

Kateřina said she would decide.

The doctors all agreed a fast decision was important. Much of her time was already gone.

On the drive home, she turned and asked Rage, "Will you stay with me?"

"Of course."

"How long?"

"As long as you need me."

"Oh," she said with a sad wink, "that long?"

Marty must have been quite persuasive.

Closing the phone after returning this call, Rage shook his head. He was surprised Colonel Repa was willing to help under any circumstances. He had expected a cold shoulder.

Rage downed the last swallow of his coffee as he stood up. It was time to see if Kateřina had awakened from her nap. The doctor's visit and his prognosis had worn her out.

When he looked in, she appeared to be sleeping soundly, but it was more than that. Rage couldn't rouse her.

"Who are you?" she asked. Then she said it again as she looked him in the eye. "Who are you?"

"Raegene," he told her, "Raegene!" He shook his head. Then he gently shook her.

She didn't come around until he wiped her face and arms with a warm wet cloth. Then she seemed better for a while, knowing him and knowing she was in her own home.

Rage brought tea and crackers. Kateřina hadn't had anything to eat or drink since the prior evening. He worried about dehydration.

Marty came and Rage parked him in the dining room. Marty knew about the surveillance and kept his voice low even though the music was playing elsewhere in the house.

"Kateřina was confused when I woke her," Rage told his friend. "She's still having problems."

"Can she sign a letter?"

Rage knew where his friend was going. "I doubt it," he told Marty. "Besides, I expect there'd need to be a witness. Do you know? Maybe it's different here in the Czech Republic."

"What if I sign it?" Marty asked. "If you don't tell, I won't." Then he added, "I will let the Colonel know what we've done."

Rage stared at him for a moment, thinking. Then he headed for the stairs. "Come on. You can type the complaint letter in Czech. They might get suspicious if it's in English."

Marty chuckled. "Yeah, they might."

When he had the computer up and ready, Rage left his friend and went downstairs to sit with Kateřina.

She was more alert now.

Rage explained what they were doing and what they hoped to accomplish. Kateřina was pleased. She understood they were trying to free Ana.

Tearfully, she reached over and gave him a hug.

When the letter was finished, Kateřina signed it and then Marty witnessed her signature. The document was ready for the Police Colonel.

"I'll stay with him until I know the outcome," Marty said. "Let's hope we delayed them enough when we were there."

Rage heard Marty's tires chirp when they hit the cobblestone street.

Someone tapped on the door and then it opened. Madam Balca's secretary announced the security chief's arrival as he walked past her.

The Chairwoman continued studying the computer screen.

Karel sauntered over and sat down.

She glanced up as though she hadn't heard him. She still hadn't decided how much she wanted Karel to know. Especially considering the instructions. If she didn't want him to have everything, extreme care would have to be taken. It would be an almost impossible task.

On a hunch, she decided to chance it. Without help of some kind, she and the Eagle Trust could lose everything. This would not be allowed to happen.

"How much do you know about email?"

Karel's eyes widened and his mouth opened. It appeared her question had surprised him.

"A little." He appeared subdued as he answered her question.

Chairwoman Balca knew her own tone was low, somewhat depressed and angry. She decided to take a chance on anything being overheard in the office. Security, as a normal routine, swept her suite for electronics. She looked at her security chief, a focused and stern expression on her face. "This is for your eyes only."

"Of course."

She turned the monitor so he could see.

"What am I looking at?" he asked, apparently confused at her inquiry.

"A threatening message," she said. "Is it possible to trace an email like this to the sender?"

Looking at the screen, he said, "Probably, but not easy. If the sender does not want to be found, it can be extremely difficult. You might even need the use of a super computer."

She did not expect this sort of answer. "Can you do it, or do I need to hire a specialist?"

"Depends on the sender," he said. "If the sender is sophisticated, even a very trained and intelligent hacker may not be able to do what you want. It certainly cannot be done fast."

The more he said, the more depressed she became.

"There has to be a way," she said.

Rage looked in on Kateřina often for a couple of hours after Marty left to meet Colonel Repa. He sat and watched as medication settled her down, but each time it was taking longer to take effect. Finally, he stood up and walked back and forth across the bedroom. His legs were beginning to cramp from being still so long.

Kateřina seemed better. Her breathing had been steady for the last hour. The soft relaxed expression on her face indicated she was not hurting.

Rage decided to take a run upstairs and see if he'd received a response from *Idona47*.

There were several messages waiting but none from his mysterious friend and helper.

There was something else though. Someone had logged into Rage's computer and sent an email since he used it last. The individual had covered his tracks well, but Rage knew what to look for.

He loved working with deception when he knew it was happening. Rage smiled as he read through the message. Though it didn't show a sender, to a good hacker the message would appear to have originated on Rage's laptop.

Whoever's doing this is good. Hmm…blackmail.

Rage smiled. He was working undercover again.

He had enjoyed undercover work from day one at the CIA. Rage had been here before and had the scars to prove it. A finger touched the raised skin at the edge of his eyebrow as Rage thoughtfully studied the information he had discovered.

This individual's good but not perfect.

Rage wasn't perfect either, but he was better than the hacker trying to set him up for a fall.

He's planning to get rid of me when this is over.

Rage needed to see where this hack had come from. Who was trying to set him up—and why? He thought he already knew.

Timing was a factor. Rage needed to use this against whoever was behind it. If he couldn't handle it himself, and quickly, Rage would let *Idona47* have a go at it.

Marty sat across the desk and watched as the Colonel read the complaint.

"You witnessed it?"

"Yeah. No one else was available."

"It probably will not come up. I will go alone and try to get in to see Miss Bambenek."

"I want to go with you. I will stay outside."

"It is probably not a good idea after last night," the officer said. "Meet me at Café Savoy after I have been to the hospital?"

"Good idea," Marty said. "If you need me in the meantime, call my cellphone."

The Colonel nodded.

"Good. What happens if you are able to see her?"

"I will know if she is distressed. If so, we will deal with the situation."

"How?"

"If she does not want to be there, I will try to get her out. Otherwise, I will call and let you know the circumstances."

The Colonel went to the administrative offices at the hospital. He was stopped at the front desk by a secretary who appeared quite formidable.

Repa held the complaint letter where she could see it. He gave his name and explained why he was there.

"We have received a complaint." He described the details to her.

The secretary's face slowly turned red and then she stood up. She was as tall as the Colonel and probably outweighed him by 30 pounds.

Given her expression, Colonel Repa thought she might strike him.

Instead, with eyes slanted and angry, she said, "I will check with Dr. Laska's secretary." After a couple of steps, she turned. "I can assure you no one is being held against their will." Then she disappeared down the corridor.

Returning several minutes later, she was alone.

"The doctor is observing a surgery and will return in thirty minutes," she said.

"I will wait, but I must inform someone," Colonel Repa told her.

He went down the corridor out of the secretary's hearing and called Marty, telling him what was happening. Then he went back to the seating area near the secretary's desk.

Several minutes later, the phone rang on the woman's desk. She picked it up and talked quietly. When she hung up, she stood and walked over to the Colonel.

"Dr. Laska is back. I will take you to him."

In the doctor's office, Colonel Repa pulled out the letter but stated his case before offering the complaint.

Dr. Laska listened in silence until Repa was finished.

"I am sorry," the doctor said. "The woman referred to in your complaint is in quarantine and has been for several days."

Marty had mentioned the mother was told about the quarantine by a hospital representative. Colonel Repa was prepared.

"There is a witness who claims this woman was seen last night on a gurney here in the hospital."

The doctor retorted, "It's quite impossible. This woman has been unavailable for several days."

Then Colonel Repa pushed the situation, "I must see her. I need to know she is alive."

"Quite impossible at this time," he stated. "We do not keep a special room for this purpose. We have not quarantined an individual since…" he turned his eyes upward and pursed his lips as if remembering, "…since the early 2000s."

"This doesn't answer the question of seeing Miss Bambenek," Colonel Repa countered.

"It does in this case," Dr. Laska told him. "The room we are using is small and has no windows. It would be too dangerous for you to go into the space."

"Why?"

"Why...? Because we do not yet know the true nature of Miss Bambenek's contamination. While we think it is an extreme form of SARS, we are not certain. Only our personnel outfitted in special clothing may enter the quarantine area."

"Then get me a set of this special clothing. I must personally verify Ms. Bambenek is alive and here in this facility."

The doctor stood his ground.

"I cannot take the responsibility," he said. "You will need a release from your department for us to allow you into the quarantine area. Until you have such a release, I cannot help you."

Repa knew he couldn't get a release with only the word of a couple of intruders.

The doctor stood up before continuing.

"Now Colonel Repa, I have a previous engagement I must attend. Also, you may tell Miss Bambenek's mother we will inform her as soon as she can see her daughter."

The doctor ushered him into the corridor.

Marty was on his fourth cup of coffee when he saw Repa come through the door. He waved. His friend was not smiling; in fact, he looked disturbed as he joined Marty.

"Bad news?"

"Yes."

"I was afraid of that."

"The doctor in charge is sticking to the quarantine story."

Repa ordered coffee too. They were silent for a few moments, and then Marty asked about last night's episode.

"It was not mentioned."

"What can we do about the young woman?"

"Let me talk with some of my people," Officer Repa said. "I have a couple of young officers on the force." He looked over at Marty and winked. "Maybe we can do something off the books."

They finished the coffee and went their separate ways. The Colonel's last comment had given Marty a bit of hope.

When Marty returned to the house, Rage nodded toward the bedroom. "Kateřina is not doing well." They walked to the kitchen. "Adina and I considered calling an ambulance," Rage said, "but Kateřina said no. She told me she's not going anywhere until we have her daughter."

Opening the liquor cabinet, he poured Marty a double Sourz Pineapple Schnapps, then a cup of coffee for himself.

When Rage pointed outside, Marty nodded.

As they walked out to the terrace, Rage glanced out toward the woods in back.

The van had not been back the last few nights. Rage regularly checked the area where they parked, once late at night and again around midday to be sure. There were tracks when he looked earlier but no van. The same had not been true last night.

Rage led his friend across the terrace, and they seated themselves at the wrought iron table. In no hurry to discuss bad news, they sat in silence, dealing with their own thoughts for several minutes.

The sun was out, and a cool morning had turned into a pleasant afternoon. Clouds were gathering, though, and showers appeared inevitable.

"Any luck at the hospital?" Rage finally asked.

Marty gave him the details. Rage was disappointed. Against his better judgment, he had allowed his hopes to build. This was a letdown. He dreaded telling Kateřina.

"One more thing," Marty remembered. "It may not amount to much, but Colonel Repa is going to talk with a couple of his younger staff and see if they can come up with any new ideas."

Rage perked up a little. "Did he tell you more?"

"Not really, but I wouldn't be surprised if he sends someone in casually, as in undercover."

Rage was paying close attention now. "Would he do that?"

Marty grinned. "He brought down an entire Russian mafia group that way early in his career."

Interesting, Rage thought. "What kind of people did he use?"

"Not people," Marty said. "There was only one individual involved."

"He sent just one?"

"Yeah, and the individual had only been with the force a few weeks."

Rage whistled and then took a big sip of his coffee.

"Want to hear the best part of it?" Marty asked.

"Sure." Rage's eyebrows lifted as he looked across the lip of his cup.

Marty took a sip of the schnapps and scooted up in his chair, leaning his elbows on the table.

"My buddy got into a knockout argument with his supervisor and quit the force. He had only been with the police for a short time when the argument broke out. Some others who were there had to hold Repa to keep him from attacking the guy."

"But…?" Rage was trying to get his head around it.

"Let me finish," Marty told him. "After he quit, it took about a week for him to go to work for the Russian mafia. He stayed with them for two years. During those years, my friend's former supervisor received several telephone tips from an unknown woman. The information was always accurate and timely."

Appearing to enjoy the telling, Marty continued. "After a couple of years had gone by, there was a knock on the door at the supervisor's apartment late one night. When he opened it, a gun was in his face, motioning him to go inside. The supervisor didn't recognize the guy, but the voice sounded familiar. The assailant had long hair and a big beard."

Marty stopped and held out his glass for a refill.

When Rage returned with the bottle, he filled Marty's glass to the top and set the bottle on the table, hoping to save time.

"When the apartment door was closed, the gunman asked for a drink. The mystery guy's voice was suddenly that of the woman who had been calling with tips. In the same voice the guy said, 'You don't know me, do you?'"

Marty hesitated for a moment and then asked, "Want to guess?"

Rage knew the end of the story now. "Your friend?"

"Yeah, but the tale isn't over."

"Okay, go ahead."

"Repa wanted his old job back. In fact, he demanded it, and there were conditions and tradeoffs."

"Conditions?"

"He wanted facial surgery and a story to make him dead as far as the Russian mafia would be concerned. The tradeoff was he had information to bring a huge hit to the group in Europe, especially Prague and the Czech Republic."

Marty picked the glass up but only took a sip before setting it down again. Then Marty told Rage he was surprised the two had never crossed paths. Rage was too; he was fascinated by the things Colonel Repa had done and the risks he'd taken.

Then, thinking back, Rage realized he and Repa probably had been close a couple of times. In the mid '90s, the FBI Director at the time, Louis Freeh, had said the Russian mafia posed a great threat to US national security. Not long after, pertinent information was passed to Prague's police and on to the U.S. These particular details provided the tools to bring down local heads of the mafia in Prague and those in several other cities across Europe.

Rage had meticulously traced everything back to one individual who was a member of the mafia. Underworld gossip indicated the man had been executed, and his body made part of a new hanger foundation at the Prague airport. Although the foundation was dug up and crushed into large gravel in the search, whatever happened, the individual had disappeared without a trace. A body was never found.

"My friend, looking completely different, was hired onto the Prague police force a year later and has had an exemplary career."

"Interesting," was the only comment Rage made.

"Oh, and one more thing," Marty added, "The woman who had provided all those tips never surfaced again either."

Rage was quiet for a moment and then said, "Oh, I'm guessing she did."

The two men looked at each other for a moment with Marty breaking the silence.

"Yeah...you're probably right."

Marty finished off his schnapps and told Rage, "I have to get back home. Jolana must be wondering where I've gone. Okay if I catch up with you later?"

"Sure. If anything changes, I'll call," Rage told him. "Oh, and let me know when you hear from the Colonel."

He stood at the front door watching Marty walk to his car.

I'm glad he's on our side.

Glancing at the sky, he noted evening was approaching and hoped this would be a better night.

The cleanup at the hospital was going faster than anyone expected. Off duty employees were called in so others could be sent home to rest and return. Management also immediately hired additional maintenance people.

Dr. Jirsa stayed close to the surgical suite. Overseeing the cleanup and catching an occasional nap in the doctor's lounge, she had been on the verge of postponing the procedure indefinitely. Though tired and stressed from everything happening in the last several hours, Dr. Jirsa took a few minutes to check on her patient.

What she found was disturbing.

Victoria Lancing was in a chair by the window. Someone had obviously helped her there. Uncombed, her dull blonde hair hung across her shoulders. Eyes bloodshot and bleary, she was holding a short pencil like a cigarette and pretending to smoke. Victoria didn't speak as Hana felt her pulse and took a BP reading.

The doctor leaned against the bed and took a moment to look at Victoria. It was apparent to Dr. Jirsa the only reason the patient was here and would be receiving a transplant was her membership in the Eagle Trust. Any other individual would have been cancelled out of the transplant surgery. Effectively though, Victoria owned her donor, and Ana Bambenek was healthy and waiting.

Finished with her cursory exam, Dr. Jirsa compared her findings against Lancing's chart and did not like what she was seeing. Lancing's signs were deteriorating rapidly.

The doctor hurried to the surgical suite, surprised to find the area almost empty. Only a few of the cleanup crew were still working. The area and apparently most of the equipment and supplies were ready. The head nurse appeared and verified the doctor's visual inspection.

"What about the donor? Is she prepared?"

Ivana indicated the young woman was prepped and ready.

Dr. Jirsa suddenly felt invigorated and ready for the long and complicated surgery.

I can grab a shower, maybe even a quick nap, and get something to eat. If the surgical team is prepared, Victoria's transplant can begin within a few hours. She desperately needs this.

It was late, approaching evening when they came for Victoria. At this point, she had no will to argue, and no wish to say she had changed her mind and did not want the transplant. She was ready to go, one way or another.

She was given an injection to start the process and moved to the transplant surgical suite. Though she was slipping into a sleepy state, Victoria remembered making those critical decisions along with others all those years ago.

I did not imagine alcohol would become a part of my life in those days. Nor did I think I would become a celebrity...

She rolled her head from side to side.

...it just turned out this way. One led to the other.

Victoria realized in some ways she had been trapped by the decision she made in 1983. Through the years and try as she might, Victoria had been unable to disassociate the Prague research from her own downward spiral. It was almost as if she drank more knowing she had a way to overcome the results. Unfortunately, her ability to cure herself came at a supreme price for a young woman Victoria had never met or talked with.

There was no turning back as the injection she'd received a few minutes earlier closed her mind and spirit to consciousness and regret.

Vaguely recalling a fall of some sort, Ana had been in and out of consciousness for several hours. She also remembered nurses giving her shots each time she started to regain her senses. There seemed to be no way for her to rally.

She was in a room and alone again. She wasn't sure if it was the same or a different room. This one was virtually bare. Then she saw the bible.

Maybe I am in the final stages of the gift and parting the psychiatrist mentioned when I first came here.

A tear ran along Ana's cheek as she remembered Dr. Seifert's words. He had spoken them in their first meeting. Ana remembered being upset.

Then her thoughts were interrupted by a noise outside. The door opened and Head Nurse Ivana stepped into the room. She was carrying a syringe.

Glancing around, the nurse saw there was no one else present. She obviously felt Ana's hazy eyes following her. Sure enough, the young woman was awake.

Ivana walked over and put the syringe tray on the bedside table before she spoke.

"Hello Ivana."

Tears welled in the nurse's eyes. Though Ana wasn't sure why, the normally gruff nurse had a soft spot for her.

"Welcome…my only friend." Ana's greeting was only a whisper. Before Ivana could speak, Ana asked, "Is this the end for me?"

She believed the nurse would tell her the truth, especially now. Certainly now.

Ivana only managed a slight nod before turning away.

After a moment, the nurse walked into the bathroom. When Ivana returned, she was wiping her eyes with a tissue. She sat on the edge of the bed, something she normally did not do.

"We will come for you in a few minutes."

"Is this a difficult thing to do?" Ana asked. Then she asked a second question. "Have you done it often?"

Ivana stared at her for a moment, obviously wondering if she should answer. Then she appeared to realize it didn't matter.

"This is my fourth experience."

Then Ivana said, "This injection will make you sleep." She held the syringe up for Ana to see. "I doubt if you will know when we are here."

"That is good," Ana told her. "It is better that my last moments be with a friend."

Kateřina had been wide-eyed when Adina arrived earlier. The headaches were not coming as often but seemed more intense than ever when they struck. A particularly bad one early that morning had Kateřina practically tearing at her hair.

Rage was afraid of what he would find later that evening. When Rage knocked and walked in, Adina was in a chair by the bed. She was holding a Bible.

Kateřina was somewhat back to her old self, at least for the time being. She was even hungry. The women were discussing what Kateřina could and would eat. Settling on crepes and preserves, Adina left to prepare the treat. Rage and Adina were both happy their charge wanted to eat.

When Adina left the room, Kateřina suggested Rage get out of the house for a while.

"You must be getting, ah…" she shook her head trying to re-member, "…what do you call it in your mountains?"

"Cabin fever?"

"Yes. You are getting cabin fever. Take a walk…or go for a ride," she said. "Take the new car."

Probably a good idea.

Rage even thought of a destination, a place he would need to drive when he went out later.

"I won't be gone long," he said.

I can't be away from you for very long.

It was late when he climbed into Kateřina's vehicle. Rage had already decided where he wanted to go. He pointed the car toward the Cambridge Center.

Not having a particular purpose in mind for when he arrived, Rage drove west on the main streets until he reached the turnoff to the hospital.

He slowed down as he neared the Cambridge Center. Rage didn't turn in, choosing instead to drive past and into the maze of buildings located near the hospital. He circled back and then slowed as the main structures of the Cambridge Center came into view.

The health center really was beautiful to behold. Subdued lighting displayed the elegance of the modern glass and chrome wings on either side of the classic wood and stone structure that was their anchor. The Cambridge Center health facility was certainly one of a kind.

Genuinely unique in more ways than one.

He remembered something else he'd noticed on that first day—the tall chimney at the end of the second building. Rage had no doubt it was connected to a crematorium.

As he looked, there was something that had not been there before when he and Marty drove by. Rage had read modern day cremation only took three or four hours and did not produce smoke and an odor as it had in the past. There was one thing though, that could not be eliminated. It was the heat.

It was difficult to see from this distance, but when Rage slowed and looked closely, with the background of the trees against the night sky, he could see sparks and heat waves emitting from the chimney. Pulling to the curb, Rage watched for a few seconds.

Since trash would produce smoke and there was none, there was only one other explanation: a cremation was in progress.

Rage slowly drove back to Kateřina's. There was a lot on his mind. The heat waves from the crematory's chimney were firmly imprinted in his memory.

Rage understood it shouldn't have bothered him—he knew that—but it did. He also recognized there were many people in the hospital and a few probably died every day. Some were probably cremated.

But it was Kateřina's daughter he was worried about now. Rage didn't want it to be Ana today. The thing that bore on his mind was three young people of Ana's age and circumstances had already died, and Rage was pretty sure each had been cremated at the Cambridge Center.

Then he remembered something he had not asked Kateřina. He made a mental note to get an answer when he was back at the house.

Adina was in the kitchen preparing sandwiches when Rage came inside.

"Kateřina is now asleep," Adina said. "She was very tired."

"That's all right," he said. "I need to inquire about something. I can ask you."

She put down a knife, wiped her hands, and turned toward him. Adina appeared concerned about what he might want to know.

"Kateřina told me what happened with your son and the other young man he knew. But I was never told what happened to Marta Melcer."

She pursed her lips before answering. "Her mother was told she took an overdose of sleeping pills."

"Why?"

Adina hesitated again before continuing. "I feel as though I am betraying a trust."

Rage reached across and touched her hand. That was all it took.

"According to what I was told, Marta had been having trouble with a boyfriend," Adina said. "He was angry to her. Is this the correct English word?"

Rage tried to help. He wanted to be sure he understood. "The boyfriend was bad? Mean?"

"Yes, mean. He went out with other young women and screamed at Marta when she confronted him. Marta loved him. Ana told Kateřina there often were red eyes from crying when Ana would see her."

"So, Marta could have been depressed because of the boyfriend."

"Yes, but I do not believe she would destroy herself!" Adina exclaimed.

"Why not?"

"Because she did not like medicine. Marta would not take aspirin. I cannot believe she would suddenly take a handful of sleeping pills." She looked at Rage. "Do you?"

With all the deception connected with the two young men, Rage agreed.

Chairwoman Balca had been waiting for another email, drumming her fingers on the desk since noon. She had expected the message earlier. When it hadn't arrived by late afternoon, she was ready to hurt someone.

Dark was starting to settle outside when Pavia Balek knocked on the Chairwoman's door at exactly the wrong time. The young woman had papers her boss had requested early that morning. She had been called in on the weekend specifically for this project.

Pavia had never seen the Chairwoman so angry. When she entered the office, the Chairwoman shouted at her.

"Where have you been? I needed to have these papers so I could sign them earlier today."

Pavia tried to plead her case. "I did not get some of the material from the departments until this afternoon. People were required for weekend duty to gather the information."

It made no difference to the Chairwoman. Still shouting, she told Pavia if she couldn't handle the job, someone else could. "When I tell you I want something at a certain hour, you must understand and get your work finished on time. You must not be the reason your Chairwoman does not get her job done."

Pavia's eyes were red and misty, ready to cry.

"Do you understand?"

Pavia nodded and was turning toward the door when Chairwoman Balca shouted, "Tell Ema to get Vlasta up here."

Pavia nodded again.

"Now, get out."

The young woman was sobbing by the time Madam Balca slammed the door behind her.

As he came into the Chairwoman's office, Karel told her immediately. "I have someone working on a trace for the email sender."

"Can we trust your person?"

"Yes, but I only gave him enough information to start the search," Karel assured her.

He had done exactly that. He was going to let Alexandr trace the email to Kateřina Bambenek's visitor. Karel would have options to make changes. Maneuverability was important when you're stealing millions of korunas.

Madam Chairwoman cut the meeting short. Karel could feel the tension in her office.

As he left, she said, "I will want your input if another email comes."

"Oh, I'm sure it will come," he told her. "People do not send messages like this unless they are serious."

She caught his glance and held it, her lips closed and tight, obviously angry and determined.

The timing couldn't have been better.

Karel looked at her and said solemnly, "Madam Chairwoman, you do realize you will have to eliminate this person when we find him?"

"Yes." After hesitating for only a moment, she asked, "Do you have someone who will do it?"

"I will."

The next email from the unknown sender landed late that evening. The Chairwoman read it with trepidation.

The demand was staggering. Chairwoman Balca stared at the amount for over a minute before she was able to focus her eyes elsewhere. Finally, she turned to the windows as she often did when there was a crisis in her world.

When she looked back at the email, the amount had not changed.

One Hundred Million US dollars!

She was finally able to look at other details regarding timing for transferring the funds. According to the instructions, twenty million dollars should be deposited at each of five financial institutions scattered across the globe. Information regarding accounts and their locations would be available minutes before the transfers were to be made. The deadline was 4:00 p.m. local time, three days hence on Wednesday, September 30.

She stopped reading, already knowing there would almost certainly be no payment of blackmail. She and the other members of the Eagle Trust had the funds, both collectively and individually, but Chairwoman Balca could easily predict the five other members, like her, would never agree to deal with blackmail. The problem would have to be solved in another manner. Something more permanent.

The Chairwoman realized she would still need to deal with the threat. Some way, somehow, she would have to find the source of these emails. Otherwise, they might have to transfer the funds and then attempt to reclaim them when the blackmailer was identified and eliminated. Chairwoman Balca could fund the initial transfer from her own resources if necessary. This would need to be done if the blackmailer had not been dispatched prior to the deadline. Otherwise, they might lose everything they had worked for since 1982.

As a last resort, she could see them closing the Cambridge Center before succumbing to blackmail. It might be better to shut down the operation than to give in to the demands of a world class thief. This last possibility would need to be decided by all six board members.

But how could this ridiculous demand be handled? Well…she knew *how* to handle the individual, but she had to find him first. Chairwoman Balca understood there was probably more than one person involved. Right now, finding the thief or thieves was Vlasta's assignment.

Karel had said 'him'—a man. How could he know? Or was it just natural to use the masculine term?

The only threat so far was the individual who sent the emails had inferred certain things were known—information to which less than a dozen individuals were privileged.

With only a passing thought, Madam Chairwoman couldn't imagine the problem coming from any of the members of the Eagle Trust. The same was true with the few others who knew. They had too much to lose from a scheme like this—including their lives.

It had to be an outsider. Kateřina Bambenek's American friend came to mind again.

She glanced back at the email as her anger grew for the individual perpetrating this fraud. If this Raegene Doyle was here right now, the Chairwoman believed she would attack him physically.

She did have misgivings though. *What if I'm mistaken? What if it isn't Bambenek's friend?* If she was wrong, killing Doyle could only cause more problems and unwanted attention. She couldn't permit this to happen, especially now.

As the Chairwoman scanned the email again, a word jumped out at her—newspaper. Newspaper? What could newspapers have to do with the demand? She concentrated now, examining this part of the email.

"Google the Personal Advertisements for this date in the following newspapers: *The Prague Post, The London Daily* in the UK, *The Santiago Times* in Chile, *The Seattle Times* in the US, and Rome's *La Repubblica.* You will find information in each of the papers indicating the seriousness of this demand."

The Chairwoman felt a chill thinking of what she might find in those newspapers. Still, she couldn't keep her fingers from the keyboard.

The first one was her own local paper. The Chairwoman quickly found what she hoped she would not.

The ad read simply, "Continue to watch this space and its online version over the next four days for information including details regarding unusual, immoral, and illegal practices in the medical field at a world-renowned hospital by its founding organization and connected individuals."

This was all there was in *The Prague Post,* but it was enough. The blackmailer was serious and appeared to have pertinent information.

Madam Chairman googled *The London Daily* and found the same ad with only the wording changed to accommodate the language. It took her a few minutes, but she checked all of the other papers too. The same information was in each of them.

It was obvious the blackmailer was capable and committed.

Rage heard the two women talking in Kateřina's bedroom when he passed on his way upstairs. Their conversation sounded normal, even a bit cheerful. Adina was spending significant time with Kateřina now.

Upstairs when Rage brought his computer on line, he noted the hacker had been there again. Rage went deeper and followed the individual's actions all the way to the email sent from his computer.

It was written in Czech. Rage ran the entire message through a translation program. Finished, he leaned back to read.

The first thing he saw was the demand: One-hundred million US dollars.

His eyes glued themselves to the numbers for a few moments.

Whew! Big money.

Rage kept reading. He had the entire demand note on his monitor.

Three business days, Wednesday at four o'clock. The hours were already ticking.

The part involving the newspapers caught his eye. He googled the Seattle ad because it would be in English. When he finished reading, Rage glanced back at the amount being demanded and took a couple of deep breaths.

Serious stuff.

Rage had immediately recognized steps were being taken to blame him. The original email appeared to come from his own computer. This one would too. Someone was probably tracing it now.

On his side was the fact they didn't know he was following the blackmailer's every move. The hacker also didn't know Rage had *Idona47* on call. Though the blackmail message was urgent, he couldn't give it his full attention. Rage's most important goal at the moment was saving Ana. Until that was settled, the Trust and the Chairwoman would have to deal with the blackmail themselves.

And…Rage realized, he would have to be very careful. He glanced at the loaded pistol on the corner of his worktable. Reaching over, he touched the weapon with the tips of his fingers.

Just after noon the same day, a young woman had walked into the lobby of the Cambridge Center's hospital. She asked for the administrative offices, saying she was looking for a job. Anything would do. She had a young child her mother was keeping, and she needed to work.

The information clerk told her they were hiring for the hospital's maintenance department. There had been an emergency recently requiring extra hours for a big clean-up. A couple of their full-time laborers had quit.

"Go down that corridor." The clerk pointed over her shoulder. "Here, you will need this," she said handing the young woman a visitor's badge. "You will see a sign for Personnel. Go inside, ask for the supervisor, and tell him I sent you. Oh, and mention the maintenance issue."

Doing as she was told, Gita Kovar filled out their forms and tinkled in a cup. The young woman was issued coveralls and within an hour of talking to the information clerk, she was mopping floors in the transplant surgical preparation room. Gita was told she would be working through the night until 8:00 a.m. on Monday.

A background check was in progress, but they needed her working now and gave her a broom and mop. Thinking about the background check, Gita smiled, knowing what they would find.

They are desperate, she thought. *Last night's fracas must have been pretty bad.*

Catching comments as she worked, Gita learned more about the incident. She already knew that two men, both outsiders, were involved.

A gurney had been overturned breaking and spilling everything in sight. The mishap even dumped the patient. Gita and others were cleaning the mess in all out-of-the-way places.

A delayed and rescheduled transplant surgery would begin as soon as the surgeon signed off on the cleanup. Gita pushed her mop into another tight corner, and it came out unsoiled. The surgical suite clean-up was practically finished.

It was evening now.

Medical personnel began entering the suite and preparing for the intricate work they would be involved in over the next several hours. The surgery would begin as soon as the cleanup crew was out. The young woman determined from gossip there would be several surgeries with more than one donor involved.

The maintenance personnel continued working in the halls and other locations. There was still a great deal of work to be done in areas where it would not conflict with the delicate labor in progress in the transplant surgical suite.

Gita watched for anything interesting or out of the ordinary. Along with others, she swept, mopped, and wiped everything. All the while, the young woman made mental notes.

After many hours, doctors, nurses, and other medical types began to exit the surgical suite. The older lady Gita worked with told her they might be released soon. Another crew normally handled the cleaning in operating rooms and connected space when surgery was completed.

With the procedures over, the cleanup, as difficult and rushed as it had been, was now complete.

Gita and other maintenance personnel were being assigned to new duties as the regular surgical cleanup crew took over. Working with the experienced older lady, she began sweeping and applying a new coat of wax to hallway floors in the transplant wing. Several hours later, they had worked themselves around to a hallway near the surgical suite.

As she returned a broom and other equipment to a storage room, two nurses came by pushing a gurney. It held a covered body. Gita watched the gurney until it passed through a set of doors at the end of the corridor.

She asked her work partner about it.

"Probably on the way to the crematorium," the woman said. "There were several transplant surgeries last night. I heard the doctors did a procedure for a financial broker from America and another for an entertainer from London. There were other transplants too. The doctors also harvested other organs from the same donors. Those were flown out to other hospitals. It's the routine."

"Who told you?" Gita asked.

"I listen," the older woman said.

Gita stared at the doors leading to the crematorium.

Her work partner had stopped and was staring too.

The partner began talking about the surgeries. "There were two donors. I heard one of them had been in an accident, and they couldn't use some of her organs." Watching, the woman added almost as an afterthought, "She was the first one to go to the crematorium."

Gita glanced toward the closed doors.

Even though there wasn't much time, Colonel Repa had thoroughly prepared Gita to go into the hospital. She was new, as her mentor had been those many years ago, and, like him, she was willing to take chances.

Gita knew the right questions and when to ask them. Among other reasons, Colonel Repa liked her because she came early and stayed late wherever he sent her. Those were times she could learn details without being intrusive or too inquisitive.

After the cleanup, Gita walked to the Metro stop with a young man who had been on the waxing detail with her. That was when she found out about a young woman who had disappeared during the night.

"There have been others," the young man said, "This was the fourth time."

Gita stopped and stared at him.

"How are you aware of these disappearances?" she asked.

"When you are on the maintenance crew," he said, "they send you to all parts of the hospital—wherever you are needed." He glanced at her. "You hear gossip, and sometimes you see things."

"So tell me more about the disappearances." Gita's smiles and friendly manner urged him on.

"There were three others before this one. The first two were men. Young like you and me." He glanced at Gita again. Then he continued, his hands shoved deep in his pockets and his eyes downcast, seeming to study the cobblestone sidewalk as they neared the Metro platform. "Then, a couple of months ago, a young woman went missing." He didn't look at her this time. It was like he was talking to himself.

"Strange things happen when there are disappearances." His voice was soft. "People come to the hospital and stay in a locked room. They are seldom seen once they're here. Sometimes someone will see a doctor or nurse go into the room. Otherwise, the only time anyone notices them was when they were out for a test or an X-ray."

They arrived at the Metro stop, and Gita sat down on a bench. Her new friend stood in front of her and continued telling her the interesting highlights of her new job.

"The rooms they are put in are outfitted a little different. There are regular things, like a bed, monitoring equipment, and a chair." He hesitated. "But these special rooms usually have a conference table, extra chairs, and a few books."

She listened closely.

"This part was different. It was as if the doctors wanted to keep these people as happy and contented as possible." He was quiet for several seconds as if thinking of items he had seen.

"It was like…" he slowly moved his head from side to side, "…it was like they were planning something special for these particular people."

He glanced at Gita.

"On the downside, there is no phone in the room. One thing is strange…"

"What?"

He glanced at her again. "When these young people arrive here, they appear to be completely healthy. Each of them."

Gita remained quiet, listening. He kept telling what he knew.

"There are no visitors, and the patients almost never leave the room." He was repeating himself. "It's like they are prisoners."

A Metro bus stopped, and they climbed on. It was crowded, forcing them to stand. He kept talking. Gita encouraged him with smiles and allowed their legs to touch enticingly a couple of times. He told her there were multitudes of medical tests, most without the patient leaving the room.

"Nurses draw blood in the room most of the time. I have cleaned those rooms sometimes when the young person is out for X-rays. It's the only time we are allowed in." He glanced at Gita. "Then a few days before a transplant procedure, someone important always arrives and is scheduled for surgery."

"Someone important how?" Gita asked. "Politicians, celebrities… who?"

"Yes, those," he said nodding his head. "The very wealthy from all over the world come here too. I have googled some of the names."

They were nearing one of the main transfer points at the center of Prague.

"Oh," he remembered, "the President of Chile had a heart transplant here just a couple of months ago. That is when the young woman disappeared. Gossip said she was transferred to another hospital, but no one saw them moving her.

"The two acts, the young person being held and the upcoming transplant, always coincide. After the surgery, the young person in the rooms I have described always disappear." He stopped for a moment, then glanced at her. "They may just have gone home or been transferred somewhere else."

He told the last part slowly, as if it was a given conclusion.

"A few of the staff have noticed and don't think the young people leave the Cambridge Center at all."

When he appeared to have run out of things to tell her, Gita said her stop was coming up and told him goodbye. She got off, walked out of sight and then returned to the hospital for her vehicle, driving directly to a coffee shop where Colonel Repa was waiting.

She told him what she had learned. Gita included the gurney she'd seen going to the crematorium and that according to her young coworker, there had been two potential donors for transplants that evening. Other than the accident, Gita didn't know what had happened to make second one a donor.

Then he asked questions, and she answered them. When they finished, Colonel Repa had a good idea of what was happening. He just didn't know why.

Milan finished his regular shift at eight o'clock and then worked several extra hours before going home. There was still much to be done. Some would be handled by the next shift and other chores would be completed the next day.

A number of organs had become available hours earlier, and they were quickly used. The transplant ICU had several patients including the London-based entertainer.

Milan had been cautious but watchful as he went about his duties. He was scrutinizing anything out of the ordinary. He had been particularly observant of Victoria Lancing who had been near death when she received her transplant. It had saved her life.

She had been taken off the ventilator, and her vital signs were where they needed to be. It was late, and she would be fully conscious soon. Lancing was already a different person in the moments when she was awake. She was pleased at the difference in the way she was feeling, but she also appeared to be expressing significant remorse for her donor. Several of the people working in the ICU had mentioned it.

Dr. Jirsa and her transplant teams had worked steadily through the hours to utilize the available organs. Now the surgical teams were rotating between patients and bringing each of them off the critical list as soon as their condition permitted. The kidney and heart patients were already looking forward to being released from the hospital.

Dusa had been transferred to the night shift and was working twelve hours from 8:00 p.m. With Milan still on days, this suited both of them. They would be able to keep tabs on the transplant unit and the ICU twenty-four hours a day with these schedules.

Without appearing suspicious, they were able to grab coffee or a snack together at least once a day. To an observer, it appeared they were good friends sharing stories about life and work. Though Milan did most of the reporting to Marty, Dusa could call if something was urgent.

Adina prepared cheese and ham sandwiches and side treats before she left. Rage would phone her if needed. Otherwise she would return around eight o'clock on Monday morning.

Feeling better, Kateřina sprawled on her favorite settee and watched Rage as he munched on a sandwich.

"You appear famished," she told him.

Rage said he hadn't eaten since early in the day.

They talked, laughing often at the things they did in the few weeks they had together all those years ago. Both of them realized just how much they had grown to care for each other in a short time.

"I loved how you would call me Sweetheart, and you would touch me unexpectedly and hold me close," she laughed, "and you always surprised me." She smiled wickedly, her face turned slightly to the side and her eyes dancing. "I can sometimes feel those sensations even now."

Rage moved over and stretched out beside her on the settee, his head propped on an elbow.

Their eyes locked, and after a few moments, he softly said, "I love you. I think I've loved you since the first time you spoke to me."

"Do you remember what I said?" Kateřina asked.

"Yes…do you?"

"Of course," she told him. "I said, 'Come.' Then I took your hand and led you away from the Ambassador's party."

They'd had this conversation before, but he let her go on. Kateřina was repeating herself more often now. Rage went along with it when he saw her special enjoyment. This was one of those times.

"Do you remember where we went?" he asked with a questioning grin.

"We went down to Charles Bridge and strolled across. Then we walked along the river for hours." She glanced at him, remembering, smiling. "You held my hand every step of the way."

Smiling too, Rage added, "We must have walked twenty kilometers."

"You also remember."

She kissed him. Then she leaned back and said in a serious tone, "My feet still hurt."

They both chuckled.

"Do you remember where we went after the walk?" he questioned seriously.

She was quiet for a few moments. Then her answer was almost a whisper.

"We took a room at a tiny hotel above Charles Bridge and made love until the sun lit up our room."

He leaned forward and kissed her forehead.

Looking up at him, she smiled. "As I told you, you called me Sweetheart in those days," she said. "You are the only man who has ever said that to me."

He kissed her again. "I find it hard to believe."

"I never loved a man before you came to me," Kateřina told him. "Did I ever tell you?"

"No," he lied softly. Then she put her head on his shoulder.

Sometime later, Kateřina said she was tired and wanted to rest for a while. Rage glanced at the big clock in the kitchen. It was nearing midnight.

He asked if she would mind if he went upstairs to his computer for a while.

She yawned and said she didn't.

He had been itching to see if *Idona47* had reached out to him. This time there was a message with details.

It began with information regarding the Eagle Trust members, secrets Rage had been trying to dig out on his own. The first detail confirmed Madam Chairwoman was one of the original members of the Eagle Trust. The authentication was based on circumstantial but reliable information. Rage's earlier supposition was true.

What had not become apparent in his investigation until now was two of the nine original members had died young. One of them, a young man, had fallen to his death while mountain climbing. The second member was killed by an aircraft that crashed into a house where she was staying.

Rage knew the architect of the Cambridge Center project had committed suicide several years after the hospital began operation. According to *Idona47*, there was also a possibility the individual was a member of the Eagle Trust, and he knew the suicide had occurred in the crematory at the Cambridge Center.

Also, according to *Idona47,* six of the original group were still very much alive and loosely involved in management of the Eagle Trust through its Board of Directors. Four of the six remaining had been identified, but two had not. The notes gave slight detail.

Reading from *Idona47's* information, Rage verified several items he already suspected. The four known members were Zuzana Balca, commonly known as Madam Chairwoman. She ran the Trust. The second—also a woman and German in origin—was

Dr. Hana Jirsa. She was the physician specializing in organ transplantation at the Cambridge Center.

This bit of information didn't surprise Rage.

The third was Victoria Lancing, the entertainer from the UK. The fourth was the President of Chile. The information suggesting she and Chairwoman Balca were friends as students at Cambridge had proven to be accurate.

Rage looked up from his computer screen.

Victoria Lancing is at the health clinic now. She's here for a transplant.

Rage had heard Kateřina and Adina talking about Victoria Lancing. They were both fans and would be excited if they knew she was at the Cambridge Center. The hospital, though, would not want word to get out that the entertainer was near death.

Glancing back at the screen, Rage read on. The two remaining members of the Eagle Trust were men. *Humm... Idona47* had not identified them yet but was close.

Finishing with the email, Rage did a little experimenting of his own. *Idona47* had provided the last of the data from Karel Vlasta's hard drive. Though he seldom let his feelings show, Rage was like a kid with a new toy.

Looking over emails Vlasta had sent and received, a particular IP Address appeared often. Over the last three months there had been several messages, both to and from the address.

Intuition caused Rage to write an email, encrypt it and fire it off. Could *Idona47* identify the address and get the info back to him right away?

It was a hunch.

After a few minutes of thought and planning, Rage shut down his computer and closed it. He doubted if anything more could come to haunt them in the short term. This day was over.

Pushing his chair back, a peculiar sensation caused Rage think of Ana. It was as though with the ending of the day, he no longer needed to search for her.

Premonition?

Glancing outside, he accepted it always made him nervous to have a feeling like that.

# 1 4

Monday, September 28, 2015

* * *

Dusa called Milan at home before dawn with an urgent message. A serious situation occurred early in the morning after the multiple transplants. She had listened to a very private conversation and thought he should notify his friend Marty immediately.

The conversation involved two of the Cambridge Center's doctors. Dr. Jirsa was particularly concerned about Victoria Lancing. The doctor was discussing the entertainer's mental state with the hospital psychiatrist.

Dusa was charting at a desk several feet away and appeared to be paying no attention to the two doctors who were speaking English instead of their native Czech. They obviously did not realize the Czech nurse was fluent in the language.

"I am concerned," the transplant specialist said excitedly, her arms and hands in constant motion. "Victoria Lancing was becoming somewhat unstable even before the surgery. Now, with the procedure over, she is having significant afterthoughts in her conscious moments. We desperately need the research involving her transplant and follow up."

"What do you suggest?" Dr. Seifert asked.

"I sedated her several hours before the surgery and for the moment, I am going to bring Victoria off the drugs slowly," Dr. Jirsa said. "She came through the operation without complications, and I am hoping she will be calm and even allow herself to enjoy her new lease on life. It's the only reasonable alternative."

The psychiatrist nodded and then told Dr. Jirsa, "I will be prepared to meet with her when she regains consciousness."

The surgeon breathed a long sigh as the psychiatrist continued.

"If she persists, you know we will have to stop her. She cannot continue." Dr. Seifert's face was flushed, and there was a touch of perspiration above his lips.

Dusa had listened as she finished the reports and casually filed them away. She walked to the lounge afterwards and poured herself a cup of coffee. Then Dusa pulled out her phone and called Milan.

"Listen," she whispered. "I have only a moment." Dusa told him what she had learned.

She detailed the conversation and the implied threat. Finished, she hung up and returned to the ICU.

Dusa didn't notice the psychiatrist standing nearby in a dimly lit doorway.

Back in his office, Dr. Seifert sent an email to the head of nursing and copied it to the Chairwoman. He called for the immediate dismissal of Nurse Dusa for discussion of an ICU patient's condition with an unknown individual outside the hospital. Not going into details, he only said she had been observed and overheard naming a transplant patient in a phone conversation.

It was enough to dismiss her, especially coming from someone as important as Dr. Seifert. The psychiatrist wished he knew who she had talked with. Whoever it was, it couldn't be good. However, he didn't want to chance a negative situation within the ICU. Interrogating her would have made it a major incident involving other individuals. Releasing Dusa and escorting her out of the building would have to do. He also didn't want to involve security other than to have them remove the nurse from the premises.

With the email on its way, Dr. Seifert headed back to the transplant unit. He wanted to be there when Victoria Lancing awakened.

The new day started well. Kateřina appeared to rest throughout the night; she hardly moved at all. In contrast, Rage slept fitfully, jumping at every small sound she made. He spent the night with his chair pulled as close to the side of her bed as possible.

She was still sleeping soundly when he went in to get an early morning shower and shave. Rage had moved his toiletries to Kateřina's bathroom so he could be close at hand.

He was in the shower when he heard the house phone ring a little after 7:00 a.m. Realizing he couldn't get there in time to keep it from waking her, he left Kateřina to answer it. When he heard her talk for a few moments, Rage wasn't concerned. It was probably Adina. Kateřina could tell him about their conversation when he dried off.

The phone call had not been from Kateřina's friend.

When Rage came out of the bathroom, she said, "Dr. Seifert, the hospital psychiatrist, called."

"Is there a problem?"

"I do not know. He asked if I can meet with him at 9:00 this morning. Will you go with me?"

"Of course."

Kateřina was nervous, but neither of them mentioned it. Instead, Rage tried to put a favorable spin on the visit.

"Hopefully there's good news," he told her. "Let's be positive. Perhaps Ana is better, and you can see her."

"Yes. Let's be optimistic," she said but didn't smile.

Dr. Seifert waved them in and motioned to the two chairs in front of his desk.

"I have bad news," he said immediately.

Kateřina slumped in her chair.

The psychiatrist glanced at her but then continued.

"As I told you recently, Ana had been exposed to something that made her ill. The exposure was the reason for her quarantine."

Kateřina's head was down, preparing for a bad outcome. Rage hoped she was wrong.

The doctor continued, repeating several things Kateřina had already been told. "We have had your daughter under close observation since we discovered the danger. Ana's health was our primary concern, but we also wanted to be sure no one else became ill." He leaned forward. "You do understand?"

Rage watched the doctor's expressions; he wouldn't look directly at either of them.

"Yes, we understand about the risk." Rage said, answering for them both.

"What about Ana?" Kateřina asked. "Is she going to be all right?"

The doctor's hesitation was too long.

"Oh, no!"

She stood up, quiet and outwardly calm, and walked to the door. Kateřina began shaking as she let herself out and walked to a nearby reception room chair.

Rage stood up to follow her, but the doctor caught his arm.

"Wait," Dr. Seifert said. "There is something you should take with you."

The doctor reached for a box on the cabinet behind him. Handing it to Rage, he said, "Tell Ms. Bambenek I am sorry."

Rage immediately realized the box contained an urn. He hesitated for a moment, looking directly at Dr. Seifert. Rage was an expert at facial expressions and knowing whether people were telling the truth. He knew Dr. Seifert was lying about the manner of Ana's death.

Kateřina took the box from Rage on the way to the parking lot. On the drive home, she held it in her lap, quietly looking out the window while wiping at an occasional tear. They didn't speak. Though the distance was only a few kilometers, it was a very long ride.

She carried the box inside and then to her settee. Rage left Kateřina to her thoughts and memories for the next hour. She remained seated, the box and urn on her lap, her arms holding it close. The only interruption was when he set a cup of tea at her side. She smiled and then looked away.

He checked on her throughout the morning and into early afternoon. There were tears on her cheeks a couple of those times.

On another occasion, he heard her humming a lullaby. Kateřina was saying goodbye to her daughter.

At mid afternoon, she saw him in the doorway and asked if he would help her do something.

"Certainly," Rage said it softly. He hadn't wanted to disturb her.

"Please bring the small table in the corner of my bedroom and place it by the window." She pointed.

When Rage had it positioned, Kateřina stood up and handed him the box.

"Open it," she said, "and put Ana there."

He noticed she didn't say Ana's *ashes*. When he had the urn in place, Kateřina glanced at him and then back at the table.

"I will not believe my daughter is truly gone until I know exactly what happened to her."

Her statement worried Rage. Kateřina was sick too. She needed to get back with her doctor for treatments or at least another consultation. Each time Rage asked about it, she put him off. He knew if treatments were to help, they needed to start immediately.

Obviously, Kateřina wasn't thinking of herself. Her mind was on her daughter. She was adamant about learning the circumstances of Ana's death.

"Ana's letter only posed more questions," she said. "There were no answers in it."

She looked at Rage and summed up the remainder of her life. "I *must* know."

Later when Rage walked to the kitchen, he found her across the room standing near the urn and looking out the windows. The day had brought unimaginable distress for Kateřina. He watched and could only imagine what she must be going through. Her own medical problems were getting worse by the hour, and now Kateřina was dealing with the loss of her daughter.

Rage noticed the urn was at the window overlooking the stone terrace and the far gardens and trees—a favorite view of Ana's according to her mother.

She wiped at an occasional tear as she gazed outside. If he hadn't known the circumstances, it might appear she was enjoying the activity. Birds were darting among the trees, and a squirrel was busy digging for food near a flowerbed.

In the hours since they left the oncologist's office a day earlier, Kateřina hadn't mentioned her illness unless Rage brought it up. From the beginning, she hadn't wanted to discuss her own situation until she knew the details concerning her daughter.

Rage was thinking of Kateřina. Ana was out of reach now. Kateřina should get treatments started right away, but she wasn't interested.

"Not until I know what happened to Ana and the other young people," she said. "This is more than I can handle at one time."

Kateřina returned to the settee and asked him to make them some soup to go with a sandwich. They ate slowly as she talked about Ana.

She had been a good daughter, Kateřina told him, never giving her trouble. "Ana was even thinking of returning to school to become a physician." Kateřina broke down and sobbed, "I could not have been more proud of her."

As they finished eating, Kateřina said, "I must rest for an hour or two. My head is hurting. Will you help me with my bath?"

He nodded.

She stood up and then hesitated. "What was I going to do?" she asked, looking toward Rage for the answer.

"Rest," he said, "You were going to rest for a while, and you mentioned a bath."

"Oh, yes," she muttered, appearing embarrassed. "The dealership returned my car," she said turning to him as she started out of the room. "Did I tell you?"

"Yes." He didn't tell her this was the third time she had mentioned it. They had driven it to the Cambridge Center.

Rage was watching her closely—physically, emotionally, and intellectually. Often, she seemed reluctant to get up and walk, and he noticed she was talking less too. It was as if pieces of Kateřina were slipping away.

Though she had mentioned it earlier, it was well into the afternoon when Rage helped Kateřina with her bath. She wanted to soak for a few minutes and then sleep. While Rage went for her gown, Kateřina decided to get out of the tub and dry off.

She had toweled her upper body and stepped onto the edge of the tub with one foot. She became unbalanced and was close to falling face down on the tile floor. Fortunately, she only slipped backwards for a butt flop.

Rage heard the commotion and hurried to her side. He helped her up, and they toweled Kateřina off and into a gown before he walked her to the bed.

Rage held her arm this time. Even with his help, she moved slow and cautiously. Kateřina couldn't believe and didn't understand what was so suddenly happening to her. In truth, only a few days ago she had appeared healthy.

When she was tucked in, Rage kneeled down and kissed her. She kissed him back with more enthusiasm than he expected.

"I love you," she said. "I did not tell you yesterday. I meant to, but I didn't."

He pulled his chair close and stayed there until her eyes fluttered and then remained closed. Rage hoped she would sleep for a while but doubted if it would happen. Restless naps had become the norm.

Kateřina had been sleeping for over an hour. It was almost dark, and Rage's legs were cramping. He had started to stand up when the doorbell rang.

It was probably Adina. She had told him she would come and stay for a few hours that evening.

Instead, Marty was leaning against the porch railing when Rage opened the door.

"I was in the area. Got a few minutes?"

"What is it?"

"Milan called again," Marty said. He didn't sound overjoyed.

They had discussed Nurse Dusa's first two calls. The news about the nurse being fired had been a setback. More disturbing, though, was the information she had overheard regarding Victoria Lancing. They were both concerned about the discussion between the two doctors. Rage and Marty each thought the conversation ended with a threat.

As an afterthought, Marty had indicated Milan was concerned about his own job. He hadn't known if Nurse Dusa had told anyone who she was phoning. It worried him. He could be next.

One other interesting piece of information had come from Milan. He had obviously known and told Marty about the Cambridge Center architect who had shot herself in the crematorium several years ago. If she was a Trust member, it meant there were now only six surviving. Rage wondered who else might know the identities of the members.

Marty began talking about the most recent call from Milan. There had been several transplants at the Cambridge Center late yesterday and last night.

Rage said he knew and told Marty about Kateřina's daughter. Not surprised, the big man expressed sympathy and then moved on to Milan.

As they talked on the porch, Kateřina's friend pulled around the circular driveway and parked. Another car passed as Rage walked out to meet Adina and tell her about Ana. He thought it better she hear the late developments before she went inside.

With tears coursing down her face, Adina said it was so much like when her son had died. She had also been given an urn. "Kamil's ashes are at Vinohrady Cemetery," she told him.

As before, Adina had brought food. She indicated there was enough to share.

Rage took the container, and Marty followed him into the kitchen. Adina wiped her eyes and went to check on Kateřina. She obviously wasn't looking forward to the expected conversation.

Rage spread the treats on two plates and poured Marty a cup of coffee. He had enjoyed the last of the schnapps on his previous visit. Rage had water.

Marty chuckled and said Rage was going to rust. Patting his stomach, Rage countered, "You're just jealous of my six-pack."

Then he grinned, remembering all the times the big man had kept spirits up with his humorous takes on serious matters.

They settled down at the counter and began discussing the business at hand. Cover music played 24/7 now, although Rage had checked and the van was not coming in the daytime.

Finished eating, Rage piled their dishes in the sink and led the way upstairs to his computer. He made notes as they discussed what they knew and what they didn't.

"Did Milan or Dusa learn anything else before she was escorted out?" Rage asked.

Marty was primed and ready. "Well, for one thing, guess how many organ transplants there were at the health center yesterday and last night?

"A couple, I would guess." Rage was staring hard at Marty. "There were more?"

Marty began. "I didn't count them, so there are probably more than I'm telling you. Some organs were used here, and others were flown out to other hospitals."

"I expect several were Ana Bambenek's," Rage said.

Marty held up a hand and started counting—a finger for each organ. He counted close to two dozen organs—from two donors.

Dusa got a glance at a list of organs being flown out. He counted those too—going to who knows where.

"That's a lot of surgery," Rage said when Marty paused to take a breath.

"They must have been using more than one team," Rage observed. "Was Victoria Lancing involved?"

"Yeah." He ducked his head, eyeing Rage. "How'd you know?"

"An educated guess," Rage told him.

"Depending on the geographical location, some estimates put black market pricing for one kidney at more than $150,000 US dollars." Rage looked at Marty, shaking his head.

Rage did a little mental math. *The plane carried quite a payload! And most from just one donor—Ana Bambenek.* And then a scary thought struck him. *What if there had been more donors and at other times?*

Though he had no definite proof, Rage was thinking the three young people who died before Ana could have also been donors. It was a clear possibility. *Perhaps there'd been no accidents at all. What if everything had happened here at the Cambridge Center?*

Rage glanced at Marty and said he had an idea.

"Let's try to answer some questions about Ana's death. I don't think she was sick," Rage indicated to his friend. Having thought it through, he had no doubts. "So why was she an organ donor?"

The question seemed the basis of all they had to answer.

"The heads at the health clinic obviously had a way of holding Ana and keeping her from talking," Rage said aloud.

But what were they keeping her from talking about? And for what reason, other than illicit organ donations? And perhaps black market trade?

Marty was thinking too. He spoke out. "Ana's death and the fact she had not been sick or injured was the anomaly: death supposedly of a virus while in quarantine at the Cambridge Center."

Rage had a thought. "If she had a virus, how could they use her organs?"

The two men looked at each other.

Rage expressed their thoughts. "They couldn't."

He went further, "Two of the three other young people had supposedly died away from the hospital. That was what their mothers were told. The bucket is starting to spring leaks. The stories of the young people's deaths aren't making sense."

Marty added, "Accidents and out of the country, both of the men. The young woman supposedly died at the hospital but from an overdose of sleeping pills." He shook his head. "I don't think so."

He hesitated for a moment remembering what Rage had told him. "Gossip had it she was breaking up with a boyfriend and didn't want to live without him."

Given all the other circumstances, Rage didn't believe it for a moment.

The big man had some other ideas, too. "Have you thought about the security out at the Cambridge Center? Overall, it's more than adequate. They seem to be trying a little too hard to keep everyone out of certain areas. Normal medical research wouldn't have security as strict as that. I wonder about the Center's testing areas. Maybe the type of research had something to do with all of the deaths. Ana's too."

Marty said it appeared security was attempting to keep almost everyone out except those who work there. He grinned and said, "Obviously, they were not very successful with you and me."

"They are probably not accustomed to having experienced CIA operatives attempting to breech the security."

Marty nodded and said, "It wouldn't have surprised me for someone to have gotten nervous and taken a shot at us during the melee. I wonder why security was unusually nervous that particular night? Regular protection is always important. Security should be strong in a hospital. Then there's the Cambridge Center's research. They might conclude the nature of the research required extra efforts. The third cause could be…"

The proverbial light bulb switched on in Marty's mind. He glanced at Rage as he considered the new possibility. Both he and Rage were already suspecting this.

"What if the Cambridge Center is doing something they shouldn't with research? Something illegal or immoral? Or both?" he added.

Rage thought they might have an answer. "Research and security might be our best pathways to the cause of the young people's deaths. The connection to both would be Ana Bambenek."

Pulling his chair toward Rage at the table, Marty started talking. Rage immediately stopped typing notes.

Marty detailed his theory regarding the connection between Ana and the health clinic's security. As he got into it, Rage sat forward, his arms on the table.

"What about the other three?" Rage asked. "Do they connect the same way as Ana? And what's the relationship? The key is the connection. There *has* to be a common link."

Rage stood up and started pacing. Marty watched and listened.

"There are four of these young people with similarities enough to question. Four, Marty. Understand?"

Marty was definitely listening.

Rage glanced at his friend, even poking a finger in his direction. "Have you thought about this? What if there are more than the four we know about?"

Marty sat up straight. "I hadn't thought of that."

"So? What if?"

Rage continued. "Then we have more potential victims. Some already dead and more in danger."

Marty's eyes narrowed and his forehead wrinkled—a worried expression replacing his usual happy one. "Where do we start?"

"Two places," Rage told him. "You and I will work the health clinic with Milan since Nurse Dusa is out. That's if they don't toss Milan out too."

"And the other place is…?"

Rage smiled. "I have an unnamed source."

Marty was immediately on top of that one. "Wait. No secrets if I'm working on this and sticking my neck out."

Rage walked over and stood in front of his friend, a hand on his shoulder.

"Two days?" he said to his friend. "Work with me for forty-eight hours?"

Marty looked at him. "Only forty-eight hours? You got it."

"One more thought," Rage said. "Isn't it interesting that the Cambridge Center has a crematorium?"

Marty stared at him.

Rage finished the thought. "What better way to hide the taking of human organs? Especially if you don't want the outside world to know what you're doing."

At that moment, Adina knocked, drawing their notice. Her eyes were drawn and wrinkles bunched her forehead.

"I am afraid and have been hesitant to ask your advice." She was looking at Rage but had glanced at Marty a couple of times too. Rage gestured for her to continue.

"Someone is following me when I leave my house," she told them. "I have noticed the same automobile on more than one occasion. It is a white Volvo, and it has a crumpled left fender. It was behind me today as I came here."

Glancing at his big friend, Rage received an almost imperceptible nod.

"It's okay," Rage told her. "We have had someone watching you."

A look of surprise crossed Adina's face. "I am in danger?" She was scared now.

Marty explained. "We don't think you are, but Rage wanted to be careful."

That was all the explanation she needed. "Thank you," she said looking at both of them. "I will leave you to your conversation." She turned to go downstairs to Kateřina's bedroom.

"I'll walk with you," Marty told her. He waved goodnight to Rage as they left The Author at the desk.

Shortly after nightfall, Rage was starting to ask himself questions that could untangle mysteries and reach to conclusions. He was also beginning the first steps of a plan to expose the terrible things happening at the Cambridge Center.

The concept was to have Marty direct Milan regarding information and events to watch for at the hospital. Meanwhile, Rage planned to work with *Idona47* to dig into current and past dealings of the Eagle Trust.

There was a list of questions. Essentials for some were already on the table; others were not. The basics concerned the purpose of the Trust, who its remaining two unnamed members are, and the nature of the hidden research being conducted at the Cambridge Center?

Rage had one other chore for *Idona47*. He wanted to examine Karel Vlasta's updated hard drive for any new details. Though he had done that recently, things were rapidly coming to a conclusion. Vlasta was probably updating material several times a day.

He was hesitant to tap Vlasta's computer during normal hours, usually reserving the chore until nighttime. Though Rage knew a great deal about the methodology, he didn't want to take a chance on Vlasta discovering him.

Somewhere on Vlasta's laptop there would be clues. He would be too wary to have anything incriminating on the Cambridge Center's system computer. Too dangerous.

Rage hesitated several times as he constructed the email. He wanted to cover everything in one carefully written message. Time was running out, and getting everything to *Idona47* in one package could make a difference. Finally satisfied, Rage put the list of information into an email, coded it, and hit the send button.

Then Rage leaned back and thought about the question he'd added to *Idona47's* email at the last minute. He hoped there would be time to research this one for the meeting he was planning.

Adina met him at Kateřina's bedroom door when Rage went down to check on her.

"She is very sick," Adina told him. "I believe it is the head pains, but I am concerned it is more."

Rage looked over her shoulder to the bed. Kateřina was there, twisted in the sheets and on her side facing away.

"She has not known who I am for most of the time you have been upstairs," Adina said. "She asks for you often, but then she will ask for Ana or some friend. She also seems to be in sorrow at times, remembering she has lost Ana."

He eased around Adina, telling her to go and have something to drink.

"I'll stay for a while," he told her.

Rage took his place beside the bed.

Moments later Kateřina's eyes fluttered. She saw Rage, obviously recognizing him, and said, "You've come back to me."

He didn't know if she meant he'd come back from upstairs, or he had returned from her past.

She smiled, obviously pleased he was there. Kateřina reached out. "Hold my hand."

Rage took the offered hand and held it for the next hour.

Adina returned and stood watching at the foot of the bed. There were tears in her eyes.

"Go and rest," he told her. "I'll call you when I need to go back upstairs."

She nodded, turned and then walked out of the bedroom. He watched, thinking, *Kateřina is not alone. She has at least one good friend.*

As he held her hand, Rage thought of the promises he had made and then broken. *There were times when I thought of coming back, and then there would be one more thing to do or another place to go.*

Before he knew it, another year would have passed.

He reached out and brushed a strand of hair from her face. *I wish I'd been here to do that a thousand times.*

A half-hour passed, then an hour. Rage was getting very little rest.

Kateřina had dropped into an uneasy sleep. Her body was constantly twitching.

Finally finding himself dozing, Rage stood up and strolled to the front window. Pushing curtains aside, he peered out into the dark that had cast itself on the houses and hills beyond them. Street lamps lit the scene but only left a soft glowing sketch of reality.

He turned, watching Kateřina from where he stood.

Given the opportunity, would I come back to her now and stay? Would I keep my promises?

Unfortunately, this was not an option, at least not for a real future. Rage felt moisture cloud his eyes as he heard Adina coming.

"Would you like to rest?" she asked again from the doorway.

Rage looked at her, his thoughts broken. "No. I need to stretch though, and I should go upstairs for a few minutes. I'm expecting a message."

He walked to the doorway, touching Adina's arm in thanks as he entered the hall.

"Call me if you need to," Rage said without looking back.

A new email from *Idona47* was waiting.

Ask and you shall receive…especially if you ask Idona47.

The communication contained much of the updated information he had requested. Rage's attention immediately jumped to the possibility of breaking into the security chief's laptop to obtain current data. He knew it could be done, but Rage expected he would need several pieces of info to enter the security chief's secret computer world.

He had been right about needing the information, but *Idona47* had provided everything necessary, including codes and instructions. There was even a short step-by-step tutorial video. Rage was ecstatic—grinning and tapping the desk three times with his knuckles.

Starting immediately, Rage was into Karel Vlasta's laptop within fifteen minutes. Another twenty and he knew his way around the updated hard drive and was searching for new information.

He watched for indications of Vlasta signing into his computer. *Idona47* had warned Rage being there would slow Karel's computer operating speed considerably. Vlasta would notice.

Two hours of concentrated effort allowed Rage to fill several pages of a legal pad with written notes and and to print fifty-odd pages of additional material. Rage was sweating by the time he finished. He had expected Vlasta at any moment. This hadn't happened so far. Rage wiped at his forehead with a sleeve as he hurried. Another few minutes and he could close down Vlasta's computer.

All the written material was stacked on the foot of his bed. Had Vlasta known, Rage's target would have shaken his head in disbelief. Vlasta was good. There was no denying that, but Rage was better. And *Idona47* was better than Rage.

Moving quickly, even with a couple of pauses for a quick review of the video, it took only a few minutes, even with numerous dead-ends, before he hit paydirt.

Rage realized what he had, whistling as he shook his head: the demanding emails Karel Vlasta had sent to the Chairwoman. This verified what Rage had read earlier on his own computer, put there—he was sure—by the security chief. Rage exclaimed aloud as he reread the first one— *"I know about your specialized research and the acts you have committed,"* and the second requiring payment of one hundred million dollars.

What spectacular evidence could Vlasta have to make his blackmail stand up against the secrets of an organization like the powerful Eagle Trust?

In Vlasta's blackmail note, he had specifically mentioned un-named research and that he was familiar with it. There was also something the Eagle Trust had done three times according to the security chief. The only trio of anything Rage was aware of were the deaths of Ana's young friends.

It would be a huge step if Rage could see whatever Vlasta had found giving him a basis for the blackmail. He glanced out the window, his thoughts wandering. As yet, he had not seen anything particularly damning that could be proven.

Rage shook his head and shuffled through some of the accumulated papers. Chances were whatever Karel Vlasta found was not on his computer. There was probably too much data and time involved for Vlasta to have copied it onto his hard drive. He must have found it somewhere else... But where?

Continuing to dig through updated files, Rage came across something interesting, a large file he hadn't noticed previously. *Idona47* had not provided this. It had been a part of the original download from Vlasta's computer, and it appeared to be a copy of another computer's hard drive. The more Rage examined it, the more the files appeared to be from Chairwoman Balca's personal computer.

Yes! The Chairwoman of the Eagle Trust! A cursory exam indicated the information was only nine or ten days old.

Rage was surprised Vlasta had not locked the data in some way. He obviously didn't think anyone was capable of hacking his laptop. Rage quickly downloaded everything he wanted onto an external drive he had brought with him. Finished, Rage was able to close out of Karel Vlasta's computer. He was confident the security chief would not discover his secrets had been hacked. Rage wiped his forehead with a sleeve, only now realizing the tension he'd been under for the last several minutes.

With the external hard drive connected to his laptop and the Chairwoman's private information available, Rage was looking through heretofore hidden and secret files in a matter of minutes. Since Rage already knew what he needed, he was immediately making copies of specific information for his meeting.

Quickly realizing the Chairwoman's hard drive had indexing, Rage scanned several topics. It immediately became evident the hard drive was where Chairwoman Balca kept information on everything secret or even private in her life. Rage was convinced he'd found the specifics of information surrounding the Chairwoman and the Eagle Trust.

A thin sheen of perspiration had formed on his forehead again as he neared the end of the process. A few final chores and Rage breathed a sigh of relief.

Rage wished he had noticed this earlier. Time had been at a premium all along. Now it was critical.

Wrapping things up, he was ready to look for answers. Before he could dig deeper, though, Adina appeared at the door.

"I am sorry to bother you," she said, "but I need to return to my home. There are some things requiring my attention."

"It's no problem," he told her. Rage glanced at his computer and then at the papers on the bed. Looking back at Adina, he asked, "Is there time to move my computer downstairs?"

"Of course. I will help you."

Rage piled everything he needed onto the bed: the computer, the papers he'd printed, and the coded information and directions he'd received from *Idona47*.

To avoid disturbing Kateřina, Rage took his makeshift computer stand into her bathroom and set up a workstation in the shower. The counter surrounding the double sinks served as a worktable. Kateřina's small printer from her desk upstairs was on the counter beside a sink.

Hope no one needs a bath, Rage thought as he finished the set up.

Fifteen minutes had him ready to do business. He was set to continue his search for details on the Eagle Trust.

With lights dimmed and the bathroom door partially open, Rage could keep an eye on Kateřina as he worked. He knew she would want him to continue looking for the motives connecting Ana's death to those of her friends. There was also the question of other young people in jeopardy—individuals still living but in danger.

It would be tragic to lose others when Rage thought they were so close to an explanation.

Things were quiet until near two o'clock in the morning. Rage had been making good progress. He had basic details from day one of the Trust and had tapped into other minor pieces of interesting information going back to the late 1980s.

The Eagle Trust had been operating for close to seven years, and the hospital was on its way toward black ink. The red of the early days was showing up much less often.

Leaning back in the chair, Rage stretched his back and then his arms and legs until he felt revived. Thinking of specific information he had read, Rage was engrossed in thoughts of the Trust's progress when he heard a sound at the bathroom door.

Startled, he looked up.

It was Kateřina. She was leaning against the door frame, a frightened expression on her face, and she had been crying.

She didn't move for a few moments. Her eyes were drawn and cast down.

Rage rushed to her side. "What's wrong?"

"I am going to die," she stated slowly, but with an assurance that frightened Rage. Her words sounded so final.

"No…," he told her, "…you're sick, but you will get better when you start the treatments."

"No…I am going to die. I dreamed it."

"You're having a bad night," Rage told her.

"Come lie with me," she said. "I need to know you are close by."

Rage took Kateřina's arm, walking her to the bed. She lay down and he climbed in beside her. A few minutes passed before steady breathing and stillness told him she was sleeping.

He remained beside her for another half hour before return-ing to the computer. He had used the time to make mental notes and had plans by the time he struck the first keys. Knowing the remaining members of the Trust seemed important. The research question kept coming up too. What sort of research? What could it involve?

Rage kept probing. He found several files showing promise, but he couldn't open them without passwords. The Chairwoman had obviously developed a random method for creating her passwords. He looked for storage software.

This took another hour, and he was lucky to locate it then. A particular corporation's name in a group of medical suppliers looked unusual and out of place. When Rage opened the details for the company, he decided to go to what he thought was a web-site. Instead, the HTTP address took him to an application, which turned out to be for password generation and storage.

He leaned back; now he was getting somewhere.

Being familiar with password storage and how they are gener-ated, Rage tried a couple of times to break his way into the pro-gram. He realized immediately that he needed someone with special knowledge and use of a supercomputer.

Idona47—Rage needed his helper again.

Preparing the email, then coding and sending it took Rage sev-eral minutes. He hoped his helper was at the desk and didn't tire of all Rage was asking. He knew doing it himself would take more time than he had, if he could do it at all.

A strange sensation kept telling him time was running out. Not only for the research but also for Kateřina.

Rage remembered the younger Kateřina, the woman-child with the unusual green eyes he had chanced to know when they were young. The Kateřina in the room a few meters away was all he had left of those early years, and Rage was all she had of those same special times. Finding out why Ana had died a premature death was one way he could show he cared.

Glancing toward the room where she lay sleeping, Rage punched the return key to send the email to *Idona47.*

1 5

TUESDAY, SEPTEMBER 29, 2015

* * *

RAGE RETURNED TO CHECK ON Kateřina, spending another hour with her this time. Morning light was peeking over the horizon as they lay talking.

She described the vivid dream making her think she was going to die. Kateřina was sure it was going to happen. "I am going to sleep, and I will not awaken."

Looking at him, her next words caused a peculiar feeling to run along his spine.

"At the end, death will come easy to me," she told him. "I will no longer be in pain, and the headaches will be gone. But…" A tear eased down her cheek. "…I will no longer have you either."

Kateřina was so sure of the outcome, it was difficult for Rage not to believe her.

Confused at his own reaction, Rage didn't seem able to convince her otherwise. He held her hand and tried to talk about other things. Still, Kateřina was sure her death was near. Rage wondered if she was becoming delusional.

Adina came early and took over getting Kateřina bathed and into the kitchen for some tea. Food was still not something she would discuss.

"She is losing weight," Adina said, concerned.

Rage had noticed it too.

Rushing through his shower and shave, Rage had *Idona47's* last email on his mind. The passwords could be a big leap forward. He had scanned a number of files he wanted to examine in detail, especially those he had discovered on Vlasta's copy of the Chairwoman's hard drive.

Rage kept wondering about other young people who might be in jeopardy. Time and attempts to find others seemed to be flashing by without results.

With his morning bath ritual behind, Rage moved his office back upstairs to the bedroom and organized himself. He desperately wanted to get to the computer, expecting a return message from *Idona47*.

I need those passwords.

Minutes later, the explicit instructions for unlocking the Chairwoman's password file and retrieving the details were in a new email.

Reaching for a pencil, he set a pad on his knee and started a list. He knew almost immediately that several lists would be on the pad before his search was finished.

The dates Rage had picked up earlier regarding the beginnings of the Trust proved correct. It had all begun in 1982 with the Eagle Trust being formalized the next year. He was almost certain the number of original members was correct at nine, and two had been lost early with another to suicide. The idea that the Trust had been drawn together, first with an idea and then with a goal, was also correct.

He started with the four members they had identified. Rage learned each individual's early wealth came mostly from family trusts. He also discovered the members had come from wealthy families scattered around the globe and each was an only child, a sole beneficiary.

Understandably, all had graduated from the best private prep schools available. Superior education was a common qualifying factor. After prep school came the educational magnet drawing them together: The University of Cambridge.

It was fascinating reading. Rage was enjoying himself, but their history was not getting him where he wanted to go. He needed to see what was behind the Eagle Trust. What mysterious things were they—could they—be hiding?

After examining several files, Rage decided the details he needed were not there either. He moved on to other possibilities. Though he wasn't finding it, a strange intuitive feeling kept telling him he was searching in the right place, the information he wanted would be found in the Chairwoman's private files. To him, it was the logical place.

Unfortunately, finding the exact ones he needed was not easy. Rage guessed there were a few thousand files on her hard drive alone.

He shook his head. *I should get some coffee.*

Downstairs, he checked with Adina. She smiled and said Kateřina was sleeping soundly and had been for some time. The good news had him moving on to the kitchen and the coffee. A bit hungry, Rage made himself a slice of toast and spread it with Kateřina's special jelly. After eating, Rage looked in on Kateřina. She had awakened and wanted to go to the settee. Rage carried her there before heading upstairs.

On the way back to his workstation and thinking, as always, Rage decided he wasn't having any luck just scanning file after file. He decided to work through the drive looking for unusual documents, no matter where they were.

He was having to translate a lot of words and phrases between Czech, English, and a few other languages. It was slowing him down.

He had gone through more than fifty possibilities before he smiled. He passed over the phrase initially, then came back. The words were in Czech and Croatian. Rage knew just enough of the languages for the words to appear strange to him.

He looked at the file name again: *Pochyby - Tři x.* He couldn't imagine what the words meant as they were arranged. Rage shook his head, almost passing them over again.

That's when his sixth sense kicked in and nudged Rage to check out the strange words.

As he had with so many others, Rage ran them through a translation program. The Czech word, *Pochyby,* and the Croatian word *Tři,* with a small x at the end, translated to Doubt and Three in English followed by an unexplained x.

Doubt -Three x.

With this unusual combination of words bouncing around in his mind, Rage attempted to tie them to something meaningful.

All at once he got it. The simplicity of it struck him with the suddenness of a lightning bolt. He couldn't help but admire the Chairwoman's creativity.

The antonym for Doubt is Trust.

Rage was starting to smile.

He glanced at the second word and ran it through the translation software again. He knew what to expect and glanced at the monitor. There it was: Three, followed by the small x.

Using the antonym for the first word and attaching the number, the name of the file became *Trust - Three x.* But the three didn't denote anything he recognized except the three earlier deaths. The file was probably generated and named back in the early '80s, so the deaths had nothing to do with it. He had another thought, but there were nine, not three names on the list of members.

Or did the *Three x* actually mean nine when multiplied, as in nine members. Or is *Three x* a coded name for an organization taking the lives of young adults? This could be the way the Chairwoman remembers her most important file—another of Zuzana Balca's intentional deceptions.

If that was it, then the code would denote Trust-Nine. If his reasoning was correct, Rage had the file containing the Eagle Trust and now possibly the identities of its members.

Now, the password to get me into the world of the Trust.

That was much easier. The passwords were almost a cinch once he had the files. Those details and software *Idona47* sent in the email took Rage directly into almost everything secret about the Eagle Trust. Almost...

The research referred to so many times was not defined. An entire wing of the main building at the Cambridge Center had been dedicated to the work, but for Rage, nor anyone else he was aware of, the specific research was totally secret and still a mystery. Its details were apparently never committed to written text.

Hours into it and needing a break, Rage stood up and walked out into the hallway. He lingered at the top of the stairs, listening for sounds from the main floor. It was as if there was no one else in the house.

He walked down the stairs, making hardly any noise. Rage was at the door to the kitchen before he saw the two women.

Adina was sitting near the small table and the urn. She was holding a book and looking out over Kateřina's landscape.

Kateřina, a blanket snug around her, was facing away from him on the settee. She apparently had been reading when sleep got the best of her.

"She has rested for several hours," Adina whispered to him.

"Has she eaten anything?"

Adina shook her head.

"Keep trying."

She nodded, her eyes drawn and sad.

Upstairs and settled in at the computer, Rage turned his efforts back to the Trust and his obsession for answers. He desperately wanted to identify the research, but he also wanted to know the identity of the last two members.

Rage looked at the computer's monitor as if the members would come walking into view...and in a way, they did.

Browsing the remaining files in the Trust, Rage saw one labeled "Tickets." *Idona47* had a password for the strange file, so Rage opened it out of curiosity. It was small, but it contained a list with exactly nine names.

Members of the Eagle Trust?

He clicked the button to print and watched a single page exit the printer. A list.

The four he already knew were there: 1) The Chairwoman, Zuzana Balca, 2) Dr. Hana Jirsa, 3) Victoria Lancing, and 4) the President of Chile, Emilia Herboso.

Then came five names he didn't recognize.

Two of the five would be the young members who had died soon after the Eagle Trust was formed. But which two? Then which one had committed suicide and which two are still unknown and out there?

Rage crossed his arms, holding the list out in one hand and studying it.

Back to the internet.

The first name he googled was a young man who had died in a mountaineering accident when he was only twenty-two. Rage drew a line through the name.

The second was an Italian, Renato Onorio Bencivenni, with a large family living in Rome. He had come from a shipping background. Judging by dates, Bencivenni would now be in his mid-fifties, about the same age as Dr. Jirsa and Victoria Lancing. Rage remembered the Chairwoman was a few years older than the other members.

Bencivenni now ran several companies scattered among port cities throughout Europe and the Mediterranean Sea. Among the enterprises, there was a shipping fleet of several hundred oceangoing freighters and tankers. Most of these were on the seas at any given hour, three hundred and sixty-five days a year.

Rage had not previously found Bencivenni's name in any of his searching. He was obviously one of the two missing members.

Next came a young woman.

Googling her, Rage learned she was the second member of the Trust fated to a premature death. This young woman could not have been more unfortunate. An airplane falls out of the sky and strikes a house where two women are drinking coffee. Both women perished. Rage shook his head at the sadness of the circumstances.

The next name, Roger Shawn Langston IV, lived in the US outside Seattle, Washington. Langston was the third in his family to be involved in the computer industry. His grandfather had been in on the ground floor of developing the modern computer. The family fortune's size, a guarded secret, was estimated to be in the billions.

Among other areas of expertise, the family held numerous patents for components and processes indispensable in constructing and flying the International Space Station.

Roger Langston IV, the Trust member, had invented, developed, and controlled processes for the use of Nanotechnology Robots in medicine and technology. The size of his individual fortune and holdings were not available to the public.

Another member found.

Rage didn't need to google the next two on the list: Zuzana Balca, the Chairwoman of the Eagle Trust, and Hana Jirsa, the Chief Surgeon and Transplant Specialist at the Cambridge Center.

That's interesting, he thought. *Up to now there had been no direct proof Dr. Jirsa was one of the members.* This was also true of the Chairwoman, the President of Chile, and Victoria Lancing. Circumstancial evidence the four were members was all Rage had until now.

He moved on. Two names to go.

Doing a double take, Rage stared at the next one, Emilia Herboso, President of Chile. Herboso's much publicized political career stood out in her profile. She was in her second year as the President of Chile, and she had been in Prague for a heart transplant only a couple of months earlier.

Bells were starting to ring for Rage.

Something else had caught his attention recently too—something that had happened at the health clinic several years ago. He concentrated but couldn't remember.

Not wanting to waste time, Rage moved on to the final name on the list. This member was a woman and an architect. One of her best-known projects was the Cambridge Center facilities.

It was a showpiece. Several complimentary articles had been written about the combination of old and new at the health center.

The central building dated back several hundred years. The female French designer had built a reputation on this project alone.

A number of innovations had gone into the project. One had been a small combination furnace system for incinerating hospital bio waste and a crematorium for the disposal of body parts involved in organ transplantation. A new and unique system of filters had allowed the latter.

There was one detail involving the furnace Rage noticed was missing. There was no mention at all of actual full body incineration.

Aware of at least three cremations that had been Ana's friends, Rage became even more resolute to find out what had happened to Ana. He was also determined to find out if there might be others in jeopardy.

Taking one last glance at the information googled on the last member, something caught Rage's eye. Alayna Moreaux had shot herself to death at the Cambridge Center. Not just at the hospital, she had killed herself inside the crematorium at the doors to the furnace. One well-placed shot, the article stated.

Isn't that interesting?

Then Rage realized the suicide was what he had been trying to remember earlier. Milan had told Marty about the incident.

Rage knew much more about the members of the Eagle Trust now. He had a mental picture of the six who were living, and he knew about the three who were deceased. But this was only one part of the puzzle.

Now, how did the four young people, including Ana, come into the picture.

Rage leaned back again. He had a thought—the same one he'd had before.

"Could this be it?" He slowly rolled his head from side to side as he stared at the list he'd compiled. The thought would not leave his mind.

"Nah…couldn't be…could it?"

Rage was having a full-blown conversation with himself.

"But its not even possible," he said aloud.

"It would be illegal." He rubbed his head.

"Everywhere," Rage added.

He climbed to his feet and walked to the window. Rage smiled as he gazed out.

"I don't even believe my own argument."

Jolana and Marty were eating schnitzel and potatoes when Rage called.

No surprise there, he thought, *the eating or the schnitzel.*

Rage said he could call again later.

"No," his friend argued, "just took my last bite. Talk," he said, "I'll chew while I listen."

Rage heard him chuckle.

Through the mumble of munching, Marty added, "I'm still capable of multi-tasking."

Rage grinned and began laying out his plan. It was time to expose the Trust and hopefully, what had been going on with research at the Cambridge Center. Rage told Marty everything he had discovered. He also told his friend about identifying the nine members of the Eagle Trust.

Rage went into detail about the gathering he planned. There were a number of other individuals Rage wanted there. Most of them were available and several would be surprised their presence was required.

When he finished, Marty asked, "How many people for the meeting?"

"Upwards of thirty-five or forty. Maybe more."

"Where?"

"The Cambridge Center has a small auditorium in the administration building. I saw it on a directory when I was searching for Ana. We'll use it."

"What about those who aren't here?" Marty asked. "Those living outside the Czech Republic?"

"No time to bring them in. We'll arrange for a conference situation by internet. They will receive the same emails I'm sending the others, last minute and direct." Then he added with a knowing tone in his voice, "I want the meeting to be a surprise, and I don't want interruptions."

"When is this going to happen?" Marty was asking all the right questions.

"One o'clock tomorrow for everyone but the Chairwoman," Rage told him. "We'll meet with her at noon. I want you and Colonel Repa with me."

Marty was okay with the plans.

Rage continued. "When we are finished with her, Chairwoman Balca will accompany us to the auditorium."

"Are you going to let anyone know we're coming?"

"And spoil the fun? No, we'll just show up at the Chairwoman's office at noon. I'll make sure she's there to greet us."

Marty didn't ask about that either. The Author had an enviable record of making things happen the way he planned them.

Per Rage's instructions, Marty needed to make a couple of visits. He made necessary phone calls and then hurried out to make final arrangements in person.

Those on Marty's list for the most part worked in shift jobs at the hospital. None of them liked the idea of coming in for a meeting during their time off. Some of his contacts were reluctant to join such a meeting on short notice and with so little information. Still, with a bit of name dropping and other gentle persuasion, Marty was able to convince most of them to attend. He simply threatened those who were still reluctant. In the end, everyone on his list agreed to be in the auditorium on Wednesday afternoon.

Nurse Dusa, free of employment for the moment, was drafted to make the phone calls. She alerted those due for emails to expect them during Prague's morning. Rage had prepared a list and gave Dusa specific wording for her calls. Everyone was led to believe theirs was the only notice. They were not to discuss the meeting.

Everyone had received Dusa's call by midafternoon on Tuesday. Emails were set to go out early Wednesday morning,

Czech time. Neither Dr. Jirsa nor Victoria Lancing would receive a call from Dusa. They would be notified shortly before the meeting. Lancing would need help getting to the auditorium.

The Chairwoman would get her own special notice.

Rage spent the remainder of the afternoon and much of the night arranging his notes. The only times he left the upstairs desk was for short periods to check on Kateřina. She had another headache and stayed curled up on her bed for most of the time. Adina remained close by.

Both of the women knew Rage was probing for answers regarding the deaths of Ana and Kamil. They left him to do whatever would get them answers concerning their children.

Rage had asked Adina if it would be possible for her to spend the night with Kateřina. He explained he needed to work into the early hours and then get some rest. A noon meeting on Wednesday, he told her, would be important for all of them.

Adina agreed and made a trip to her own home for items she would need. She was back at 8:30 in the evening.

Saying good night to both of them, Rage hurried upstairs and began searching for some dates in the Chairwoman's files. He had reached conclusions regarding the research in those early years at the Cambridge Center's facilities.

Two lists were set up. One was the names of the members. The second involved any medical visits they'd had to the health clinic over the years. Those were secured for him by *Idona47*. The list took significant time because health records of the clinic were written in Czech and had to be translated.

In the dead of night, Rage was still working on the emails going to individuals. Those requiring their presence had to be very precise. Though the meeting was only hours away, Rage did not want anyone to discuss it. Instructions in the emails cautioned recipients. They were warned of possible unnamed consequences and left to wait for the meeting. Because of the number of individuals involved, there was no way to assure they would not talk. Rage could only hope.

The blackmail factor played into the picture too. By keeping the meeting and its subject confidential, he believed Karel Vlasta could be caught by surprise and perhaps give himself away as the blackmailer.

Hours before dawn, Rage still had a great deal more to do. He wanted the notifications to go out in time for recipients to arrange their schedules.

There were special messages for the three members who lived abroad. Time differences were taken into account. Rage wanted them glued to their screens at the appointed time.

The message content going to a core group was written for each specific individual. Dusa was prepared to send the information out by early morning, Czech time. The messages would appear to have come from the Chairwoman.

Finally, near four in the morning, Rage set up a folder on his iPad to use during the meeting. His suspicions had been accurate all along. Now he could prove his theory and other previous uncertainties.

Finished, Rage dropped onto the bed fully clothed and slept for two hours.

The first email to a member of the Eagle Trust arrived in the western United States at 11:00 p.m. Tuesday evening. Since his heart-lung transplant thirty-four months earlier, Roger Shawn Langston IV had feared he might receive such a message. He had actually been dreading the possibility since 1982. Now he was facing the reality.

A woman with a heavy Europeon accent had called earlier in the day and simply told him when to expect an important email based on Seattle time. It should not be missed, she told him. In a subdued voice, he thanked her and hung up.

The email lit up the screen of Langston's cellphone at the exact time the woman had given him. The message was somewhat strange but appeared to be from Zuzana Balca, his fellow Trust member and the Eagle Trust's Chairwoman.

An outside demand had been made against the Eagle Trust, the message said, and a meeting was scheduled for 1:00 p.m., Prague time, on Wednesday. Since timing and distance would not permit him to be present, he would be able to participate in the meeting via the internet and Skype. Details were given. It was indicated he should not miss the communication.

The message went on to mention the specifics of his surgery. Obviously, this was to deflect any uncertainty he might have as to legitimacy. After reading the email, Langston had no misgivings.

For security purposes, the message stated he was not to make contact with anyone regarding the email, the conference, or the Eagle Trust prior to the scheduled meeting. Questions would be answered then and in subsequent communications. Prior and un-authorized correspondence could jeopardize all the Trust had ac-complished since its founding.

Langston reread the email a number of times, almost memo-rizing it. There was no one he had any desire to contact. He saw other members only at meetings and had no significant relation-ships with anyone in the group. With time to reflect, he wondered if his decision in the early 1980s would be the same if he made it today. He guessed his questioning attitude would be typical for several of the other members of the Trust too.

1 6

WEDNESDAY, SEPTEMBER 30, 2015

* * *

THE NEW DAY DAWNED COLD and rainy in Prague. Standing at the window, Rage glanced back toward the alley where the security van had parked. He checked his camera and recording equipment. No sight or sound of it this morning.

After stretching his limbs, Rage had a shower and a shave. He dressed and laid out his fedora and long leather coat before heading downstairs to check on the women.

He found them having toast and coffee. Rage had a favor to ask. He wanted both of them at the Cambridge Center at 1:00 p.m. Glancing at Kateřina, Rage had no doubt attending the meeting would be a significant effort for her, but considering its purpose, he knew she would want to be there.

When he explained, they both agreed.

Rage took his coffee and walked out onto the terrace. Beyond the door's cover, a thin mist was still falling. He sipped the coffee as the day's schedule played out in his mind.

The email arrived early.

Appearing to be from the individual demanding the blackmail and saying she was being watched, the message ordered the Chairwoman to remain in her office during the morning hours. She was to take no visitors or calls, and not to contact anyone otherwise.

The notice also said she would receive a call on her private cellphone before 11:00 a.m. She would be told where to meet an individual who would give her further instructions regarding the demands on the Trust.

The Chairwoman spent several agonizing hours before the call came at 10:05 a.m. It was a man who spoke in her native language. She did not recognize the voice.

Chairwoman Balca wrote on a notepad, ripped off a page, and immediately went out to her car, leaving the hospital grounds without a word to anyone. The meeting place was several miles away in the Lesser Town area. She would be near Charles Bridge where the trams and buses made their connections.

Nearing her destination, Balca was slowed by heavy midmorning traffic. The Chairwoman hardly gave Prague Castle a glance today. There were too many situations demanding her attention—too much on which her future and that of the Eagle Trust depended.

Parking on the street, she hurried to the area where passengers normally awaited their travel connections. The Chairwoman found the food vender she had been told to use as her waiting point. She glanced around but saw no one who seemed to notice her. There was a bench nearby so she sat down and waited.

A few minutes later, a vagabond came and occupied the other end of the bench. He glanced her way and mumbled a hello. She nodded at his greeting and then looked away. Turning back, the grimy man produced a banana from a dirty coat pocket and started to peel it.

After a couple of bites, he gazed over and then slid toward her. "You going to give me some money?"

"What?" She was not sure she understood his garbled words.

"Are you the Chairwoman?"

Shocked, she started not to answer. Then she realized this foul-smelling individual was the connection she'd been sent to meet.

"Yes," she managed to say, "I am Chairwoman Balca. Who are you?"

He stared, ignoring her question. His eyes were bloodshot, squinted and piercing. Now he was in command of the situation.

"The woman who sent me said you would pay for this envelope." He exchanged hands with the banana and then held his dirty coat open with the other, revealing a brown letter-sized package poked inside his belt.

She hesitated. Looking into his eyes again, Chairwoman Balca realized he was not going to give her the envelope unless she paid.

Opening her handbag, the Chairwoman pulled out the roll of bills she normally carried. As she started to peel off a couple, the man suddenly dropped his banana and reached a dirty hand over grabbing the roll of korunas.

The Chairwoman still held the money too, and their eyes locked.

"Give me what I came for," she said.

He passed the package to her with his other hand while holding onto the money. Now both of them held the envelope *and* the money. One more look into his greedy eyes convinced the Chairwoman there was only one way this could go.

She released the roll of bills. He immediately let go of the envelope. The money went into his pocket, and the vagabond picked up his half-eaten snack.

"Want a bite?" he asked, grinning and holding the banana out toward her.

Before she could respond, he was up and away faster than she would have believed. The last she saw of him was when he took the final bite of the banana. The peel was tossed on the cobblestone sidewalk as he disappeared into a crowd of commuters.

Nurse Janalynn Dusa had observed the entire episode from a shadowed doorway a hundred meters away. The plaza was crowded, leaving little possibility she would be seen. Chances of recognition would be low anyway. Dusa was not in her nursing uniform today. She was dressed in business clothes for something a little more formal.

The delivery of the envelope had gone exactly as planned. The stranger she had picked now had some unexpected funds, and Chairwoman Balca had the envelope. The message inside it would give her something new to consider.

Karel Vlasta's email notification of Rage's meeting, like others, appeared to have come from the Chairwoman. It came as a routine communication and showed up on Karel's computer at midmorning. It ordered him to the auditorium at one o'clock in the afternoon. Unlike most of the others, Karel had not been scheduled for a phone call. This was his first and only notice.

Karel assumed he and the Chairwoman would have their regular daily meeting after this conference. He would not let this nor anything else interfere with his own plans. He read the email, noted the time, and mentally put it on a back burner until closer to the appointed hour.

He had spent the morning ready and waiting for Henri to send final instructions for transfer of the blackmail money. The email was scheduled for one-thirty in the afternoon. By evening, Karel expected to be wealthy. Contrary to what the Chairwoman might be thinking, he would not be back for more in the future.

If this transfer went as he planned and expected, she and the other members of the Trust would never see or hear from him again. If they accidentally passed on the street, the Chairwoman would not recognize Karel. His three phases of cosmetic surgery were already scheduled in Sweden. He would have a new look and a new life. Karel would live this life wherever he pleased.

He briefly wondered what this hastily called meeting was about. The thought it would have anything to do with him never crossed his mind. Karel had been adamant in his communications—there should be no contact outside the members of the Eagle Trust. As far as the Chairwoman knew, he was still searching for the blackmailer and monitoring all activities at the Bambanek home. His plans were still to tie the blackmail to Raegene Doyle.

The final demand message would reach the Chairwoman's computer at 3 p.m. This would give her the time she needed to meet the four o'clock deadline.

Who knows? I might even be in her office when it arrives.

He leaned back in his chair thinking of other possibilities. The Chairwoman had not requested any special security for her afternoon conference. Deciding the meeting must be routine. Karel had passed normal instructions on to his assistant. Alexandr could handle things.

If he didn't forget, he would put in an appearance at 1:00 p.m. Karel laid out a notepad in case he wanted to add to his own plans as the Chairwoman droned on about the Cambridge Center. He didn't like to waste time on things that could have no future value to him.

Karel smiled. *I will be gone...gone...*

Tucking the envelope into her handbag, the Chairwoman hurried back to her Jaguar, then toward the Cambridge Center.

Along the way, she could no longer contain herself and drove into a small park alongside the street. She killed the engine, glanced around, and then pulled the envelope out of her handbag.

There were no markings on the outside of the sealed package. Ripping it open, the Chairwoman found a single page. The instructions were simple and maddening. It directed Madam Balca to return to her office. There she was to wait in solitude again. Someone would contact her at noon. As before, no communications allowed.

I have been had.

No other instructions. Obviously, someone had wanted her out of the office. Nothing else was logical.

Who could have wanted me gone? Who would have needed me gone? And at this particular time.

She'd not even had time to make a final call to her Swiss financial institution. A call to her banker on Monday had reserved the blackmail funds in the doubtful possibility they would be required. She would work it out with the other members if it became necessary. Her security chief had given her every reason to think it was Kateřina Bambenek's friend and he would be able to prove it. Then, Karel had said, he would dispose of Raegene Doyle.

Thinking of the dirty man who had delivered the note, whoever sent it had certainly achieved their mission. Her thoughts were all over the place.

The character had said it was a woman. *Who...?*

She glanced at her watch—11:21 a.m. The Chairwoman put the note away and drove back to the Cambridge Center. On arrival, she had fifteen minutes to worry and watch the time drag by.

Scant minutes before noon, her office door opened with a preceding knock and Pavia Balek hurried in.

"I must tell you something," the young woman said.

The Chairwoman expected Pavia wanted to talk about some chore she had been assigned. Under normal circumstances, she would have listened but not today.

With a hand on the young woman's shoulder, Balca pushed her toward the door.

"I cannot take the time now," she said. "I am expecting someone for a conference." She added, "Perhaps we will talk later today."

Then the Chairwoman practically shoved her out the door. Pavia looked apprehensive, probably because of their angry encounter on Sunday.

"But this meeting at one..."

"Later," the Chairwoman emphasized.

As the door closed, she glanced at the clock. *Three more minutes.*

Wanting no more interruptions, Balca buzzed Ema and told her not to let anyone else in unless she announces them first. "No one!"

The secretary, caught in the middle, told the Chairwoman she would handle it.

Noon, but there was no knock at her door.

Another ten extremely uneasy minutes went by, then twenty. Finally, there was a sound outside and someone knocked. Quite sure this one was about the blackmail demand letter, she hurried to the door.

Seeing who awaited her, Chairwoman Balca raised a hand to her mouth in surprise but stood her ground. Three men were facing her, along with Ema. Balca immediately became angry. The audacity of these men presuming to come directly to her office without an appointment or giving notice.

A thought…*They did give me notice. Just not in a manner I would have expected.*

Of the three, the Chairwoman recognized only one of them: Raegene Doyle, Kateřina Bambenek's house guest. He appeared to be the leader. The others were not familiar. She studied them. One wore a police Colonels uniform. It concerned her. What reason would the police have for coming to her office?

She thought of asking her secretary to call security and have Karel join them. As was her manner though, the Chairwoman quickly decided to handle this on her own.

The third man was dressed in a business suit and was very large. He looked familiar, perhaps from the trouble in the transplant wing a few of nights ago. There was a big man involved in the altercation.

With Doyle leading, they started inside.

"I tried to tell them they could not come into your office without an appointment," Ema said in her own defense.

Rage Doyle turned and interrupted. "We are here to discuss the demand you received."

This shocked her a second time. She held his stare for only a moment before turning to dismiss her secretary.

"It is not a problem," the Chairwoman assured her and closed the door. Moving behind her desk, she motioned the three men to available chairs as she remained standing.

Doyle remained standing too. "Ms. Balca, my name is Raegene Doyle, but you probably already know. This gentleman," he said pointing to the giant, "is Martin Mayhem Cutler."

She listened but did not appreciate him using her name rather than her title. It was disrespectful, though this was probably not a time to argue the point. She glared at Doyle, realizing all this was a calculated strategy on his part.

Turning to the third man, Doyle's last introduction brought the most singular apprehension to the Chairwoman.

"This is Colonel Tibor Repa of the Prague Police." The man stood up and stepped forward offering to shake her hand. The Chairwoman only glanced at the officer, noting basics were all Doyle had given. She had no doubt the colonel was important, but there would be no handshake. Her immediate unease was difficult to hide.

"Ms. Balca," Doyle continued, "without you knowing, a meeting has been scheduled to deal with the blackmail demand you received."

How could he know?

"Some additional important matters concerning the Eagle Trust and the Cambridge Center will also be discussed."

"Mr...Doyle, is it?" Her eyebrows raised, Balca's words barely suppressed her anger.

"Yes...Raegene Doyle."

She stared at him. "I do not know what this is about or what you think you know. Whatever it may be, I do not believe it is your business."

Rage studied the Chairwoman for a moment.

"Madam Chairwoman, I can assure you the subject matter is the business of everyone who has ever had contact with the Eagle Trust or the Cambridge Center." He let the words hang.

Suzanna Balca had always feared this day would come.

As the Chairwoman's thoughts twisted and turned, there was a soft knock from outside. Intuitively expecting more of the same, she glanced at the men one more time and then walked over to open the door.

Nurse Dusa stood in the corridor. Instead of her usual uniform, she was wearing a dark skirt and blazer, a tan blouse and heels. The Chairwoman was now quite familiar with the young woman.

Surprised, Madam Balca asked, "What are you doing here? You were dismissed."

Dusa countered, not disrespectfully, but not retreating either. "I am back under different circumstances today. For your information, I arrived with the police contingent and Mr. Doyle."

The young woman's words sent a shiver down the Chairwoman's spine.

Dusa stepped away from the door and said, "Now please follow me to the auditorium." The nurse turned and stood waiting in the middle of the corridor. The three men walked toward Madam Balca at the door.

Balca had no reasonable choice but to fall in behind Dusa. The men followed.

Walking a couple of meters ahead, Nurse Dusa held the auditorium door open for the small procession and followed them inside.

Madam Chairwoman's name and each of the men was marked off a list by a police officer. Chairwoman Balca noticed the list was rather long.

She turned to the room which was filling rapidly. Rage Doyle motioned her to the lone chair on the speaker's podium. Hesitating initially, she then walked over and stood beside the chair. This would give her a better view, but, she realized, it would also make her more visible to everyone seated in the auditorium. She would need to be mindful of her emotions and expressions.

The Chairwoman thought it odd for there to be so many policemen with the Colonel. She also thought the young policewoman who took a seat beside Repa bore a striking resemblance to a maintenance worker who had filled in on a couple of shifts recently. Remembering, she realized it was during the cleanup in the transplant surgical suite.

Grudgingly taking the chair Doyle indicated, Chairwoman Balca glanced at the audience. She knew most of the attendees by sight. Guessing, she thought about forty people were present.

With her heart rate increasing, the Chairwoman noticed two of the remaining surrogate mothers sitting side by side. Adina

Dobias was there along with Kateřina Bambenek. Another surrogate sat a few rows away with her daughter. This one was Hana Jirsa's. Though she recognized the woman, Madam Balca had never met her. The fact that this woman was in the auditorium raised another concern for the Chairwoman. Why was she there?

Balca watched Rage Doyle help to get the Bambenek woman settled. There was obvious tenderness in the way he dealt with her. She was in a wheelchair and did not look well at all. The Chairwoman remembered Karel implying the woman possibly had cancer.

Ana Bambenek's ashes had been returned to her mother only two days earlier. The mother was obviously sick *and* grieving. Watching her for a few moments, the Chairwoman wasn't sure Kateřina Bambenek would make it through this meeting.

Waiting on Doyle to begin his show, Chairwoman Balca suddenly recalled the two surrogates who were deceased, one of an overdose of sleeping pills and the other who had died in her house at the end of a rope. The deaths had been investigated, but no foul play had been proven.

If only the two women had behaved in a less aggressive manner after their children's deaths. There had certainly been setbacks in the Cambridge Center's research, but there had also been great success.

The Chairwoman noticed her young assistant sitting alone on the aisle leading to the door. The Chairwoman was pleased that she'd had the foresight to bring Pavia onto her personal staff quite early. Now the young woman was dedicated, loyal, and able in her duties.

As she looked about, Madam Balca noticed several medical personnel were seated together, including the tall nurses who were a part of the transplant team. Dr. Laska and Dr. Seifert were next to each other. She watched as they whispered.

The psychiatrist had been very valuable to her as the unofficial Administrator at the Cambridge Center. That he had become known as the Warden was common knowledge. He was somewhat infamous for his leather shoes too. No one on the staff wanted to hear those well-known clicks coming in their direction.

Father Anděl was not far away from the Chairwoman. He had placed himself on the front row—his hearing, she expected. He kept looking back over his shoulder. She wondered if he was looking for someone in particular or only interested in who was there as the auditorium filed.

The head nurse was on the back row. Ivana had held the position in the transplant surgical suite for over twenty-five years. Though the woman had a dark reputation, the Chairwoman knew another side of her. If she liked you, she could be accommodating and sincere. However, she didn't like many people.

Madam Balca realized almost everyone there was on the medical team in some way, even her old friend Milan. He smiled when she glanced at him. The Chairwoman thought of the near crash she and Milan had a few days earlier. It had seemed rather comical at the time. Now a different thought crossed her mind.

Where had he been going in such a hurry?

Scanning others, Chairwoman Balca caught the eye of Hana Jirsa. The doctor still looked tired. She and her teams had completed many hours of surgery beginning late Sunday and continuing into the early morning hours of Monday. Some of the patients were still in serious condition and required constant monitoring. The surgical teams had transplanted numerous organs taken from Kateřina Bambenek's daughter. In doing so Jirsa saved Victoria Lancing's life, along with a number of others.

The Chairwoman focused on Victoria Lancing. The entertainer sat in a wheelchair a few rows up, an experienced ICU nurse at her side. Dr. Jirsa had said Victoria had been on the threshold of death prior to her surgery. Then afterward, the entertainer had almost hemorrhaged to death while still on the surgical table. The doctor had saved her again. Now she was improving rapidly.

Victoria's skin was no longer the jaundiced yellow of a person with liver failure. Her eyes looked better too, closer to a healthy white than they had been for several weeks. She looked sad, though. The Chairwoman wondered how their patient was doing emotionally.

She thought of the young people their endevors had fostered. Of the six they had started with, only two of these very special young people remained. The Eagle Trust research had claimed the others.

Madam Balca caught Pavia glancing her way. She looked unhappy. Was she upset the Chairwoman had been so abrupt with her earlier. Or could it be something else?

Balca gazed at Dr. Jirsa again. She appeared concerned too. Another result of their 1980s experiments belonged to the doctor and was sitting with her surrogate mother in the middle of the auditorium. The most recent report the Chairwoman had received on Jirsa's clone indicated everything was well and the young woman was living a normal life.

Dr. Jirsa kept close scrutiny on the situation. The doctor had fabricated a story of a weak heart valve in order to do periodic tests on the young woman. This allowed personal contact that was unique considering the nature of the research being conducted at the Cambridge Center.

Thinking of the young woman, Balca glanced at Dr. Jirsa again. The Chairwoman wondered again if Hana would be able to utilize her clone given the close contact. Four of those young people were already gone, and only Victoria had come close to leaving the program at the last minute.

Glancing at Doyle, she remembered him in another context now. He and the big man, Cutler, were the two who had nearly destroyed the transplant center on Saturday night. Security cameras had caught glimpses of the men as they attempted to seize Ana Bambenek and remove her from the hospital.

Yes, it was these two men who had caused the havoc. She was sure of it now.

Glancing back, the Chairwoman noticed Victoria Lancing was now watching Kateřina Bambenek. Did Victoria know she had a new lease on life specifically because of that woman's daughter? She might have pieced the story together from gossip she'd heard while in ICU.

Madam Balca surveyed the crowded room again and made a discovery. Her security chief was not there. Where could he be? She couldn't imagine his presence had not been required. Alexandr was there. Where was Karel?

No longer thinking of herself as Chairwoman, Balca now had a sudden deep dread for the purpose of this gathering. She had been brought here against her will and knew this could come to no good.

The Chairwoman suddenly could not visualize an end that would justify the decisions she and her eight fellow classmates had made all those years ago. To the four young people already sacrificed to science, it would not matter. To those who were left, Madam Balca dreaded they would now survive to know their own dark story.

Doyle was at the podium preparing to speak. Janalynn Dusa was next to him, outfitted with a microphone.

Chairwoman Balca watched Doyle closely. Her professional future and many others were at stake and could be decided in this meeting. She glanced around the auditorium. Nerves were on edge. She could see it in scattered faces.

The Bambenek woman's head was down, but her eyes were on the podium. Adina Dobias held her hand.

Seeing someone she didn't recognize give a thumbs-up, Balca noticed equipment off to the side of the podium and a camera mounted at the rear of the auditorium.

Doyle bent over, telling Chairwoman Balca, "We are using video to reach the members who are in other countries."

The fact Doyle appeared to know the Trust members surprised the Chairwoman. Their identities had always been secret. The Chairwoman knew the three who were not present. Their names had been guarded. How was Doyle aware of them?

She expected if he really had found those particular members, they would certainly be watching and listening. Especially since all three had been beneficiaries of decisions made in the 1980s.

As Doyle was about to begin, the entrance door suddenly burst open. The security chief rushed in and took the nearest empty seat on the aisle.

Balca watched as Karel immediately began making notes on a pad he brought with him. He busied himself for several moments before looking up. Finally, he raised his eyes and glanced around the auditorium. Karel appeared thoughtful, yet still not quite comprehending what was happening.

Then he noticed Rage Doyle on the podium. The thoughtful expression disappeared immediately. For a moment, Karel's eyes grew wide. Then he managed to control himself and his expressions.

Even at a distance, the Chairwoman could see perspiration pop out above his lips and on his forehead. Karel had also sneaked a glance at the entrance and the big man standing nearby.

What is Karel's problem?

Her attention was drawn back to the podium as Doyle began speaking.

"Ladies and Gentlemen, there are several subjects we are here to discuss." Turning to the nurse, Doyle added, "Nurse Janalynn Dusa will be interpreting for me."

Dusa repeated what he'd said in Czech. There was a bit of chatter as everyone began to suspect what was happening. Several appeared concerned.

"My name is Raegene Dorryen Doyle. Most who know me—friends and enemies alike—call me Rage Doyle. I'm a former United States CIA operative."

After Dusa interpreted this, Doyle let it settle for a moment.

"First, you should all know there has been a blackmail demand on the Cambridge Center, the Eagle Trust, and its six surviving members. The demand is for One Hundred Million U.S. dollars."

The Chairwoman cringed.

Dusa again translated.

Madam Balca noticed Karel Vlasta lean forward in his chair.

A buzz of speculation went through the audience and then settled as Doyle raised a hand.

"For those of you who may be unaware," Doyle said, "the Eagle Trust owns and operates Cambridge Health and Research Center."

He hesitated again, allowing for confusion and several surprised gasps and comments.

"The blackmail, unfortunately, is not our main concern."

The speaker had everyone's attention now. As Balca watched and listened, the Chairwoman surveyed the audience. She knew how many the auditorium would hold. Including police personnel scattered about and the one stationed at the door, the space was nearly to capacity at fifty. As she had considered earlier, the Chairwoman hated to think they were all going to learn the Trust's secrets.

Thinking of that, she made a decision. Balca was not going to allow the meeting to continue. She stood and walked to Doyle's side. Reaching out, she looked at him while placing a hand over his microphone.

A murmur ran through the audience. Every eye was on her; she could feel them.

"Mr. Doyle." She said it softly but in a stinging tone, "I will not allow this." Her eyes were dancing with a fire that was well known at the Cambridge Center. "Anything you have to say can better be handled in our conference room or in my office. All these people are unnecessary and have no right to hear any accusations you may be going to make. I am going to adjourn this meeting immediately."

The audience watched silently as if everyone had ceased breathing so they could hear her whispers.

Balca started to take her hand away from the microphone, but Doyle covered it with his.

"Madam Chairwoman, unless you return to your seat, the only thing going to happen immediately is you being arrested. You will be handcuffed and removed from this auditorium—forcefully, if necessary." His eyebrows lifted slightly when he uttered those last words, his stare both disturbing and intimidating.

The Chairwoman glanced toward the audience, noticing only one person. Police Colonel Repa was standing now, staring directly at her. Then she noticed all of the officers were standing.

Being arrested could serve no useful purpose. She knew that. After a few moments, the Chairwoman slipped her hand from under Doyle's and returned to her seat.

After a final glance at her, Doyle continued.

"I have operated a security firm in the years since leaving the US Central Intelligence Agency. My company does investigations and inquiries of varying sorts and for many different individuals and organizations. Most of the time, I work alone, but I have sources."

Doyle paused, giving Nurse Dusa time to do the translation. Then glancing across the audience, he said, "I tell you these things so you will understand I am qualified to make the investigation I've just concluded."

He took a moment to scan his audience.

"I recently received a letter from a friend in Prague. I had not seen or spoken with this person for many years." He glanced at Kateřina Bambenek. "This individual asked for my assistance. I remembered her fondly and couldn't refuse to come and help."

The Chairwoman looked over in time to catch a kind glance from the Bambenek woman toward Doyle. Her attention then shifted back to the audience. Father Anděl was sitting with his hand cupped to his left ear. Nodding, he seemed to understand what was being said and what was happening. He looked sadder than usual.

Not surprised, she noticed both Hana Jirsa and Victoria Lancing sitting straighter. A couple of rows back, Dr. Seifert leaned forward in his seat.

A number of individuals in the auditorium were looking more familiar now. The Chairwoman recognized they were employees she did not see much and did not know by name. By this time, she had determined everyone present had something to do with the transplant unit. This would mean they almost certainly knew or suspected what was happening there.

Doyle thinks everyone here helped to murder the four young men and women. It's the way he would see it from an investigator's point of view. But that's not how it was.

She looked at Victoria and also thought of the three who were watching the meeting on their computers.

These four would not think of the research as murder.

Doyle continued. "The letter I received stated that this person's friend had recently lost her daughter under strange circumstances. The daughter was in her twenties and in good health until shortly before her death. Then the mother was being handed the young woman's ashes."

He scanned the audience again, circling the entire room, stopping with his eyes on Adina Dobias.

"That particular mother thought there were unusual factors involved in her daughter's death. My friend thought so too. Unfortunately, the mother became so distraught, she took her own life. I am referring to Elita Melcer and her daughter, Marta."

Several individuals were beginning to move uneasily, Dr. Seifert and Dr. Laska among them. Vladan Kocian, the Organ Transplant Coordinator, was concerned too. He had shifted in his seat several times.

The Chairwoman particularly noticed the quick dark stare directed her way by the psychiatrist. She hesitated to speculate on his thoughts. Glancing over, she caught Dr. Laska looking at her.

A number of others glanced her way. Most who had looked were from the hospital medical teams, but some were not. Even the police were watching her. She could see Milan and Head Nurse Ivana. Almost everyone had stared at her accusingly when she returned to her seat. Approaching Doyle had probably been a mistake.

Again, the Chairwoman speculated she knew why most had been summoned to the meeting. However, there were people she didn't know seated throughout the auditorium. Those particularly worried her. *Could they be health board officials or outside policing authorities?*

Doyle suddenly stared her way and said, "Four young adults, two women and two men, have been sacrificed for the ideas and principles of the nine individuals who originally founded the Eagle Trust and the Cambridge Center. Two unknowing others await their fate if their organs are needed."

Another murmur, louder this time, swept through the auditorium. More than one individual glanced toward the entrance and the big man standing near it.

"Since notice of this meeting was short, three of the remaining members of the Trust could not be here in person. The other three are sitting among us."

Doyle motioned toward the video equipment. "We are missing Renato Bencivenni from Rome, Roger Langston from the United States, and Emilia Herboso, the current President of Chile."

Doyle's eyes swept the audience again.

"Each of the three who are not present have benefited from the scientific research conducted here at the Cambridge Center."

Doyle turned to directly address the camera's live feed.

"Had they known what we would be discussing, I doubt they would have attended this meeting anyway."

Turning back to the auditorium, Rage continued. "Some of you are probably familiar with the three who are here with us today. I will not name them here. This can be expected later when charges are brought against them."

People began glancing around the room again.

The Chairwoman found it difficult to keep her composure.

Outwardly, she stared at Doyle in a way that had served her well for so many years and situations. With him, her glare and attitude had no effect.

Inwardly, Madam Chairwoman was on fire. Rage Doyle was degrading everything to which she had dedicated her life.

She and Hana Jirsa had totally committed their lives to the research and practical application of using human clones. Other members of the Eagle Trust had lived as they wanted to and used their clones whenever it became necessary.

They had not been here in Prague to deal with grieving surrogate mothers when they were handed the ashes of their children. They also had not awakened in the night to worry with important details regarding the operation of the Cambridge Center. They had not been front and center as she had.

The Chairwoman now noticed Victoria watching her.

She didn't care what the entertainer might be thinking. The woman was alive because of her. Let Lancing have sympathy for the clones. She could have the Chairwoman's portion too. Madam Balca had decided long ago she had no time for those emotions.

Now she felt Doyle watching her. She knew he could discern discomfort in her expression. A frown covered her face as she glanced at those in the audience. Balca now expected only the worst of possibilities from this meeting.

During Doyle's accusations, the Chairwoman had occasionally let her eyes settle on her security chief. Karel Vlasta was doing things that were not usual for him. Normally calm and collected, Vlasta was now running fingers through his hair as he twisted in his seat and glanced about the auditorium. He was obviously nervous; they all were. But Karel had something extra going.

What is wrong with him?

Rage was also keeping tabs on Karel Vlasta and his restlessness. The security man seemed to know he was in a precarious situation. Doyle's discussion was the basis of the blackmail demand. Doyle also knew about the deadline coming later in the afternoon. Vlasta's computer had given up all its secrets to *Idona47* and Rage.

Karel's eyes darted about, appearing to search for a way out.

Watching him, Rage went on. "With connections I developed over the years, I have been able to narrow down an interesting list of individuals who either work here at the health clinic or have been involved in its history." Rage glanced around the room, this time with his eyes halting on the security chief. "In all cases, the individuals have access to information worth the amount of blackmail being demanded. At least one of the people involved obtained the information by virtue of their duties here and the access that comes with those duties."

Doyle scanned the audience again and once more stopped on Karel Vlasta.

He's not going to break easily, Rage thought.

"One of you is aware of everything I'm saying, and I can prove it," he told the audience, nearly all of them on the edge of their seats now.

"There are two choices of action relating to what should be done. The first involves the police."

There was a stirring in the room.

"Almost everyone here could be arrested as an accessory to murder for what they've done, and for many, what they have known for years and failed to report." Rage scanned the surgical teams, the doctors, and the psychiatrist. There was an observable flinch from several of them. Dr. Seifert stared at Rage in anger, an expression of defiance on his face.

Some had now leaned back and dropped their heads—many in shame, others in dread—at what could be coming their way. Some were whispering to the person next to them.

Doyle tapped the podium sharply to regain the audience's attention. When all eyes darted his way, he said, "Everyone here surely is aware human cloning is not only immoral but is considered illegal internationally."

Finally, having said the words, Rage now had them all on the same page.

"The Cambridge Center—your very own hospital—has been involved in this undertaking since the 1980s through both research *and* practice."

He gave those listening a moment for the basics to penetrate their thinking. Then Rage Doyle stated the real grounds of this meeting.

"Research here has shown one of the purposes of human cloning is to have compatible organs available for transplant, if needed. This would also make cloning specific to certain individuals." He hesitated for a moment. "Given the thought, what would be better than having organs available from a clone of oneself?"

The room became totally silent. Kateřina Bambenek's head dropped into her hands. Sitting beside her, Adina Dobias stared toward the Chairwoman in sadness.

"The problem is this. To use most cloned organs, the human clone and donor would be lost. The taking of organs from a human clone involves murder if the individual is sacrificed in the process." Again, Doyle hesitated. "Murder of this type has happened four times here at the Cambridge Center."

He waited for the chatter to subside as he watched Victoria Lancing choke back tears.

Rage checked his audience again. "An employee here, an outsider, has stolen this information and threatens to release the details unless one hundred million U.S. dollars is paid immediately. The deadline for delivering the funds is 4:00 p.m. today."

Startled, almost every soul in the room glanced around them, obviously wondering to which employee Doyle was referring. There were a few whispered speculations. Only Karel Vlasta sat perfectly still and quiet.

The audience quickly settled down. Some heads were bowed, not in prayer but in fear. A few others wondered what Doyle was talking about. A small number were ready to run for the hills.

Doyle's last words had shifted the focus back to the blackmail demand. Without appearing to do so, he was watching Vlasta even closer now. Marty was too.

One of the police officers standing in back whispered something to another and then they walked to the door. One continued outside while the other remained near the entrance, joining the officer already stationed there.

Rage continued speaking.

"An individual who works for the Cambridge Center or an accomplice who has been given information by the insider has made this demand for money."

All eyes were back on the speaker—even Vlasta's.

Rage looked around the auditorium as though searching. He glanced at several individuals before letting his attention come to rest again in the area where Karel Vlasta was sitting. Then his gaze settled directly on the security chief.

Almost everyone followed his eyes.

"In this case, we know who is making the demands."

The security chief now knew it too. Karel did not understand how Doyle had traced the blackmail to him, but he was immediately convinced he had been discovered.

A loud discussion had broken out toward the rear of the room. The door guard's attention had been drawn that way.

His eye on the door just three meters away, the security chief suddenly broke from his seat like a racehorse from the gate. The big man who appeared to be guarding it was twice as far away. To Karel, it was no contest.

Vlasta was at the exit before the nearby policeman heard him and could react. To Karel's surprise, when he reached the door, he was not alone. The big guy in the suit was there with him.

As Karel reached for the door handle and his way out, an iron grip encircled his left wrist. *It can't be,* Karel thought as he tried to shake the big man's grasp. *He can't be this fast!*

Karel almost laughed as he reached under his coat for the Czech pistol in his shoulder holster.

This man will wish he'd never confronted Karel Vlasta—if he lives that long.

The gun was on its way out of his blazer when a crushing judo chop struck Karel's right arm just above the wrist. Onlookers as far away as the back row heard bones snap in the double break. Karel's scream was audible throughout the headquarters floor.

The weapon flew from his hand, tumbling and skidding along the floor. In an aisle seat, several rows back, a woman felt a thud against her shoe, but she couldn't take her eyes off the action at the exit. In the continuing chaos, the jolt she'd felt was forgotten.

One of the police officers near the door hurried to take custody of the security chief. It wasn't difficult; Vlasta was in no condition to resist. He was doubled over, holding his arm in pain.

The young policeman glanced at Marty and appeared surprised at how efficiently the big man had disarmed the security chief. The officer held Vlasta's good arm and waited for instructions. The prisoner moaned.

Colonel Repa issued orders to others in their group to spread themselves around the auditorium. He had warned them in a morning meeting to expect trouble of this sort. The officer who had stationed himself in the corridor had now moved forward to help secure the door.

Almost everyone else in the auditorium was waiting, talking, and dreading what was to come.

The focus returned to the Cambridge Center's security chief. "It was not me," Karel shouted, pain showing on his face. "It was the American." He nodded toward the podium.

People were staring at him now.

"I found the emails on his computer," Vlasta shouted with a grimace breaking up his words. Raegene Doyle is who you want. I was gathering information for Madam Chairwoman. I was going to turn everything over to her this afternoon."

People lost interest in the security chief and were soon back to conversations around them. Karel was becoming frantic.

As his good wrist was cuffed, the security chief stared across the room, a shocked look in his eyes. He seemed to be searching for someone—scanning back and forth, looking…

The noise and confusion only added to the desperation that had descended on the auditorium.

Now, though in obvious pain, Karel painstakingly scanned the room again…

The Chairwoman watched, feeling self-reproach for hiring Karel and giving him so much authority and license to use it. How could she have been such a fool? Balca didn't feel a hint of guilt for those she and her fellow members had brought into the human cloning research. The doctors and the psychiatrist had come willingly. Money had bought their allegiance and silence. No one had been forced to the Cambridge Center's research wing.

The same could be said of the surrogates. Only two of them had become verbal and active after the deaths of their children. Both had died shortly after their children. No questions were raised in cursery investigations, and the two women's deaths were officially ruled suicides.

After those deaths, the remaining surrogate had been quiet. Glancing at Adina Dobias, the Chairwoman wondered if she hadn't made the connection about her son or was afraid to voice her concerns.

The Chairwoman and Vlasta had kept tabs on her for several months after the son's death. Dobias had been a typical grieving mother. No problem, they had finally decided.

But there were other matters to attend to right now. She approached Rage Doyle in the uncertainty following Karel Vlasta's rush to the door and then his continuing tirade.

With her attention focused on Doyle, she almost spat her words at him. "You cannot prove any of the things you have told these people."

"Madam Chairwoman—"

"You have brought great discredit to a proper and outstanding hospital. The damage may never be repaired."

Rage let her rant. What he had said was true, and she knew it. Guilt, mixed with anger, was evident in the Chairwoman's eyes and expression. Finally, she turned in obvious disgust and moved away from Doyle. Madam Balca stood on the podium and watched as her former employees obviously discussed her part in this planned tragedy.

Colonel Repa and his people were asking everyone to be seated. There would be information to gather and people to arrest. Vlasta's assistant, Alexandr, was sitting quietly near the middle of the room. He had watched Karel, disbelief etched on his face. Now, his hands folded in his lap, Alexandr sat still, resignation evident in his demeanor.

Marty had moved into the entrance and stood blocking the doorway. The Cambridge Center's psychiatrist and Dr. Laska had both tried to leave, but there was no way to reach the corridor except around the big man. Everyone had seen Karel attempt that with violence. No one wanted to take the same approach, and words had no effect. Several had verbal exchanges with the individual and then returned to their seats.

Various conversations developed as the police prepared to question individuals. It soon became clear the doctors and the psychiatrist had kept the exact nature of research and experiments from most of the staff. A few obviously had suspected but had no real proof young people were being killed for their organs. It didn't matter death for the donors came in an easy manner from chemicals developed in the Cambridge Center's own labs. Death in these cases was murder and must be punished.

Word quickly spread that several individuals were slated for serious criminal charges. Dr. Jirsa, Dr. Laska, Dr. Seifert, Head Nurse Ivana, and several others were among this group—and the Chairwoman too.

Doyle was glancing around the room. Satisfied Colonel Repa and his contingent had control of the situation, he walked over to Kateřina Bambenek, nodding to Adina as he kneeled down.

Pavia Balek looked at those around her. There was not a friendly face among them. Several knew she had been seeing the security chief and had watched as Karel was taken into custody. He had never been popular at the Cambridge Center. Now, flanked by police, he had burned all his bridges.

Could he be what Doyle said he was? A blackmailer? A thief?

Karel had admitted he killed a man in France. She had believed his story that it had been an accident. Now this. Could she believe anything he had said?

That's when they looked into each other's eyes.

Pavia felt tears on her cheeks. Her forehead wrinkled, and her eyes grew tight as she returned a stare from the man she had only recently begun to trust. She thought of his questions about her business relationship with Madam Chairwoman. Remembering, she realized Karel was using her to gain information for his own purposes. She thought of the intimate evening they recently shared and suddenly wanted to slip away and take a shower. How could she have been so wrong about him?

Holding Pavia's eyes and confused expression, he shouted out to her in a menacing voice, "Pavia, watch yourself! You could be next!"

Karel's words echoed across the auditorium. The room fell silent again, all eyes on him and Pavia.

"Listen to me!" he shouted.

Pavia wanted to look away, to close her ears and mind to his words. What could he possibly say that would be important for her to hear?

"There are only two of you left," he called out.

Two what? Pavia thought. *What could he be talking about?*

"You may be next!"

The policemen couldn't shut him up. The officers began forcing Karel toward the door.

She couldn't help looking at him now, her stare focused on his face.

"Ask Dr. Jirsa." He had managed to get a leg against the door frame and was looking back.

It was suddenly as if the two of them were the only people there. Looking directly at Karel, she could understand every word he said.

"Ask Dr. Jirsa!" the security chief repeated. "She has a clone too."

I don't understand. Why is he telling me about Dr. Jirsa, and what does he mean 'she has a clone too.'

Pavia remembered Doyle's earlier words about Eagle Trust members having clones of themselves in case they were injured or ill and needed replacement organs…

As the officer's dragged Karel into the corridor, he screamed to Pavia, "Ask the Chairwoman! You are Madam Balca's clone."

The Chairwoman heard him too. Her expression darkened as she glanced at Pavia.

The two women's eyes met.

Scattered gasps were the only sounds besides those of the police as they scuffled to control Vlasta and take him away.

Though Pavia knew little about cloning, she quickly realized if Karel's words were true, she had been destined to die if the Chairwoman became terminally ill or had an accident. She thought of the four who had already been sacrificed. Pavia had known each of them and had been friends with two.

She glanced at Ana Bambenek's mother. The woman's head was down as she wiped at tears. *Had she known about Ana?*

Pavia turned back to Zuzana Balca. Their eyes met, and the Chairwoman was the first to look away. She couldn't endure her daughter's accusing expression.

Astounded, she studied Madam Balca. Eyes don't lie. Pavia suddenly believed in her heart that if she was truly the woman's clone, then the Chairwoman would have sacrificed her if the need presented itself.

Balca chanced one more glance toward her clone. The young woman met her with a stare that sent shivers through the Chairwoman's body.

Finally, Pavia's anger consumed her as Madam Chairwoman's expression pleaded for understanding. Pavia had no desire to look at her anymore. She only wanted to leave this madness. The young woman lowered her eyes, attempting to calm and hide her anger.

As she looked down, something underneath the seats caught her attention. Pavia shifted her legs to see. There was a pistol on the floor. She remembered something striking her foot earlier as the fight at the entrance erupted. She immediately realized this was the weapon Karel lost in that altercation.

Without hesitation, Pavia picked up the gun, sliding it behind her handbag. She glanced around. Almost everyone was in conversations concerning how this would affect their own futures; no one noticed Pavia.

Standing, she stepped into the aisle and purposely walked toward the podium. A few, including Colonel Repa, glanced her way but had no particular reason to hinder her.

The weapon was heavy and large, but concealing it was easy. Pavia released the safety as she stepped around the female police officer.

A few others were milling about in the room while several remained seated. Groups had formed, and Pavia could hear many of them talking about the blackmail demands Karel had made and the way he was arrested. At the podium, the Chairwoman was talking with the old priest.

Pavia reached Madam Chairwoman but didn't wait for her to finish the conversation. She didn't excuse herself or even acknowledge Father Andĕl's presence.

Her voice shaking, Pavia asked, "Is it true what Karel said?"

The Chairwoman turned to her. "Could we talk about this—?"

"No!" Pavia's face was red with building anger; tears clouded her eyes. "Answer my question. Is Karel telling the truth? Am I your clone?"

Kateřina Bambenek was watching, glaring at the Chairwoman. Pavia could see her over Zuzana Balca's shoulder. The young woman stepped closer, her manner becoming more aggressive.

"If you have some illness that requires an organ, will I be sacrificed like Ana Bambenek?" she demanded. "Is all this true?"

Then Pavia raised her voice above the noise of the crowd. "Tell me the truth! I will know if you lie."

Hesitating, Zuzana Balca answered with downcast eyes. "Yes… yes to all your questions. You are a human clone—my clone." She finally looked at Pavia. "You are a copy of me."

Pavia stared back, her demeaner calm, before exclaiming, "I do not want to be your clone!"

In a flash, she drew the pistol from behind her purse and pressed the barrel to the Chairwoman's chest. Their eyes met for an instant before Pavia pulled the trigger.

Madam Balca was dead before she hit the floor.

Screams and confusion filled the auditorium.

In a split second, Pavia closed her eyes, thought of her mother, and softly whispered, "I'm sorry," as she pressed the barrel of the gun to her own chest and pulled the trigger.

Acrid smoke filled the air.

Rage had his back to the podium and was talking with Colonel Repa when he heard Pavia's loud words demanding the Chairwoman tell her the truth. The Colonel and Rage both turned toward the women as the Chairwoman reluctantly affirmed Pavia was indeed a human clone. Then came the final declaration before the shots.

Rage and the Colonel were two steps too far away to stop the violence.

When the first blast rang out, Repa's eyes widened, and he reached for his weapon. Rage was drawing his own pistol in the moment before the second explosion.

They were both too late. The killing was over.

Weapon in hand, Rage glanced across the room for other threatening movements. Everyone was suddenly still, and all eyes were focused on the podium and the two women lying there. There had not been time for anyone to duck or to hide.

The scene was tragic.

Coming out of a crouch, Rage holstered his pistol and rushed forward, the Colonel moving with him

Rage could tell by sight it was probably too late to save them. He had witnessed scenes like this before. Kneeling, he touched the neck of each for a pulse. Too late...

Dr. Jirsa rushed to her friend's side. She ripped open the Chairwoman's blouse, touching fingers to her chest. The doctor's other hand was holding Balca's wrist, hoping for a pulse. Several seconds passed before the surgeon, still kneeling, looked across at Rage with tears in her eyes. There was a slight side-to-side movement of her head. Dr. Jirsa could do nothing to help.

The doctor then moved to Pavia Balek and went through the same procedures. The younger woman, too, was dead.

Since this was a crime scene, the women's bodies would remain where they were until certain facts and evidence could be gathered. Though this was a hospital where transplant surgery was the norm, there would be no harvesting of these organs.

The Chairwoman lay on her back, arms spread at odd angles. Her unseeing eyes were open. Pavia Balek lay on her side at the Chairwoman's feet, a small pool of blood spreading from her chest onto the floor.

Rage stood and surveyed the scene. There was a pistol a few inches from Pavia's hand. She had been the shooter. He would ask Colonel Repa to substantiate. They had both witnessed the action.

As Rage searched for other evidence, Colonel Repa gestured for his people to keep close control of the onlookers. Gita Kovar and one of the other officers moved toward the door. Others of Repa's group scattered themselves about the auditorium, reassuring some, directing others to calm themselves and overall bringing a nervous composure to what had been total confusion.

The Colonel told Rage he was calling for more officers. There would need to be interviews and perhaps some would even be held for further questioning. "We will be working into the night," he told Rage.

Dr. Laska and one of the new doctors were standing at the back of the room where they were joined by Dr. Jirsa. Rage was watching as the new man obviously asked a question of Jirsa. She answered and then the doctor shook his head. Jirsa said something else before he turned and walked away. Dr. Jirsa called out, but the young doctor kept moving.

Getting no response, she immediately went toward the exit where she was met by the policewoman. Officer Kovar placed herself between Dr. Jirsa and the door.

Though close enough to see and hear them, Rage was not able to understand their Czech conversation. It was obvious though, Dr. Jirsa intended to leave the auditorium. There were loud words and then the policewoman reached behind and pulled a set of handcuffs to show the doctor. She looked at the restraints and then at

Gita. Finally, the doctor nodded and retreated to the rear of the auditorium where she took a seat.

Dr. Seifert had returned to his seat after his and Dr. Laska's ill-fated attempt to get past Marty. The psychiatrist's only discernable movement had been to turn toward the back of the room. Not one of the Eagle Trust's members, Rage wondered if the psychiatrist felt any guilt or remorse for the research being conducted at the Cambridge Center. Dr. Seifert was certainly involved.

Rage could see his face. It was expressionless, and his eyes displayed a thousand-meter stare, though they were in the closed room. Having watched the confrontation between Dr. Jirsa and the policewoman, Dr. Seifert turned slowly and slid down in his seat. He seemed to understand life as he knew it had ended.

Glancing across the auditorium, Rage saw the priest, who had retreated off the podium and to his seat when Pavia Balek interrupted his conversation with the Chairwoman. The old man was still sitting with his head tucked between his legs. Rage touched the old man's shoulder and watched as he slowly raised himself to a sitting position. Gazing around the room, he seemed to be all right, just nervous and still afraid.

Victoria Lancing was alone a few rows up. Her eyes were closed, lips pulled tight, and her arms drawn tight across her chest. Rage wondered if Lancing might be having second thoughts about Kateřina Bambenek's daughter. The entertainer looked as if she might pass out at any moment.

Rage asked if Colonel Repa could spare one of his people to accompany Lancing to her room and stay with her until she could be interviewed. They would certainly want Victoria's statement.

Glancing across the room, Rage wondered if any of these people were feeling remorseful or if they were only thinking of possible repercussions for their acts?

The security chief's assistant had come out of his seat and dropped into a crouch when the shots rang out. There wasn't much he could do since he and Karel were the only ones attending the meeting from the security office. Rage guessed Alexandr also understood the gravity of his part in what had been happening.

After looking around, he eased back down into his chair, a rather sad expression on his face. Glancing around, Alexandr realized the next few weeks would be traumatic, not only for himself, but for most of these individuals.

Most everyone was averting their eyes from the bodies on the podium. Someone had come up with a couple of jackets to cover them. Everyone knew the Chairwoman. Many others had been friends with Pavia.

Rage knew Kateřina and Adina would be devastated knowing the details of their children's deaths. He went to them and knelt beside Kateřina. Adina was holding her hand. The two women had much in common now. They had each lost their child to others who had decided to overrule God's laws. Getting a grip on their sadness and anger would take a lifetime.

Kateřina and Rage whispered to each other for a few moments. She slipped fingers behind his neck and pulled him to her. "Thank you," she said with her eyes and her words. "Now I know about Ana."

Motioning to Nurse Dusa, Rage asked her to help the two women to their vehicle. He knew Kateřina would need rest after this ordeal and witnessing the shootings at the podium. It had happened only twenty feet from where they were sitting. Statements could be taken later.

Nodding, he stood and walked toward the front of the auditorium. Rage was joined by the Police Colonel. In his broken English, Repa said he had seen the shooting coming in the final moments but had no time to change the results. He confirmed everything Rage saw with only a few words.

"The women were talking," Colonel Repa said and then pointed to Pavia. "The younger one was angry. She pulled the weapon from behind her purse and touched the Chairwoman's chest with it before pulling the trigger."

Colonel Repa nodded toward them.

"Then the young woman shot herself the same way," he said. His eyes squinted in a puzzled expression, then the Colonel added "She seemed to whisper something before pulling the trigger."

It was as though Repa could not believe what had happened even after watching it with his own eyes. "She wanted to make sure they each were killed," he said. "I have witnessed murder/suicide this way before."

"It's shattering to watch," Rage said, "and very difficult to understand."

Repa only nodded.

1 7

AUTUMN 2015

∗ ∗ ∗

THE DAY WAS COOL AND fair, and the sky azure blue when Ana's cremains were interred at Vinohrady Cemetery. The service was held three days after the tragic pivotal meeting at the Cambridge Center. Kateřina had wanted the interment over now that she knew the details of Ana's life and death. Though the answers were not what she would have wanted, Kateřina finally knew the truth.

Rage stood beside Kateřina's wheelchair as they watched and listened to the Catholic Priest from her church say a few words. Adina and other friends, mostly from church, were there too. Kateřina held tight to the hand Rage had placed on her shoulder.

Two roses, one from Rage and one from Kateřina, were the only flowers there. The single stems had been her idea.

The service was short. Kateřina, though solemn, had appeared at ease as they returned to her automobile. Getting into the vehicle was difficult. She had to have help doing most things now.

"I have thought of Ana many times in these last days," she told Rage as they were driving back home. "She could have had such a wonderful life; being a physician, marrying, and having a husband and children." She sighed and then glanced his way. Smiling slightly, she added, "I might have become a grandmother."

With tears in her eyes, she touched his arm.

In the days following the meeting at Cambridge Center, Rage had several conferences with Colonel Repa. They attempted to tie up loose ends with the Colonel coming to Kateřina's house for their talks. Rage seldom went out. Through Marty and Repa, he passed on details gathered in the investigation. Rage also gave a written statement.

The Colonel was allowed to copy work papers and other information Rage had accumulated. *Idona47's* input was discussed off the record and evidence included for Repa as though coming from Rage.

The Colonel was charged with investigating the deaths and accompanying circumstances of the four young adults. Repa also told Rage interviews were being conducted with those involved with the human cloning research and experiments.

Dr. Hana Jirsa, Dr. Laska, a second transplant surgeon, two other specialists, and Dr. Seifert were now implicated in the human cloning research. Other medical personnel, mostly from the transplant surgical teams, were running scared. All of those implicated were now on paid leave.

Though the authorities had no doubt they would develop a case, there was not enough direct evidence to confine anyone immediately. This would come later when details had been linked to specific individuals. In the meantime, everyone involved had been warned to report any planned travel and have it approved before leaving the country. Some were not given the option. They had all signed documents agreeing to the restriction.

The old priest, Father Anděl, ailing and not fully understanding what was happening, had been told his services were no longer needed at the Cambridge Center. He used his savings to purchase a small cabin in the Romanian mountains where he grew up and had friends. The cleric had walked his last unfortunate clone to their death.

Though she was under minimal travel restrictions, Victoria Lancing, with the help of relatives and in the dark of night, had quietly slipped away to return to her home in London. A chartered aircraft was waiting and ready to roll at Vaclav Havel Airport when she and her entourage arrived there. Victoria was gone before Prague authorities knew.

The three members of the Eagle Trust who lived in other countries were not expected to willingly return to Prague for any reason. They had said as much.

Dr. Hana Jirsa was the only member of the Trust still living in the Czech Republic. Authorities had restricted her travel. The doctor had not been seen in public for several weeks. It was as though she had disappeared from the city.

Weeks later, on a cool morning in mid-October, Kateřina and Rage had finished a light breakfast and were sitting on the settees. He had carried her there to have a second cup of coffee. Kateřina was reading the newspaper.

Looking up, she asked, "Did you know this?"

"What?"

Her eyes returned to the article. "Both the Chairwoman and her daughter were interred at Vinohrady Cemetery yesterday."

"Together—in the same plot?"

"No, separately," she told him.

"Does it mention how they died? Is there anything about the meeting?"

"It is almost like an editorial. Only a few friends of each were there, and it was raining and cold." After glancing his way, Kateřina read aloud, "'Dark clouds fit the mood at each of the two small gatherings.' It actually says that."

She added one more thing. "It does say the surrogate mother of Pavia Balek was at her funeral."

They each reached for their coffee as Kateřina laid the paper aside.

Articles had run in various newspapers around the world after Prague's sensational news regarding human cloning. Details were scarce, but few had doubts about the truth of the information. News channels on the internet had updates as often as there was anything to report. As with many internet stories, if there was nothing fresh, online writers would make it up. It was difficult to separate truth from fiction.

Several stories had implied the Cambridge Center was not unlike a vehicle with no driver, speculating the five remaining members of the Eagle Trust were still running the hospital.

Other information indicated the city of Prague had taken over temporary operation of the hospital. Patient load had dropped off significantly, and there were questions regarding closure of the facility. No one wanted that. The large hospital was important to a city the size of Prague. Though one of several, no one wanted to lose the Cambridge Center.

The core group running operations day to day were new doctors who had been with the Cambridge Center for less than a year. Everyone who appeared to have knowledge of the transplant unit was on leave until the human cloning investigation was complete. The transplant unit was shut down until the investigation was complete.

A group calling itself Cambridge Center Administration was in charge of negotions with the Eagle Trust members and reported to the city of Prague.

Marty worked with Colonel Repa and kept Rage informed of the latest developments. They tried to talk several times each week, but with Rage caring for Kateřina, sometimes a week would pass without a call.

On a morning near the end of October, Marty phoned and asked if he could come over.

"Sure. When?"

"Now."

"Come on."

They sat in the big chairs on the front porch to keep the house quiet for Kateřina.

Hardly containing himself, Marty began.

"There was a conference in Paris yesterday," he said. "I was invited to go with Colonel Repa."

"You hadn't mentioned anything being on the schedule. Was this a surprise?"

"The meeting was secret until it happened," Marty said. "The foreign members are being careful. They don't want to get caught in a situation where they could be dragged back to Prague."

"Tell me more."

"The subject concerned the Cambridge Center and the Eagle Trust. All the remaining members of the Trust were there along with their attorneys. Several people from the hospital attended too."

"What about Dr. Jirsa?" Rage asked.

"She was there," Marty told him. "I heard she flew in from Switzerland. She walked into the meeting a few minutes before it began and left immediately after. She didn't comment at all, just listened. I only saw her nodding once. That was when the members said they wouldn't return to Prague."

Rage was surprised. "I didn't think Jirsa could travel."

"You didn't hear about her escape?"

"No."

Marty grinned. "She disappeared from Prague a couple of weeks ago. No one knew about it until she walked into the meeting."

"What do you mean 'disappeared?'"

"Jirsa left during the Chairwoman's funeral. Without anyone knowing, she chartered an aircraft out of France to secretly fly her and a small amount of luggage to Zurich. It was timed for the exact hour of Balca's interment. She's gone."

He glanced at Rage, who showed no reaction.

"Dr. Jirsa's old phone numbers are turned off, and no one can reach her. Her house here in Prague was owned by the Eagle Trust. Did you know that?"

Rage shook his head and made a rolling motion with his hands, gesturing for the big man to continue.

"Her residence was deserted when someone went to check on her," Marty said. "All the furnishings and her other belongings had been shipped to an apartment at Lutry, Switzerland, on Lake Lausanne." He glanced at Rage. "She did everything in total secrecy."

"Tell me about the meeting," Rage said.

"The individual members are trying to stop the bad press," Marty told him. "Money doesn't appear to matter. They don't think they can be brought back to face charges, but they're trying to shore up their reputations.

"The guy from Rome spoke for them. What's his name… Bencivenni? Yeah, that's it. Renato Bencivenni. He acted as their speaker."

"Who ran the meeting for the people from Prague?" Rage asked. "And who was there from the Cambridge Center?"

"One of the new doctors was the Prague spokesman." The big man started to name the others, checking individuals off on his fingers. "Me, Colonel Repa, Janalynn Dusa, Milan. Oh, and the last two doctors hired at the hospital."

He took a breath.

"Adina was there," he remembered, "and the other surrogate mother. You know, Pavia's, the one who shot the Chairwoman." Marty took a breath, then added, "Oh, and neither Jirsa's surrogate nor her clone showed up. Someone said they are moving out of the country."

"What are the remaining members after?" Rage asked.

Marty had an answer, but it was joint—his and the Colonel's. "We think they're attempting to make it so the Czech authorities won't try to extradite them for the four murders."

Rage was shaking his head again. "How is it possible?"

Marty held his hand up, rubbing the thumb against the index and middle fingers. "Money," he said. "Money…"

"How much?"

"They're willing to deed over houses, vehicles—everything personal—and pay the families for the deaths."

"What if there is no family?" Rage asked.

"Funds go to the hospital."

Rage raised an interesting point. "The Eagle Trust owns the Cambridge Center," he said, "and the members own the Trust."

"The five of them would give up their voting rights but would consider staying on board in an advisory capacity."

"Okay. And what about funds for the families?"

"Twenty-five million for each death and surrogate and the same for living children and their surrogates. Where surrogates and the children are deceased, the funds would go to the Cambridge Center."

"How was it left?" Rage wanted to know.

"There will be another meeting in two weeks," Marty told him. "Paris again but an undisclosed location."

"What happens now?"

"Meetings here with local attorneys, new ones." Marty indicated the Cambridge Center Administration group didn't want to use lawyers who had previously dealt with the hospital or the Trust. "Two local meeting will be held in the next ten days."

"Can I get a look at their proposal?" Rage asked.

Marty smiled, pulling folded papers from his pocket. "Colonel Repa thought you might want to be involved."

Still holding the pages, he patted them against his hand. Marty seemed to have thought of something else.

"A couple more things," Marty said. "Colonel Repa heard there's a move on in Chile to remove Emilia Herboso from the office of President. The military might even get involved. I guess the opposition has started rumors Herboso is thinking of doing research at hospitals in Santiago. She might resign to get out of the spotlight."

Rage was shaking his head when Marty finished.

The big man handed the pages to Rage and left, saying he had things to do.

On a misty morning, Kateřina pulled Rage close and told him, "My head hurts so much, I wish to die." Tears clouded her eyes.

Her lucid moments were coming less often now. More and more she was slipping away. Rage wasn't prepared for this. He was used to controlling things in his world. There was no control here. He could only watch a beautiful life slowly fade away.

Marty kept Rage abreast of developments in the investigation. Further searches had determined there were no other young clones. There had been only been the original six. One had survived.

Now that Kateřina had answers about her daughter, she agreed to see her doctor. They had been able to schedule an emergency appointment with the oncologist.

"The cancer is quite advanced," he told her. "We will only be working to manage the symptoms."

Tests indicated Kateřina had waited too long for any preventive treatment. Refusing earlier chemo and radiation was having dreadful effects on her. The symptoms of the damaging disease were multiplying, both in number and intensity.

The doctor took a chair beside Kateřina and held her nervous hands as he explained hospice and palliative options. They also discussed new problems she should expect in the days and nights ahead.

"I will see you periodically, and hospice nurses will watch over you on a daily basis when it becomes necessary. Together we can give you some relief from your pain and the stress you are under."

A nurse who spoke English translated for Rage. He told the doctor he and Adina would be Kateřina's caretakers. Beyond administering medications, she had made it clear she did not want strangers touching her.

The oncologist continued. "The drugs you take will help reduce swelling. It will also help to control seizures and reduce nausea and stomach sickness."

Kateřina glanced down. Her hands were in constant motion. Clasping them, she tried to restrain their movement. Kateřina often wondered if the cause was the cancer or the stress. Her oncologist had told her it could be stress related to her condition and the death of Ana.

Outside the doctor's office as they were leaving, Rage knelt beside Kateřina's wheelchair. He pulled her close and held her in his arms. He heard a single sob. Kateřina went home without significant hope.

Rage met twice with Colonel Repa and Marty in the weeks before Christmas and between meetings. One of the group's new attorneys was present each time.

The five remaining Trust members acknowledged they could not control the legal actions taking place in Prague. They also let it be known they would spend whatever it took to avoid being returned to the Czech Republic for trial.

The media had gone on to other stories after an initial sensational series of articles regarding human cloning and Cambridge Center's research and experimentation. Emilia Herboso had made news again when she resigned the Presidency in Chile. Other information and interviews became newsworthy as the investigation continued. The four murder investigations were a part of the original publicity, as was the identification of the Eagle Trust members. In time, action in the Middle East took over headlines and relegated human cloning research articles to lesser back pages.

Now the remaining members only wanted to be away from public notice. They were each offering lots of money toward this end. In addition, they were collectively proposing to continue funding the hospital.

Rage studied the agreement. Other than a few wording changes, the Cambridge Center Administration group and their attorneys were satisfied. Rage was not. He could see the Eagle Trust members failing to fund the hospital at some point. There was also no provision to continue funding when the members were deceased. Rage recommended a very large endowment instead of volunteer payments. The number he had in mind was five hundred million US dollars. He also suggested Czech International University take over the hospital's management.

In lieu of those arrangements, Rage recommended selling the Cambridge Center and distributing the funds according to the Eagle Trust's original agreement. In that case, Doctors Without Borders and UNICEF would receive a great deal of new funding.

Doubting members would allow this to happen, Rage expected they would rather fund a large endowment and let the University take over the hospital. After all, the Eagle Trust, at least on paper, had been originally formed to do good in the world.

Rage thought they might also like to make sizable donations to the two charities in lieu of selling the hospital. This might help with their reputation problem.

After much discussion in a second Paris meeting, Rage's suggestions were made a part of the tentative agreement.

Disregarding their arguments, plans were being made to try and bring the remaining members of the Eagle Trust back to Prague for a trial. With their wealth, Rage doubted this would ever happen.

After the Paris meetings and approval of the updated agreement, Rage sat beside her bed and explained the details to Kateřina. She seemed to understand most of it but said it fell far short of having her daughter at her side.

That same afternoon, Rage received a call from Marty. The big man had received an important update on Victoria Lancing through Colonel Repa.

The entertainer had overdosed on a pain medication she had been taking after her surgery, and she had left a note. Though not implicating others, Lancing talked about decisions made early in life that affected others near the end of her life. It was evident she was talking about the research and organ transplant surgeries at the Cambridge Center. Lancing also wrote she could never repay her donor or the young woman's family for the gift she had been given.

"She wanted her will read immediately," Marty said. "Everything she owned went to the Cambridge Center."

"Good," Rage replied.

"I'm not finished."

Rage nodded.

"I wasn't given a number," Marty said, "but Colonel Repa indicated it was a vast amount. The interesting part is the funds are to only be used for children's cancer research."

There was a moment of silence and then Marty said, "I guess in the end she did accomplish something good in life."

Conditions were bad most of the time now. Though Kateřina tried to be active, she spent much of her time in bed. She tried to read but couldn't concentrate. Sleep claimed more time than the stories.

Breaking the routine one day, Kateřina's lawyer rang the doorbell.

"I called him," she told Rage. "There are some matters I want to put in order."

She gestured for the elderly lawyer to pull a chair up close to her bed. "I need to give you some instructions."

Rage found other things to do while they were talking.

As the lawyer was repacking his briefcase, Rage happened by the bedroom on the way to the kitchen. Kateřina introduced them. She had to translate for both of them, so there was little conversation.

The next time Rage saw the lawyer was a couple of days later when he returned for Kateřina to sign documents. She had wanted to go to the settees for this meeting. Rage had tucked her into the wheelchair and took her there, lifting her onto her favorite seat.

Finished and on his way out, the elderly man asked her to inform Rage he would send some papers in a few days. Surprised, Rage smiled and said that would be fine. He expected this would be the last time they would have reason to communicate.

Rage turned his attention back to Kateřina. He could tell she was tired from the activity.

"I think I will rest for a while," she said. He turned the wheelchair toward her bedroom. Surprising him, Kateřina asked Rage to dance with her.

"The Blue Danube" was playing. Without hesitating, he lifted her into his arms, and looking down she placed her bare toes on the tops of his shoes. They danced a few turns to her favorite waltz. Holding her close, Rage slowly whirled through the steps as though they were a couple out for a pleasant evening. With her head on his shoulder, she obviously relished the dance. This was all that mattered to either of them.

When the music ended, Rage swept her up into his arms and carried her to the bedroom. He watched as Kateřina stretched out on the bed. She smiled up at him and then turned on her side. Closing her eyes, she immediately dropped off to sleep.

Rage worried as he stood watching her. He thought she had lost more weight, but he moved to the thought he would always remember: how she felt in his arms during the dance.

Over the next two days and nights Kateřina didn't leave the bed except for aided trips to the toilet. Otherwise, she slept most of the time. Rage knew the hospice nurses were medicating her for the headaches.

What little food she accepted was brought to the bedroom.

Adina had rejoined them and helped Rage care for her. They took turns at her bedside.

Kateřina was becoming more confused, and even with the medicine, the headaches were disabling her more frequently now. Her speech was often slurred. The disease was claiming her.

Rage tried to do things he thought would comfort her. Restless one night, she had tossed and turned for over an hour as he watched from the chair beside the bed. In an effort to ease her, Rage lay down and rested his arm across her body. Surprising him, Kateřina immediately eased herself back into the contour of his body and appeared to settle down. She remained this way for over an hour.

Kateřina softly called out to Ana several times as she slept.

She was slipping away before his eyes.

"Each time I do something, I wonder if it is for the last time," Kateřina told him during one lucid moment.

Rage touched her arm gently and smiled into those big green eyes. They were as beautiful as the first time he'd seen them.

Kateřina sighed as she glanced in his direction. "There are so many last times," she said dispiritedly.

Christmas was upon them, and Adina brought a few decorations, some lights, and a wreath over to brighten the house.

"I didn't realize the holidays were so near," Kateřina said.

They were on the settees across from each other one evening. He had carried her there. It had been a bad day, and he wanted her to have some time out of the bedroom.

During the day, Kateřina had become angry at him for things she imagined. Rage had made tea for her and set it on the side table. It was unsweetened—the way she liked it. But today she complained vigorously it was not sweet enough. Becoming irate when he tried to explain, Kateřina had thrown the full cup and its saucer on the floor.

Rage had cleaned up, picking up pieces of china and sweeping afterwards. She had complained about his efforts and said the floor would be slippery.

He had run the mop again, but she had still been unhappy. Things of this sort happened often. It had occurred with Adina, too. Little nonsense things. It was difficult dealing with her much of the time. She had to have help with almost everything, but they loved her, so…

The anger would come from nowhere, and it was often directed at Rage. Things were difficult, but he loved her, and to him it meant taking the challenging along with the easy.

So many things were going wrong with Kateřina's body and her mind. More symptoms added themselves to a growing list each day. Those that were already there became more pronounced.

Watching over her consumed the days and nights. There was little sleep for Rage—always one more thing to do. There were funds for her needs, but no amount of korunas could have purchased the dedication Rage gave Kateřina as the days and nights ebbed away.

Friends from her church stopped by daily. Adina and others quietly kept food available. They slipped in and out without disturbing the relative quiet that finally settled on the house.

A few days after the lawyer's last visit, an envelope was delivered by UPS. It was addressed to Rage. Expecting it was information regarding Kateřina that he would need later, Rage took the package upstairs and left it unopened with his other papers.

Adina became his standby. She came without being asked and often stayed for hours. Rage occasionally left the room when Kateřina's friend was there. The women's relationship had strengthened during those trying days. Leaving them alone allowed words they might not have said with Rage there.

Napping from time to time, Rage knew sleep would not be possible without someone like Adina to watch over Kateřina. Caring for her had become an around the clock endeavor since they had returned from Vinohrady Cemetery and Ana's ceremony

Days had passed since they last embraced, and he carried Kateřina to her bedroom. She never left her bed again; Rage seldom left her side.

Hospice had been asked to begin daily visits. Their nurses now oversaw all treatment and medications. They kept Kateřina bathed and monitored her overall condition, but Rage was always there. Both he and Adina understood the end was near.

Occasionally, Rage would slip outside when Adina was there. He strolled across the terrace countless times in those last days. He had often noticed Adina watching as he stood looking out toward the trees, remembering…

There was not much in life Rage regretted but having never returned to this woman was the most disturbing. As with so much in life, there was no way to change it now.

When she peeked in, Adina found them on Christmas morning, her hand in his, as Rage sat in his chair resting his head on her arm.

Looking up, he said, "She's gone. Let the others know."

Kateřina had passed quietly in the early morning.

He eased her hand down onto her chest and stood up. Rage walked to the window as he wiped a mist from his eyes.

Kateřina 's final ordeal was over and her prophetic dream had finally come true. The pain and headaches were gone forever.

As with Ana's service, there were only a few individuals at Kateřina's interment beside her daughter. Rage stood a distance apart from the others. Marty and Jolana looked on from a few meters away. Adina and several women from their church also attended. The elderly attorney who had prepared Kateřina's papers stood near a large tree with his young assistant holding his arm.

Wet snow was falling. Umbrellas shielded most everyone but Rage, Kateřina's lawyer, and his young helper. They were also without umbrellas or rain coats. The old counselor wasn't even wearing a hat.

Words were spoken and then everyone moved through the increasing snow to their transportation. A few, including the lawyer, acknowledged Rage. Adina gave him a brief hug.

Afterwards, as he stood alone, the young woman from the law office came over and shook Rage's hand. Though she wore a leather hat and coat, the snow had gotten to her around the collar. She held her arms tight across her chest and was shaking.

The woman lingered, asking, "Have you read the material my employer sent you?"

"No," Rage told her. "There has not been time." In fact, he had forgotten the large envelope delivered to him a few days earlier. There had been too much happening.

"Find a few minutes to read it, Mr. Doyle. There is a copy in Czech and one in English. I did the translation for you." She smiled, appearing proud of her forethought. "After you have examined the material, I am sure you will want to visit our office."

Rage gazed after her as she turned and hurried to catch up with the old attorney.

Back at Kateřina's house, Rage exchanged his soaked clothing for a dry turtleneck, slacks, and footwear.

The house was still and quiet—not a sound except his own. Leaving the bedroom, Rage walked the halls of the second floor, opening a door here and there. There were several bedrooms and baths and another room set aside for crafts.

In this room, there was an easel, paints and brushes, and other materials near a window where the light was best. He had examined the room for listening devices earlier but hadn't paid attention to detail. Now he did.

A landscape canvas, sketched and partially painted, was on the easel. It must have been Kateřina's last work. Several paintings decorated walls in the room, both watercolor and oils. Rage had noticed works in a similar style in various rooms of the house. She was obviously an accomplished artist.

Rage wished he had known that of her. Pausing as he started to move on, Rage walked back to a corner of the room and picked up one of the paintings. It was a pastel, done in oil, of Kateřina's house. Rage hesitated for only a moment. He took the painting and another—this one a watercolor of Kateřina and Ana—a copy of a beautiful portrait of them on the table downstairs. He set the two paintings against the wall outside the door.

He continued to wander through the house and remember the woman he had given second place in his life. She had waited for him— Kateřina had told him—but he'd always had some more important place to be. Rage couldn't help it; he wished he had one more chance. He thought of Marty and Jolana and the relationship they shared.

Maybe if I had cared more for Kateřina...

Dry and warm, Rage made coffee and slid onto one of the barstools at the counter—one foot on a rung, the other on the floor. Without great interest, he opened the lawyer's envelope.

The English version of the documents was on top. There was a short three page will and then a copy of Kateřina's property.

He scanned the several pages of assets first.

"Whew!" Rage couldn't help the exclamation after reading the list. Among her assets were assorted items and several bank and financial accounts. No amounts were shown. Rage guessed this was because amounts change continually. Institution names and account numbers would lead the beneficiary to whatever funds were available when the time was appropriate.

Moving on, Rage realized the house and the Porsche were not listed. He understood the Eagle Trust owned those.

He had read an early version of the agreement regarding the Eagle Trust's members and the Prague group which was slated to take over the Trust and the hospital. In the last draft, houses, vehicles, and significant funds had been slated to go to each of the young people and their surrogates. Rage had not read the final papers; he didn't know the outcome of the agreement though he had made suggestions. Now that Kateřina was deceased, Rage wondered if the assets from the Trust would go to her estate.

He dropped the attorney's papers on the counter and walked to the windows overlooking the terrace. Rage had to think. Perhaps she had wanted him to handle the distribution of her assets.

After a few minutes spent thinking and looking out the back windows, he returned to the counter and picked up Kateřina's will. Rage read it over, then again…and again.

Concentrating was suddenly difficult considering the details in her will.

The lawyer's assistant had been right. He would certainly need to go to their office before he left Prague. In fact, he would probably need more than one visit.

There were details to discuss, and he would need to have the attorney check on the assets from the Trust. Those were still a maybe.

Kateřina had left an assortment of small items to Adina and other friends.

He went over and dropped onto the settee, the three pages of her will lay beside him. There was some thinking Rage needed to do. After a while, he picked up Kateřina's will and read it one more time.

Kateřina had left cash, financial accounts and all other assets to Rage.

There were two visits to the attorney's office. The young assistant acted as interpreter for Rage each time.

On the first visit, the lawyer suggested Rage sign a Power of Attorney allowing him to handle account transfers and other transactions. This would allow Rage to return to the US without the need for a trip back to Prague.

Sounded good to Rage.

The second visit was to sign documents.

Now Rage was free to return to Tennessee and his log cabin.

But there was one last thing to do.

Rage wanted to say a simple goodbye to several individuals he'd had contact with in Prague. A table was reserved at the restaurant, *Terrace at the Golden Well.*

Everyone gathered around a secluded table overlooking the city and talked softly. Marty, Colonel Repa, Milan, Janalynn Dusa, and Gita, Repa's young policewoman, were all there. The panoramic view on this clear night was simply stunning. Several commented about it.

Conversation was informal, mostly Rage telling everyone how grateful he was for their efforts. There was ample schnapps for Marty, beer for Milan, water for Rage and whatever the others desired. The food was extraordinary too, as it had been for Kateřina and him on a night not so long ago.

Rage missed parts of the conversation as he stared off across the city. He was remembering how beautiful Kateřina had been that night with the lights of Prague sparkling in her eyes. She was gone now, but he would always have the memories of both the young woman and the mature lady he'd been privileged to know in this life.

At a point, Gita noticed and inquired why Rage was smiling.

"Oh, just a special memory."

She watched him for a few moments before Rage told her, "You'll have them too. I promise."

The old maintenance man at the cemetery was stoop-shouldered and moved with a slight limp. His coveralls were worn and needed washing. He could have used a shave that morning too.

Though he appeared unkempt and scruffy, the small pile of broken twigs and other debris at his feet indicated he was still capable of doing his job. A stiff wind during the night had cleared most of a light snow off the sidewalks, mounding it under nearby shrubs and trees.

He had stopped sweeping, and now, propping himself on the big broom, he stared across the forest of graves near an entrance to Vinohrady Cemetery. Though winter had just begun, the brisk chilly wind and occasional snow reminded everyone this was to be expected in Prague.

With a free hand, the maintenance man gathered his collar close around his neck and tugged his hat lower.

Leaves blew from his pile, the wind scattering them along nearby paths and among the tombs and headstones. Paying no attention to the minor distraction, he stared instead at the visitor who was kneeling at a fresh burial plot a hundred meters distant. The man was placing something against a granite headstone.

Pointing him out, the maintenance man told his helper, "He has brought red roses again."

The visitor wore a fedora and long black leather coat. His shirt and pants were black too. The only color was in his tie. Even this was only a soft plaid. He was dressed as he had been at the small funeral several days earlier.

Dark shades hid the stranger's eyes, but his observer didn't think he would want to see them anyway. There was something about this man that stirred a feeling of unease in the old maintenance worker.

Adding to the earlier explanation, he glanced at his helper and said, "He brings but two roses each day."

The helper spoke. "It is strange that he does this."

With the blossoms standing against the headstone, the visitor, still kneeling, removed his fedora and remained there, his head bowed. The man did not appear to be praying, only remaining close to someone who was important to him.

As the two men stood watching, a vehicle's horn sounded near the cemetery's entrance. The visitor and the maintenance workers glanced that way.

A taxi was waiting; a sign at the edge of a window indicated it was going to the airport.

After a few additional moments, the visitor donned his hat, then stood and kissed the tips of his fingers on one hand. Reaching out, he touched the headstone and remained still for a moment.

Apparently satisfied, he turned and without looking back, walked toward his observers and the gate beyond them. He tipped his fedora as he passed and then walked on.

The maintenance workers watched until the taxi drove away.

"I am going to look," the old man told his helper.

Dropping the broom, he walked to the headstone and small plot where the stranger had left the roses. He examined the inscription.

Behind the blooms, only four notations were engraved in the polished granite.

Ana a Kateřina
2015

He was saying goodbye, the old worker thought.

Glancing toward the gate, the man doubted if he would see the stranger again.

ACKNOWLEDGEMENTS

As with most writers, this novel is not a product of my efforts alone, and I would like to thank those who helped along the way.

First of all, readers come to mind. These are individuals I've asked to take a look at the novel during various stages of the writing. Without pay and with good heart, several have read the story, resulting in new thoughts for me to consider, and overall, a better book. I would like to thank everyone by name, but I am afraid I would miss someone. Please be assured that I appreciate everyone's time and assistance. You were important to me and to this book. Thank you.

Wayne South Smith of Atlanta, my editor, stuck with me through the fun and the not so fun. He provided developmental editing for the content and copyediting to seal the story. Even when we weren't on the same page, we always found a creative solution that worked well for the novel, our shared goal. I grew as a writer through our work and have never been so proud of a book. Wayne knows what to look for in a story. Now I am more skilled about it too. Thanks Wayne.

Dianne French of Edits by Alpha Omega in Savannah, Georgia, provided a keen eye, well-honed skill, and even some additional suggestions during final proofreading. Couldn't do without you. It's always a joy to work with you.

The cover for this novel, as well as my first three novels, was created by Barry A. Hodgin, my friend from the Tennessee Mountains.

Barry is a man for all seasons, and graphic design is only one of his many talents. Barry is also responsible for most of the videos found on my/his website. Take a look at www.SilverSageMedia.com.

Other unnamed souls have helped and encouraged too. A very special thanks to all of you.

ABOUT THE AUTHOR

JOE SHUMOCK WAS BORN IN a rural setting near Mobile, Alabama, and spent his early years there before joining the US Army in 1959. Ending his military service in 1962, Joe labored in several fields including insurance and finance before attending the University of New Orleans where he received a BS in Accounting. He worked as a CPA and Certified Financial Planner for over 30 years, retiring from his firm in 2002.

Joe currently lives in Foley, Alabama. Away from his desk, Joe enjoys fresh seafood and an occasional walk on the beaches of the Gulf of Mexico.

Extensive reading through the years kindled and strengthened Joe's desire to write. In his early teens, Joe began reading serious fiction from renowned authors, such as Ernest Hemingway, John Steinbeck, Jack London, and Tennessee Williams. Later, he has been inspired by the writings of Robert Ruark, Harper Lee, and Taylor Caldwell, among others.

Joe has been writing seriously since 2007. His newest, *Sacrifice of the Lambs*, is Joe's fourth novel in his *Letter Series.* Currently, he is completing *Briana and the Dog*, a children's story for all ages set on the Gulf Coast in south Alabama and due for release in early 2018. Meanwhile, he is also plotting his next suspense thriller.

For information on upcoming titles, as well as purchasing from his current catalog, visit and join Joe's Fan Club at www.SilverSageMedia.com.

Books by Joe Shumock

* * *

The Letter Series

A Letter to Die For

The Lost Letter

Letter from the Dark

Sacrifice of the Lambs

For Young Audiences

Briana and the Dog (coming 2018)